THE SLEEPER'S SERENADE

SERENADE

THE GOD SINGER: BOOK I

JACOB OAKLEY

Admittedly Bad Publishing, LLC

Copy Editor Lydia Craig
Editor at Large Keith Winkelman

First Printing, October 2021

Art by Jacob Oakley

To my wife and family, thank you for supporting and tolerating my excessive nerdiness

For my kids, don't ever stop dreaming, and write down the really good ones.

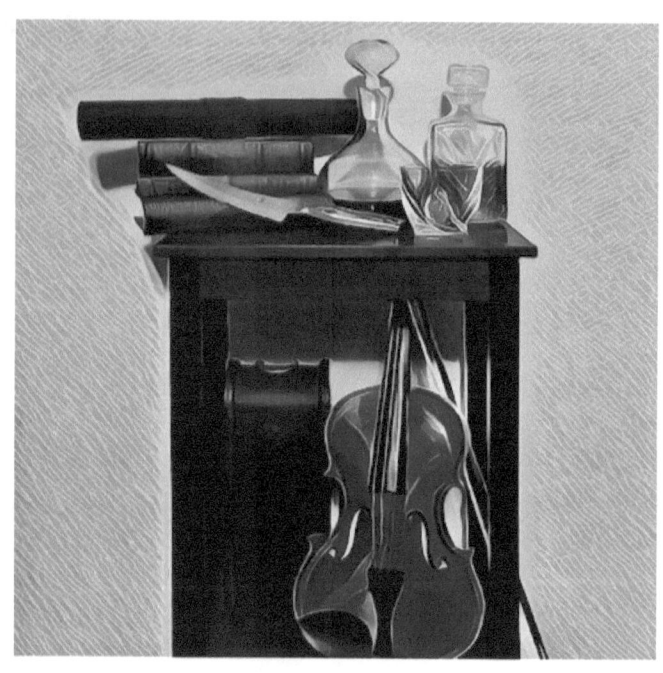

Quaj Island

★ The Hall

Tuath

N

★ The Sanctum

Mer
★ The Archdiocese
The College

Lake
Gitche

Fjall

Fjall River

Ravnice

Glasdville

Kalt

Lodestar Island
The Syndicate

THE SLEEPER'S SERENADE

Chapter 1
Death and Life

Sirul stunk. The cool drizzle that moved in over the city of Kalt near midnight soaked through his ragged clothing. When not wearing the guise of a beggar, he was a strikingly handsome figure. Curly blond hair sat shortly cut atop a chiseled jaw that framed intense grey eyes against a backdrop of olive skin. The jagged scar that ran from his right cheek to the bottom of his face accentuated the perpetual stalking nature of his gaze.

Patiently, he began his vigil outside the shop owned and operated by his current target. It took immense discipline not to shiver while the growing puddle he was sitting in steadily drained precious body heat.

As the minutes became hours, Sirul wondered what the man inside had done to warrant sentencing. It was unlikely the man even knew he had committed a transgression worthy of death. Such was the price The Syndicate charged for steering the island towards the greater good. Shadows such as Sirul simply collected the payments. Not that he minded the slaying, far from it, he knew and enjoyed nothing more.

However, being told who to deliver to The Great Dream, and when to do so increasingly infuriated him. Sirul often followed his prey for days or weeks before receiving the execution order. It was a ravenous agony. He endlessly starved for the nourishment of fatality. The Syndicate too often and too long kept his meals tortuously out of reach, their sights and smells endlessly afflicting him while he obediently observed.

Despite his growing disgruntlement with his masters, he still found their professional title for him, The Needle, more than agreeable. It was surgical. Precise. His namesake implement was slightly longer than his outstretched hand, with two-finger loops on the bottom. Crossing his arms against the chill, he slipped his right hand in his left sleeve, hiding the weapon.

When the man inside eventually doused his candles, the street had been quiet for hours. Hungry with anticipation as Sirul was, the last few moments passed excruciatingly slowly. His target finally exited the shop and came down the steps to the muddy street. As he reached the ground, a cough from Sirul drew his attention. Once the man noticed him, Sirul muttered incoherently under his breath.

"What's that?" the man asked, taking a step towards Sirul before bending down to hear him better.

Sirul's left hand grabbed the man's hair with impossible speed as his right plunged the needle into his ear, the pithing action immediately incapacitating the man. Sirul gorged on the adrenaline coursing through his veins. Killing seemed to be the only time he felt anything anymore.

Easing the paralyzed body to the ground, he cradled the head in his lap. Then, covering the nose and mouth, he stared fervidly into his victim's unmoving eyes as their light faded. Sirul relished the brief reprieve he found in the instant of mortality before yielding back to the deliberate professional restraint that made him peerless amongst assassins.

"Another for The Sleeper and The Syndicate," he said with a tinge of reverence. "Daybreak, forgive me," he muttered as a pragmatic afterthought.

After checking for any witnesses, Sirul quickly dragged the corpse up the stairs to the shop and unlocked the door with the key from the man's belt. Pulling the body inside and latching the door behind him, he removed all potentially identifying jewelry and placed it on his own hands and neck before switching clothes with the dead man. They were not the same build or quite the same height, but it would not matter. Putting the forged farewell letter on the desk at the entrance to the shop, he took a moment to look around at the gadgets and devices within it. He was unable to discern which, if any, had been the motivation for ending this man's life and endeavors.

The rain let up, and he carried the body to the outhouse behind the shop in the early morning darkness. Propping it up inside, Sirul dumped the vial of acid he brought with him to disfigure the face beyond recognition. Lighting a candle from the shop, he dripped wax into the man's ear as he removed his needle to prevent bleeding. After staging the corpse, he broke the latch on the outhouse door so that it would not freely reopen and headed back inside to wait the last hour or so before dawn. When someone walking past eventually smelled the rotting flesh, the remains would be unidentifiable.

As sunlight started spilling into the windows of the shop, Sirul put the dead man's traveling cloak over his shoulders and pulled the hood low across his face. He took the man's horse out of its stall next to the shop and saddled it. Riding north out of the city that morning, several people beginning their day and opening their shops waved. Sirul waved back and spurred the horse to a quick gallop.

*****

The cool rain of the night before may have subsided, but the humidity refused to relent, resulting in an abnormally hot Kalt summer afternoon. The late-day sun drew forth rum-scented sweat from Harpis' neck and brow as the black and silver-haired man stepped from the railing of the *Steady Wind*. He felt the edge of the fishing boat dip with his weight and heard it rise behind him like a giant bobber as his boots landed fully on the dock.

The buoying boat caused the ship's captain to nearly stumble overboard.

"Damn it, Harpis," he said after regaining some composure. "Consider this your severance!" he grumbled, throwing two silvers at the younger man.

After sluggishly catching the coins, Harpis turned his brown, bloodshot eyes on the captain in a dismal glare.

"This is only half a day's wage, Emrae!" He shouted.

"And you deserve less than that." Captain Emrae retorted. Wagging his finger, the shorter, pudgy, and balding man continued his berating. "You show up here every day this week still drunk from the night before. On your best day, you hardly put in work worth your pay. Today was by far the worst of it, so you know what, don't bother showing up tomorrow."

Harpis stared back blankly, offering no response.

3

Emrae huffed and crossed his arms in front of his chest. "The lads aren't too happy at being overworked to make up for your abysmal effort today. Gods, if I tried to pay you for a full day, I think they would track you down and beat it out of you in compensation. I should have listened to the other captains' warnings when I first hired you."

Harpis didn't even bother responding as he fingered the two silver coins in his palm. Then, dismissing Emrae with a glare, he turned toward the Kalt wharf. His eyes, aching from sunburn and sea salt, began searching for the nearest drinking establishment amongst the shops ringing the village-like sprawl of vendor tents and wagons that spread across the cobblestones.

His stomach growled in protest, reminding him that he had not eaten since snagging a half-eaten loaf of bread from a serving girl's tray as she cleared the table next to him the night before. But, despite his belly's complaints, his mind had other plans for his limited funds.

Trading the warmth of the setting sun for the stuffiness of the dim, candle-lit Squid's Tavern, he plopped down at the empty chair nearest the exit and motioned to the bartender with one of his precious coins. "Two glasses of rum if you would."

Downing them one after the other, he struggled to hold in a cough as the dark, spicy fire coated his throat. With no food to slow its progress, he soon felt the tingle of the alcohol creep into his thoughts and relax his body.

The two drinks were not enough to temper his daily self-loathing at eking out an existence as a deckhand, scarcely making enough each day to get him to the next. For nearly a year, he had unsuccessfully tried to drown his grief at losing his father in barely afforded rum. Unfortunately, with his stint on the *Steady Wind* abruptly ending, he had run out of potential employers at the Kalt docks.

Aside from working the railings of a fishing vessel, Harpis was not sure he had any other marketable skills. Young, relatively well-muscled, and an adept drunk, he did not have much to offer an employer.

Raising his last silver coin at the bartender, he requested two more drinks. He did not permit the bartender to set them on the bar. Instead, he took them from the man's hands and tossed them both back, handing the empty glasses back with a wink.

Concern for Harpis' pace showed in the green eyes of the pale brown-haired Kalt bartender before the man took the empty glasses and turned his attention to other patrons.

Maybe his father had been right, and he should get away from The Siren and her sea. After all, he was confident that he could stand watch as a member of a city militia just as readily as he could man the railing of a fishing boat. Better yet, posted at a street corner or gate, there wouldn't be rolling waves to reveal the wobbliness of his legs from nightly imbibing. With a smile to himself at that thought and welcoming the fog beginning to take hold of his mind, he decided he did need more to drink.

"Two more, and then a break for a piss and some food!" he half-shouted to the bartender at the end of the bar, who nodded and fetched a bottle as Harpis pretended to reach for coins in his empty pockets.

The man deposited the two drinks before holding out his hand for payment. Harpis quickly snatched the drinks from the bar and downed them. Then, placing the empty glasses in front of him, he shrugged at the bartender apologetically and stood up to leave.

With a look from the bartender, the two large bouncers walked from the nearby door and grabbed Harpis, holding his arms and hands firmly behind his back. The bartender made his way around the counter to stand in front of Harpis.

"Care to pay for that last round?" He asked with his hands on his hips.

"You see, I would, but I am still waiting on payment from your mother for last night. So, if you wouldn't mind keeping my tab open or fetching her to pay it while getting me another round, that would be perfect."

Unimpressed by the drunken belligerence, the bartender shrugged at Harpis.

"I'll be having those back then."

The bartender answered Harpis' questioningly raised eyebrow with a punch to his gut, causing him to double over and deposit the evening's indulgences onto the tavern floor. Then, still choking on rum flowing from his belly instead of into it, he was thrown out onto the street.

Staggering to his feet, he brushed off his white cloth pants and leather tunic before resignedly gazing around the wharf. Walking away from the Squid's Tavern, he paused mid-step to turn and spit at the establishment. His half-hearted retribution was interrupted when he nearly collided with a young boy running and peering back over his shoulder as if being pursued.

Harpis' drunkenly executed dodge caused his self-righteous spittle to dribble down his chin and tunic instead of being slung vehemently at the tavern.

The boy stopped a few paces away and judgingly looked Harpis up and down.

"Watch what you're doing, ya drunk oaf!" the child yelled accusingly.

Putting his hands on his hips to steady himself, Harpis narrowed his eyes at the adolescent.

"Shouldn't you be in bed? Where are your parents, you little miscreant?" he asked indignantly.

The boy scoffed and laughed from his belly, "I have no need for parents!" Then, crossing his arms, he spoke in a feigned parental tone, "shouldn't you take a bath? Being a homeless beggar is no excuse for sitting there covered in your own slobber and bile. Especially when the harbor waters are right there to bathe in."

Throwing his hands frustratingly in the air, Harpis yelled after the child who had already fled, "I am not homeless and no beggar!"

With the youth's laughter receding around the tavern, Harpis frowned to himself at the realization that he was, in fact, out of money and no longer welcome to sleep in the hammocks hanging within the *Steady Wind*.

While daylight and its warmth faded, the typical chill of a southern summer night swept in with the darkening evening sky. He began wandering the wharf in a swerving saunter, lamentingly noting ship after ship that had banned, dismissed, or evicted him. After a while, he found himself passing by an unrecognized vessel. His focus on the unknown boat caused him to stray into a dock post which he shot a long indicting glare before looking back at the oddly named *Sea Goat*.

"It's a bit early to be so drunk, isn't it, lad?" a weathered and greying man asked from the ship's gangplank.

Harpis shrugged in response.

"The name is Captain Fynhar. Where you headed?" the older man asked.

"Nowhere," Harpis answered with a forlorn look at the Kalt wharf and harbor.

"Well, that much is obvious, I suppose," Fynhar stated flatly. "And who might you be to seek so lofty a destination?" he asked

Harpis paused before responding. Given his well-earned and distinguished reputation, he wasn't sure about giving the surly captain his real name, but he decided he was too tired and drunk to care.

"Harpis, Harpis Akkeri," he answered.

"Well, Harpis, for a few silvers, I can take you somewhere, and by the looks of you, anywhere is better than nowhere," Fynhar offered.

"And where is somewhere?" Harpis asked suspiciously, noticing the Ravnice flag fluttering above the ship's mast.

"A few small villages to drop off and pick up goods, but ultimately we will arrive in Ravnice harbor the morning after tomorrow," Fynhar said.

The thought of abandoning his familiar cage was disconcerting, but perhaps fleeing from his torment was better than hiding from it in the bottom of a bottle. Staring up at Fynhar, he decided that if he was going to end up drinking away his days, at least he could do it somewhere warmer. Somewhere that wasn't Kalt.

"I can't pay, but I can work for the passage if you're willing to let me," he said with a hopeful look.

Captain Fynhar tapped his fingernails against his teeth for a moment.

"I do not need an extra worker, especially one who looks like they'd more than likely just get in the way, but that will get you the passage you seek," Fynhar said, pointing at the necklace hanging around Harpis' neck.

Harpis' immediate reaction was to scowl at the captain. Instinctively reaching for the talisman, he ran a finger over the blue lapis lazuli cut in the shape of a raindrop and the silver mermaid visage of The Siren which held it.

The necklace was the only thing remaining in his possession from his father. He'd had it around his neck for as long as he could remember.

Somehow it had survived the storm where the boat and his father had not. When he woke on the beach, his first memory was

7

of wanting to throw the necklace into the sea.

It was part desperation, part depression, and part rum reduced inhibition that led to his decision. He begrudgingly tore the necklace from his chest, snapping the chain, before handing it to the captain. Fynhar snorted at the brash display. "Go on then, pass out where you like, but we won't wait for you, so you'd be wise to do it on the ship."

*****

Wren had taken up his position on the rooftop across from the Kalt governor's office just after dusk. A century earlier, he would have stayed crouched painfully at the very edge of the roof, gladly enduring cramped and burning muscles. He would have remained there tirelessly, glued in excitement to his perch, desperate to observe the espionage taking place at the hands of his fellow Syndicate agent.

Those days were far behind him. The old gnome's joints and bones had decades ago begun to groan and ache to the point that they prevented the adequate stealth necessary for sneaking about. However, the diminutive stature of his race, made concealment easy enough as he was barely the size of a human toddler. Clad in his wool-lined black leathers and resting with his back against chimney bricks halfway up the roofline, he was just a slightly darker shade within the shadows that grew in the fading light.

Wren casually plucked a twig from a long-deserted bird's nest wedged beneath the chimney crown and nonchalantly picked his teeth with it while keeping an eye on the governor's office window.

The peaceful silence was disturbed by a nasally voice near his right ear.

"How long is that young dimwit going to take delivering the letter? Don't you have to board the *Water Donkey* by morning?"

"*Sea Goat*," Wren corrected as the owner of the voice, a tiny undead fire sprite floated from his shoulder down to the roof tiles in front of him. She stretched her red, demon-like wings and ashen-skinned limbs as if she was some feral alley cat before putting her hand provocatively on her bare hip. Flipping her purplish hair out of her face she raised a questioning eyebrow at the old gnome.

Taking his gaze off the distant window for a moment, he crossed his arms and gave the barely one-foot-tall fire sprite a look of mild exasperation.

"Sweet Xissay, you make me think I should have pursued the undead company of a kinder woodland faerie. Maybe they would be less quarrelsome," he stated.

"I think you mean less interesting," Xissay replied with a snort as they both looked across the street at the still motionless office.

Pretending to ignore her, Wren shifted to alleviate an aching tailbone.

"I don't even know why we are here in this dreary five-forsaken southern city," Wren said. He briefly stared up at the cloud front moving in with the evening before continuing.

"The Syndicate Hand and Eye in Kalt should be taking care of this," he grumbled.

Narrowing her eyes, Xissay tried focusing her vision on the building across the road. After a moment, she shook her head, lavender hair tumbling around her shoulders like dripping flames.

"What's this, your fourth Eye in the century or so you have been their Hand in Ravnice?" she asked.

Wren sent his gaze skyward in thought for a moment. "The fifth actually, and I am about fed up with the Navigators sending me short-lived humans to train."

Xissay laid seductively with her elbows on the clay tiles and her chin in her palms, staring up at Wren.

"Maybe if you were better at training them, they would live longer," she said accusingly.

"Bah," he responded, "the first two retired of old age, as did the fourth. The third happened to be incompetent, and his early death was unsurprising and his own doing."

"What of this one then?" she asked as they both strained their eyes in the near-complete blackness of a cloudy Kalt evening.

"He is young and overeager," Wren said.

Suddenly the office across the street was bathed in golden candlelight as the door to the hallway was thrown open by what appeared to be one of the mansion guards and a late-night female companion. Wren sat up straight, and Xissay returned to her original position floating over his shoulder.

The Syndicate agent stood frozen behind the Kalt governor's

desk as the light silhouetted him. The figure in the doorway shoved the feminine companion aside and unceremoniously skewered the unarmed intruder.

"Damn! The Sleeper keep the poor fool," Wren said bitterly as the guard killed his colleague.

"Hey, I know you left your robes on the ship but come on necromancer, why don't you just ask your sleeping goddess to let you reanimate yonder corpse so that the human can prove somewhat useful in completing the task at hand?" Xissay asked enthusiastically.

"I think we've caused enough of a scene here already, thank you very much. I am not doing that, and you are not going over there either," Wren answered with a stern look.

The gnome grimaced, but professionalism quickly buried the guilt he felt at the young agent's fate and at not being with him as he left the living to join the dead in The Great Dream. With a quick prayer, Wren pulled his necromancer scythe from the realm of the dead as if from thin air.

It had a black wooden handle upon which sat a blade of obsidian protruding from an eagle skull fashioned of pure silver. Inlay along the blade's edge depicted the nude sleeping goddess he worshiped.

Continuing the ritual words while holding his scythe to focus his gift, the world before him greyed and discolored. He saw the wispy white form of one of The Sleeper's handmaidens floating to the dead man's side.

The feminine form bent beside the corpse for a moment, and Wren whispered to himself the words he knew the handmaiden was reciting. Then as quickly as the apparition appeared, it floated away and dissipated with the man's soul in tow.

As Wren let go of his focus, the grey vision faded away. He calmly observed the commotion as more guards quickly searched the mansion grounds. Before long, the house grew quiet again. The number of guards visibly doubled around the mansion's exterior before the lights inside were blown out or subdued.

"Late night romantic rendezvous will be the undoing of us all," Wren stated matter-of-factly.

Xissay shot him a look of concern from under arching eyebrows. "Shouldn't you be finding out what happened to the fabricated letter yonder dead man was supposed to have placed?"

she asked.

Turning and stretching his head to each side, Wren was rewarded with satisfying cracks from his neck. "The letter's discovery could indeed unravel years of work by The Syndicate. If it is destroyed, The Syndicate will simply find another way. Eventually," Wren said in acknowledgment.

After a long moment and a determined look at the mansion, the gnome spoke again. "However, if I could see it placed as intended, neither need to happen, and the mission will be a success. At least as far as the Navigators are concerned," he stated flatly.

"It will be fun listening to your archaic bones creak, click, and pop as you sneak your way over there to fix this mess," Xissay said with a bemused look on her face.

Her humor turned to dejection as she faded into a sulfuric smoke when Wren dismissed her before heading to the street below.

Despite the increased guard presence outside the mansion, the men had no hope of spotting the barely two-foot-tall, black leather-clad gnome with decades of experience at not being seen. He made his way silently up a downspout and across a gutter. Landing quietly on one of the windowsills to the governor's office, he quickly unlatched it.

Creeping behind the desk, he spotted the letter he had forged earlier that day, crumpled into a ball, and thrown into the corner of the room. Wren spared a thankful thought for the Eye adhering to some semblance of tradecraft even while facing certain death.

He uncreased the parchment and gave it a disconcerting look. It would raise suspicion for a battered document to be sent from the governor. Using the governor's chair as a stool, he grabbed an inkwell, quill, and parchment. With the governor's own writing implements, he reforged the same letter.

Even with the enhanced night vision of his largely subterranean race, it was difficult to compose in the near blackness of the office. He finished the letter and returned the tools to their original place. Spotting the governor's seal, he dumped some ink on the crumpled letter from before. Dipping the seal in the pool, he stamped the newly forged letter, blew it dry, and placed it with the outgoing correspondence.

He folded the ink-covered, wrinkled forgery from earlier to

11

ensure the words were obscured and crushed it into a ball again, tossing it in with the governor's trash.

Wren shook his head at the irony of creating a more convincing forgery due to the unfortunate events that had transpired. However, he derived solace from the fact that the mission was more likely to succeed despite what had happened. As the subdued light of pre-dawn illuminated Kalt under overcast skies, Wren made his way hastily to the *Sea Goat* and passage home.

*****

Enky nervously paced his tiny, windowless one-room abode with the short strides of a small childish frame. His body was that of a human boy of six or seven and did not reveal his forty thousand years of existence across the better part of two ages. He stopped for a moment in thought and plopped down into his cushioned comfy chair, peering around at the dozens of picture frames that hung crooked and uneven in every shape and size. They almost completely covered the two walls that were not dominated by bookshelves or what looked to be a dormant stone-filled portal.

In each frame, a scene played, showing various beings and goings-on. Most were of the living realm, but some showed happenings on the other planes as well. Enky's gaze settled on the one that sat propped up on his tiny writing desk. Standing again, he took two steps and was before the desk where he reached and reverently picked up the frame from its top.

"My marionette is set in motion, the commencement of my commotion," he whispered to the view of a beleaguered man in Kalt city.

Setting the odd wooden frame back down, he reached into one of his vest's many pockets and pulled out a coin which he then flicked into a spin across the desk.

Chapter 2
The Sea Goat

Begrudgingly, Harpis lay awake in the hold of the *Sea Goat* as his hammock rocked gently with the movement of the waves. Each swing sloshed his innards around, and it was all he could do to keep the contents of his stomach in place. His headache had faded sometime around dinner, thanks in no small part to finally consuming something other than rum.

His clothes were stiff and uncomfortable from being dried in the sun. Crouched in a huddle on the ship's deck in the late morning, he was awakened by the crew dumping buckets of seawater on him. They said he smelled like he hadn't bathed in a week.

Though he wanted to argue the point, his patchwork of sober memories did not afford him proof of recent hygiene. His first clear memory of the day was clutching his chest in a panic that the necklace was gone. After that, rage at potential thieves on the boat taking advantage of a poor drunk gave way to a piecemeal recollection of last night's events.

In vain, he tried to overcome the personal disappointment of trading it away. Maybe the necklace depicting The Siren was bad luck. Maybe she did want him dead. Maybe it was for the best he let go of everything from his past. Maybe he was just a miserable drunk.

The drones of several sleeping sailors had already interrupted his attempts at slumber. They were now actively interfering with his contemplation. He considered drinking some of the overly spiced rum but reconsidered when the mere sight of the bottle caused his mouth to water and stomach to convulse.

It took biting hard on his tongue and focusing on that pain to stave off losing his meager dinner. Lethargically, he returned to his inner debate regarding the reasons for his current lot in life.

Homeless, out of money, and with no living family, he wondered which of The Five he had so offended as to deserve his current position.

Given everything that had transpired over the past year or so, The Siren was a likely suspect. Perhaps the goddess of storms, wind, and seas found his continued existence an annoyance.

Certainly, Konflict was not angry with him. On the contrary, the fiery god of battle would laud the employment he currently pursued as a militiaman.

It was probably not The Wild. Harpis had been sailing this and other forsaken ships too long to draw the ire of the nature-friendly goddess.

Had it been Daybreak or The Sleeper that he had offended, he doubted the goddesses of life and death would suffer him to remain alive, pondering which of The Five was responsible for his fortunes. Therefore, it must be The Siren.

With the question of godly aggression settled, he stared intently at the beam above him. Countless previous passengers of the *Sea Goat* had defaced it with names, sayings, and crude carvings. Who names a ship the *Sea Goat* anyway? Perhaps they had run out of more regal sea creatures.

Given the state of its slumbering crew around him, the rum probably had more to do with the vessel's naming than anything else. Abandoning unassisted sleep and internal debate, he swung out of his hammock to escape the wheezing snores. Perhaps he would find peace while taking in the sky outside.

Before heading out of the ship's belly, he gave the rope belt around his waist a tug. Earlier in the afternoon, one of the crew had asked him about it. So, he showed the man how to tie some rope to the broken-off head of one of the boat hooks used to pull the ship in to dock, noose it around his waist and then wrap it until it was slightly snug.

Placing the boat hook in the noose would hold the belt in place. Harpis' father had always said it was helpful when falling overboard, pulling in nets, coming into a dock, and other things.

*****

14

The *Sea Goat* contained four cabins in its half-deck, which sat on the main deck above the hold with the helm atop it. Two of the cabins were for the captain and first mate and the other two for high-paying passengers.

One such passenger was Wren. The gnome was a comical sight, sitting atop pillows on the human-sized chair so that he could more easily reach the top of the small desk on which he was writing.

Squinting by candlelight at the parchment before him, each stroke of the pen caused the wide cuffs of his deep purple, almost black robe to nearly brush the wet ink. He lamented the clotting nature of the ink, the blotting tendency of the pen, and other sources of smudges and stains covering the embroidery on his sleeve.

Symbols of The Sleeper shone in silver thread across the purple hood hanging off his shoulders as it did on the cuffs. The embroidery identified him as a death speaker, second only to the Death Herald herself.

Pausing his writing, he took a sip of the rum he had requisitioned from some of the crew and pulled a face as the overly spicy fire hit his mouth and then belly. At least it did its job, he thought, as his nerves and emotions dulled.

The report was due to The Syndicate upon landing in Ravnice. The writing was draining work. He left out his unprofessional questioning of being sent to do tasks usually assigned to the Hand and Eye stationed in Kalt. Finally, he confirmed the delivery of the forgery.

After finishing the rest of the rum, he sighed and documented the death of his Eye. Guilt and frustration ran their course across his face as he wrote. Such a tragedy would not have happened back at their posting in familiar Ravnice.

Leaning against the chair back, Wren rolled the parchment and used candle drippings to seal it. He poured a small amount of wax, letting it cool halfway. The gnome then made a well with his thumb and dribbled some ink into the cavity before sealing it in with more wax. Then, slipping the letter into his robe, he decided to get what rest he could before the *Sea Goat* sailed into the port at Ravnice the early morning.

*****

Harpis was halfway up the ladder when he paused, straining to hear the growing commotion above. Suddenly, the impact of something slamming into the side of the *Sea Goat* threw him off the rungs and into the bulkhead.

Blinking stars out of his eyes, he heard the ship's whistle sound the alarm frantically over men shouting. He bounded up the ladder and burst through the hatch to the grim scene unfolding on the ship's deck.

The full moon and clear skies bathed everything in a macabre pale light. A slightly larger vessel was alongside the *Sea Goat* and well over thirty armed men poured over the rails.

Harpis spotted the stoic Captain Fynhar. The captain was the embodiment of a grizzled and salty sailing man, fending off several attackers with broad sweeps of his cutlass. Thankful that no arrows flew overhead, Harpis rushed towards the man, but was cut off by the slashes of a nearby attacker. Then, as the pirate confidently stalked in, Harpis watched in dismay as the captain was run through by a sword, and his slumped dying form fell into the sea.

His focus turned to the pirate in front of him, Harpis stumbled over a corpse as he backed away before frantically searching for a weapon. He snatched the dead man's sabre up just in time to block the heavy cutlass coming down again and again in overhead chops. Harpis' hands vibrated as the other man's sword repeatedly rang off his feeble blocks. Fear began to overwhelm him as the screams of men dying, and shouts of battle surrounded him.

*****

Wren awoke in mid-flight as the collision jolted him out of bed and onto the floor. He quickly got to his feet and put his robe on amongst the alarms and shouts. Making his way up the stairs to the helm, he grumbled about the inconvenience of being so abruptly roused from a rum-induced sleep.

He casually climbed the last few steps, noted the dead first mate's corpse still clutching a pike pole, and stepped over the body to survey the scene below.

At once, he noticed the members of the *Sea Goat* were hard-pressed and sorely outnumbered. Worse still, they appeared to be much less adept at combat than their enemy. Nearly half of the twenty-odd crew and passengers were already dead or dying, while only a handful of the enemy had suffered similar fates.

Alone on the steering deck stood the helmsman. Struggling to peel his eyes off an approaching knot of men from the other ship, he glanced perplexed at the robe-wearing gnome.

Wren winked at him. "Try to be useful and keep trying to steer this flotsam away from them, won't you?"

Not waiting for a reply, the gnome calmly turned to face the group of assailants almost upon them and drew his scythe and called upon his goddess-endowed gift. Concentrating on the corpse before him, he murmured a request to borrow the bodies of the recently deceased, reanimating them to his will for a time. Rising to his commands, the headless corpse of the first mate ascended from the steering deck, still clutching the pike pole in its hand.

At his instruction, the corpse stepped in front of him and promptly impaled the two lead assailants as they reached the top of the stairs.

The other two immediate enemies hacked the headless corpse to pieces. As they stepped over it to attack him and the helmsman, the bodies of their two compatriots rose from the bloodstained planks.

Still connected by the pike pole, the reanimated corpses slashed at the backs of the two living assailants before clearing a few more of the pirates away from the base of the stairs. As Wren's words to his goddess ended, they fell to the deck in a lifeless heap. He nodded thanks to The Sleeper's handmaidens as the wispy feminine creatures performed their ritual of taking souls to The Great Dream.

With the immediate threat to his own livelihood dealt with, Wren unhurriedly looked over the ongoing struggle. Letting out a long sigh he glanced back at the helsmen, who promptly vomited his dinner across the deck.

"Away from the other ship," Wren reminded him with a finger held up in reprimand.

With a thoughtful look, the gnome returned his scythe to the air. The visage of the handmaidens bent over corpses disappeared with it. No longer needing to borrow the bodies of the dead from

17

his goddess, he walked to the railing of the steering deck to observe the battle below.

*****

Harpis was not weak by any standards, and his recently acquired saber was a decent enough weapon despite its rust. He did, however, regret a lack of formal training.

The much larger man kept swiping away at his head without relenting. It was all he could do to keep stepping backward and block the heavy blows. In his heart, he knew he was likely to die. Another step back brought him into the bait cleaning table, which he promptly fell backward on.

Lying back on the table, he blocked one last blow before the pirate pinned the saber to his chest and leaned in with a near toothless grin.

For a moment, Harpis considered the irony of being gutted on the bait table. Besides the stench of dead fish, he also noticed a filet knife on the table. Grabbing it with his free hand, he slammed it, handle deep, into the side of the pirate's neck. In a silent surprise, the man stood up and fell lifelessly backward.

Standing up and gripping his saber with white knuckles, Harpis was terrified by what he saw before him. Maybe ten others of the *Sea Goat* remained, and double that was attacking them.

His legs were already rubbery, and his breath was coming in gulps. Harpis thoughtlessly responded to the fatigue in his muscles the same way he had when pulling in long fishing nets with his father, by chanting the words of a fisherman's work song.

The notes dictated the rhythm of his movements and the melody seemed to take over his weary arms. When he faced the nearest enemy, he thought not of dying or fighting with his saber only of the rhythm of hauling ropes. As he sang the song, his blade danced with the pirate's own, and he drove the man back. He could feel a strange swelling in his pulse that grew with each note and cadence.

From deep within him, the unknown emanation flowed. Another note, another lyric from his gravelly voice and another sword stroke possessed of unbound fury, this one through the pirate's heart.

*****

Wren felt an unbounded surge of some other being's gift that sent a chill down his back. He worriedly canvassed the fray for an enemy mage or some other magical doom that might have been about to assail them. Finding no such threat, he instead noticed the change taking place below him.

All the remaining fighters from the *Sea Goat* seemed to now fight as one. Almost tirelessly and together in unison, they beat back the enemy's advance.

It was a dance of melee and death choreographed to the rise and fall of one man's voice. They seemed to strike faster, in time with each other and without tiring.

Two more fell, but so too did nine of their enemies. The unity of the attacks had the pirates wholly taken aback. As one sword thrust, another fell behind it with seemingly inhuman, relentless speed, synchronized with the ebb and flow of the song.

It had been ages since he had seen a bard weave magic into and through song and never with such effect. He was shocked that it seemed the man below had done it as an afterthought and with a significant effect on both himself and the others. Even more surprising was the man's ability to maintain the magic of the song while fighting for his life.

He pensively rubbed his short white beard stubble while considering the black and white-haired young man on the lower deck.

The odds a of human being born magically gifted were worse than one in a thousand, and most of those were elementalists, not bards. Wren knew of only one other being alive that could weave the gift of magic into song. However, unlike what he had just witnessed, when the Impresario, head of The Bard's Hall, did so, it was more a paltry trick than a magically gifted spell.

*****

The last of the pirates leaped back to their ship and began hacking at the lines mooring the two vessels together. His song and the battle concluded, Harpis felt the intensity of his pulse ease. Clenching his hands and flexing his arms for a moment before releasing them, he was in awe at the fading vigor. After months

19

spent turning hours into flashes of consciousness with rum, for once he wished the lingering moments of his performance could last an age. For the first time since his father died, he yearned to remain possessed by the present.

Around him, the other *Sea Goat* warriors shared confused glances at still being alive. The helmsman above, following Wren's advice, was turning them away from their attacker, and the ships were soon separated.

Harpis' gaze fell to the filet knife handle sticking out of the neck of the first pirate he had killed. He decided he should keep the weapon. Even if it was an odd choice, it had been a thing of luck lying there on the gutting table. After all, it saved his life.

The ornate carving of The Siren in the whalebone handle was undoubtedly beautiful. An omen perhaps that she was no longer so mad with him. Smiling at that thought, he yanked the blade free. He wiped it clean and sheathed it in his boot before pausing to take in the confusing reality of what had just come to pass.

The realization that he had just killed this man and several others washed over him in a cold sweat followed by vomiting all over the deck.

"Tisk, tisk," a voice said from above. "You humans just can't hold your innards when there is death about, can you?"

Harpis looked up at the stairs to the steering deck with confusion, not just for the gnome atop them chastising him, but the pile of corpses at their bottom.

"Quite the performance, lad, I am Wren, and you have my thanks," he said. "Let me buy you a drink or three when we arrive in Ravnice for saving our asses."

"The name is Harpis Akkeri. Did you kill all those men?" Harpis asked dumbly after stating his own name.

"The first mate had lost his head before I arrived, sadly. However, his corpse proved useful in dealing with the first two, and theirs were useful in finishing the task," Wren answered.

Behind the gnome, the helmsman stood staring down at the corpses, pale and shaking.

Wren peered up at the stars and then at the helmsmen. "Mind the wheel now, just as you were. Ravnice is that way," he said while pointing to the left. "We ought to be there in the next hour or so and arrive at dawn."

The gnome then turned to face Harpis Again. "It gets easier, you know."

Harpis stared back blankly.

"Not the vomiting, though maybe that too." Wren shrugged. "But the killing, that gets easier."

Harpis nodded back at the gnome.

Chapter 3
The Siren's Scream

It was closer to noon than dawn when the *Sea Goat* finally moored at the Ravnice docks. The state of rolling plains contained most of Quaj's farms. As a result, it was the only state where most of the population resided outside the city proper instead of within it.

Wren stood with Harpis at the railing while the remainder of the crew tied the beleaguered *Sea Goat* to the dock. The gnome's ear was at belly level to Harpis as the man's stomach growled violently for sustenance.

"Suppose we grab some food and drink before your stomach turns itself inside out or convinces your eyes I might be good for eating," he said, looking up at the young man.

Harpis looked down sheepishly. "That sounds about perfect."

Before they could make their way down the gangplank, the helmsman of the *Sea Goat* stopped them. "Thanks to you both, we would have all perished without your efforts."

Reaching out and shaking their hands, he looked from the gnome to the man and back. "Feen Masterson is the name. I'll be in Ravnice for some time trying to repair the ship and rebuild the crew. Here and later, if the *Sea Goat* or I can ever be of service, you've not but to ask," he said, waving them off. Before turning back to the boat, he pointed down at the handle poking above Harpis' boot.

"You're already a better owner than Fynhar was. I never understood why the old man always used such a pretty thing to gut fish." He said, shaking his head.

Harpis went to draw it from the boot and hand it back, but Feen stayed him with a raised hand. "Please, keep it as a token of

22

our appreciation lad."

Once they made it to dry land Wren paused to scan the wharf area. "We'll find food, drink, and beds fine enough in there," he said, pointing at the sign which read Siren's Scream Inn. Harpis followed the gnome through the wide cobblestone wharf toward the inn.

The open wharf was maybe three hundred feet deep. Still, navigating the crowded cobbles to the row of narrow two-story taverns, inns, and other businesses aimed at serving the typical customers and purveyors of the wharf took some doing.

As they stepped into the half-empty inn, Wren waited, watching Harpis blink several times as his eyes adjusted to the dimly lit and damp-smelling stone and wood structure. The gnome then took them past the bar and fireplace that smoldered along the wall at the entrance. They made their way to the back-most booth tucked behind the stairs to the second level.

Walking around to the seat that afforded a view of the tavern entrance, Wren gestured for Harpis to take the other. As the man did, he whispered a call to The Sleeper for a spell of revealing to see if the man had any hidden magical items or the like. The ability to detect magical enchantment was one of the few endowments all god-gifted magic wielders could call upon.

He quickly saw the bright aura that flickered around the dagger in the man's boot but nothing else. Finally, he sat down with what he deemed to be a relatively safe drinking partner.

"Know much of magic then, lad?" he asked, his head unmoving as his eyes surveyed the other patrons.

"Never in my life," Harpis replied.

"So just the once then, eh?" he continued, garnering a surprised look from Harpis.

Satisfied the man knew nothing of his gift, Wren felt further assured he was not being conned or lured into some ambush.

The barmaid approached, and he asked for a whiskey and a bowl of stew. Harpis ordered a mead and stew for himself with a raised eyebrow aimed at the gnome.

Furrowing his own in response, Wren looked at Harpis questioningly. "What?"

Harpis shot him a grin. "I just didn't expect they'd serve you alcohol at all on account of looking like a partially bald, malnourished youth."

Wren flashed him a look of disdain and opened his mouth to scold the man but was interrupted by their server.

"If I didn't serve the likes of Wren, I'd only be making half my money, good sir," the barmaid said, flashing a smile as she deposited their drinks.

Wren beamed and handed her coin enough for ten times their order. "Keep us filled up, please, lass, and he gets whiskey next," he said.

As she curtsied and hurried away, Harpis raised his eyebrows again at Wren. "Whiskey with lunch?"

Wren snorted as if the question was preposterous. "We are in Ravnice City, of Ravnice State, where the finest corn is grown and the darkest, smoothest, whiskey is distilled from it. I'd have it to break my fast if somewhere around here that sold it would open early enough."

Harpis' growling stomach did a flip at the thought of whiskey for breakfast.

Their bellies full and stew bowls empty, the barmaid cleared away their dishes and placed two glasses of whiskey on their table. The drink and weariness from the last night's battle began to creep in, and the odd pair of drinking mates visibly relaxed.

Wren looked the man in the eye. "So Harpis, what plans do you have for yourself here?"

Harpis paused awkwardly for a moment in thought before shrugging almost helplessly at the gnome.

"To be honest, I have worn out my welcome in the south, and I am sick of working the rails of fishing vessels. The Siren killed my father and will probably do the same to me if I make my life on her waters. My father always suggested I try my hand with a city militia, so here we are, I guess," he said in a voice that didn't sound like it believed itself.

Wren gave him an approving nod. "A fine enough life you'd make for yourself protecting the people of Ravnice, its governor or gates, but how would you feel about serving the greater good of this whole forsaken island?"

Harpis shrugged. "I don't know what good I'd be as a necromancer. I don't worship The Sleeper. Or any of The Five."

"I speak not of my religion but instead of something clandestine," Wren said quietly before leaning in to continue. "If you have the perseverance and the wherewithal to make it through indoctrination, you will find a life and a career far more satisfying than that of a local militiaman. Perhaps we can help you explore that gift of yours as well."

Harpis tilted his head inquisitively at the gnome. "You are an acolyte, right? Those are the robes of a necromancer, aren't they?" He asked, holding up a finger in warning. "I'll not be convinced to join you for some evil lovemaking experience with a corpse."

Wren glared at him for a moment and then laughed from his belly. "Not much of an education in the pissant fishing village you must have come from, eh?"

Harpis laughed nervously at the gnome's barb, spreading his hands apologetically.

"I am indeed a necromancer and have worshiped often at The Sanctum. I am no acolyte anymore; I attained the rank of death speaker a century ago. We are no eviler than Daybreak's Exarch or his clerics at their archdiocese in Mer. We are simply the other side of the same coin," Wren explained.

The barmaid returned and poured more of the dark liquor for both. Wren waited until after she left before continuing.

"Just because people fear death does not make its goddess evil. I worship her with the same reverence as those of the light worship her sister," he explained.

Harpis grinned drunkenly at the gnome and continued his alcohol enabled oversharing of his thoughts, unable to keep a straight face as he pushed Wren's patience.

"So, you're telling me you worship a naked dead lady but don't engage in corpse fornication? I suppose that's all right then."

Wren's knuckles whitened as he clenched them before he let out a long breath and gave the man a steely look. "Consider that you will die of old age long before I will, Harpis, the human. One more insult at the expense of my goddess or my faith, and I'll hunt down your corpse and reanimate it for the sole purpose of pleasuring farm animals at the Ravnice Wharf," he growled at the semi-intoxicated man.

Harpis cringed at the threat but continued largely unabated. "What about the other thing then, this other order you serve?" he asked.

Wren made an obvious scan of the tavern before leaning forward and speaking in a whisper, "If you are interested in joining my organization, then stay at this tavern for the next week. I will pay for your room, food and then some. If you are still here on the final day, you'll receive further instruction and more coins in case you choose to stay."

Harpis raised his eyebrows at the statement. "And what if I just take the coin and make my start here in Ravnice, joining the militia?" he asked.

Wren crossed his arms and stared at Harpis for several long moments until the man started fidgeting. "I welcome your decision. Consider the silvers a thank you for what you did on the *Sea Goat*. However, based on the smell and look of you that first morning we left Kalt, I am guessing you are more likely to drink your way through it. I'd bet you'd quickly find yourself haggling the Ravnice wharf for work just as you did in Kalt."

The man seemed taken aback for a moment. Instead of arguing, he gazed distantly at the table and then looked Wren in the eyes.

"Well, either way, I would probably be better off than making love to the dead with you and your mysterious friends," he said in a voice that pretended confidence.

Wren did not flinch or speak. Instead, he took a long sip of whiskey. Setting his glass down gingerly, he gave Harpis a tight smile.

"Have it your way then, lad. Maybe you'll wake up twenty years from now with two thankless children, a fat wife, and a career of escorting vomit encrusted drunks to the city jail to look back on. Or perhaps, you'll wake up dead, a miserable drunk who drowned falling off the side of a fishing vessel. I am honestly unsure which would be worse."

Harpis stared intensely at the ceiling for a long moment in contemplation.

"Hey," Wren said, drawing his attention, "look, it's your life, Harpis. I am just offering you purpose. Enough talk of that then. You have my thanks and, as I mentioned, some silver. You are as interesting a drinking partner as I have had in some time. Tell me about yourself."

After several more glasses and discussions ranging from fishing villages to The Five, Harpis could hardly see or speak straight.

With sunlight disappearing from the inn's windows, Wren

got up from his seat and walked to the barmaid attending customers at the front of the tavern. He paid for one of the rooms upstairs and gave a wink and instructions to her.

He walked back to the table and an inebriated Harpis. "Come with me to your room. There is something I must tell you."

The man rolled his eyes and followed Wren upstairs. When they arrived at the second door in the hallway, the gnome paused and glanced at the stairwell before speaking again in a whisper, "Look, I know you said you did not want to get involved, but as we made our way up the stairs, I spotted two men taking an over-abundant interest in us. I doubt they care about you, so I will do my best and lead the older skinny looking sailor and his ox of a friend away from here. If anyone asks you about my employers or me, you should pretend to know nothing. There are rival organizations that work counter to my own on this island."

"But I don't know anything," Harpis said

Wren held up his finger to quiet Harpis and took a few steps down the stairwell to peek at the first floor before returning to the man leaning heavily against the wall.

"You know my name, and that is enough. I think they've left. Remember, take the coins and do as you please if you want. But if you are indeed interested in something more for yourself, stay here for the week. Someone will deliver instructions regarding what to do next," he explained.

Harpis grinned at him and nodded stupidly. He drunkenly reached for the doorknob, missing twice before turning and opening it. The gnome followed him inside, shutting the door behind them.

"Hey, what did I just tell you?" he asked.

Harpis gave him an exaggerated wave of the hand before slurring his response. "Drink my life away for a week and await instructions," he said before promptly flopping onto the bed face first.

"Amateur," Wren commented. He hastily produced some parchment, pen, and ink from his robe and scratched out the same instructions for a more sober Harpis to read the following day. He slipped the note and some money under the man's elbow and latched the door behind him as he left.

Heading out of The Siren's Scream, he stopped the barmaid and tipped her twice as much again. He then bid her bend down so he could whisper in her ear. "See to it that none bother my companion while he stays here."

Blushing at the amount of money he had given her, she nodded in agreement and returned to her other, less thankful patrons.

The night was young, but Wren always felt it best to leave bars, taverns, and inns well before their closing time. That was the hour thieves and worse preyed upon the overly drunk customers streaming out of such establishments.

Besides, he had better whiskeys at home he could enjoy. A few blocks away, Wren stopped at the door to one of the city's morgues. Noting that the small piece of cloth he had shut in the door as he left was still in place, he picked a key ring from inside his robes and unlocked the door. The shred of cloth fell without the door to hold it to the frame. While surveying the street behind him, he picked it up before entering the small first-floor office of his establishment.

"Home sweet home," he muttered aloud to the shadows. He truly did love this shop and the one-room apartment on the second floor. What luck, or more likely a well-planned strategy, that his Syndicate posting, as a gifted necromancer, was as one of the city's morticians. It offered him ample time working for The Sleeper and Syndicate both. It also gave him a unique grasp on information and goings-on in the city.

He climbed rickety stairs that creaked under even his small weight at the back of the office to the one-room living space on the second floor. He thought of having the stairs fixed for a moment but decided he preferred hearing the approach of a would-be attacker instead. He opened the apartment door and locked it again behind himself.

The apartment was small but had plenty of space for the solitary gnome. His small bed was around the corner from the stairwell wall. At the far end of the room was his comfy chair and fireplace.

He walked through the kitchenette and eating area, which held a small wood table he had procured from a nearby bar along with the two wooden chairs that sat at it. On one side of the fireplace, wood was stacked floor to ceiling with a ladder leaned against the pile. On the other was a bookcase with religious and magical texts and a dozen or so various whiskey bottles.

He thought of falling into his comfy chair and drifting off but instead sat in one of the wooden chairs at the small table. A shot glass and a cup sat next to several bottles of brown liquid. He blew the dust out of the glass cup and poured himself a drink.

No need to drink alone, he thought, snapping his fingers. A small amount of smoke appeared on the table in front of him, and through it stepped Xissay.

She was Wren's familiar bound to him through the ritual he carried out a century ago in earning the rank of death speaker. Others of his order would call forth spirits out of The Great Dream of giant demons or other physically impressive creatures.

Wren thought it more prudent, given his occupation as a Hand of The Syndicate, to go the more inconspicuous route. Besides, it was nice having someone around smaller than him. Wren could also keep Xissay in the plane of the living longer and with greater ease than fighting to keep the undead soul of a wyvern or some other monstrous, unwieldy thing from returning to The Great Dream.

Though she was not as physically strong as other larger familiars, she made up for her lack of size with an ability to fly and cast some of the fire magic she mastered in life. To Wren, she was more companion than creature or tool.

Strutting past the smoke, Xissay looked Wren up and down. "Drinking alone again? You look like hell."

Wren shot her a glare and poured her a drink in the shot glass. "Not anymore, it seems, and not before either. I met someone."

In her high-pitched nasally voice, she taunted the gnome, "Oooooh, and was she pretty?"

"Not like that," he replied. "I think I met someone who could be a new Eye for The Syndicate and us here in Ravnice."

She spread her hands apologetically in peace, and Wren harrumphed away the pang of guilt at the passing of his late charge. He poured them both another glass and before long was himself snoring away in his bed.

Xissay gave the sleeping gnome a fond look. "Amateur." She snickered and stepped back into the once again appearing sulfuric smoke. She smiled as she returned to the plane of those eternally sleeping. At least these past hundred years with Wren, she got to enjoy the adventures of the living from time to time.

Chapter 4

Lodestar Island

His palms flat on the ornate marble banister of his office balcony, Seulman Tuath inhaled the sweet tropical air of the city-state his family had ruled for generations. He had the tan, olive-skinned complexion shared amongst most northerners, and his sun-bleached hair was more grey than golden blond.

His almond-colored eyes scanned and flicked about as he looked out at his city. Tuath sprawled out below him from his mansion atop a giant hill as it sloped to the water. The north-facing bay before him bustled with ships and merchants.

He spared himself a few indulgent thoughts envisioning a return to when Tuath was the most prosperous island region and held the lion's share of its wealth. Still, it was second only to Mer in population and wealth and maintained one of only two formal navies along with the pseudo-capital.

Motion in the courtyard caught his attention as a rider dismounted and tied up his horse. Seulman turned from his balcony and walked back into his office. He gripped the back of his chair and then sat in it slowly before looking at the older woman who sat in stately silence awaiting his command on the far side of his expansive desk.

"Fetch my son, will you, Niverna." He directed the white-haired sage from The College of Elements. "Perhaps he will learn something of the world and how it runs."

Nodding to the governor, the woman made her way out of his office without a word, her flowing orange elementalist robe barely shifted with her measured steps as she left.

*****

Knowing where to find the governor's son was easy enough. Niverna had known him his entire life. Her posting as court representative for The College of Elements in Tuath had happened several years before he was born.

Myrlman's mother had died in childbirth, which didn't help the boy's cause with his father. She had helped educate him as a youth and still as a young man and was the closest thing to a motherly figure Myrlman had. She knocked on his door as she swung it open.

"I'd recognize the rap of those old knuckles on my door any day, Niverna," the young man said from his seat in front of a large easel, a paintbrush held in his hand. The practically nude woman on the bed shot Niverna a look for the interruption.

"Myrlman, your father wishes your attendance; Dillion has returned from The Hall with news," Niverna said, altogether ignoring the model wrapped in sheets.

Myrlman Tuath rolled his eyes and reverently laid his paintbrush down. "I shall return before long, my dear." He said softly, and it was hard to tell whether he meant the brush or the woman.

As they left, Niverna offered some counsel to the young man walking in front of her. "At least feign interest and spare us both a tirade from your father if you wouldn't mind."

Myrlman slowed his stride as they approached his father's office door, letting the woman catch up with him.

"Ever have you attempted to protect me from my father's wrath, good Niverna"

She gave him a shove through the door and took a seat on a wooden bench along the wall.

Myrlman sprawled into one of two cushioned chairs on the other side of the office. "Beautiful day, is it not, father."

Seulman was about to lay into his son when the office door swung open again, and the city's court bard stepped in front of his desk. "Good day to you, Governor," he said, after raising his eyebrows at the lounging Myrlman.

"What news of the world Dillion, and how fares my cousin?" Seulman addressed the bard, deciding to deal with his son later.

"The Impresario is in good health and sends his best to you

31

both," Dillion said, indicating the father and son. "Of other affairs, in the south, it seems tensions between the wood elves and city proper in Kalt have eased some."

Seulman snorted. "Of southerners and foreigners, I care not."

"It is feared pirates are getting bolder. Tales of an attack on a Ravnice ship are circulating at the Hall," the bard said, undaunted.

Seulman turned to Niverna. "Take note to let the admiral know we might need to step up patrols or even escort some of our more valuable shipments in the near term."

Returning his gaze to Dillion, his voice became a bit surlier. "And you send word via The Hall of our intentions and mention that I expect those commoners down in Mer to do the same." He paused and raised his voice further. "I will be bringing it up at the next council meeting too!"

Dillion rattled off several more happenings and goings-on. Niverna sat quietly, taking note of his statements and Seulman's responses. She would pass her recordings along to the local vicar for archival with other historical records at the Tuath Diocese. The room finally grew quiet, and she looked up from her paper.

"You are dismissed," Seulman said from behind the immense desk. Then, as they got up to leave, he stabbed a finger in the air at his son. "Not you, boy."

As they left the office and closed the door behind them, Dillion nodded to Niverna and headed off towards the kitchens. Niverna turned and headed towards her quarters. The sound of Seulman's berating on responsibility and ruling fading away behind her, she shook her head at the thought of Myrlman's eventual ascension.

Entering her quarters, Niverna tucked herself into her writing desk. Then, pulling a blank roll of parchment from its drawers, she began her report for The Syndicate. It seemed the situation in Kalt had been resolved, for now.

The woods are calming.

She wrote in case news had not made it back to the island through another channel. She also noted that she felt Seulman's disposition towards the other city-states was worrisome. She further reiterated that she did not think her adviser role would enable her to steer him from likely violent attempts at regaining control over more of the island.

> *Tropical waters, unavoidably near boiling*
> *The pirated sea will grow more watchful*
> *A breeze may sway the apple from the tree*

Niverna was more than a little concerned. She felt by now The Syndicate would have acted on the recommendations provided by herself and the Hand. Not that she would know ahead of time. The timely passing of Seulman Tuath would be their only indication of the Navigator's decision. So compartmentalized was The Syndicate that she had no idea who its handful of assassins were, those few mysterious Shadows of The Syndicate.

The more sensitive, shorthand parchment she rolled and sealed with candle wax. As the wax seal cooled, she indented it with her thumb, making a small bowl into which she poured a minuscule amount of ink. Then she added more candle wax to seal it in. If the document were opened and resealed, the ink stain would indicate a potential compromise of The Syndicate's messaging system to the Navigators on the other end.

That done, she took a calming breath of Tuath's thickly humid air. Her joints hurt less in the warmth of Tuath than they had during her time spent further south teaching at The College of Elements. She was a natural fit for Tuath's court, given Seulman's suspiciousness of magic in general. Lacking the gift had not stopped her from becoming one of the senior members of the college, and she never lamented much over its absence.

The door of her quarters opened, and she was nearly startled out of her chair.

"Good evening, Sage Niverna." The serving girl said with her head bowed until the door shut behind her. "I have your dinner for you."

Niverna smiled at the unassuming young woman and exchanged the two parchments for her plate, which the woman promptly tucked in her bodice.

Too old for the sneaking about she had done as The Syndicate's Hand in Mer, Niverna was happy now to be the Eye in Tuath. "The sealed one for the Helmsman and the other for the local diocese."

The woman squeezed her arm and left. How clever of The

Syndicate, Niverna thought to herself. Their Hand in Tuath was a comely younger woman with easy access to most rooms of the governor's mansion.

She also had a daily excuse to go to the market to buy foodstuffs from merchants, especially the one who was in truth a Syndicate Helmsman. Such individuals were responsible for getting messages to one of The Syndicate fronted merchant ships that couriered supplies and information to and from Lodestar Island.

If ever the Hand was caught in the wrong place, bringing with her a food tray with refuse on it to clean up would surely provide an easy excuse for being there. But, if that failed, batting of eyelashes and a bit of flirtation could handle almost any situation.

*****

Seulman's tirade at his son's expense complete, the younger Tuath left the office seemingly unfazed. Seulman sank into his chair and grabbed the decanter of wine off his desk. Not even bothering with a glass, he drank deep. Sirul had seen enough through the peephole his needle had made in the ceiling above. He slowly rolled onto his back in the cramped attic space above Seulman's office.

The tasking he had received in Kalt to head north had made this mission seem rather pressing. He had noticed the order of execution the day he arrived in the Tuath harbor area. To any passerby, it would appear as drunken graffiti. At some point, the disgruntled shop owner would naturally paint over it, covering any trace of The Syndicate's message. After a quick rest, he had spent the last hours of his first night in the city making his way into the cramped attic space he now occupied.

He preferred to observe his prey longer before deciding how to dispose of them, but his mission was urgent. As he lay flattened above the office ceiling in the mansion's attic, he had seen Seulman consuming vast amounts of wine and stumbling around his office. The drunk man was mumbling curses to himself on his balcony into the waning hours of the evening before passing out drunk in his bed in the chamber next door. Sirul decided no one would second guess the cause of death upon finding the governor's corpse dead on the street below his balcony, shattered wine decanter in hand.

No one would notice the small hole from his needle in the man's ear among the bloody mess the fall would make. Seulman's method of death decided Sirul hoped to catch a quick nap while the man snored below in his adjacent quarters.

His mind had other plans and his thoughts went to the political theatre he had witnessed in the office below. Sirul wondered if it was the bard or perhaps the sage that was an agent of The Syndicate here in Tuath.

Surely, they had planted someone close to this raging buffoon to keep an eye on him and provide enough information to warrant his assassination. Sirul was not supposed to know the identity of Eyes or Hands, but his money was on the sage.

It had struck a nerve with Sirul how oddly similar he and Myrlman Tuath looked. They were both olive-skinned and grey eyed, with short-cut, curly blond hair. They were even of similar build. Such strange fate that two men so alike in looks had lived such different lives, he thought to himself.

Unaccustomed to distraction, he could not shake the coincidence of their lives from his mind.

"One who draws women in bed, and another who paints only in red," he whispered to the rafters above him in a voice that sounded quite like the son of Seulman Tuath. Sirul pictured Myrlman twirling his paintbrush in his fingers just as he twirled his needle.

Not quite the same, though, Sirul thought to himself, running a finger along the scar from his right eye down his entire cheek. It was a reminder of a fight at the age of twelve with a baker over a loaf of stolen bread. That was the last battle he had ever lost.

He understood that, for most, the position of Shadow in The Syndicate was not a long-tenured one. Lately, he couldn't keep fantasies of retirement from his mind. Maybe he should retire.

Not from murder. What else would he do? But from The Syndicate's tasking. He had more than earned that.

He knew he needed to be very careful, or he would be enjoying his retirement as a corpse floating in Tuath Bay. He decided a trip to Mer was in order. A quick trip at that. If his plan were to work, he would need to be back in Tuath before The Syndicate sent another Shadow.

*****

It had been six days since Harpis had parted ways with the *Sea Goat* and Wren. Amid a pounding headache the morning after their evening together, he found the instructions left by the enigmatic gnome. Despite how much whiskey he had drunk that night at The Siren's Scream, he clearly remembered the look of concern on Wren's face as his gaze kept darting around the tavern.

He also recalled the gnome's parting words regarding the two sailors he had spotted taking an interest in them as they supped and drank downstairs. Waiting on more instructions, he had spent the following days eating, thinking, and drinking.

During the day, he would stroll around Ravnice, imagining himself one of its uniformed militiamen. At night he watched his future colleagues dragging belligerent customers from taverns and inns or chasing thieves on the wharf. After almost a week of observation, he decided the job of enforcing law and keeping peace excited him not at all. Each day that passed, the intrigue around what Wren had proposed gnawed at his resolve.

On the seventh morning in Ravnice, he woke to a leather pouch sitting on the pillow next to his face. He was more than a little shaken that someone had snuck into his room and placed it there without stirring him.

The purse had silver coins enough for him to buy armor, a good sword, and stay another two weeks at the inn. Enough to start his new life, just as the gnome promised. There was also a bronze coin with a one-eyed elven face on one side and nothing on the other and a folded parchment. The letter told him to arrive at the southernmost docks without being followed. At noon he was to present the bronze coin to the crew of a schooner named *The Albatross*.

Shrugging at himself in the room's poorly polished mirror, he flipped the coin, letting it hit the floor of his rented room. It skipped and then rolled in a circle in front of him a few times before falling flat. The one-eyed depiction of an elf stared up at him ominously from the floorboards.

"Why not?" he asked, looking from the coin to the man in the mirror. He picked up the coin and parchment, sticking them in his boot along with his knife before heading downstairs. Leaving the tavern, he thanked the barmaid for the stay.

36

*****

Harpis reached the edge of the specified dock a little before midday and readily found *The Albatross* tied off at its end, bobbing amongst several other boats. He tried to catch a glimpse of anyone aboard but did not see or hear anything. Finally, after a few long moments, he decided to try and hail the crew.

"Hello? Is anyone there? I have the coin, and I am ready to go!" he shouted.

Suddenly the world went black when what felt like a grain sack was pulled over his head. An impossibly firm grip swept him from his feet and flung him down face first. He felt smaller hands deftly search him, stopping at his boots to snatch his knife, the coin, and the letter. He tried to struggle, but the larger man had his hands expertly locked behind his back.

"Get off me, you ape! Help!" Harpis wailed from inside the thick sack.

One immense hand kept an iron grip on both his wrists while the other palmed his head and slammed it to the dock.

"Shut your mouth, or you'll be taking a little nap," the man on his back said.

"You sure this is the man we saw the other night with the gnome?" the other assailant said.

"Yeah, that's him for sure. He must be one of them. What does the note say?" the larger man asked.

"To look for this boat right here, *The Albatross*. It looks empty for now. We should probably get out of here before his friends get back," he said, pausing for a moment, "It also says don't be followed!" he snickered.

Both men laughed, and Harpis heard the letter get crumpled and thrown to the water.

"Hey, I don't know any gnomes, and I don't have any friends. I was down here looking at the fish," Harpis pleaded.

"Oh, my apologies, good sir, we must have the wrong man. I guess we should let you go," the standing figure said with a chuckle.

Realizing the moment was becoming more desperate, Harpis panicked. "Help! Anyone!" he screamed as loudly as he could. If anyone noticed, he would never know. A muscled arm slipped

37

around his neck and choked him unconscious.

Chapter 5
The Syndicate

The day after Harpis was supposed to have left, Wren could not help his curiosity as he made his way to the Ravnice wharf area. He had other business in the waterside market, but he first stopped at The Siren's Scream. He spotted the barmaid who had served them the other night sweeping off the entryway and hailed her with a wave. "Good morning, miss."

She smiled and paused her work. "And you as well, Master Gnome."

Wren found it odd that he was almost nervous to know the answer despite having not seen Harpis around Ravnice once since they parted.

"My companion the other night?"

The barmaid winked at him. "He was all dressed and ready for the day when I went to wake him. He left before lunch, and I have not seen him since."

"My thanks again," Wren said, waving goodbye to her. Visiting the wharf shops was his weekly errand. He would pick up supplies for the mortuary, mostly linens and oils, to prepare the bodies. Today though, it was just linen that he needed. His usual vendor exchanged a stack of white sheets for a few of his silver coins, and a few pleasantries later, he was on his way home.

Passing near The Siren's Scream on his way back, he fought an internal debate about a bite and a sip. Something about the look in his linen vendor's eyes sent him straight back to his morgue. Locking the front door and checking that he had the closed sign placed out, he headed upstairs. Closing his apartment door behind him, he set the stack of linens on his table.

39

He then walked over to the apartment's singular window, which overlooked the street below. Staying in the shadows of his curtain to not be seen from the road, he surveyed it for anything suspicious. For several agonizing moments, he waited to see if he saw anyone from the wharf who may have uncharacteristically made their way to his street. Finally, he let out a long breath at not being followed.

Undoing the ties around the stack, he began taking them off one by one. He made a new pile next to them until he picked up a linen halfway down and revealed a parchment sealed with wax. He scrutinized it for signs of ink droplets. Seeing none, he sat on his chair before snapping his fingers. Sulfuric odor and a puff of smoke later, Xissay stood on the table before the two piles of linen.

"So, old gnome, when did you take up quilting?"

Wren ignored her and broke the seal on the parchment, noting thankfully the several drops of ink that spilled out.

Xissay provocatively stretched her lithe form as she stepped between the linen piles and continued. "I'm just saying, Wren, if you're going to make a quilt, I think you need linens of two separate colors."

Wren looked over the parchment at her with one raised eyebrow. "Word from the Navigators, and they seem unusually skittish."

Her interest piqued, she floated without a flap of her wings onto Wren's shoulder to read with him.

Sorry to hear about your eye.
Well done abroad.
Go Pray for Sirul Amun.

"Looks as if we are bound for Fjall and The Sanctum," he told Xissay as he handed her the parchment. "Be a help and take care of that."

Xissay left his shoulder holding the parchment in her hands, and it burst into flames almost immediately. The ashes fell to the floor below her as he stood from his chair. "We shall leave in the morning."

Being a devout death speaker of The Sleeper and one of the senior necromancers meant that Wren always had an excuse to leave town for religious reasons. As such, it was never suspicious for the morgue to be closed for weeks at a time with little notice.

It was a coincidence that this time his journey was truthfully to The Sanctum. He had no idea who Sirul Amun was, but apparently, the Navigators wanted to know if he or she was alive or dead. There was only one who could ask that of Lady Death. So, it seemed that he was to head west in the morning, to the mountains of Fjall and The Sanctum.

*****

They had been at sea a little over a full day, and Harpis had lost his sense of direction long ago. Not that it had mattered. He was locked below deck in a tiny cabin at the front of the boat's hold while still unconscious, so he had no sense of his surroundings. Since one could sail around the entire Island of Quaj in just over two days and Ravnice was only a day's sail from any major city, he had no idea where they were going.

There was only the two crew on the ship as far as he could tell. He was sure they were the same two Wren had seen at The Siren's Scream, an older thin man who seemed to be in charge and a burly sailor who fit the gnome's ox-like description.

The past two times, it was the bigger man who had brought him food. On both occasions, Harpis had tried to reason with the man and solicit information but received only smirks and grunts. When the brute got him his dinner, he had a surprise in mind. Finding a sharp nail head on one of the walls, Harpis had taken off his shirt and rubbed it against the metal until he cut a line almost entirely down the back of it.

His pulse pounded in his throat, and adrenaline coursed through his veins as he heard the man approaching. The wood cover slid open on the grate at the top of the door, and the sailor peered at him suspiciously before sliding it shut and cracking the door open to throw some bread and a waterskin into the cabin. Once the man turned to go, Harpis took a steadying breath.

"Hey, ass face!" he shouted through the door.

The man's footsteps paused, and he smiled to himself before continuing his taunting.

"Oh good, so you know your face looks like an ass. And let's be honest, we both know I'm not talking about the lovable

41

livestock. I wouldn't insult the animal so. I am talking about the lumpy thing your mother puts in her customer's laps at the cheapest brothel in town!" he yelled.

He grinned at the approaching angry stomps. The sailor snapped open the wood cover to the grate.

"Watch your mouth, idiot, or you are going to regret it," he growled.

Harpis sucked in a breath through his nose and spat in the man's face.

Bellowing in rage, the man unlocked the door, flung it open, and grabbed a handful of Harpis' shirt before pulling back his other fist to strike. The larger man almost fell backward as Harpis' shirt effortlessly tore off, and his punch swung wide.

Harpis quickly shouldered into the off-balance sailor and sprinted for the ladder at the other end of the hold as his shouting captor chased after him. Harpis made the hatch at the top of the ladder and heaved himself onto the ship's deck facing the stern. He didn't see the other sailor, only an unmanned helm. As he swiveled his head to look around, he barely caught sight of the swinging oar before it knocked him unconscious.

*****

The city of Mer sat mostly contained on a peninsula jutting outward from the middle of the island's eastern coast, with the harbor opening to the north. The College of Elements sat on the southernmost portion where no ships could port, providing easy access to a mostly private beach area where science and magic could go awry with minimal destruction to the surrounding city.

Rallis was one of the newest trainees of the college's Tower of Stone. It seemed that the gifted and non-gifted elementalist trainees alike often aspired to manipulate the more exciting fire, wind, or water.

Stone may be dull, Rallis thought to himself, but his plans for today most certainly were not. He had found the dusty book covering the life and works of Stone Magus Breyva left open in the apprentice area the other night and was determined to know if the writings were rumor or fact.

If Stone Mage Vennil possessed the Stone Mask of Breyva, it could allow Rallis to don someone else's face and have all kinds of fun.

He waited for the stone mage to take his lunch in the courtyard like he did every day. As soon as the older man passed the trainees and went out of the tower door, Rallis rose and headed upstairs. As he passed the two apprentices who happened to be on the second floor, he held up a bag that contained his books.

"Errand for Stone Sage Mara," Rallis offered and carried on to the third floor unimpeded.

He could not believe his luck that the stone mage had not locked the door. He slipped quietly into the room, hoping he did not alert Stone Sage Mara in the other quarters and locked the door behind him. He spotted what he was looking for on top of the bookshelf against the far wall.

Grabbing the stone coffer from the bookshelf, he gingerly placed it on Vennil's desk. He used one of the few spells he did know and sensed the chilly tingle along his spine from the magic of the coffer and noted the aura of the item within it as well. It must be this, he thought.

*****

A commotion from outside the room caught his attention, and the thief spun around in panic. The locked doorknob jiggled once, and then the door exploded inward. Behind it stepped a dwarf-sized stone elemental familiar followed by the fuming Stone Mage Vennil and a confused Stone Sage Mara.

The middle-aged mage from Ravnice had short-cut red hair that only accentuated his aggressive demeanor.

"Rallis, you are one of the most impudent, know-nothing, belligerent trainees I have ever encountered. I'll have you painting rocks in the courtyard until your dotage. You dare to steal the Clay Mask of Breyva?" Vennil said as he looked down at the thief's trapped fingers. The stone of the lid held firmly all ten.

"Serves you right for opening the coffer," he said, closing his eyes, he laid a palm on the lid, and it released the thief's fingers.

"Master Vennil, I wasn't going to steal it. I just wanted to use it to prank the apprentices."

The explanation did nothing to cool Vennil's temper as he continued to glare at the trembling young man.

Vennil pointed an angry finger at the thief. "Now put this

43

back and forget it exists. It is nothing to be trifled with."

"But master...the Mask was not in the chest, and I did not unlock it..." the would-be burglar stammered while still holding the coffer.

Vennil's gaze slowly drifted down to the empty coffer, looking as if he would be sick. For her part, the much older Stone Sage Mara was rubbing her grey temples in frustrated thought.

"Rallis, if you speak of this, I will have you expelled from this college," the stone mage said, pausing in thought before continuing. "You were up here at my bidding, the coffer's magic trapped you, and I had to burst in here to save you from it. Now leave. Stone Sage Mara and I must consult the Arch Mage immediately."

Chapter 6
A New Life

The next day Harpis felt the boat slowing, and even with the sack over his head, he could hear waves lapping against a stony shore, a sound which he hoped meant his journey had come to an end. Then, at last, the boat stopped and bobbed in the water as he listened to the crew tying it to a pier.

His door swung open, and he felt the familiar strength of the more considerable sailor grab his arm and lead him above decks.

"Well?" Harpis heard the older sailor behind him ask.

A new, soft-spoken voice responded. "Let me see his face first."

The sailor ripped off the hood, and Harpis sucked in the fresh air with a chill that was more than he expected this late in spring. Salt from the sea was everywhere in the endless howling gusts on what must have been the windward side of this unknown island. Above him, in front of two black leather uniformed and pike bearing guards, stood a short but fit, fifty-something man with grey hair. He had scarred and wrinkled brown skin that reminded Harpis of the Quaji natives. The man wore a well-trimmed goatee and weathered dark leathers.

"He'll do, twenty silvers as agreed," the man said in the same quiet voice, throwing a coin purse to the older sailor behind Harpis, and the sack appeared once again over his head.

As the guards escorted Harpis away, he heard the older sailor handle what sounded like a sack with parchments in it and address the man. "For the bosses, Master Arken."

"Fair winds and following seas, lads. Good work, see you in a few weeks," Arken said to the departing sailors.

*****

When Arken removed the hood again, Harpis' eyes found little light to adjust to in what smelled like a cellar that had only a few lit candles to fend off the gloom. Next, the guards shackled his ankles to a chain cemented in the floor. They then bent him forward, shackling his wrists together and to his ankles, forcing him into an arched position.

There was not enough slack for him to sit, and standing was now an impossibility. A shake to make sure the shackles were secured, and the guards seemed to leave.

Arken stepped in front of Harpis. "Who are you, and why were you on that boat? Surely you did not knowingly board a slave traders' vessel?"

Wren had warned him to keep quiet about what they had discussed until he arrived safely with the gnome's compatriots. Harpis answered the man with silence.

Behind him, Harpis heard a chuckle and a thump. He could not see the source of the laughter or that the person behind him had picked up and turned an hourglass over before setting it back onto the table.

"I'll ask you again, who sent you and why?" Arken pressed.

This time Harpis' silence was rewarded with a punch to the kidney and a few slaps to the face. Arken then pulled a large bucket of water in front of Harpis, grabbed his hair, and shoved his head into the water.

As furiously as Harpis struggled, the shackles would not allow him to free his head from the waters. Just as he thought he would die drowning in what was probably a latrine bucket, Arken ripped his face out of the water.

Coughing and gagging, he heard Arken repeat the question and remained silent. In response, Arken slid the bucket forward and grabbed the back of his hair again.

"Fine, I'll ta-" he muttered, with the last word coming out as mostly bubbles when Arken shoved his head back into the water.

After what seemed like forever to the drowning Harpis, his torturer pulled his face from the bucket again. Once he recovered his composure, Arken spoke, "I am sorry. I couldn't understand you there. What was that?"

Harpis responded in a half shout, "I said I'd talk!"

Arken grinned. "Well then, why were you on the boat?"

After catching his breath, Harpis paused for dramatic effect and responded as sincerely as he could manage. "I thought I was going on a pleasure cruise with your mother."

Arken's grin turned to a frown as the figure behind Harpis chuckled again and tauntingly tapped the hourglass several times. Then, with speed and strength unfitting his apparent age, Arken grabbed Harpis' hair again, but instead of slamming him back into the bucket, he licked his pointer finger on his other hand and jammed it into Harpis' ear, pressing harder and harder.

It felt as though the man could reach his brain as pain and heat exploded in his ear and along his cheek as Arken pressed on.

"All right, all right stop, I'll speak true," Harpis screamed. Arken pressed for another long moment before letting up.

Harpis practically spat the words of his confession. "Some corpse humping gnome I met on a boat out of Kalt convinced me to go to the docks that day with tales of grandeur and service!"

Arken and whoever was behind Harpis laughed together.

"You'll have to do a lot better than that in the future, young Harpis." Arken taunted, softly patting his face.

"About ten minutes, Arken, you're getting soft in your old age," said the unknown voice over fading footsteps.

"Just out of practice is all, Braffen," Arken replied before turning back to Harpis. "We needed to make sure you weren't an infiltrator or worse," he said with an innocent shrug.

Arken undid the shackles around his wrists and ankles. "Apologies for the roughing up. We can't be too careful, you see."

As Harpis painfully straightened his back and stood upright, Arken wagged one finger at him. "Quite effective, no?"

Still clutching his ear, Harpis could not argue.

"Come, it's time to meet the bosses," he commanded, offering Harpis his dagger back before turning and beckoning him to follow.

They emerged from a cave not far from the lone dock he had arrive on, and the constant wind struck Harpis again. The island was small, maybe a mile around. A jet-black dormant volcano rose above the scant ring of shrubs on its lower slopes. Ahead was a path cut into the side of the mountain which climbed away from them around towards the island's leeward side.

After a few minutes of walking, a simple three-story light-house tower rose out of the side of the volcano. In addition, there was a small two-story building attached to its base that could be considered a house of sorts.

When they reached the door, Arken pulled a rope hanging from the soffit overhead. The result was the sound of a bell ringing somewhere inside.

"Coming, coming!" a grating voice said, flitting out the windows above as the stairs creaked from someone making their way down. The door swung open to reveal an aged man of some seventy years with bushy white eyebrows, long white hair, and beard to match. He wore simple worn clothing which framed the lean features of a man who had spent many decades at sea.

"Good afternoon, gentlemen, come on in." From off to the side, the two uniformed soldiers who had escorted Harpis to the cave acknowledged them and disappeared into another room.

The older man shut the door behind them and shuffled back up the stairs. Arken led Harpis straight towards the back wall of the hallway, tugged a torch sconce, and the back wall slid away, revealing a tunnel into the side of the volcano with light visible some fifty paces down.

"This is amazing," Harpis said, gawking. "How many of you live here?"

Arken was silent as they walked through the tunnel and emerged onto the circular floor of the dormant volcano crater that stretched over two hundred yards before them. The path across the crater was intersected in the middle by one perpendicular to it. The walkways split the courtyard into quarters, one of which fenced in some goats and sheep.

Harpis spotted two cows with a large chicken coop against the rock wall. The crater walls themselves stretched up thirty feet, yet the mid-day sunlight illuminated its entirety. On either side of the animals, two-quarters of the courtyard contained gardens and fruit trees. The last quarter was mostly dirt and had racks of wooden and iron weapons as well as archery targets.

Arken put his hands on his hips and peered around the crater. "There are some thirty or so of us that live here and another handful who pass through."

As they walked across the courtyard, Harpis began to make out windows carved into the rock face opposite them.

Immediately upon entering the hewn rock hallway on the far wall, Arken took him to the right and up a curving stone staircase to the second floor, down a short hall, and arrived at a thick ironbound wooden door. He pounded it twice, and a voice inside bid them come in.

The room they entered was not deep but was very wide and faced the courtyard with many windows. On one end were three desks and bookshelves with twice as many books as they should hold. There were maps and scrolls beyond that stacked, stuffed, and strewn about the place.

A low fire burned in a small fireplace, and two black-robed figures sat at a triangle-shaped table near the other wall. The table itself looked as if it came from a single piece of enormous driftwood.

In the center was an engraving of a ship's steering wheel with a palm-up hand that stretched from top to bottom of the wheel and had an eye engraved in the center. There was an empty chair on the side nearest Harpis which Arken motioned for him to sit in.

Arken himself leaned against the wall just behind him and Harpis had the feeling that even if he wanted to make a move at either of the two across from him, Arken would have killed him before he finished the thought.

To his left sat a short woman with the same dark complexion as Arken. Her hair was stark white and hung loosely, framing a face that looked slightly older than Arken's fifty-some years. Almond-colored eyes bored a hole into Harpis for what seemed like forever before she spoke quietly and deliberately.

"Well met, Harpis, I am Trilia Saboghan, youngest of the three Navigators of The Lodestar Syndicate. It seems you have already met Arken Hester, our master instructor," she said, gesturing to Arken, who gave her a short bow.

Harpis tried not to visibly squirm as she stopped speaking but never lifted her gaze.

"And I am Qarn, second eldest Navigator," the ancient-looking Gnome to Harpis' right said gruffly.

Qarn paused to glare at Harpis for a moment before softening his gaze. "So, you want to join our merry band of misfits, eh? You, on the words of a too-often drunk gnome with a strong case of necrophilia, sailed halfway around the world to Lodestar Island on a whim. Why?"

49

Harpis gulped and answered, "I wanted to do something worthwhile. I thought that was in the Ravnice militia, but Wren convinced me there was potential here for more. I want to make my mark on the world, and he told me if I made it through indoctrination here, I would get to do that."

Qarn leaned forward. "Oh, you'll make your mark and then some, so long as you are all right with never being able to claim that you were the one who made it."

The gnome leaned further across the table, as far as his short frame would allow while still touching the floor. "Can you live with such anonymity?"

Becoming surer of himself despite the austere company, Harpis answered more steadily this time, "I can, Master Qarn."

Trilia sat drumming her fingers on the table. "Your knife please," she said, holding out her hand for it.

Harpis reached down into his boot and drew the knife. He could sense the tension in Arken's muscles behind him as he slowly handed it, handle first, to Trilia.

"This," she said. "This is quite special." She turned the blade over in her hands. "The Siren blesses you to own such a weapon. I implore you, do not lose it."

Trilia looked above Harpis at Arken. "That, he may keep, and Wren was quite right about his gift." Then, turning back to Harpis, she continued. "If and when you complete your indoctrination, I will reveal its powers to you, and we may discuss your gift."

Qarn climbed on top of the table, earning a disapproving look at his filthy sandals from Trilia.

"Well, suppose we make this official and all before we feed him to the dogs." Qarn paused and glanced at Arken. "No offense intended, Master Arken."

The man snorted in response.

Walking over to Harpis' side of the table, Qarn motioned for Harpis to stand. "As eldest Navigator present and Vicar of Lodestar Island…."

Trilia put her head in her hand, drawing a glare from Qarn.

"What of it? I am the senior-most member of the clergy on this island, and as such, I am therefore its vicar, so what if I've been off Quaj since before the current Exarch was but a babe," he said.

Trilia rolled her eyes. "You're the only member of the clergy

50

on the island," she said and waved a hand at Qarn to continue.

"What's your family name, lad, and where do you hail from?" Qarn asked.

"Harpis Akkeri, and nowhere." He answered, receiving an uncaring shrug from Qarn.

"All right then, Harpis of nowhere, do you swear on your life and your soul, to crew the vessel that is Quaj, keeping safe her passengers, to keep the wind in her sails, her hull off the rocks, and point her true to the greater good of all?" the gnome finished, out of breath.

"I swear it," Harpis said, bowing his head slightly. Then, when he looked up, the gnome backhanded him with surprising force across his cheek.

"You've made your oath, and that was so you remember it," he said, climbing back into his chair, huffing.

Trilia stood slowly, walked up, and kissed Harpis' other cheek. "And that, she said winking, was so you really remember it."

From behind him, Arken slapped the backside of his head. "And that was simply because I wanted to, and don't be expecting a kiss to follow."

Settled back into his chair, Qarn addressed Harpis again. "Consider yourself accepted for indoctrination."

He stopped to draw in more breath. "The Syndicate has existed for several hundred years to protect the people of Quaj from the malice and greed of the individual from dooming the lot. As you may have deduced from talking with Wren, each city-state has a Hand and an Eye."

The old gnome paused, running his hand along the crest on the table in between them. "The Hand is typically the more senior and allowed to manipulate the course of the island. The Eye learns and takes direction from the Hand and is instructed to gather information but not act on it. We only train one operative at a time here at Lodestar."

Qarn sat back and laced his fingers together before staring Harpis in the eye. "The Syndicate is an espionage organization, you see. Three Navigators to chart the course, based on information from our Eyes. We turn the wheel using our Hands to keep the island on the right course."

Qarn then seemed to become more careful and deliberate in

what he divulged.

"Lady Trilia, an accomplished water mage, will instruct you on laws and geopolitics, and I, servant of Daybreak, will cover the histories," Qarn finished.

"And I will ensure you learn everything else," Arken commented from behind him, putting a hand on Harpis Shoulder. "Truthfully, I will teach you but three things, and when you leave here, you will never forget them. Everyone may be a threat, everyone may be a mark, and every piece of information may be vitally important."

Trilia smiled at him. "If Wren has vouched for you, I think you will make it through indoctrination just fine. We believe your intentions, Harpis, but we still need to test your soul, train your body, and fill your mind," she said.

Arken ended his lean against the wall and took a step back. "Come, Harpis. I will show you the rest of our facilities and your quarters. Indoctrination begins tomorrow."

Harpis stood out of the chair, but he could not resist a question before turning to go. "Where is the other Navigator, who sits in this chair?"

Qarn chuckled. "Not all our secrets at once, lad. Eat well tonight. Tomorrow starts the toughest month of your young life. Make it through these weeks and the assessment that follows, and we will consider you worth the while of being truly trained back on the streets of Ravnice by a certain necromancer. If you become an Eye for The Syndicate, you may spend years or decades in that role learning from the Hand before being deemed capable of further responsibility."

*****

Sirul had been stalking the Tuath wharf for days after his decision to let Seulman live. He had spared Seulman's life not out of mercy but for a purpose. The governor would not live long. It would not take The Syndicate but days or weeks to find out that Sirul had not completed his mission.

For his retirement plan to succeed, Sirul needed to be there when Seulman Tuath drew his last breath. But, for that to happen, he needed to know when the next Syndicate Shadow received their tasking.

It was a stormy spring day, even for tropical Tuath. He was looking for The Syndicate runes he was sure would appear as graffiti in the city's poorest and more dangerous area. There were times where death was to be obvious, a warning to others. His instructions received weeks ago, for Seulman's death, had been to make it appear an accident. That may have served whatever grand plan The Syndicate had in motion, but it would not help his own.

Sirul was one with the shadows of a storage shelter near the docks, allowing him to view as much of the wharf as possible. It was essentially empty given the hour and the weather.

He almost jumped when he saw a slim feminine figure pause near the side of a particularly unsavory tavern. The figure bent down with what must have been charcoal and quickly wrote on the bottom of the wall.

She was done after a moment and then straightened, pulling her green cowl and cloak tight against the rain. Finally, she paused, surveying the rest of the wharf.

Sirul, for his part, attempted to become one with the pile of grain sacks behind him, despite knowing she could not possibly see him. Still, if she was writing what he hoped she was, she too was trained and likely experienced in espionage, and her senses may have been nearly as keen as his.

Seemingly satisfied no one noticed her, the woman stepped away from the wall and disappeared into an alleyway. Sirul's tradecraft-driven paranoia and excited curiosity waged an excruciating battle for his will. He wanted more than anything to run over and see what she had written but knew he needed to wait until she was truly gone.

Perhaps she was as good as he at sneaking and prying, and he could not risk that. She could also, out of curiosity, contemplate breaking protocol to try and catch a glimpse of a Syndicate Shadow. Maybe she had waited out of sight to see who came to inspect the runes. Then again, if he waited too long, he might run into the other Shadow, or worse, miss him or her and lose his chance to be present at Seulman's killing and set his planned events into action.

Curiosity won after an hour as dawn's light began to break. He would become increasingly noticeable and suspicious-looking backed into an alcove of grain sacks. He strolled towards the markings she'd made, gazing around at every window and every doorstep acting as calm as his nerves would allow, and walked past the graffiti.

He saw an anchor casting a shadow, the sign that the Shadow was to move forward with the plans to stop someone's journey on the sea of time. A small crescent moon next to the anchor indicating the death still was to appear as an accident. If it were instead a sun, the death was to be an apparent assassination.

Over the anchor, a crown with Tuath's city seal indicates that the city's leader was the target. In his excitement to return, he almost missed the rope hanging from the top of the anchor, a knot tied in its end, the sign to dispose of loose ends.

He felt hot rage wash over his entire body. Did they send another Shadow here to not only finish his task as he expected but look for, and if possible, dispose of Sirul himself? His training kept him walking, his steps measured. His fists were clenched so hard several knuckles popped, and the tendons of his hands silently screamed for mercy.

He had sent hundreds of souls to The Sleeper for The Syndicate over his decades-long service. They had let other assassins who gave up on their service disappear into the shadows of their own accord. What made him different?

He had intended for his transition to retired killer to come in comparatively bloodless terms, requiring only the deaths of a few choice individuals.

His former employer's actions regarding his own life would not go unpunished, he decided. He was Sirul Amun, the foremost dealer of death on all Quaj, maybe even the world. He ran rain from his hair with his hand and traced the scar on his cheek with his thumb.

Sirul Amun, The Needle, longest Shadow of The Syndicate, decided he had personal and unfinished business regarding his former employer. His pace quickened as he made his way back to the mansion's stables, where a dry change of clothes awaited.

He slipped into the exposed half-basement of the mansion from the stables, wearing clothes like what he had seen another stableman wear. Sirul was halfway down the musty hallway to the scullery and kitchens when he stopped dead in his tracks, unable to move.

On a drying hook outside the kitchen in the basement hall of Seulman's mansion, there was a soaking wet green cloak of exactly the color the woman who left the runes wore. Slowly his gaze drifted into the kitchen, seeing one of the young serving girls staring straight at him as she squeezed water from her hair, the drops sizzling on the stones around the kitchen fireplace. She smiled and threw him a wink and turned herself towards the fire to continue drying off.

It took every ounce of sheer will to peel his eyes from the back of her head as he mentally commanded his feet to continue walking. Why had she winked? Did she think he was the Shadow for whom she had just left instructions? Did she know of his own identity and impending death sentence? Sirul forced the paranoid thoughts from his mind. She would be dealt with if necessary. He made his way to the attic access and his cramped, makeshift quarters.

Wedged again in his space above Seulman's office, the day had passed in a boring fashion. An emissary from Kalt had come in the late afternoon, bringing with him what he claimed to be several gallons of scarce ice wine from last winter.

The two men ate together in Seulman's office. They drank late into the night complaining about the foreign elf tribe together, lamenting the popularity of the capital in Mer and reminiscing on past days. The southerner also favored hereditary rule and repeatedly mentioned he was some half-attached descendant of the ancient line of Kalt.

Sirul wished the two drunks would just pack it in for the night so he could rest hidden in Seulman's quarters and wait for the other Shadow to appear. His impatience slowly simmered into anger at the two below him as they carried on, and he felt any chance at sleep slipping away with his calm.

So it was that his eyes were wide and his mind sharply awake when the wrinkled, sixty-something man from Kalt suggested one more drink before bed, which Seulman, of course, accepted. He saw the older man draw a vial from his robes and dump it into the glass he eventually handed Seulman, who was already half passed out in the chair behind his desk.

"Cheers to you, Seulman Tuath, may your family reign as long as it may," the man toasted.

Seemingly spurred by the anger of thinking about what his son would do to his legacy, Seulman chugged the glass in two gulps and fell back full into his chair. His breathing got more and more labored, and his heartbeat slowed until both stopped.

The man from Kalt calmly watched Seulman die while finishing his own glass. Once it was empty, he walked across to Seulman's corpse, dumping some wine on the man's clothes. He then urinated on Seulman's crotch, chair, and the floor in front of it.

Sirul watched intently as the killer put Seulman's glass on its side and spilled more of the wine before grabbing some of the scrolls and books from the desk. He then took a glass decanter of rum from a bookshelf, walked next to Seulman's now limp hands, and let the decanter slip, shattering on the floor as if the man dropped it to the floor before passing out.

Sirul knew he had to be quick. He had to get into position before the man from Kalt fled the mansion. Sirul made his way to the stables, where he had seen the man tie up his horse earlier and hid in the next stall over before the older, slower man arrived.

*****

The man from Kalt saddled his horse while looking around frettingly despite knowing Seulman's corpse would likely lay undiscovered until morning. His old bones creaked and cracked as he pulled himself onto the horse's back. They were barely outside of the stable when he felt the weight of someone suddenly behind him and the horse sagging under two riders.

That sensation was the last he ever knew as Sirul's needle ended his thoughts. Sirul rode with the dead man in front of him out into the streets of Tuath in the cover of night and quickly dumped the man's corpse where he hoped no one would find it. Then, with all due haste, he made his way back to the mansion. He snuck into Seulman's office, drew a knife he had liberated from the kitchens, and slit the throat of the corpse.

How nice of the other Shadow to stage the scene. A dropped decanter and soiled pants could just as easily come from self-intoxication as well as an assassin slitting one's throat from behind. The man had been dead for an hour and did not bleed as well as Sirul had hoped. He pumped the man's chest with both of his hands until he was satisfied with the amount of blood on the floor and Seulman's clothes.

Chapter 7
The Sanctum

Wren had been sailing upriver from the ferry station at the border between Ravnice and Fjall for two days. At last, the mouth of Fjall was within view. The namesake mountain which contained the city stretched to the clouds above him.

The mouth of the River Fjall was a gaping one-hundred-foot-wide chasm entrance in the mountainside from which the river flowed to Ravnice city and the sea.

As the ferry passed under the thirty-foot-high cavern mouth, Wren's eyes quickly adjusted to the dark, giant cave that stretched before him. He could see the docks and slips with ferries and small merchant vessels tied off along the left side. However, he was more interested in his immediate destination, where the docks ran into a rock ledge at the cave's back. There, where the river went underground, two dwarves in plated armor guarded the entrance.

Their shields were almost as tall as their five-foot frames and rested on the ground. One dwarf had a hammer in his belt loop, the other an ax. There had not been open warfare on Quaj in a hundred years. For dwarves though, old habits die hard, Wren well knew, especially when most of the Fjall dwarves had been alive for the disastrous War of Magi a century before.

Wren appreciated that while no other city kept more than a policing militia, Fjall maintained a professional standing military. With a thousand actively employed and another five hundred reserves working other jobs day to day, its active ranks were a fifth the size of the Kalt or Ravnice militia and maybe a tenth the size of those in Mer or Tuath.

Wren made the short jump off the ferry and onto the docks,

thanking the crew. Then, he headed for the two dwarves and the passage into Fjall.

"Good day," he greeted them.

"What's your business in Fjall, Master Gnome?" the one with the hammer in his belt asked.

"I am bound for The Sanctum and have a couple stops at the shops below." The dwarf nodded to Wren as he walked by them into the squatter, lengthier passage, which split a few paces in. The tunnel to the left would take him upward and into the city proper.

Wren, however, was headed downward via the other tunnel, which angled towards the heart of the mountain. Living quarters and vendor shops lined the underground thoroughfare, all lit by a combination of mage enchanted light and the flames of torches.

Halfway down, Wren stopped and went through the doorway into what, to him, was the most beautiful place a gnome could find on the island. The shop was one open cave the size of a large human house with rows of counters and display cases holding every type of jewelry conceivable.

There were endless combinations of every type of jewel and metal worked together that one could imagine. The most prominent grouping of gnomes on Quaj ran the shop. They could have easily afforded mage stone lights for their shop but used dancing flames instead. The effects of lantern and torch fires waltzing across the gems and jewelry had Wren momentarily enthralled.

An elderly gnome woman shuffled from behind a counter after rummaging behind it. "Ahh, Wren, so good to see you. Your order is ready," she said as she handed him the platinum wristlet.

The Sleeper's image, nude and resting on her side with her head laid on her hands, twinkled in the light on the solid band. The gnomes had carved it from a single amethyst that must have initially been the size of his fist.

The beauty and weight of it took Wren's breath away. He had initially ordered the piece for himself, but he had changed his mind on its eventual purpose.

"It is perfect, as always." He gave the gnome woman the rest of the payment for the piece and took a moment to stroll around the store. His spirit leaped with the flames flickering in the jewels as he walked. Finally, he bid the gnomes farewell and headed further down the tunnel. It did feel good to be back below ground and seeing his kin and their marvelous work always brought a smile to his face.

Wren was virtually at the end of the downward thoroughfare. The Fjall Mining Company platform was before him, but he first made for the last door before it. He knocked twice and waited.

"Who be it?" The familiar, gruff dwarven voice greeted him from the other side.

"It is Wren, Lorkin," the gnome answered.

The thick stone door swung open, revealing the oldest living mage on the island. Despite his three hundred years, his long black hair pulled up in a knot atop his head showed no grey. His cherubic face and shortly kept beard further hid his long years.

He wore the customary orange robe of The College of Elements, the black cuffs and edging marking him as a mage. The embroidery on his chest depicted Fjall mountain, the symbol of the Tower of Stone. Smiling at Wren, the dwarf welcomed him in. "Good day, Death Speaker."

"Sorry for the brevity, but I have a task at hand myself," Wren apologized. He produced the wristlet and a parchment describing the intended enchantment and handed them to the dwarf, who silently admired it for a moment after scanning the parchment.

"Your kin work with jewels like mine do metals," he complimented. "The enchantment is an odd choice and a difficult one. It will take some doing."

Wren nodded his agreement but did not explain as he handed over the coins to pay. He then bid the stone mage and his five apprentices a good day and departed the Tower of Stone's annex. He could have had the item enchanted at the college but preferred the spiritually gifted work of those that lived under the mountain. The dwarf and gnome mages and sages of the annex had an almost religious love and familiarity with the stone.

Wren knew even Stone Sage Mara and Stone Mage Vennil in Mer would agree that Lorkin was chief among them. His ability to wield magic and control stone garnered him much respect from his younger compatriots of other races.

From the mining platform at the foot of the stone causeway were six tunnel entrances. Five headed to different mining operations and one to the deeper places that Wren sought. It had another pair of dwarven guards and a gate.

"Headed down to The Sanctum?" one of the dwarves asked. Wren nodded. "I should return in three days."

The dwarf produced a ledger and motioned for Wren to fill it out. The Sanctum was almost a half a day's march through the island's underbelly, and there was considerable risk of the inexperienced getting lost. Checking his information, the dwarf bid Wren good luck and raised the portcullis that blocked the tunnel.

The walk through the tunnels would have been cramped and stifling for a human. For Wren though, it resembled what an elf must experience on a stroll through peaceful woods. The pitch blackness and near silence would be troubling to most, but they were welcome solace to Wren.

The shifting humidity and temperature as he passed side tunnels and channels were as soothing as so many soft breezes. The drips of water making their way down from the mountaintop were like beautiful bird songs to the gnome. So it was that the hours-long trek passed by like moments as he walked, often letting his fingers slide along the smooth rock walls.

Slowly he felt the air begin to change, and the incline he walked on was starting to increase noticeably. The upward slope of the tunnel floor continued until he was in the stairway to The Sanctum itself. He smiled as he began upwards along the spiraling stairwell.

After ascending for half an hour, Wren's legs tired as he reached the last few stories. The air had cooled and was almost refreshing as it crept in from small windows the size of arrow slits that dumped cold mountain air in from outside and afforded Wren quick glimpses of the outside.

At last, he arrived at the midnight-black doors of The Sanctum. A gemmed mosaic of The Sleeper, as tall as a man and twice as wide, adorned the three feet thick slabs of slate. The doors loomed like the entrance to a giant mausoleum.

When the dwarves installed them, they had been so perfectly balanced that even Wren could have opened them from the inside with little effort, so long as the locking mechanism was undone. He struck the gong hanging on the wall to the left of the great doors, and moments later, they silently swung inward. A pale, dark-haired man of no more than twenty years stood inside the doorway wearing the unembroidered, plain, purple robes of an acolyte.

The man was almost halfway done with his rehearsed welcome speech when he confusedly stopped mid-sentence staring at the gnome's robe. "Who amongst the living dares journey to The Sanc…."

Wren crossed his arms at the impudent youth. "Death Speaker Wrennulmatlkuonoksug Svatnurlak"

The acolyte grew even more confused and suspicious. "Never heard of no Death Speaker wrench cookout maggot lock," he said, narrowing his eyes.

Tiring of the young man, Wren reached into the air in front of him and drew from it his scythe. Snapping the fingers on his other hand, Xissay appeared lounging atop his left shoulder.

With a yawn, she floated to hang in the air slightly above Wren. "Oh, good, we're finally here. Who's this idiot?" she asked, glaring at the acolyte. Her high-pitched voice seemed to titter in echoes off the walls.

"You," she said, pointing at the befuddled acolyte. "Your mouth is for talking, not breathing."

Wren stopped Xissay with an upheld hand, sparing the poor man. "This is just soon-to-be-thrown-in-The-Dreamer's-Door Acolyte Nobody if he doesn't go and tell the Herald that Death Speaker Wren has arrived and seeks an audience at her earliest convenience."

The man shut his silently open mouth and ran off as Wren entered The Sanctum, shaking his head.

"Don't worry about the door!" Xissay shouted after the man as loud as her little voice would allow. She then whispered, "idiot," quiet enough for only Wren to hear as the gnome closed the slate slab doors.

"Are you going to behave?" he asked his familiar.

Xissay pulled a face and then exaggeratedly closed her lips before pinching them with her fingers.

Wren shot her a skeptical look and snapped his fingers again. As the smoke appeared around her, she threw a parting insult at Wren's expense. "Fine killjoy, but when you're done seducing corpses, take me to the miner's tavern deep in Fjall. I miss the warmth of the deep places, and you look like you need a drink or five."

Leaving the entryway behind him, Wren caught up with the

61

acolyte who was standing, head bowed, at the door to the reliquary.

"Apologies, Death Speaker Wren, please forgive my earlier rudeness. She is alone at prayer inside. The other necromancers are currently about their duties. We just finished our daily commune."

Wren gave the man a warm look. "No need for forgiveness, acolyte...?"

"Acolyte Jabruelle Kalt," the young man answered with a low bow,"

"Well met Jabruelle, The Sleeper's blessing to you," the gnome said and went inside the cavern-like amphitheater known as the reliquary as the acolyte softly shut the door behind him. He walked down the center aisle, past rows of stone benches that would hold over a hundred necromancers but of late saw barely thirty.

Another reason not to alienate the young and newer member, he thought. It was not the youth's fault that Wren was the only one of the six death speakers that spent most of his time away from the temple rather than in it. At the end of the amphitheater was a raised stone platform with what looked like an oversized well and a stone bench curving a "U" shape around it facing the rest of the reliquary.

Alone in the middle of the bench sat a hulking, hunched figure wrapped in a flowing purple robe with the same silver embroidery on the cuffs and hood as Wren's but with the stars of The Sleeper's constellation emblazoned in diamonds on the breast and back of the robe. Wren had been a newly minted death speaker when she had washed up on the shores of Quaj eighty years ago. The lapping waves had pinned her unconscious form into the rocks of the island's western rocky coast. Eventually, a dwarven patrol had found her. When they finished digging her an unmarked burial hole, her regeneration had brought her back to life.

The dwarves had nearly been frightened to death themselves when she sat up halfway through being covered in dirt. She had no memory of her name and would speak at length about The Great Dream and the beautiful goddess within it to anyone who would listen. The dwarves thought perhaps the necromancers in The Sanctum might be able to help reach her sanity.

The Herald did not remove her hood, move, or speak as Wren approached the dais and sat near her. Bowing his head and holding his scythe across his lap, he began whispering in prayer.

After finishing, he stood and walked up to her. He took a moment to peer into the blackness of The Dreamer's Door. The small, well-like stone structure sat atop a fissure that rumor said reached the center of the world. Dropping a stone or coin into it would never result in the sound of it hitting bottom. The necromancers worshiped The Sleeper in this holiest place where they assumed their words would reach her ears as she slept in The Great Dream beneath the mortal plane.

"Greetings, Death Speaker Wren," the female mountain troll said as she removed her hood, exposing her red pupils, crooked, toothy smile, and greenish-grey skin.

The regenerative powers of her race had allowed her to visit The Sleeper again and again. Each time she was slowly returned to the living. Those numerous intimacies with death enabled her to rise to the rank of death speaker and ultimately granted the Herald's Scythe from within The Great Dream by The Sleeper Herself.

"Greetings, Herald. I have an urgent question for Our Lady," Wren said, bowing.

"A question for Our Lady in service of your organization?" Wren nearly dropped his scythe in surprise at the apparent mention of The Syndicate.

"Do not worry, Wren, had you fallen from her favor, you would lose sway over your familiar, and your scythe would be lost to The Dream forever."

Wren did not feel the need then and there to inform the Herald that he was not quite sure he ever had sway over Xissay.

The Herald continued in her broken and guttural use of the common tongue. "The Sleeper has informed me of your shared loyalties and that she sees no conflict between the two. She knows your devotion well.

Ask your question then, and I will listen and see if she feels that the question and the one asking it are worthy of a response." Wren grasped his scythe in both hands and prayed to The Sleeper, asking her of Sirul Amun's fate. Almost immediately, the Herald's back snapped straight, and her eyes opened.

Her hands clutched the eight-foot-long handle of her intricate scythe. A leopard's skull made of platinum with fist-sized rubies for eyes held the three-foot onyx blade atop it in place. The weapon quivered and then steadied in her hands.

"Rarely has she answered so quickly. This soul is known to her as well as you or I are," she said, rising to stand with Wren.

"This Sirul Amun has personally given more souls to her handmaidens than any being still living."

The Herald's response puzzled and troubled Wren. He knew full well how odd it was for The Sleeper to respond so hastily. He hadn't expected to get an answer for The Syndicate at all, but orders were orders.

The knowledge that his Lady knew and accepted his role in The Syndicate brought him some comfort. He joined the Herald for a ritual with the other death speakers and supped with necromancers.

He later retired to an unused room. Struggling to calm his mind, he pondered why the Navigators needed to know of this Sirul's fate. Tomorrow he would find peace in the tunnels of stone and visit a particular tavern in Fjall with a certain thankless familiar.

*****

The complete blackness of Harpis' room disintegrated as his metal-clad door was flung open, slamming against the stone wall. The resounding clang turned the space into a giant bell that wrenched him from slumber. He sat up, squinting his eyes at the light, and held his hands to his ears until the toll of the door dissipated.

"Get up. It is time to get started," Arken shouted at him from the hallway.

Harpis moaned and rolled out of bed wearing only his pants. His bare chest bore a sizeable black fishhook tattoo he had gotten to match his father's several years ago. In addition, tentacles of a massive kraken tattooed on his back peaked over his shoulders and encircled the base of his neck.

He crossed his arms in front of his chest. "You said we would start tomorrow!" he responded accusingly.

"It has been tomorrow for several hours now," Arken said from the hallway. The spymaster raised an arm, pointing at

Harpis' chest. "Any more of that on your body?"

Harpis shook his head. "Just this and the back," he said, turning to give Arken a full view of the kraken that covered his back and shoulders.

Arken motioned for him to turn back around. "Get dressed, and next time you are with the Navigators, have them record their presence and location."

Rubbing the sleep out of his eyes, Harpis yawned and raised a questioning eyebrow at the other man.

"In case we need to identify your body, or in case we catch wind of some dangerous folks looking for someone with your specific markings," Arken said, indicating for him to follow him out into the hallway.

Harpis finished donning his boots and tunic and followed the other man through the narrow stone tunnels as they made their way towards the volcanic crater of a courtyard.

"I wouldn't recommend getting any more of those, especially any you can't easily cover up in normal attire. Being easily identifiable can be a professional hazard if you make it that far," Arken advised him.

Harpis paused for a step as the implications of his tattoos and the institution he was currently trying to join sank in before catching up with Arken, who had kept walking.

"You should start keeping a mental tally of folk who have or end up seeing your tattoos. That way, you are more aware of who may be able to recognize you in various circumstances," Arken continued when he was once again close.

The men stepped out into the dim courtyard under a heavily clouded early morning sky. As they did, the air noticeably became cooler and brought with it the salted notes and sounds of the sea.

Arken stopped and faced him. "What did I tell you I would teach you?"

Fully awakened by the cool sea air and used to waking early as a fisherman, Harpis echoed what Arken had said the day before. "Everyone may be a mark or a threat, and all information could be valuable or save my life."

Arken nodded at him. "How many doors did we pass on our way here?"

Harpis shrugged unknowingly. "Uhhh, I think five?"

Arken shook his head. "Seven. How many exits are there to

this courtyard?"

"Four, one at the end of each of the paths that cross here in the middle," he answered confidently, having taken in the courtyard with great interest the other day.

Arken pointed at the navigator's office window that looked down on the courtyard. "Could you not climb through that?"

As the sky above began turning from black to grey, the courtyard became lit with a drab grey hue. Harpis started looking around at his surroundings with a different perspective than he had the first time he passed through.

Arken interrupted his observations by drawing his sword and thrusting the point at Harpis' neck. Stumbling as he backpedaled, Harpis stared wide-eyed as Arken slashed at him again before stopping his assault as suddenly as he started.

"Close your eyes right now!" Arken commanded.

Harpis warily closed his eyes. He was reasonably sure that if Arken wanted to kill him, it wouldn't matter if his eyes were open or closed, so he obliged the man.

Harpis heard the snap of Arken's sword returning to its sheath. "Now, which exit are you closest to?"

Harpis felt helpless, having no idea which direction Arken had just forced him to move.

"I don't know," he replied meekly.

Arken was unrelenting. "Keeping your eyes closed, tell me the nearest item you could use as a weapon to defend yourself?"

Harpis simply shrugged unknowingly and opened his eyes. Arken indicated for him to turn around. Doing so, he realized he was almost to the coop where the chickens had been sleeping. An ax lay resting against the outside wall. Harpis was exasperated at not noticing the sounds of the agitated chickens inside.

Arken crossed his arms. "If you are predictable, you will quickly find yourself dead. If you are unpredictable, it is hard to be set up or followed without notice. Pay attention to everyone and always be looking for a way out, a way back in and keep track of things you could use to save your life on the paths you travel," he said in a heavy tone.

Harpis returned the stern expression Arken was giving him, but his serious demeanor was lost when his stomach grumbled loudly enough for his teacher to hear.

Arken's face did not soften. "Go quickly and take care of that.

Return here with haste, and I expect more accurate answers to my questions. Don't be followed either."

Harpis started walking towards the tunnel to the kitchens but paused when he saw the growing anger in Arken's eyes.

"The quickest path is the most predictable, and I thought I was clear when I said with haste!" The spymaster shouted at Harpis.

His voice boomed and echoed off the crater walls, and the chickens in the coop sounded their displeasure at being startled.

Harpis' face flushed with humiliation as the feeling of embarrassment washed over him, and he took off at a sprint.

Chapter 8
Indoctrination

Myrlman looked to Niverna. "It feels very odd to sit on this side of the desk, Niverna," he said to her lamentingly from what had been his father's position.

"We will punish those who are responsible," he stated flatly. Niverna shifted uncomfortably in her seat. She had assumed this day would come, where she would sit opposite the son and not the father in hopes of guiding Tuath and the Quaj to a brighter future.

However, this abrupt transition was not the well-orchestrated and strategically planned process she had hoped it would follow. Still, she felt hope that Tuath might join the other city-states in democratically elected leadership at long last. However, she had also never seen the hard look in the eyes of the typically flippant and overindulgent Myrlman.

"Myrlman, we have no idea who could have carried out this horrific act."

The old sage visibly jumped as Myrlman reacted, slamming his finger into the pile of letters on what was his father's desk.

"Oh, but we do!" he shouted, picking up the stack of them and shaking them at her.

"I was up reading these through most of the night last night. They are threatening, nasty letters from that pretentious scum of a governor from Mer."

He threw the papers, and they drifted to the ground around the room like leaves in the autumn. "We are at war, Niverna, an economic war that Mer is waging to unseat this house from its rightful position ruling Tuath. The threats and words from Governor Edwin Lurras of Mer make it clear!"

Niverna cleared her throat, and Myrlman seemed to pull himself partially from his anger.

"Myrlman, even if that is all true, what benefit would Mer see in such an endeavor with your father dead?" She was not about to indicate that she was fully aware of the ongoing silent war between the two city-states. She also decided not to mention that the words of Governor Lurras paled in comparison to what Seulman had often written and sent to Mer.

The man was unfazed. "Their reason is me, of course. They probably see me as a pawn they can control or push out!"

At this point, he was shouting at the top of his lungs from across the desk. Niverna could not argue his self-criticism, given her own and the Navigator's intentions with him as ruler.

"Niverna, you must write The College of Elements, with them on our side, we could likely oust the governor and bend Mer to our will!"

She planned to write a letter this afternoon, but not of the topic, nor to the recipient that the young new governor of Tuath had in mind.

For once, Niverna found herself agreeing with the man who used to occupy the office. Myrlman would indeed have benefited from some geopolitical education and knowledge of rulership.

"Myrlman, the college is a non-partial organization when it comes to the city-states and their politics," she said and paused for a moment to let her next words sink in. "As is The Bard's Hall in your lands, they will not participate in any feud between Tuath and Mer."

Myrlman seemed to regain some poise. "We shall see what my cousin the Impresario has to say about that!" he said, admonishing Niverna with self-assumed cleverness.

"Perhaps," she replied, in hopes of appeasing Myrlman some. Seeing no immediate benefit from her continued presence, she excused herself to her quarters.

*****

Bending her old frame into her writing desk, Niverna hastily wrote on the parchment in front of her. She was finishing her message as the serving girl Eiyna knocked and entered. Latching the door behind her, she set the lunch down next to Niverna's

69

parchment and pen. Niverna glanced at it before rolling it up and sealing it with wax and ink.

Open Incursion was problematic
Collision potentially unavoidable
Rudder likely damaged

"With haste," Niverna said, handing the sealed letter to Eiyna.

"So soon?" the girl asked, tucking it into her blouse.

"I fear we may have erred," the sage said sadly, rubbing her temples. "I fear for Tuath and Mer and all those caught in between."

*****

"Enter," replied Myrlman to the soft knock at his door. His favorite model slipped into his room. Stepping past him, she gazed back longingly. Letting her dress fall to the floor, she splayed herself on the bed.

"How do you want me?" she asked flirtingly.

Myrlman sat staring blankly at the canvas in front of him for several awkwardly silent moments. The model pursed her lips and then complained.

"Myrlman…" His eyes shifted off the empty canvas and to the woman, but he did not speak.

"How would the governor have me?" she said seductively, leaning forward and continuing her advances.

Myrlman's hand holding the paintbrush trembled and then snapped it. He grabbed paint from his easel then threw it as hard as he could at the canvas. It flew partially on the canvas, also splattering the woman and his silk sheets.

"Leave," he said, so quiet the woman hardly heard him. She was so stunned at his outburst that she did not move a muscle.

"Get out!" he screamed a moment later, kicking over his easel and boring into her with eyes that had traded their customary smiles for burning rage.

*****

70

After a childhood in a poor fishing village that had starved his intellect, Trilia and Qarn were force-feeding Harpis' voracious appetite for learning. Each night he was required to read a Navigator assigned book, and each morning he was to write a several sentence letter that only someone who knew what book he was reading would understand.

The reading had been easy and enjoyable enough, though his penmanship was a work in progress. Two weeks on in his stay at the island, he had begun to improve that too, though Qarn still referred to it as drunken chicken scratch.

He had very much enjoyed his last night's reading, the hundred and some year-old History of Democracy in Kalt, that covered the transition from hereditary rule to an elected government by the people. Essentially, as the second to last state to still embrace the law of inheritance, Kalt did not want to cede to democracy.

It amused him that after hearing of the bloody coup that had taken place in Ravnice, where revolutionaries had butchered the entire Ravnice family, Uberthall Kalt had reconsidered his position. Unlike the Ravnice family, the Kalt family transitioned power on their terms.

That move allowed Uberthall to devise the terms of resignation. Nearly half of the city-state, the woodlands that fed its timber industry, remained in his family. Thus, ensuring his family wealth for generations and guaranteeing the Kalt line held considerable sway and clout in the local economy. Harpis scratched his head in thought and then wrote his message to the Navigators.

Impending storm forced hand
Controlled felling in lieu of certain uprooting
The forester yet wields half the saw

Harpis felt very clever as he folded and sealed the letter just as Arken had shown him. He dribbled some ink into the bowl his thumbprint left in the warm wax and then covered that in more wax.

Once it cooled, he headed to the Navigators, stopping at the kitchens to break his fast along the way with some eggs and bread. Knocking as he entered, Trilia bid him take his seat, and he pulled out the letter and went to hand it to her. Qarn snatched it from his hand before Trilia could take it, and the gnome nearly fell off his chair for the effort.

"This some new watermarking technique, lad?" the gnome grumbled at Harpis. He wiped the drop of egg yolk off the letter with his finger and then stuck it in his mouth.

"That poor drunk chicken you keep paying to write these letters know you're eating its young?" he asked Harpis with a raised eyebrow.

"Ahh, no sir, I have taken to paying said chicken in corn kernels instead of whiskey, with marked improvement."

Qarn chuckled despite his attempts at gruffness with the young man.

"We shall see," he said, cracking open the letter and giving a satisfying nod at the stains from the ink.

Qarn handed the letter to Trilia to read. "Well, the chicken does appear to be partially sober this time. However, I think you may be overly clever with this message."

Trilia handed the letter back to Harpis. "It is concise and as brief as needed, and the point is well received." Harpis beamed at the apparent compliment.

She continued her evaluation. "However, the overuse of forestry and timber industry-related terms too obviously indicate the message is of Kalt, and the rest is fairly deducible by anyone living in the context of the times."

Deflated, Harpis put the letter back in his tunic.

"There will be no lesson this morning. Arken is already expecting you in the courtyard," Qarn said, dismissing him with a wave. "Best not keep him waiting."

Harpis left excitedly. On the way to the courtyard, he stopped at the kitchens once more, asking for breakfast on a tray for Master Arken. Harpis made his way into the still shaded courtyard not yet lit by direct sunlight due to the high walls of the volcano crater around them. He spotted Arken leaning against the rack of practice weapons and approached him.

"You won't mind if I quickly finish this before we begin for the day, will you, Master Arken?" Harpis asked.

As Arken was about to respond, Harpis tripped and fell into him, spilling the food tray and knocking some of the wood weapons off the rack.

Apologizing profusely, Harpis tried to separate himself from the other man. Unfortunately, he found his fingers trapped in Arken's vest pocket, locked painfully in place by the other man.

"Nice try," Arken said, squeezing the knuckles of Harpis' hand together and inducing pain for a few moments before finally releasing him. As they stood and faced each other, Arken flipped a bronze coin with a cooking pan emblem engraved into it to Harpis. With a panicked look, Harpis caught it and immediately slapped his own now empty pocket where the coin had just resided and groaned.

"Still, you've stolen a coin three days in a row now without being caught, even if this most recent one belongs to the over-imbibing cook," Arken said. Crossing his arms, the spymaster continued. "Today, though, your training will change. You will at times be followed and must either evade those pursuing you or force them to reveal their intentions."

Arken paused for a moment, drew a blank bronze coin from his person, and flipped it to Harpis. "Return the cook his coin and keep that on your person. Folks will be trying to take it from you from now on. Do not let them."

Harpis caught the second coin and put it in another, smaller pocket he hoped he would notice someone rummaging through. Looking up he noticed a dwarf approaching from the far end of the courtyard.

Arken hailed the dwarf with a salute. "I will be with you less for these last two weeks. Keep practicing the tradecraft I have been teaching you. Remember, you are constantly being tested and evaluated. Most of your time now will be at Braffen's disposal," he said, leaving them.

Harpis was excited about the change in pace. He had been practicing espionage and the tradecraft of not getting caught and not dying with Arken for twelve hours a day, every day since his first morning on the island.

"Well met young Harpis, Braffen Frothbrew at your service," the dwarf said, shaking Harpis' hand.

Harpis had seen the dwarf in passing but had not been formally introduced. Having heard the voice, he recognized him as the other person present at his initial interrogation upon arriving at the island. Braffen was short for a dwarf, maybe four and a half feet tall. He was also not as plump as the few dwarves

73

Harpis had run into over the years.

Not to say he was not strong, Braffen's muscles were corded and well-practiced. However, where most dwarves perhaps weighed as much as a large man despite their height, Braffen was maybe two-thirds that.

"I am aiming to teach you a thing or two of combat, young Harpis, if you would step over here with me," the dwarf said as he walked with him into the circular pit of sand beyond the weapon racks.

"I am not so young," Harpis said defensively as he turned to face the dwarf.

"Well, I, being two hundred and seventy-eight this year, I'd go ahead and claim you young until you can convince me to call you otherwise," Braffen retorted and then stretched his arms and twisted his back before grotesquely cracking his neck to each side.

"I won't be teaching you many things, but the things I learn ya, I intend to beat into you until they're instinct."

Harpis stared at the dwarf for a moment, seemingly confused. "Well, where is your ax or hammer?" he asked.

The dwarf now looked equally perplexed. "Me ax or hammer?"

Harpis looked back at the weapons racks. "Right, every picture I have ever seen of a dwarf they were wielding some ridiculously heavy ax or hammer, where is yours and what shall I pick off the rack? I favor the saber."

The man did not get, but the first hiss of the "s" in saber on his lips before the dwarf was toe to toe with him, his fist exploding into Harpis' gut so hard he thought he was going to lose his breakfast.

He instead lost his wind and bent, attempting to recover it while holding onto the dwarf's shoulder.

Braffen gave him a comforting pat on the head as if he was a child. "There, there, lad, racism is the progeny of ignorance."

As Harpis began to recover his breath, Braffen slid his right foot forward, heel to heel with him. Nudging forward, so they were hip to hip, he tossed Harpis to the sand, holding firmly onto Harpis' right wrist with a crushingly firm grip.

Braffen's admonishment continued. "No weapons besides your mind and your body. Remember, you're supposed to be as innocuous, unsuspicious, and forgettable as possible. Weapons

74

make folk nervous, make them see you as a threat."

The dwarf fell to his back perpendicular to Harpis, crossed his legs over the arm he still held, sliding his feet under Harpis' shoulder and back. He straightened and locked Harpis' arm, tucking it into his own armpit and arching his back to apply pressure, resulting in a howl from Harpis.

"Hey now, focus, lad, look over here." Harpis turned his head towards the dwarf, who wiggled his hands at him.

"These and the body I can help with. Seeming to me though that the mind may be a lost cause with you."

He released Harpis arm and rolled to his feet. Harpis was less graceful in his return to a standing position.

"Now, I'll be letting you go when you say give, but the enemy will not be offering you the same grace."

Rotating his sore elbow, Harpis grimaced at the dwarf. He was less than enthusiastic at the prospect of spending eight hours a day for the next two weeks being the ragdoll for an overly surly, undersized dwarf.

"Did Wren have to suffer through this same hand-to-hand beating at your dispensing?" Harpis asked sarcastically.

Braffen crossed his arms indignantly. "Master Wren can summon the corpses of his enemies to fight for him, has the favor of The Sleeper herself, and the company of an overly attractive, inappropriately dressed miniature friend that can melt a man's flesh with her hands."

Though Harpis could not see his face in a mirror, he was confident it wore an idiotic look.

Braffen gave him a smug look. "Oh, he hadn't introduced you, eh? In good time I suppose. Xissay is quite the spectacle."

Harpis was no less confused.

"I worry for your mind lad, maybe try sleeping on some of those books they give ya. Perhaps some of that knowledge might leak into that head of yours," Braffen said with a feigned look of concern.

"Feel safe to assume that starting with tomorrow, all members of this island will attempt to physically attack you at their convenience. I expect you to make a decent showing of yourself and respect pleas of submission, as will they to you," Braffen instructed.

Harpis nodded at the dwarf and decided he was terrified for

his body.

****

It had only taken Wren three days to ride a ferry down the river from the mouth of Fjall to the sea. There he booked passage on a ship that took only a few hours to reach the port at Ravnice. Typically, he would have taken the time and saved the coin and just journeyed back by land but his need to return was urgent.

By design of The Syndicate, he did not know who the Eye or Hand in Fjall were, so he could not send word to the Navigators until he was back in Ravnice. Wren was also getting sick of working alone. He had thought of selfishly enjoying the company of Xissay. However, a fiery-haired and fiery-tempered undead sprite from the nether regions of the world floating at your side was less than inconspicuous.

Alive

His pen hung over the parchment after writing the singular word. It was odd, he thought, this single word had such an unknown meaning and impact. He paused for more than a moment, wanting badly to ask more questions about who this Sirul Amun was. After sealing the parchment, he made his way from the wooden table and started a fire. Passing the message to the Helmsman would have to wait for morning when the vendors opened at the wharf.

Wren got up and grabbed himself one of the dustier decanters of whiskey from his kitchen shelf and poured himself a glass before settling into his comfy chair and enjoying some thoughts of Harpis entering his second half of indoctrination at the island and getting to suffer through a couple of weeks as Braffen's plaything.

Smiling to himself, he sighed and snapped his fingers. The smoke and smell of rotten eggs faded, and Xissay walked right into the fire he had made and sat on a log amongst the embers.

"Good to be home," she said as she closed her eyes for a moment as if to soak in the heat before addressing the gnome again. "What's got you smirking?" she inquired.

Before he answered, she floated over to the kitchen to grab

the shot glass she used for her imbibing. "Hitting the bottle without me got you all smiley?"

Rolling his eyes, Wren poured her cup full of the same dark vintage he was currently sipping,

"No, I was just enjoying the quiet and thought to myself how wonderful it would be to have you ruin it."

Chapter 9
The Two Deaths

Myrlman was angrily pacing the balcony of what was now his office overlooking the city. He constantly paused to glare down at the Exarch's entourage as they made their way to the Tuath Diocese, where the local vicar waited to greet them. After each pause, he snarled to himself and resumed pacing.

Niverna sat silently on the far side of the grand desk, noting the growing rage and resentment she now saw in Myrlman. She also appreciated the irony that the father thought Myrlman would never come to resemble his rule.

Her analysis was interrupted as he stopped with his back to her and clutched the railing. "Who does he think he is, refusing me!" Myrlman said, half shouting and half growling.

Niverna straightened in her chair and laid her hands in her lap, preparing for the verbal onset she thought likely to follow. "He is the Exarch," she said.

Myrlman spun around at the overly obvious point, prepared to tear into her for assuming him stupid.

She held up a finger and clarified, "The Exarch adheres to neutrality when it comes to Tuath. Just as he does when it comes to the other city-states, he knows that to confer the power of governorship to you could be seen as an endorsement to hereditary politics. A fact which could cause him to have issues with the other city-states."

Myrlman stalked in from the balcony and put his hands flat on the desk across from her before responding. "I will have their whole little gathering expelled from our city-state, the Tuath Vicar and his clerics included!"

Niverna raised an eyebrow at the exclamation from the young man she had thought well educated by her hand. "Shall I have someone fetch a necromancer to perform the burial rites instead then?"

Myrlman sat back in his chair as he realized the implications. "I'll not have the corpse worshippers usher my father's soul." He stood and thrust his finger triumphantly in the air in front of her face. "I shall expel them after my father's burial rites!"

Niverna remained stoic. "And then who would your people go to for healing in Tuath? Gifted, or otherwise, the clerics are all trained at the hospital in Mer," she responded.

Myrlman spun around and threw his hands up in frustration as he walked back to his balcony and resumed pacing and glaring at the distant diocese.

*****

Whether a necromancer or cleric performed them, the burial rites and body preparation commonly happened within a day or two of death. Seulman Tuath's corpse lay in the cool second basement of the diocese for almost five full days. The local vicar had delayed the rites and examination upon hearing word that the Exarch himself and several of his attendants were due to arrive in Tuath after visiting some of the more remote communities of the island.

Exarch Hameki Cooperson was a squat man who showed every one of his seventy-two years in the wrinkles in his face. Though not overly fat, he had given up healthy eating for daily indulgence several years ago, and his belly showed it.

Though Daybreak had not gifted him with healing magic, he was a practicing doctor for over fifty years. Joined by his two attendants and the local clergy members, he began examining the corpse of Seulman with both the forensic attention of an autopsy and the reverent care of a blessing.

Before beginning the autopsy, he sat staring at the corpse while rubbing his bald head and stroking his waist-long, red, and white beard in contemplation. He removed the black and gold cloak of his station and the white cleric robes beneath it. The vicar and other attendants followed the suite, donning black work smocks more appropriate for the bloody work at hand.

79

The Exarch cutaway bloodied and soiled clothing, which he handed to one of his attendants to burn. They would show Seulman's blood the respect that the rest of his body would receive at the pyre next dawn. As the Exarch continued cutting clothes away, he examined the lethal throat wound. His attendant Ezera, who was a vicar in her own right, interrupted his commentary on the various arteries, veins, and muscles that had been severed.

"Your holiness, there is something odd about the way his clothes are burning," she said.

Even a first-year student at the school in Mer would recognize the odd hue of the flames coming from the bloodied clothes to indicate some unnatural agent had been coursing through Seulman's body at his death. The unmistakable blue flames of alcohol flared here and there as they consumed the garments, but the odd green flame and its acrid smoke persisted until the clothes were gone.

Without a word, Hameki grabbed a scalpel, cut open Seulman's abdomen, and sliced a large chunk from the liver, and threw it into the fire. The resulting smoke was of the same thick green hue and then was entirely consumed by green flames.

He turned to the rest of the room. "There is enough poison in this man's veins to kill a horse or two. The venom of a cave spider from the underbelly of the world, if I am not mistaken."

The clerics shifted nervously and began whispered conversations. Had two men tried to kill Seulman? Was it an assisted suicide? The possibilities were many, and their repercussions were all severe.

"Silence!" the word dropped from the Exarch's mouth like a hammer fall.

He made sure he had everyone's attention. "This information and any conclusion drawn from it will have far-reaching implications for the island, and I fear none of them are good."

He stopped for a moment to caress his beard in thought. "Myrlman already knows his father was murdered. It has thrown the young man and likely this city-state into a vengeful mood. I will not feed their rage or cloud their judgment further by telling them of this."

Hameki pointed straight at the head of the Tuath Diocese. "Vicar, you will not record what we have witnessed here in case

Myrlman takes to reading the recorded histories in these dioceses. I will have it recorded in Mer so that the information is not lost."

He examined the corpse one last time before dictating their course of action. "Let as much of his blood as possible and burn it, his liver and kidneys here, before preparing the body. Triple the amount of anointing oil used at his pyre to try and hide the poison's smoke. You are all here now to swear to Daybreak before me that you will obey my wishes."

After murmured oaths from all in the room, they finished the burial rites in private and left to wash and put on their formal robes for the ceremony to be held at dawn tomorrow.

*****

Qarn was resting his elbows on the office window ledge, staring out into the courtyard below, when he heard Trilia thank someone at the door.

She walked over to him and laid her hand on his shoulder. "News from Wren and Niverna."

Qarn turned to see the two sealed parchments in her hands. "To business then," he said as they made their way to the triangular table.

Opening the first one, Trilia read aloud Niverna's message.

Open incursion was problematic
Collision potentially unavoidable
Rudder likely damaged

"So, she doesn't feel as comfortable in being able to control the situation in Tuath as before, despite the son now ruling," Qarn commented.

"And things between Mer and Tuath may, if anything, be getting worse," Trilia concluded.

"What's this business about Seulman's death then?" Qarn asked.

Trilia only shrugged. "Niverna has always been succinct. I can't figure out what she means by the incursion being open? The Brewer and The Needle before him both had orders to make it look organic."

Qarn cracked the seal to the letter from Wren and his face

81

furrowed. "I am surprised Wren was able to get an answer. Given Niverna's letter, I think Sirul Amun hasn't simply hung up his Shadow."

Trilia's face tightened as he turned the paper for her to see.

Alive

"We need to seek clarification from our Hand and Eye in Tuath as soon as possible, as well as send an inquiry to The Brewer," Trilia offered, and Qarn nodded his agreement. "I also think we ought to consult Turin and probably tell him to forego his planned return to Lodestar until we know more details about Sirul's whereabouts and intentions.

*****

As the mid-summer rain carried on outside, Harpis was making his way to the kitchens to grab some lunch. In his four weeks on the island, he learned much of the place, its people, and The Syndicate.

The geopolitics were as intricate as they were intriguing. It was a testament to The Syndicate that there had only ever been two attempts by Mer and later Kalt to establish their own espionage and intelligence operations. Both of which The Syndicate operatives successfully infiltrated and ultimately dismantled over a generation or two.

After grabbing a warm roll and eggs from the kitchen, Harpis made his way back to his room to eat his breakfast. He made his way through the halls towards his room with tense, light footsteps.

His senses had been successfully honed to near-constant paranoia by the random assaults and burglary attempts that had beset him almost daily, just as his instructors had hoped.

Opening his door, he turned to set the breakfast tray on his small writing desk and felt the hair on his neck stand up.

The tray had barely touched the desk when he saw a blur as Braffen jumped from his bed. He could not react fast enough to prevent the dwarf's arm from encircling his neck. It formed a triangle with the dwarf's other arm and hand wrapped around the back of Harpis' head, locking it firmly in place.

Starbursts began to appear in his vision from a lack of air in his lungs and blood. Harpis reacted instinctively. Both his hands shot to the forearm under his chin. Pulling down with all the strength he had, he turned inward to the left towards Braffen's torso and stepped behind the dwarf's feet.

His efforts on the dwarf's arm felt like he was trying to pull a grown tree out of the ground. Slowly though, the choke yielded enough for Harpis to suck in a breath of air.

Abusing the dwarf's height and the awkward angle of his arm, Harpis leaned into him, hip on hip, as hard as he could. The move sent both tumbling in a heap together over his left knee. As soon as they hit the ground, they were both already scrambling to find an advantage.

Harpis spun on his back, still holding Braffen's forearm with both hands while quickly crossing his legs over the dwarf's arms. He attempted the same lock he had been victim to the day they met. Unfortunately, the dwarf had been put in thousands of such grappling holds, and his experience and considerable strength kept Harpis from locking the arm straight and forcing the dwarf to yield.

After several moments of struggling, Harpis decided to embrace less scrupulous methods. He bit the dwarf's arm hard, and as Braffen squealed in response, the flex of his arm gave for a second, and Harpis was able to lock it straight.

Braffen quickly snarled a disgruntled "I give!"

As they both straightened their clothes and got to their feet, Braffen crossed his arms. "I didn't be learning ya that."

"No, but you did teach me to win," Harpis responded with an air of superiority.

"Did ya then?" The dwarf responded to Harpis' widening grin.

Suddenly Braffen punched Harpis square in the gut and was rewarded with wheezes from the man.

"Aye, ye did win, and right dirty too," he said. Walking past Harpis' doubled-over form, he patted the back of Harpis' head admonishingly.

"Took ya long enough, and well done. Enjoy your breakfast!" he said before departing the room with a chuckle.

After regaining air in his lungs and an appetite in his belly, Harpis finally finished his breakfast. While he had not planned the encounter with Braffen, his meeting this morning with Arken was something he had been excitedly anticipating since last night's successful foray. The two men met in the courtyard entryway, staring together for a moment at the unrelenting deluge outside.

Arken addressed him without turning and held out his hand. "Well, young Harpis, how did yesterday's thieving go? A coin this time?" Harpis placed two coins into Arken's palm, and the man looked down at them with a satisfied look before rolling his eyes.

"You must stop picking on the chef, or he will start feeding you spoiled food," he said.

He flipped the first coin back to Harpis. "Ahh, and the lighthouse keeper, not two impressive pulls, but stolen all the same."

Harpis caught the second coin tossed back to him and could not hide his smugness as he handed the man the third coin. Arken turned it over and did not respond for a moment, just staring at its emblem.

"How did you get this?" he asked, looking Harpis in the eyes.

Harpis rubbed his hands together as he began his tale.

"A few days ago, Trilia recommended that I get to know all the folks around the island. Given the random assault order on my person, the task was both interesting and entertaining. One of the more fascinating folks I have met on this island is the lighthouse keeper."

Arken looked on impatiently.

"You see, after meeting the two guards who were coming off shift in the lighthouse, I went upstairs to talk with the keeper. It turns out the old man just absolutely loves whiskey from his days back in Ravnice where he was from."

Arken narrowed his eyes. "Everyone knows that. Get on with it!"

Harpis' confidence grew as he went. "Now, I thought to myself, surely, getting two coins in one day would impress you. I knew I could steal again from the cook. With some of that whiskey I saw delivered on the same boat that brought me, I thought maybe I could get the lighthouse keeper's as well. Now let me tell you, it is obvious that man was never an operative of The Syndicate. A few drinks in, and words never stopped. By the way, I think he is lonely up there."

Arken motioned for Harpis to get to the point.

84

"Anyways, he tells me about his niece who works as one of the staff here at the island and how she cleans quarters, does linens, and often brings breakfast to some of the more senior folks. Now that got me thinking, it would be too hard to steal your coin from your person, but maybe she could start checking for it in your laundry for me or something," he said, sticking his finger in up with an air of superiority.

"So early this morning, I met her in the kitchens and asked if she would not mind having coffee with me and listening to the rain. After chatting her up, I found out that she sees that coin of yours sitting on your nightstand every time she changes your linens. Now I was quite surprised. Surely the great spymaster Arken Hester wouldn't cheat this great game of his own concoction by not having his coin on his person."

Arken was quickly becoming visibly agitated.

"I told her about the training and how it seemed grossly unfair that you didn't keep your coin on your person. She agreed that if you had been cheating, you deserved to be cheated. While you ate your breakfast before dawn broke this morning, she grabbed it for me and handed it over when I grabbed my food an hour later. Thankfully Braffen did not see it during our scrap. And so here we are. Cheater!" he said, backing out of striking distance as he finished.

"Well, that took you long enough," Arken said dismissively.

Harpis' demeanor became deflated as Arken's lack of surprise undermined his triumphant accomplishment.

With a grin appearing on his face, Arken tossed Harpis' own coin back to him. "Courtesy of Braffen Frothbrew."

He could not hide his disappointment at being pickpocketed mid grapple with the dwarf nor the anticlimactic reaction from Arken.

"The Navigators wish to see us, come."

The two men took the spiraling stone stairs to the second level, and Qarn's gruff reply from inside bid them enter. Standing before the two seated Navigators across the triangle table, Arken addressed them without looking at Harpis.

"He has done well. Braffen and I feel he is ready to be assessed for on-the-job training with Wren."

"Thank you," Harpis stammered as Arken shook his hand.

"Don't thank me yet. We leave the morning after tomorrow

for Quaj and your final test," Arken said.

The spymaster departed with a nod to the Navigators, who motioned for Harpis to join them in the third seat.

Qarn Spoke first. "I will reveal further details about the operations of The Syndicate upon successful completion of your final indoctrination task. As to your question regarding the chair you currently occupy, yes, there are three Navigators. That way, there can be no tie concerning our decisions about actions on Quaj. Turin Deadeye is the eldest of us three and the founder of The Syndicate. He is a wood elf sailor who shipwrecked on Quaj centuries ago."

The gnome rubbed his hands over the symbols engraved into the table in front of him. "After seeing the island tear itself apart in a war between hereditary rulers, he set in motion clandestine mechanisms to see to the transfer of rule to more peaceful democratic means. He used The Syndicate and its agents to keep the island's inhabitants headed unwittingly ever towards the greater good. One of us is always away from the island. It is typically Turin."

Trilia spoke next. "As for the knife you brought here and your gift, I can tell you only what I know. How familiar are you with the two gifts?"

"Well, to start, I guess I didn't know there were two different ones," he answered.

"There is the gift that is given via devotion to, and favor from, one of The Five. Then, there is the gift some are born with. We elementalists typically discover our gift when we are young. It manifests as an innate ability to interact with one of the four elements."

Harpis could hardly wait for her to finish answering before he asked his next question. "Which of the two is mine then?"

"That is a question whose answer is the topic of much debate. However, through Syndicate texts and research, it seems the scarce ability to sing gift-woven verse is a talent that one is born with," she said.

"I never noticed the ability before; don't most mages know of their gift before reaching adulthood?" he asked.

Trilia shrugged. "That is true, though many discover they can manipulate an element through a stressful or intense act. Perhaps you just needed the most desperate of circumstances to bring your inherited gift to light."

Harpis was happy for the answers but still mightily confused. "Even once discovered, though, mages spend years practicing before they can bend the will of an element to their whiles. So how do you explain my very first foray resulting in exactly what I needed to happen?"

"That is what makes you so perplexing, Harpis Akkeri. An elementalist does not become an apprentice until they spend at least several years crafting their Cynosure," she said, holding up her jeweled scepter. "It lets us concentrate our focus and improve our meld with our element. Only then can we begin the decades it takes to perfect the process of Anamnesis, wherein we can imbue the memory of the element into another object through enchantment. This type of enchantment is what lets a fire mage place the latent memory of a fireball into a staff and later summon it forth with an activation."

Harpis was enthralled by the beauty of the finely crafted and jeweled scepter as she handed it to him to examine.

"The practice of Anamnesis typically culminates when we mages are ultimately able to impart our persona into our element and summon forth the elemental familiar required of reaching the rank of mage," she said, taking back the scepter.

She motioned for him to hand her his dagger. "Which brings us to this," she said softly, turning the blade over in her hand and admired the seductive form of The Siren in its handle.

"Apotheosis," she whispered.

"What?" Harpis asked, at a loss.

"Few among us gifted elementalists, typically those of the longer-lived races, attain the rank of Magus through the creation of an elemental Apotheosis. It is the true and utter command of an element resulting in a permanent enchantment that slowly consumes its wielder's life force when enacted."

She gave the dagger back to him reverently. "This is the work of some long-dead Air Magus. Whomever it pierces, it will create a void of silence around them, sustained by draining their energy. Treasure it, Harpis. It is invaluable."

He took the knife in his hand, cradling it a moment in appreciation before returning it to his boot. "I have certainly never heard of a bard enchanting an item like a mage. How does any of this apply to me?" he asked.

"Where we have our Cynosures, you gifted bards have your instruments. Where our intimation is to earth, air, fire or water, your innate connection is to other beings, and music is your conduit."

Trilia stopped with a saddening expression and stood from her chair, as did Qarn. They both walked around to Harpis, who had followed suit in rising from his chair.

She kissed him softly on the cheek. "You'll not see us again for some time. If you pass your assessment, you'll be sent to The Hall for formal training and sanctioning as a bard. May the winds be ever at your back, young Harpis."

Qarn clasped his hand. "We have high hopes for you lad, don't cock it up."

Still reeling from the information Trilia had told him, Harpis clumsily gave them both a short bow and excused himself from the room as pangs of sadness struck him.

Chapter 10
Assessment

As the vessel from Lodestar Island neared the large port of Mer, Harpis made his way above deck to join Arken next to the helmsman.

"I have never seen such a sight; it is so much bigger than Ravnice or Kalt," Harpis said, taking in the city from their northern approach.

Arken snorted. "You'll see this and the rest of them in the service of The Syndicate if you do well today."

Harpis noticed the odd mechanical device of spherical metal bands with measurement notches sitting on the ledge behind the ship's wheel.

"What is that thing for?" Harpis asked both Arken and the helmsman.

Arken addressed him first. "You are aware of the limitations most islanders have in navigating the sea, I am sure, given your time spent in a fishing village and aboard ships."

Harpis nodded his agreement to the statement.

The helmsman picked it up and handed it to Harpis. "It is an astrolabe. It lets us use the stars to navigate accurately. It is how we can find Lodestar Island and how we avoid unwanted attention from the ships that cannot safely stray far from the coast."

Harpis shrugged unknowingly at the helmsman. The ship slowed as one of the other crewmen pulled in the sail once they got closer to the docks and piers of Mer.

Arken turned to Harpis. "Don't go embarrassing me out there. You will jump off here in a moment as we pass some empty docks, well before we tie this ship up across the harbor. You are to find the ship *The Lady Ghost*. Take note of what is loaded aboard her before she departs later this morning and report your findings at the Muddled Mage Tavern before nightfall."

Arken grabbed his shoulder. "Remember, everyone may be a threat, everyone may be a mark, and every piece of information may be vital to your survival or the survival of this island. Do not get followed. Do not get caught, but if you do, die for our secrets rather than live by giving them, or I will find you myself and kill you."

And with that, Arken shoved him hard enough that he took two steps backward, tripped over the low railing of the steering platform, and fell onto the dock below. So it was that he began his Syndicate assessment with a bruised ass and a swift farewell.

He quickly looked around and noted that the dock where he landed was empty in the early hours. Making his way towards the already bustling wharf vendor stalls, he pretended several times to be lost or act as if he had forgotten to check something at a vendor.

He was constantly reversing the direction he was walking at random to see if he could find anyone following him. Having never been to Mer, he found the great expanse of its wharf quite impressive.

He had no idea where *The Lady Ghost* was. However, he knew a fair number of sailors would likely still be drinking in the bars along the wharf. The first one he passed was The One-Eyed Otter, but he continued to The Flirty Mermaid.

After pushing his way through the doors, he waited for his eyes to adjust before he made his way to the wooden counter and asked for a mead. "A drink on me to the first soul who can tell me who to talk to about buying passage on *The Lady Ghost*," he shouted.

"Who be asking!" questioned a tattooed giant of a man who smelled like he had not bathed in weeks.

"I am Har…" he said, falling from his stool as if overly drunk in an exaggerated greeting to the sailor. As he fell, he grabbed the man's belt to ease his fall and help himself back up.

He apologized for the blunder but not for removing the small pouch of coins the man had tucked in his belt. "Sorry, Harpis is the name, I was just drinking the night away over at The One-Eyed Otter, and when I mentioned looking for passage out of here someone there mentioned she was leaving later today. I figured she'd do as good as any for passage out of Mer but no one at the last establishment could point me her way."

The sailor looked Harpis up and down and ordered his free drink from the barman.

"Cap'n is likely still onboard taking in our cargo at the northern harbor docks. If you make your way with haste, you may be able to book passage."

Harpis paid for their drinks with the stolen coins and left as quickly as he could before the sailor realized his coin pouch and its contents were missing.

Leaving the bar, he glanced around, looking for anyone paying too much attention to him. He quickly spotted the ship and found a wharf stall within view, where he could covertly observe both the boat and the bar.

It looked like all of what the crew was loading were whiskey barrels and some grain. However, that was the extent of Harpis' surveillance of *The Lady Ghost* because a particular roaring drunk sailor emerged from the Flirty Mermaid moments later railing about how some dark-haired man named Harpis had robbed him. At that moment, Harpis decided against using his real name when on Syndicate business and quietly slipped out of the wharf and into the city proper.

He kept quickening his pace up the street before stopping for a moment, realizing he had no idea where he was going.

Glancing around, he noticed a hooded and cloaked person on the same street as him who was peering into a shop window. Harpis was not sure, but the person felt familiar. Perhaps he was in one of the bars or out in the wharf.

In either case, Harpis became instantly paranoid. He forced himself to calm and think about how he might find the Muddled Mage Tavern. After a tense moment, the name struck him, and he cursed himself for missing so obvious a clue. Doubtless, a drinking establishment with that name would be near The College of Elements.

He remembered the description of the college in The Founding of Magi Trilia had bid him read. It was supposedly a construction of four towers and with an overall squareness to the structure. So Harpis began peering over the buildings around him until he spotted the college towers to his south.

91

The figure in front of the shop still stood unmoving as the minutes passed. The person's position in front of the shop window was probably affording a view of Harpis in its reflection, and he convinced himself that the figure was watching him.

For the rest of the morning and early afternoon, Harpis slipped in and out of establishments, changing his gait, the way, and direction he walked to shake the supposed stalker.

He always kept the college towers in view, knowing he eventually had to make his way there before nightfall.

He even stopped and bought a jellied scone from a baker he passed and ate it for lunch. As he satisfied his rumbling belly in front of the bakery, he realized he had not noticed the hooded figure in quite some time.

Having nothing better to do, Harpis continued the game of cat and mouse despite not having seen the person for some time. Finally, as the sun began to dip in the evening in the sky, Harpis made his way towards the college.

There was only one tavern near it, and it was, in fact, The Muddled Mage. With one last glance around, he went inside. He sought out the seat furthest from the entrance but within view of it so he could watch in case whoever was stalking him found their way here as well.

He had been sitting there in unshakeable anticipation, which slowly transitioned over the next three hours and three meads into self-doubt. Once the sun's rays left the tavern's windows, the poorly lit interior shown with orange and red hues of candlelight. Had he failed? He tried to figure out where he had erred. Perhaps The Syndicate simply left him, unsatisfied with his performance, to begin a life here in Mer?

Harpis nearly leaped out of his skin as the hooded figure from the streets slid into the other bench of his booth, across the small table from him. Harpis went for his knife, but the figure's foot snapped forward under the table, crushing his wrist against the boards of the bench before he could draw it.

"Well met, Harpis Akkeri of nowhere." The figure spoke, and immediately Harpis relaxed, as did the boot on his wrist. The person across from him pulled back the hood revealing the face of an ancient-looking wood elf. He knew elves could live to be over a millennium old, but this elf wore all thousand and then some years on his wrinkled face like so many tiny scars.

More than just his face, his eye carried the weight of an entire age in its gaze. An old-looking elf was something he had never seen. A thousand years at sea had weathered him mightily. Harpis could barely pry his gaze from the empty eye socket where the elf's right eye had been.

"I am Turin Deadeye, and it is good to meet you finally." The elf said in a raspy voice.

Turin cleared his throat and sipped his whiskey before continuing. "So, what about your report?"

Harpis straightened, proud to provide his information and theory about it to the revered founder and oldest Navigator of The Syndicate.

"I found the vessel and noted that she was flagged under Ravnice state but was loading whiskey and grain onboard. What need does a Ravnice merchant have of Mer whiskey and grain? I assume the crew was hiding something in those contents."

The old elf shrugged. "Perhaps, and how did you find it?"

Harpis described his adventure at the wharf earlier that morning. Turin nodded and asked to see the sailor's coin purse.

Harpis grew excited to learn what he was supposed to have seen. "What is it? Does it contain a sign of their intentions?"

A serving girl approached them and asked if they would like another drink. Turin ordered whiskey for them both and handed the girl the coins.

"No, it's going to pay for our next round."

Harpis sank a little in his bench seat. "Was I correct regarding *The Lady Ghost*?" he asked.

Turin shrugged again. "Oh, I don't know what else Arken told you to do besides meet me here, but it was entertaining watching you escape the sailor at the wharf. Your commandeering of the poor drunk's coin was a bit heavy-handed, but he was too intoxicated to notice. Also, try not to see too hard into things. There was nothing suspicious on that vessel."

Harpis was dejected, and though he was afraid to know the answer, he asked anyway.

"I did not see you that early in the day, but I did lose you sometime after lunch. Of that, I am sure."

Turin smiled. "Oh, you lost me all right when I left at lunch for this establishment to get some food and drink. It was a little impressive that you stayed out there running around the streets of

Mer trying to lose your own shadow for that long. I'd had enough of watching you slowly nurse mead any more from across the tavern and figured I ought to come to join you at last."

Harpis still was not sure if he had passed their test or not. "So then am I graduating into the…. from my training?" he asked, catching himself before accidentally mentioning The Syndicate aloud.

"You graduate when you are dead, and your training starts every morning when you thankfully open your eyes once more," Turin corrected.

"Welcome officially to our little family," Turin said as he handed him some papers and coins. "We arranged to send you to The Hall on behalf of the governor of Ravnice, who is currently in need of a new court bard. He expects you in Ravnice come autumn, after your training at The Hall is at its end. You will then begin working with the one who convinced you to take this journey."

Harpis took the papers, unable to hold back a smile at being reunited with Wren.

A few drinks and a farewell later, Turin disappeared.

*****

Inside The College of Elements, the Arch Mage paced the expanse of his second-story quarters above the now empty and still library. Uridyll Vatra was a tall and thin man with long, white hair and bushy eyebrows but almost no beard. His eighty years had hunched him considerably, but his mind was still as sharp as a razor. As such, instructors and students alike did well to remember lest they suffer the wrath of the intellectual old man.

Many at the college joked that Uridyll was appointed to his position because he was the physical epitome of how an old Arch Mage should look. As he paced his quarters, the black embroidered orange robes and black cloak of his position flowed behind him like a flag angrily snapping in the wind. The cloak had the college's symbol, a giant lit candle, depicted in golden embroidery.

He was increasingly impatient waiting for his summons to be answered and was nearly startled by the eventual knock on his door. He knew it to be Stone Mage Vennil and Stone Sage Mara at the late hour, so without going to the door, he bid them enter while taking his seat.

"How may we assist you, Arch Mage?" Vennil greeted him, even though the two were keenly aware of why they were before him.

He motioned them to join him at the five-sided table in the middle of the room. "I have spent the weeks since you informed me of the theft contemplating our path forward. Please sit." One edge had his chair, which he took, and each of the other sides sat two. Vennil and Mara made their way to the side of the Stone Tower and took their seats.

Uridyll gave them a stern look. "This discussion and the related information are not to leave this room, understood?" The instructors of the Tower of Stone nodded in agreement.

His gaze softened some at their concurrence. "I have decided that we must keep this quiet for now. I will not disclose the item or the fact that it is missing at the council's next meeting as I originally had planned. To do so would only throw the entire island into pandemonium. Imagine every leader, who knew someone was potentially plotting against them, started questioning the identity of everyone they talked to in suspicion that they wore the mask and were, in fact, an imposter."

He crossed his arms and stared for a moment at Vennil and then Mara, daring them to offer their opinion before continuing. "No, the repercussions of the item's ability and its unknown location would destroy the very fabric of trust that keeps the city-states of this island in relative harmony. I will keep an ear out at the meeting and listen for any news or decisions that seem out of place while you two try and find a way to discern its location. Perhaps I will consult the leaders of the other institutions as they do not fear magic as the governors do. Save the Impresario. I do not trust his ability to stay truly impartial, given his family ties. What could you find regarding the item?"

Stone Sage Mara laid a parchment on the table and glanced over it before speaking. "The Mask of Breyva is made from enchanted primal clay. It can allow the user to wear the face of someone they view while donning it. Uttering the activation will cause it to transform into the face currently being viewed. I had to find this information in various texts here in the library. Unfortunately, the notes we had regarding it in my desk are missing as well."

The Arch Mage turned to Vennil. "And what of its power?"

The stone mage looked from Mara to the Arch Mage uncomfortably. "It is exceptional, which is why I had it secured, or so I thought, in my quarters. The enchanted coffer caught a bumbling novice and not the real thief. The duration of the face changing and the number of uses possible is not known to us. It was no normal enchantment. It was the Apotheosis that earned Stone Magus Breyva her title. A work that took almost her entire last decade among the living to complete. Given her considerable magical gifts detailed in other texts, we can probably assume it will not run out of uses, and the duration of the face change may be indefinite."

Arch Mage Uridyll put his head in his hands and groaned noticeably.

Sitting up straight in his chair, he gave the stone mage and stone sage a long glare. "I do have one last question of you two before we conclude this business. How was it that this mask escaped destruction after The Treaty of Mer?"

Stone Mage Vennil gave him an unknowing shrug.

Stone Sage Mara, much more studied in the history of The Tower of Stone, did speak up. "Arch Mage Uridyll, the mask, though certainly powerful and dangerous, was ultimately deemed not to be an implement of war."

Uridyll rubbed his forehead several times before finally responding to the two.

"I will summon you both in the late hours again once I return from the next council meeting. Try and have something figured out as to how we might identify or locate this thing."

*****

It had taken a day and into the following morning for Harpis' ship out of Mer to dock in Tuath and the rest of the second day to get to The Bard's Hall on horseback. The road to The Hall wove its way up the coastal cliffs, turning several times, putting The Hall in and out of his view. It sat atop the sea cliff's highest point, easily a hundred times the height of a man. The Hall was at the edge of the northernmost part of the entire island.

After a day's ride in the clingy humid heat of Tuath in early summer, he and his rented horse were both completely lathered in sweat. Dismounting at the entrance to The Bard's Hall, he handed his papers to a woman who walked out of The Hall and hailed him.

"Ahh," the woman replied. "Come to fill the vacant position in Ravnice, I see. That is if you succeed in becoming a bard. Come this way. I am Maestro Olimir, and I will introduce you to the Impresario."

Harpis rolled his eyes at the statement, doubtful his experience at The Hall would be near as trying as his past month. Nevertheless, he followed the woman up two sets of stairs and was left with the Impresario in his office on the third floor above the Hall.

Taking his papers from Olimir, the Impresario dismissed her and motioned for Harpis to follow as he walked down a hallway past his quarters, his sandals smacking the bottoms of his heels as they went. As they stepped out onto the sizable third-floor balcony at the back of the Hall, the tropical heat of the sun once more beat upon Harpis' skin, and he lost his breath gazing out from the balcony over the sea.

With no other land in sight ahead and the sea over six hundred feet below him, he imagined this is how gods must view the world.

The Impresario was a hand taller than Harpis. The blond-haired man seemed to carry an air of distinction about him in his every movement. Despite his stately presence, the Impresario had a half-smile that didn't seem to leave his face or his green eyes, and Harpis felt at ease in his company. The loose, low V-cut shirt he wore exposed much of his olive-skinned chest. A wide black belt and large gold buckle stood out above baggy pants of the same cream color as the blouse.

He handed Harpis his papers back. "Glad are we to have a chance to post a bard in Ravnice again. Harpis, is it? I am Impresario Benali Tuath. These papers suggest the governor of Ravnice believes you to be not just a superior candidate but gifted as well."

Harpis nodded at the man as they shook hands.

"Rare is it that we have a gifted among our ranks. Maestro Bravit, who will be one of your instructors, Virtuoso Mahala Shelta, one of our most senior roaming bards, and myself are the

97

only ones I currently know of besides, allegedly, yourself," Benali stated.

The stated rarity of a gifted bard shocked Harpis. "I am surprised, to be honest, of the size of quarters here on the premise. I thought there were only Bards of The Hall at each city court?" he asked.

Benali joined Harpis at the railing overlooking the sea. "That is true, though as I mentioned, like Mahala, we have several members who are more nomadic. It helps us learn of and deliver news and information from the smaller villages and towns throughout the island in addition to what we gather from, and provide to, the cities' governors."

Benali turned his back to the sea to look over the grounds, leaning against the railing comfortably despite the drop behind him. "Still, we are a small organization. Counting myself and the teachers here, our postings at each court, and those roaming the countryside, there are less than twenty sanctioned bards of the Hall. Some of those here simply want to master storytelling, seek out news or learn music. Additionally, there are quarters for visiting bards and our staff, of course," he said.

He pointed at the long buildings on either side. "It is important, you see, for us to have a formal educational process and sanction our members. Otherwise, there would be no trust in the news we spread between cities and towns. Bards come here, some weekly, but at least monthly, and bring news from their posting to share with us here and take any new information from the other regions back with them."

Harpis was beginning to understand why The Syndicate was so excited for him to become a bard.

The Impresario kept his gaze on the sea. "You will learn the ways of journalism and impartiality. You will learn an instrument and the oral barding traditions of poetry and song. Compared to the other institutions that train gifted folk, here at the Hall, magic plays much less of a role in our ability to affect people, Harpis."

"What do you mean?" Harpis asked.

"There is no magical gift required to rehearse a well-written song or poem that will stick in the mind of those listening such that they never forget what you share with them. A mother singing a lullaby to her children requires no gift to induce irresistible drowsiness. A soldier's rallying cry can, with but the force of his voice and choice of his words, cause his compatriot's hackles to stand up and hearts to leap just as they cause his enemy's will to waiver," the Impresario explained.

"And will I be trained in how to use my gift through song to enhance such effects?"

Benali held up a placating hand. "If you learn well what we teach you and embrace the traditions of our Hall, Maestro Bravit and I will teach you to weave your gift into your craft, and I will sanction you as one of us few. If you prove worthy."

As if on cue, a short, pudgy man made his way onto the balcony to join them. He was still breathing heavily from making his way up the two sets of stairs as he raked curly brown hair out of his face and finally gathered himself.

"Fair evening to you, Benali…I mean, uh, Impresario," he said, with an exaggerated bow.

Benali grinned at the other man. "Harpis, this is Maestro Bravit. Believe it or not, he had at one time been a nomadic bard of the Hall. But, as you can see, that was several inches of waistline ago."

Bravit put his hands on his hips indignantly, returning Benali's grin and turning to address Harpis. "Well met, lad, don't let The Impresario's bluster here fool you. His Royal Highness Benali Tuath has never had dirt under his fingernails or slept on anything but the thickest of mattresses!"

With a more serious demeanor, Benali clapped Bravit on the shoulder. "Bravit has been sanctioned for some thirty years. He has instructed here at The Hall for almost ten of them and is one of only a handful of maestros and the only gifted one. He will take you to your quarters and handle much of your instruction, involving the gift or otherwise."

Harpis followed the shorter man as they made their way down the stairs. The going was slow as Bravit accommodated creaking knee and ankle joints during their descent. However, before they exited to head to the lodging building, Bravit halted them in front of a large board with parchments nailed to it at the entrance to the main concert area. In the wood was engraved the title of each city-state. A parchment was nailed up under each engraving, save the Ravnice court spot.

Turning to Harpis, Bravit pointed at the blank spot. "Eventually, if you become sanctioned, that will be yours to fill.

Each of these postings is from bards at other city-state courts or those roaming the countryside. I expect you to add a date of posting and your name, along with a simple list of the major events in your locale that you think is worth wider dissemination."

Bravit pointed back towards the classrooms on one side of the Hall. "We keep more detailed descriptions of news and events in the library. The board is a quick reference for bards as they visit to post their news and take back information from others to their posting. While in training, I expect you to take note of the changes to what is posted here each day and bring them to class."

Harpis nodded in acknowledgment. "Seems straightforward enough, Maestro."

Bravit slapped him on the back with a haughty laugh. "Please, just Bravit! I'll also give you sets of detailed news from the past out of the library each day, and you can practice journalistic interpretation and then post the summary here below the official board, but don't worry, we will work on that over the coming days."

With that, Bravit led Harpis back out of the front doors into the deepening dusk, where he paused with his eyes closed, sucking in a deep breath of the still and humid tropical air. The sound of insects slowly grew with the dimming light of day, and the dense air seemed to reverberate the evening concert all around them.

"That, good Harpis, is the sound of the real maestros around here. Come, let me show you your quarters and then an ale or two at the kitchens!"

Chapter 11
The Hall

Wringing hands sore from report writing, Harpis sat in the practice room while awaiting Maestro Bravit. Almost a month into his training at The Bard's Hall, much of it had come easily to him. Much that did not involve the reading and playing of music anyway. The whole process of spreading news and recounting it became a simple routine to Harpis. Several weeks into his training, it was the one thing he was growing tired of at the Hall.

"Well met, Master Harpis," Bravit said to him, entering the small practice room and shutting the door.

Harpis gave Bravit a nod.

"I see that you have settled on an instrument then." The maestro said, acknowledging the case at Harpis' feet.

Harpis shrugged. "The fiddle's sound is more familiar to me than any of the other instruments. Several folks where I grew up played them, and I enjoyed the songs they called forth."

The maestro sat down in the chair opposite Harpis with a huff. "Some people call it a violin, you know. Some people being those who play beautiful music with such instruments."

Bravit went rummaging through a stack of sheet music. "Well, let us hear it then, a simple song for the…fiddle," he said sarcastically.

Harpis took the instrument out of the case. He ran his hand across its smooth wood finish. Despite being less than exceptional at playing the thing, he truly appreciated the quality of its crafting. Then, drawing the bow across the strings, he attempted to read and play the music on the sheet.

It was slow and uneven, with some of the notes requiring

more thoughtful interpretation than others, and some he missed altogether. The results were an off-tune and off-time assault on the strings at the expense of the bow.

Bravit sank his forehead into his hands and sighed as Harpis finished. Then, he pulled his hands down and off his face and looked up at Harpis.

"I don't get it. I truly don't. I have asked you to read and play me simple music that I have seen children play after their first week with an instrument. In return, you use that poor violin to call forth the tortured screams of a dying animal that has been lit on fire while being skinned alive."

Bravit leaned back and crossed his arms. "Yet, I ask you to play me some sea shanty drinking song from your village, and hypnotic beauty flows forth from it, even without you weaving in your gift."

All Harpis could do was shrug with an apologetic look at both the maestro and his fiddle.

Bravit shook his head. "Well, we've got to get you at least somewhat better at this before the Impresario sanctions you, and I think it will take every bit of the time we have left. However, magically gifted as you are, and with how much joy I see music brings you, we must get through this. I would mourn the loss of a bard such as you to our ranks if you ultimately failed to get sanctioned."

Hours later, and with little progress, Harpis bid Maestro Bravit farewell.

He dropped his fiddle off in his quarters along the concert hall walls and took the two flights of stairs up to the Impresario's area.

His genuine love for barding was developing from his evening lessons, which covered the weaving of magic into songs. Discovering the Impresario was not yet in his quarters, Harpis went out onto the balcony.

Standing at the edge of the world, many hundreds of feet above the sea below, was Harpis' favorite place he had ever been. The wind never stopped rushing up the cliff face, and there was a strange familiar peace in the howling gusts that enveloped him when he stuck his head out over the edge.

Benali and Bravit had taught Harpis the only three songs they knew to work well with the gift of magic. Ones that, in their experience, channeled the gift well into a response from those around them. *Temurellin's Lullaby* was a low, slow song meant to calm those around the bard.

Harpis thought it very similar to the lullaby his father had sung when he was a young child. The next was *Panoryla's March* which resulted in a similar effect to those around the bard as had the fisherman's work song Harpis sang during the battle on the *Sea Goat*. He found he could use both to decent effect.

One he still struggled to sing at all, let alone with his gift woven in, was *Clario's Cacophony*. He did not particularly enjoy the song, which had no apparent pattern or musical intent. The random disharmony of it was painful to rehearse.

It made all who heard it struggle to keep their thoughts together or focus. Benali had even said that when extremely gifted bards used it in the past, it prevented mages from calling forth their enchantments. It may have even stopped clerics as they cast their healing spells, but he was not sure that was more than an old wives' tale for bards.

As he heard the footsteps of the approaching Impresario, he became determined this would be the lesson where he finally performed *Clario's Cacophony*.

*****

Vicar Ezera, the Exarch, and his other attendants had spent many weeks weaving their way through the small towns on their way out of Tuath. Finally, they were now making their way across the countryside of Ravnice. At last, she felt some respite as the burdensome humidity of Tuath faded while they made their way from the rolling tropical hills to the plains of Ravnice state.

The caravan had arrived in a small farming community with the mountain ranges of Fjall rising in the distance behind it. Hjalmstad was a town of several hundred and one of the most remote in Ravnice. It was at the northern-most point of the state, with farmlands tucked between the hills of southern Tuath and the mountain ranges of north Fjall.

The Exarch turned awkwardly in his saddle to glance back at her. "I do so enjoy spending the mornings abroad greeting the morning sun and heralding Daybreak. Perhaps we shall spend the night here in Hjalmstad," he said, a smile further creasing his wrinkled face.

Ezera met his warm smile with a forced one of her own. "I suppose that means once again staying in the only lodging available here, just as last time then, Exarch?"

Hameki nodded as they made their way to the only inn the village had. It also served as Hjalmstad's only tavern, which she decided should make for a night of frustration as she would be the target of many single, sometimes not so unmarried, tavern regulars while she ate.

Daybreak allowed her to marry. She just had not thought to explore the option much. Her beautiful blond hair bounced unkempt around her shoulders and almost elfish face. Like the Exarch and all clerics, she wore the white robes of Daybreak.

The rank of vicar afforded her the black stole, emblazoned in gold thread, that was draped around her neck and hung to her waistline. Her blue eyes narrowed at the thought of unwelcome advances yet to be endured. She decided that there was at least one disadvantage to roaming from town to town, eating and sleeping in taverns and inns to speak the word of Daybreak.

Spreading the faith was an undoubtedly cherished task to her and the Exarch. Equally important, though, was the healing medicine and magic they afforded remote peoples as it was difficult for many to get adequate medical care outside the major cities.

Town folk who needed healing were already besetting them as they tied off their horses. An older woman made her way somberly through the crowd with a wrapped breadbasket. As she got to the side of Ezera's horse, she stopped and lifted it towards her with a pleading look.

Ezera held her hand up to pause the elderly woman. "I appreciate the offer, but we cannot accept your gifts, madam."

The woman closed her eyes in pain and pulled back the tiny cloth covering the basket to reveal the still form of a recently dead baby girl.

Ezera's heart sank into her stomach. The infant's blued lips and popped blood vessels around her eyes, indicating it had somehow suffocated. Trying not to choke or weep, Ezera closed the babe's eyes and said a prayer to Daybreak.

Not one that would bring life back to the baby, that prayer did not exist.

"I am so deeply sorry for your loss, but I am unable to help her," she said. Ezera fought back sobs as she gingerly placed the cloth back over the baby.

The woman clutched the basket close to her chest and made her way back through the crowd after spitting at the feet of Ezera's horse and cursing Daybreak.

Tears flowed down Ezera's cheeks as she watched the woman go. So many villagers and other less educated people assumed she could use her magic to bring the dead back to life. But, unlike the belief that prevailed on the island, she could not resurrect people from The Great Dream.

She looked over the dwindling crowd at the Exarch, who gave her a sorrowful look of his own. "We help those that Daybreak and our medicine let us Ezera. We cannot bear the guilt of those we cannot."

The initial onslaught of those wanting healing did not last overly long in the small town. The early evening hours found the small clergy contingent supping freshly cooked meat and somewhat recently baked bread in the simple wooden inn. As much as Ezera enjoyed these trips, she was fretting internally about getting back to Mer and passing along to The Syndicate what she had seen in Tuath. She imagined the Navigators would be interested that the late governor's corpse bore the evidence of two separate murders. Despite her promise to the Exarch, Ezera felt obligated to pass the information along.

*****

Harpis rose from the writing desk rubbing his eyes before picking up the foot-tall stack of parchments he had just finished reviewing and taking them back to their home in the library. On his way out of the classroom wing, he stopped and grabbed the notes he had made regarding a winter month in Ravnice city some fifty years ago.

He paused and gave an understanding look to one of the newer students who had just begun the journalistic portion of her time at the Hall.

"Keep studying and practicing, and it will start coming naturally, and then you can spend more time on the true craft. I think you'll find the experiences learning the music make the toil worth it."

The young woman gave him a tired farewell wave without looking up from her task of combing through notes of some other month in some other place for valuable information worthy of the Bard's Hall news board.

He cracked a smile at the other trainee's expense. She would be doing similar work off and on for the next few months, whereas this was his last recording. He made his way to the news board with a smirk. It had been months since he had failed a review, and he certainly didn't expect to this last time.

Triumphantly tacking the notes to the board section labeled for training, he paused to look over the postings from real bards of actual recent events. Typically, most of the cities' bullets seemed to exclusively relate to trade and politics, which wasn't really all that surprising but wasn't entertaining either.

He read the notes all the same. An icy winter in Kalt meant lumber had moved more slowly from forest to mills and from mills to the northern states, so prices were higher than usual.

Strong currents on the Fjall River had sped up shipments of metal works from the mountain city at its mouth. The lists from the other city-states besides Ravnice, where he was due in less than two months, were predominantly the same.

The only difference he had noted over his time in training was that Mer had a typically longer list, accounting for goings-on at the city's gifted institutions.

He found those notes more interesting than the business dealings and had kept up with them throughout his practice postings.

It seemed the Exarch had recently returned from a month's long journey spreading the faith of Daybreak around communities large and small across the northern half of Quaj.

Satisfied with his work and not seeing anything else worth reading, he made his way through the heavy wooden double doors at the entrance, opening them with a grunt. The refreshing mid-evening air of Tuath in late winter greeted him as he stepped outside.

Maestro Olimir passed him at the doorway. "You the last one in there, Harpis?"

Holding the door for her, he shook his head. "No, Maestro, one of the newer trainees still looked like she had a good deal left for the day."

She passed him with a harumph. "Young Yelsha, no doubt. Thank you, Harpis."

Harpis crossed the worn dirt road in front of The Hall and stepped inside the dense, heavily flowered woods surrounding the grounds on three sides.

He had made a relaxing routine of taking in the sounds and smells of Tuath evenings after his days of study or practice. His time with the bards had felt like an entirely different life from everything before it.

Just a year ago, he would have been spending the late winter days struggling in the bitter cold seas south of Kalt. Instead, he was taking in the drones of the crickets and cicadas, which he decided were much more enjoyable than trying to pry The Siren's bounty from frigid waters.

Bravit had been right about one thing, the songs played by the orchestra of the woods were some of the best music to be heard at the Hall. Even though the pleasantly cool air of a tropical winter made the insects lethargic, the rise and fall of their notes were no less hypnotizing.

He closed his eyes and smelled the sweet perfume of the moist, pollen, and salt-ridden air that swirled around him. Before he got a chance to exhale, a mechanical click, just out of sight inside the woods, snapped him out of his trance.

"Don't move, stupid!" came the harshly whispered command from a distinctly feminine voice right in front of him. The tip of a giant crossbow appeared just far enough out of the foliage for him to recognize, confirming his suspicions about the source of the clicking sound.

He struggled to oblige the command as adrenaline coursed through his body, pleading with him to act. However, as hard as he strained, his eyes couldn't discern any further details about the voice's owner.

When she spoke again in a calm, unstrained, high-pitched voice, she dispelled any mystery surrounding her motivation.

"You've been getting lazy and predictable, Harpis Akkeri. Do not let the reason you are here slip from your mind for even a moment."

"I am aware of why I am here. I have not forgotten," Harpis said, glowering as the woman scoffed, unconvinced from behind the foliage.

She lowered the aim of the crossbow from his chest to the ground. "I suggest you start remembering and practicing the craft of our trade before you are forced to in earnest at your posting. Suspicion and unpredictability can go far in extending your already short human lifespan."

The crossbow disappeared back into the woods, but Harpis could discern no other sound or movement.

"Are you an elf?" he asked, not expecting an answer. He waited another few moments while straining his senses, but he noticed only the continued concert of the bugs and birds.

Making his way back to the residential wing of the Hall, Harpis conceded to himself that he hadn't even thought of The Syndicate in weeks, and he wondered how long he had been under observation. Nevertheless, he decided the woman elf or whoever she was, had been right to correct him.

*****

Wren grumbled to himself as he made his way out of his warm shop and into the Ravnice winter. The young moon was at its zenith in the sky and provided almost no light to Ravnice city below. The gnome was surly towards sneaking about but glad for the luxury of cover from the near-complete darkness. It had been decades since the gnome had been the one in Ravnice responsible for sneaking, observing, stealing, and placing things at The Syndicate's behest.

Wren did not know who at The Syndicate was responsible for forging the papers Harpis had taken to The Bard's Hall for admission. It did not matter to his current mission anyway. He had the next month to convince Governor Aanaman Reaper of Ravnice to accept Harpis into his employ.

The Syndicate had long wanted a bard of their own, and The Bard's Hall had spent the entirety of Aanaman's tenure as governor trying to staff the position in Ravnice. However, Wren knew well that the former farmer turned governor was as stubborn as the pigs he once raised and did much to avoid outsiders influencing or observing in the Ravnice court.

Though the position was vacant when Aanaman took over, he had inherited a sage from the college when he was elected. The poor fellow was summarily dismissed from his duties and sent packing back to Mer.

In truth, the Impresario had long ago given up on replacing his bard in Ravnice. The letter Wren forged and would deliver this night indicated otherwise. If he was successful, Ravnice, the Hall, and The Syndicate should be better off.

He had written words as the Impresario, indicating that he understood Aanaman's preconceived notions that a bard in his court was essentially a spy for others to learn of his dealings. Wren penned that the candidate was a local from a Ravnice Fishing village. It noted that Harpis loved Ravnice above all else but yearned to learn the bard craft.

The Impresario was sending him to Ravnice without any responsibility to report back to the Hall, only to gather news from it for the people of Ravnice. Wren's forgery had the Impresario essentially giving Harpis' tasking to Aanaman instead of The Hall to better the people in Ravnice.

They would receive more up-to-date information, as would the governor himself. Then, at a time, and in a method of his choosing, he could let Harpis take the news back to the Hall.

Wren knew not all of it was accurate, but hopefully, it was enough to allow Harpis to show up in Ravnice to an expected, if not welcome, reception at the governor's office.

Wren wore a thick black cloak with a high cowl to hide his face instead of his recognizable purple necromancer garb. In truth, he knew he probably ran a higher risk of someone spotting him out in the late hours, failing to identify him as one of the city's morticians, and confronting him in the belief that he was a lost child.

A street down from the governor's home and office in a quiet alley, Wren snapped his fingers and called forth Xissay while opting not to draw forth his scythe.

"You look ridiculous in that," she chastised the gnome.

"Shh!" Wren responded in a violent whisper. "Look, we need to be quick and careful about this and be gone back home. Take this letter, go in through the chimney on the left. It has not had a fire burning in it as far as I have seen," he said, pointing at the governor's house.

Xissay floated with her hands on her hips for a moment before taking the letter from him. "Does your real employer know

I do most of your dirty work for you? You should let them know. Maybe they would let you go on embracing necrophilia full time while I carry on spying for them."

Wren glared at her and contemplated dismissing her. The thought of his arthritic joints and bones cracking and popping in the winter chill as he tried to sneak his way into and out of the governor's office though prevented her banishment.

"Bah, get on with it," he whispered harshly.

Xissay floated off laughing silently at the gnome's expense.

Wren was soon growing anxious. She had been gone much longer than it should have taken to simply fly down the chimney, drop the letter and depart.

Several agonizing moments later, she appeared above him and floated down to face level. In her hands was an overly dusty bottle of Aanaman's first batch of whiskey from his distillery, barrel-aged for over two decades.

"You went into his basement!" Wren could not help himself but yell at the sprite.

"What, that stuff is worth its weight in gold, and we haven't had any in the years since your drunk of a governor stopped making longer aged whiskey. Besides, if he notices at all, he will just assume he drank it in a stupor with his militiamen friend one night."

Wren shot her another glare and then glanced fondly at the bottle she had dropped in his hands before dismissing. On his way home, he took to walking out of the alley shadows now that his covert action was complete.

He was frustrated at his oft impudent familiar, but he also quite thoroughly loved the twenty-year-old Reaper vintage. Maybe he would consume the dark golden contents of the bottle without calling her forth to join him until he had finished it. Wren chuckled aloud at the thought, and then it occurred to him that he did not want an overly pissed-off undead sprite from the deep places of the world burning his house to the ground.

Chapter 12

Reunited

Harpis slowly made his way up to the third-floor balcony. Other days he would bound up the steps in excitement at another lesson on gifted songs with the Impresario or Bravit. Tonight though, at sunset, he would begin his final moments with the two senior bards and hopefully leave in the morning, a sanctioned member of The Hall himself.

As he reached the balcony, he saw both other men sitting relaxed in lounge chairs. A lonesome stool stood in front of them.

Bravit addressed him first. "You've some task ahead of you in proving to us that you should become a sanctioned bard. Some real proving too with that violin, if you're not to be the first bard sanctioned to play the triangle or tambourine."

Benali chuckled at the maestro as Harpis took his seat nervously, holding his fiddle and bow in his lap.

Bravit stood and reached behind his chair, producing a stand and a few music sheets, which he put directly in front of Harpis. "Play it," was all he said before sitting back down.

Harpis fought back panic as he glanced at the sheet music in front of him. He had learned to read and write musical notes after agonizing weeks of practice, but he found it impossible to feel the song unless it was something he had heard before. A fact which Bravit knew well and Harpis assumed was the reason these unknown, obscure sheets now sat in front of him.

He began the song slowly, off-pace and out of step. He played the right notes as they appeared on the page, but they sounded nothing like the flow of a musical composition.

As he finished the first sheet, he looked up at a cringing

Benali and then to Bravit, who buried his head in his palms.

"Next," was all Bravit said in a resigned voice, as much to the balcony floor as to Harpis.

Harpis played the subsequent two sheets of music with no marked improvement. The fourth was one he had heard before, recognizing it by the first few notes written, as there were no titles on any of the sheets.

This time he played with his eyes closed, feeling the past performance he had witnessed of the song and not needing to read the notes in front of him. As he finished, he lay the instrument and bow back on his lap and noticed the bemused expressions both men wore.

Benali closed his eyes and rubbed his temples. "One last chance Harpis. Convince me right now that you are capable of this craft."

Harpis stared back blankly, unsure of himself. It took him long moments to shake free of the mounting pressure from his yearning towards becoming a bard and the possible consequences of failing The Syndicate. He gingerly laid the bow to his fiddle on the ground and cradled the instrument in his left hand. With his right, he slowly began plucking the strings in a steady pattern.

In barely a whisper, he began a song he had not heard in decades about a fisherman lured into a seaside cave by a siren.

Eyes closed, he focused all his concentration, weaving himself into the verse and pouring temptation into each inflection through his gift.

His foot tapped hypnotically in a coaxing rhythm. Harpis could feel the power in the string's resistance and, as he released it, felt the resonance ripple through his very soul.

The beat of his heart and release of the string fell in time with his foot. The music entwined itself into his being in the same way that he wove his gift into its notes. Every pluck became an echo of dripping water at the back of the cave.

As Harpis sang on, Benali shivered and felt his skin prickle. His vision blurred until he could see only the visage of a black cave. The whisper of Harpis' voice became the soft, distant, crashing of waves outside the entrance. The steady dripping of water bouncing off the cave walls replaced the pluck of the fiddle. Each drop beckoned him deeper into the cave.

Harpis ended the song and opened his own eyes again to see

the befuddlement across Bravit and Benali's faces. Benali let out a low whistle, and Bravit shook his head vigorously as if he could physically dismiss what had just happened.

His composure regained, Bravit addressed Harpis fondly. "I tell you true Harpis. You may be the most magically gifted bard I have ever heard of or met. So long as you don't attempt playing any sheet music for folks, you may even be able to convince them you are a musician after all."

Benali stood from his chair and walked in front of Harpis, motioning for him to stand. "What am I to do with you, Harpis Akkeri? Your singing voice has improved little in a technical sense. You have barely achieved the musical literacy of a young child. On the other hand, you have mastered our craft's oral traditions and can recall the verses and poems that contain the histories of our island and city-states with ease. Also, your ability to devour and recite information of the news boards is second to none."

Benali put both his hands on Harpis' shoulders.

"For these reasons alone, I would sanction you as a bard of the Hall. Instead, I will do so most importantly because of your potential with song and magical gift, things this profession and this institution were centuries ago founded upon."

Benali then embraced him. Bravit rose from his seat and shook his hand. Harpis couldn't stop smiling. Bravit raked his curly hair from his face and disappeared momentarily into the Impresario's quarters, returning with several bottles of wine.

"How about some celebrating and storytelling before you leave us in the morning for your posting?"

As the men sat around drinking, the conversation quickly turned to Harpis' favorite topic of magical gift through song.

Pouring himself another glass, Benali raised it towards Harpis. "To the future of gifted song, may your voice carry it further than Bravit, Mahala, or I have been able to!"

Harpis joined the toast but with somewhat muted exuberance.

Bravit noticed his expression and interrogated him. "What's got you glum?"

Harpis spread his hands apologetically. "I just expected the magic of barding to be more impressive. Compared to the necromancers, clerics, and mages of the realm, it seems gifted bards are more like performing curiosities than impressive magic

113

wielders."

Bravit scoffed at him. "If you were under the effects of your performance earlier this evening, I think you might disagree."

Benali offered Harpis his opinion on the matter as well. "A mage can powerfully affect a singular thing with enchantment over days, weeks, or even longer with proper meditation, preparation, and execution. Likewise, a necromancer or cleric may cast a powerful spell after years of practicing and having their deity's favor. However, a gifted bard can affect all those around him at any moment, albeit typically in a less outwardly observable or spectacular fashion."

The Impresario paused and drained the rest of his cup before pointing it authoritatively at Harpis.

"Let us consider the other gifted folk. Clerics may actively enchant the light around them into a defensive bulwark against assault, magical and otherwise. Mages must maintain their concentration on an element of their specialization and have some of that element on hand to summon forth their elemental familiars. Necromancers can even pull their familiars from The Great Dream itself through sheer will, but only keep them amongst the living so long as they can maintain their mental hold on those beings."

Benali shook his empty glass to request more drink, his voice getting louder, and he became more animated as he prepared to bring home his point. Bravit obliged him by taking the empty glass and simply handing him the rest of the bottle.

The Impresario raised the bottle in thanks at Bravit. "Do you know what happens if those actively commanding magic with their god-given or innate gift involuntarily lose concentration?"

Benali paused for a long moment, but Harpis offered no response

"Their powerful enchantments shatter their minds into thousands of pieces, and they live out the rest of their days as an unthinking, unfeeling husk. We gifted few that weave magic into our song do not have such weakness!"

Unsure of his ability to argue around the wine in his head, Harpis accepted the explanation and poured himself another glass. He decided to keep to himself his theory that the three of them, and maybe even Virtuoso Mahala, were barely the bard equivalent of an apprentice elementalist. He dismissed the doubts he had of his gift. Better to happily enjoy his last evening in the company of the two bards while listening to the song the wind made rushing up the cliffs from the sea below.

*****

Harpis had left the Bards Hall behind him two days ago, a fully sanctioned bard, heading for his post as the court bard for Ravnice City. He had not thought to question what extensive covert operations had taken place on his behalf. They must have been impressive to guarantee his attendance at The Hall and his position at the Ravnice governor's disposal.

Regardless, he was glad for it. The dryer chill of winter was beginning to creep into the air, and the coolness became more and more noticeable as the ship he rode made its way south along the eastern coast, bound for the port of Ravnice and less tropical climes.

When at last his ship finally moored itself to the Ravnice docks, he disembarked with abandon. He missed the raw beauty and peaceful pursuits of Tuath, but he longed to get to work as The Syndicate's Eye in Ravnice. His gait showed his excitement as he made his way through the wharf to The Siren's Scream.

As his eyes adjusted from the bright sun of mid-day to the dark of the lantern-lit inn, he spotted Wren at the same table they had shared so many months ago. He made his way to the back and sat down across from the smugly grinning gnome.

He picked up the already waiting whiskey glass on the table in front of him and clinked glasses with Wren.

"To you, Harpis of Ravnice, bard to the governor and of the Hall." Harpis nodded his appreciation and drank deep.

"I think I was more excited about getting to drink more of this stuff than seeing you again," he told the gnome with a laugh.

The taunting drew a snort from the gnome. "I am proud of you, lad. By all accounts, you have done well. Tonight, we drink in celebration of our reunion, but tomorrow, we've got work to do, and you have a governor to report to."

To him, that sounded like a perfect idea. "Hey now!" Harpis exclaimed, his mind loosened by whiskey. "I've been told you have a companion I've yet to meet. When will I get to be introduced?"

Wren grumbled, raising an eyebrow at him from across the table. "Old Braffen must be running his mouth again. I tell you that dwarf has got an unhealthy infatuation with Xissay. You will meet her when it is appropriate, and appropriate is not me summoning my undead familiar here in this bar and calling attention to us."

He barely heard the last part of what Wren said as the mention of Braffen's name reminded him how badly he wanted to tell Wren of his victory in combat against the dwarf and how he had been able to get the coin from Arken. He was also desperate to know if Wren had faced some of the same challenges during indoctrination.

"Wren, I have to tell you how I was able to get Arken's coin. You see, the lighthouse keeper…." He got no further as Wren kicked him as hard as he could under the table.

"Ow, what was that for?" Harpis complained in a not wholly sober voice.

"Given all you know, do you think that story is appropriate for an inn full of listening ears or prying eyes?"

Harpis' shoulder sank in defeat as he realized his blunder, and he held his hands up apologetically. He instead switched their conversation to The Bard's Hall and his experiences with his gift.

*****

Myrlman had started pacing the steering deck of the ship when they had left bound for Mer in the morning and was still doing so after the sun had set. Niverna was surprised his boots had not dug a trench into the wood planks. Suddenly he stopped and turned to the sage who was staring out to sea.

"They will learn to respect Tuath and me if I have to force them to at the point of a blade!" Myrlman said through clenched teeth.

"Myrlman, most of the men on the council are nearly twice your age and have held their positions since before you were born. In the case of Governor Ingar Hammersmith, he is hundreds of years older than you. These folks will not impress easily, and every single one had a contentious relationship with your father. So perhaps the best way to gain their recognition is to offer them a new face of Tuath. One that will negotiate rather than dodge their requests," Niverna said, trying to soothe him.

Myrlman spat at the mention of the dwarf, and Niverna doubted he had even listened to what she had said after speaking the name. They were all but thrown from their feet as the helmsman lay the ship on its side, spinning it into a turn.

The sailor was cursing loudly, and several shouts came from the crow's nest above and some crewman below as another ship almost hit them head-on, its bow dragging along the ship's side slowed both vessels due to the friction of rubbing together. Huge grapnels with hooks the size of a man's arm on the ends of thick chains were thrown from the other boat, lashing the two ships firmly together, and torches and lanterns sprang to life.

Scores of relatively shorter, dark-skinned men of apparent Quaji descent poured over, and battles began in earnest all over the Tuath governor's ship.

Myrlman began screaming at his crew and sailors to defend him. In response, the ship's helmsman shoved a sword into his hand and told him to help. Niverna produced a dagger from under her robes and stood in front of Myrlman.

They faced the ship's main deck preparing to battle against some of the assailants approaching from below. Unfortunately, neither Niverna, the helmsman, nor Myrlman heard the shadow swing on a rope from the other ship's rigging land silently on the back railing of the steering deck. Standing at the top of the stairs to the helm, Niverna and Myrlman did not notice the helmsman behind them suddenly become quiet as he was lowered, lifeless, to the ground.

Niverna gasped a voiceless scream as she felt the cold steel of the helmsman's saber explode through her lungs, entering near one armpit and almost clear through to the other. Myrlman's eyes widened in horror, and he let out a scream.

The Quaji kicked Niverna's crumpled form overboard after releasing the saber. He then promptly knocked the blade from Myrlman's shaking hands and slashed the young governor's cheek from eye to jaw.

The man then jabbed Myrlman in the throat as the young governor screamed in pain and threw him over his shoulders like a sack of grain.

With a labored run at the side railing, the attacker leaped with Myrlman from the higher steering deck of the Tuathian ship to the main deck of the attacking ship. Landing in a roll cushioned by the now semi-unconscious governor's body, he dragged Myrlman below deck.

Many of the Tuath sailors had seen their court sage murdered and their governor slashed and taken hostage.

Their shouts of, "Save the governor, save Myrlman!" and attempts at rallying the battle seemed to be pushing back their opponents.

The Quaji attackers almost at once all retreated to their ship, taking their grapnels as they went. As the last of them jumped off the Tuathian vessel, the two ships slowly started drifting apart.

*****

Below decks, Sirul removed the Mask of Breyva, losing the guise of a dark-skinned Quaji and for a moment revealed a face almost identical to Myrlman's own. Myrlman tried to scream again, but Sirul had precisely crushed his windpipe with his fist. Grinning at the young governor, he put the mask back on and uttered its activation so that it would henceforth take on the form Myrlman Tuath. Once again removing the mask, he took a steadying breath, free of the enchantment's pull on his life force that maintained its illusion. Returning it to the safety of his tunic, Sirul took out his needle and scraped it down his own scar opening his skin into a fresh wound, just like the one pouring blood from Myrlman's face.

He then calmly silenced Myrlman forever, pithing him in the ear. Sirul hastily stripped his and the governor's clothes and donned the tunic, cloak, and pants Myrlman had been wearing.

Before he went up the stairs back to the main deck, he took one of the lit lanterns off its hook and threw it onto the puddle of oil and rum he had made right before the attack began. Flames snaked across the ship's belly as Sirul appeared on the main deck, screaming for help at the other ship now almost a hundred feet away.

Once he noticed the sailors on board shouting Myrlman's name and pointing at him, he turned to the nearest Quaji pirate and put a saber blade into his face.

If there were any on the Tuathian ship who had not noticed him yelling, they undoubtedly heard the pirate's dying screams as the man flopped on the deck like a freshly caught fish. Then, taking advantage of the pirate crew's stunned surprise, Sirul leaped into the water and began swimming.

The pirates were soon too occupied with the flames ravaging their ship to care to pursue him. As the remaining sailors hauled him onto the Tuath ship, Sirul smiled as he heard the commotion from the pirate ship as they abandoned it.

Flames on the pirate ship were now raging above decks and consuming its sails as the burning vessel slowly succumbed to the deep of the sea.

Water dripping from his clothes and blood running down his cheek, Sirul faced half the crew who had made it through the assault without the mask, hoping his likeness to Myrlman and the blood and seawater would make any difference indiscernible in the flickering torchlight. He knew he would need to ween himself from using the mask for the sake of his health and to avoid it becoming a vulnerability.

"We turn back to Tuath immediately. As I fought my way free below decks, I saw a chest of silver and gold stamped with the seal of Mer. I will not now go to that den of snakes they call a council like a lamb to slaughter. As for the pirates, we will leave them to drown on the open seas."

Before the battle, to a man, the crew would have laughed at the thought of Myrlman Tuath fighting anything. Now though, they looked up at the conviction in the steeled eyes of their young governor and saw a leader.

"No longer will the rest of this island underestimate Tuath." He said, mimicking Myrlman's voice as much as he could, and then spit towards the pirate ship.

The ship from Tuath turned homeward, and Sirul thought himself quite clever. The Syndicate had taught him of the Quaji natives who ran pirating operations from tiny atolls and how to contact them. There was indeed a chest of silver and gold below decks on the sinking ship. It had paid for the raid, but not with coins from Mer. Instead, he had stolen it from Tuath's own coffers throughout the past few months.

The Quaji pirates had executed the plan flawlessly. During the raid, no one had noticed that the pirate who grabbed their leader was oddly tall, almost the exact height of Myrlman himself. Neither had a soul noticed that the face Sirul wore during the assault was identical to one of the other Quaji attackers.

He smiled again at the thought of stabbing the Quaji pirate in the face. That part of the plan he had left out when describing the raid to them and paying them. It was necessary to help convince the Tuath sailors.

Sirul had learned of the mask's existence years ago while rifling through the Navigator's office library late one evening out of boredom while he awaited his next tasking on Lodestar Island. The Syndicate recorded and maintained the whereabouts of powerful artifacts of concern that had survived the scavenging and destruction following the War of Magi. He thought the mask could be helpful someday, especially given its location was the easily accessible College of Magi.

He had enjoyed procuring it from the Tower of Stone months ago and was proud of how flawlessly he had obtained it. Initially, he entered as a new novice from another tower and planted the notes about the mask with the apprentices in hopes that he could follow one of them into the stone mage's quarters or frame them for the theft.

When he had seen Rallis come spying on the apprentice's conversation, he knew he had his stooge. While Rallis executed his plan, Sirul was one step ahead of him. He had paralyzed the novice with his needle, crumpled his form under Vennil's desk, and grabbed the coffer.

As the stone solidified around his hands, he held it over his head, letting the mask fall onto his face. He uttered the word of activation while staring at Rallis' unmoving face. He barely made it around to the front of the desk as the door exploded inward.

He would have killed the mage and sage, if necessary, after being freed from the coffer. Luckily for them, in their haste to consult the Arch Mage, they had left at once, letting Sirul cleanly dispose of the body. It was not surprising to Mara and Vennil that the novice, caught in the act of stealing some relic, had left the college never to return.

As much as he wanted to keep it, Sirul thought it better that it never be discovered as part of his plot, or worse, stolen and used against him. Besides, the only thing that would have distinguished the blond and grey-eyed assassin from the blond and grey-eyed Myrlman if they were standing next to each other before would have been Sirul's scar. Slashing the governor's face in front of his crew and cutting open his skin along his scar had just solved that problem, so now all he had to do was ensure his own face became taken as Myrlman's.

Sirul had been watching Myrlman's changing demeanor over the months since his father's death, and the changes suited him. He had no doubt he would be able to play the part of Tuath's enraged young governor convincingly.

The surviving crew of the raid would do well in convincing the people of the relentless and vengeful Myrlman that had fought his way out of a pirate hold. Sparing himself a smile, Sirul decided he was pleased with how his retirement plan was unfolding so far.

Chapter 13
Loose Ends

Barely a week after arriving at his posting in Ravnice, Harpis was sent by the governor back north to gather news from the Hall. He hoped his haste and diligence in making it to The Hall and back in three days would, if nothing else, help show he was dedicated to his craft and his position.

He finished making his way from the wharf to the governor's mansion at the edge of the city as the sun sank over the distant mountains of Fjall.

Though Aanaman Reaper was the only governor Harpis had met, he was confident that the man was likely the least political one he would ever encounter. Aanaman had been plowing and harvesting the corn and wheat fields of Ravnice since he could walk. His face wore his forty-some years like they had been eighty, yet his body still held the muscular frame of a farmhand, and his curly red hair had yet to show any grey.

Harpis neared the governor's home and nodded to the two militiamen who stood guard day and night outside the wrought iron fence surrounding it.

Passing through the home's entryway, he made straight for the stairs to the second story and Aanaman's office. He was halfway across the foyer when two tiny voices shouted "Harris!" at him. He paused to wave at Aanaman's young twin girls, who had yet to pronounce his name correctly, and exchanged a smile and nod of greeting with their mother, Shanowen, who stood behind them.

As he made his way up the staircase, he heard her chide the twins. "Off to bed now, you two, or I'll have the bard sing you to sleep."

Harpis was certain the comment was more for his benefit than a threat the girls would take seriously. Shanowen had been grateful on Harpis' second day in Ravnice when he had gotten the exasperatingly energetic girls to nap with a lullaby. He had decided before initially reaching Ravnice that he would keep the magical gift he wielded secret from the untrusting governor and his family, weaving it sparingly, gently, and only when necessary.

Approaching the door to the office, he could hear the militia captain, a near-constant fixture at the office table, and Aanaman heatedly debating something about corn and distilleries. The governor was far more likely to talk about his crops or his whiskey than discuss politics. The guard outside motioned for him to pause and struck the door with the butt of his spear.

"Yes?" came the short reply from inside. "The bard has returned. Shall I send him in?" the guard responded.

"That's fine," Aanaman answered. "See him in, thank you."

The guard opened the door and motioned Harpis inside.

"The bard has a name, you know," he said to the guard as he passed.

"Does he then?" replied Aanaman from his desk. "Come in, Harris!" Aanaman said, clearly amused at using the name his children called the bard.

The door shut behind Harpis, and Aanaman bid him sit in the seat next to the captain at the small wooden meeting table in the office.

"Should I be worried that your bard comes in here armed, Aanaman?" the captain said while glancing at Harpis' boot knife and the odd boat hook and rope belt around his waist.

"Well, Harris, should I be worried?" Aanaman asked from behind his desk, his frosty green eyes still belying some distrust.

"Only if you're a fat, freshly caught fish," Harpis answered, hoping his levity would resolve the matter.

"There, see Captain Kilannry, no need for me to worry. Although if you keep putting on the weight, Harpis here may mistake you for a fat fresh-caught fish in need of fileting."

"I suppose you could keep the knife," the captain huffed.

Aanaman held up his hand to end the banter. "Well, what news from the Hall?"

Harpis drew out the parchment he had taken notes on and

123

went through some discussion of trade and other minutiae from other corners of the island before clearing his throat and covering what he considered the important news.

"Sir, it seems that pirates attacked the Tuath governor's ship on its way to Mer for the council. That is what delayed the quarterly meeting. They suffered heavy casualties in the fighting, and apparently, the governor himself was kidnapped and taken to the other ship. He later escaped, diving overboard after killing one of his captors."

Aanaman took his boots off his desk and sat up straight. "This is unfortunate. It seemed that Tuath had already been on a rough road. This attack is likely to send them over the edge of reason."

Harpis paused for a moment. "There is one more item, sir."

Aanaman waved for him to get on with it. Harpis was not sure how he felt about spreading the information. It had been odd for the news to not come from the unified ledger the bards of different regions kept at the Hall. Instead, the Impresario had personally brought the bards present at the time to his quarters and told them Mer perpetrated the raid on the governor's ship and likely also the murder of his cousin, the former governor.

"There is…rumor, sir, that it was Mer who both murdered Seulman Tuath and attempted to kidnap of Myrlman."

Aanaman scoffed loudly. "What absolute horse dung! I have no love for the man, but Edwin Lurras of Mer is incapable of such conniving or cruelty on his worst day. Despite how much he and Seulman hated each other, it doesn't seem likely."

Harpis could only shrug in response. He felt he had kept his integrity. He was content in passing the supposed news from the Impresario as rumors heard and nothing more.

Aanaman looked at his desk thoughtfully for a moment before addressing Harpis. "Well done. My thanks for the hasty trip to Tuath and back, Harpis. I leave in the morning to make my way to Mer for the postponed council meeting. By the sound of it, the experience should be quite an interesting one. Perhaps for once, I won't spend the entire time regretting my foray into politics."

Aanaman then stood and made his way around his desk to stand in front of Harpis. "Admittedly, I was not sure I saw much of a point in having a court appointment from The Hall or The College of Elements ever again, but you have thus far proved quite useful. Get an earned drink or three and some rest. Captain Kilannry will be in charge in my absence. Please at least check in on him some time daily and make sure he isn't up here asleep or drunk."

In response, the captain raised an empty glass, shaking it at Aanaman. "You'll be taking at least ten of our senior men at arms with you to this likely quarrelsome council meeting, my lord."

Rolling his eyes, Aanaman poured the man's glass full. "As you wish, Field Marshall Kilannry."

Harpis bid the men farewell and headed out towards the wharf. He had his own drinking engagement with a cantankerous old gnome and mysterious third companion.

*****

It was already dark when Harpis reached the morgue door. The first floor was lightless, and the door locked. After knocking several times to no avail, Harpis unslung the fiddle from his shoulder and began playing. After only a few notes, the second-story window was flung open.

"Weren't they supposed to teach you to play that confounded thing?" The gnome said.

"I am better after a few glasses, and there is no drink out here to improve my talents, so unless you let me in, I shall continue this sober rehearsal where I now stand," Harpis smiled as the window slammed and after a moment heard the door in front of him unlatch.

Wren only had two chairs, and the small wooden one at the gnome-sized table would not hold him, but the cushioned chair near the fireplace was built for a human and was comfortable enough. As Wren got them glasses, Harpis quickly recounted what he had learned at the Hall. Wren seemed even more concerned than Aanaman. Harpis shared the odd fashion in which the Impresario had implicated Mer.

Wren scoffed at the report. "That song-pandering cousin of the Tuath governor is probably spreading whatever propaganda best suits his family and his city-state. True or not, the fact that such information is circulating is troublesome indeed. Those two northern idiots who happen to be governors have been itching for conflict with each other for years. It sounds like the young man

125

from Tuath is keen to create it."

The gnome pulled the wooden chair to a spot across Harpis by the fireplace and handed him a glass.

Harpis stopped him before he began pouring. "Now, you promised a third for our company this evening."

Wren pointed at Harpis in a warning. "Don't say I didn't try and spare you."

He snapped his fingers and turned to get the shot glass off the table. The sulfuric smoke appeared on the arm of the cushioned chair.

Through it, Xissay strutted, eyeing Harpis up and down. "This must be the musical moron you mentioned. He's more handsome than you said."

Wren handed her the glass. "I didn't say he was handsome at all. Harpis of nowhere, this is Xissay of The Great Dream, my poor excuse for an undead familiar."

Xissay winked at him. "Nice to finally meet you. Old corpse lover here won't stop going on about you." Wren had been moving to fill her glass but stopped instead and simply glared at the sprite.

Harpis picked up his leather fiddle case from beside the chair, and opening it, he took out an unopened bottle of whiskey and handed it to Wren to pour instead. "Courtesy of Governor Aanaman's finest barrel."

"I like this one already, Wren. I think we should keep him," she said, sipping the whiskey he had poured.

"As opposed to what, throwing him back into the sea? I had been considering it, but I doubt we could lift him," Wren huffed, setting down the bottle.

"You any good at playing that thing?" Xissay asked, pointing to the fiddle.

"Actually, I am quite talented," Harpis said with a grin.

Wren choked on his drink, spitting and spewing whiskey from his nose and mouth into the fireplace. The momentary flare of the flames accentuated Xissay's anguished expression as he began to play.

*****

Relying on others made Sirul extremely uncomfortable.

Depending on the mask's illusion made him doubly so. Until he could get by as Myrlman entirely without its illusion, the mask was a liability, and his retirement plan was at risk. Worse, the drain on his vitality that the mask incurred while he wore it was debilitating by the end of each day.

However, what agonized the solitary killer most, was that he was seldom alone in playing the part of Myrlman Tuath. Transitioning from a life where his shadow had been his only company for over a decade to being the center of attention was fraying Sirul's sanity.

At times he felt almost trapped in what was supposed to be a life of carefree frivolity. Each day he was growing more impatient for the next steps in his plan to unfold.

Finally looking up from the desk in front of him, he stared in silence at the fidgeting admiral who oversaw the portion of Tuath's navy that patrolled its harbor area. The post-battle Myrlman Tuath, played by Sirul, seemed to make a lot of folks nervous. Many had started talking about how difficult he was to read and how the death of his father and the attempted kidnapping had drastically changed the young man.

"There is a merchant vessel flagged out of Kalt carrying salted meats and furs. It has green sails, and you should see at least one of its crew ventures to the wharf vendor who sells netting and repair materials. You will arrest them and likely find them passing intelligence. If that is indeed the case, you will execute them on the spot and burn their vessel as a message to any other agents of Mer in our midst," Sirul said.

The admiral sat up straighter. "Of course, Governor, how did you know of these traitors?"

Sirul almost panicked. He was skilled in slaughter and stealth, but he had little experience in weaving great lies.

"Uh, it was brought to me by someone," he said, looking for a suitable answer.

The admiral provided it for him. "One of your cousin's bards, I assume?"

"Of course," Sirul replied, dismissing the admiral with a wave.

As he watched the admiral leave, he almost told the man to forget the matter and that he would handle it himself. He forced himself to let the officer depart. No governor, or spoiled former son of a governor, no matter how delusional and vengeance fed, would have offered to do so.

The other Syndicate loose end he would fix himself tonight before he made his way tomorrow to Mer for the crucial council meeting.

He needed to prevent close observation from The Syndicate agent playing kitchen girl and avoid any of those working at the mansion challenging him as an imposter as he spent more and more time without the mask. So, as soon as they landed back in Tuath, he had ordered a rotation of the entire mansion staff. Playing the paranoid and angry leader, he had told his militia he thought spies from Mer among the previous mansion and family attendants.

Sirul had noted where the woman he suspected a Syndicate agent now worked, barely a stone's throw from the mansion. Of course, an agent of The Syndicate would try and stay as close to the ruler as possible.

Making his way to his quarters, the rooms Seulman had occupied earlier this year, Sirul changed out of flowing governor's robes for his worn black leathers.

He took the mask off and secured it against his chest under his tunic. He sat for a moment on the bed, taking in several breaths and shaking his head to rid himself of the smothering and taxing sensation the item induced. He was pleased with his progress in wearing it less and less. The first few days back in Tuath, he had worn it almost constantly out of paranoia which had left him wholly exhausted each evening. Nothing made the experienced assassin more concerned than feeling depleted and weak.

Pulling his hood low over his face, he slipped off the room's balcony. He quickly crossed the small yard before going effortlessly over the mansion wall and landing silently on the quiet street below. He would have moved on the Syndicate agent sooner, but he could not ignore the advantage this particular evening provided the task at hand. The spring equinox had been the night before, and in tropical Tuath, it was celebrated with as much wine and revelry as participants could stand. The benefit to Sirul being that the next day and night, the streets and taverns were as silent and empty as they would be all year.

He made his way into the shadows of an alley between the tavern she worked in and the path he had seen her taking home late at night and waited. Finally, after several hours she appeared.

One moment she was taking her short walk to her home and bed after a tiring day at work, and the next, she was in The Great Dream.

Sirul lowered the body quietly to the ground. Grabbing a knife that he had confiscated from his kitchen after dinner, he cut her open. Cutting a piece of her clothing off, he used it to paint 'FEAR MER' with her blood on the side of the building. The whole activity was all done in mere moments, and Sirul was shortly climbing his way back up onto his balcony when he heard a shout from below.

He dropped from his position halfway over the railing like a hunting cat. Facing the two men confronting him, he was more than ready to add to the evening's tally.

"Hey, is that you, sir?" one of the uniformed guards patrolling the mansion lawn asked in a shaky and confused voice.

Sirul froze for a moment, thinking through several ways of disposing of the guards when they recognized him as an imposter. Forcing his killer instincts aside for a moment, he realized this was just another opportunity to test how well they would accept his face as Myrlman's. He slowly pulled off his hood but did not explain his actions.

"You all right, sir?" the other asked.

"I am fine. I couldn't sleep. Carry on with your duties," Sirul answered.

Both guards raised their eyebrows in confusion and stared at him for an awkward moment before the first one to hail him responded, "Uh, all right, sir, you have a good evening."

Sirul nodded in response and went back to climbing up the balcony, this time making sure to do it in a strained and clumsy fashion.

After he disappeared back into his quarters and was out of earshot, the guards turned to each other. "He was an ass before his father died, but he's downright odd nowadays."

The other guard nodded and smiled. "One slain pirate in desperation on a ship, and he's out here sneaking around pretending he is some great assassin."

They laughed at each other and continued their patrol.

Chapter 14

The Council

Wren took a deep breath of spring air as he made his way to the wharf vendors for his regular linen purchases.

His usual vendor gave him an intense stare as he purchased his linen. He knew at once that the pile of sheets he would use to wrap the fallen of Ravnice held important news. He made his way to his home as quickly as possible. If he hurried, he could read the message safely in his apartment and still meet Harpis for lunch at The Siren's Scream.

As he locked his apartment door behind him, Wren made his way to his desk and hurriedly unstacked the linen into an unorganized pile revealing the sealed parchment note. He broke the seal, verified the fresh ink stains, and read the message from the Navigators.

Northward bound.

An Eye in the Hall.
Song for one or for all?
A Hand for the vicar.
A Name for the killer?

We Lost our sight.
As quiet as the night,
Inquire after Eiyna.
A hand feeds the crown.

Wren stared for a long moment at the parchment. Never had

The Syndicate so named an operative in a message. Sending him and Harpis to Tuath must mean something was seriously amiss. The gnome snapped his fingers, and Xissay appeared sitting on his table as the smoke cleared.

"Where are we headed this time?" she asked, glancing at the parchment held unsteadily in Wren's hands.

"I think the Eye in Tuath must be dead, and The Syndicate is worried enough about the Hand to send Harpis and me north to look for her. They even sent her name and that she works in a role that gets food to the governor. This message breaks protocol on several levels. Naming an operative of another area and indicating their posting as such. It seems they need Harpis to see whether The Hall stands with the Impresario's family connections or remains neutral."

"Seems likely there could be danger around the corner, old gnome," Xissay said.

He nodded somberly and handed her the letter. She walked over and sat in the fireplace, her hands glowing red, the parchment burst into flames.

"Indeed," Wren said, pulling his scythe from the empty air in front of him. He ran a finger along its blade.

"The next time I beckon, expect it may be in dire circumstances," he said to the scythe and himself as much to the familiar.

"I live for dire circumstances." Xissay returned almost gleefully.

Wren nodded at her solemnly. "You live for nothing at all anymore, dear Xissay."

The sprite crossed her arms and shot him a glowering look. "And neither will those who face me."

Wren raised his hands in peace. "Until next time," he said, snapping his fingers.

"Just make sure there is a next time, death speaker," she said, disappearing into sulfuric smoke.

Wren gave one more look at the now-empty fireplace, sent his scythe back into The Great Dream, and made for The Siren's Scream with haste.

*****

Harpis was already waiting with two drinks in the back of the inn when Wren got there. They were an odd couple for sure to be meeting over drinks, the governor's bard and one of the city's morticians. Most of the regular customers of the inn knew well the story of how the two met and why they were so close, and why they often chose the dingy wharf bar.

"Well met, Mortician," Harpis said as Wren scooted into the booth bench across from him and slid over a glass.

"Well met, Bard," Wren said, looking around at the mostly empty inn. It seemed most of the city was not ready for whiskey with lunch.

"I am glad to hear you are going back to the Hall. It sounds like Aanaman would like fresh information after he returns from his council meeting," Wren said, finishing with a severe look at Harpis, who was about to argue he had no such plans but instead simply nodded at him. "Won't you be lonely here without me?" he asked his friend sarcastically.

"Well, I am off to The Sanctum," Wren lied for the benefit of any potential eavesdroppers. "I will tell you, having been north before, in seven days, the Northern Winds tavern in Tuath's wharf should be bringing in its autumn catch of tuna. You should try some while you are up there. If you do not see what you like that day, though, the fish has probably gone bad, and you might as well head back here."

"I will do my best to give it a try. I do so love fresh seafood," Harpis said.

Both sipped their drinks quietly for a moment, thinking about the tasks at hand.

Wren met his eyes with a serious look. "Safe travels when you leave in a few days by the sea. It's probably for the best you get a chance to hear Aanaman's account of how the council meeting went. I, for one, will set out over land tomorrow and need to prepare." With that, Wren finished his drink in one gulp and slid out of the bench.

He walked over to Harpis and squeezed his arm. "I will see you in a week," he said very quietly.

Then he made his voice a bit louder as he departed. "Travel safe, troubling times bring out troubling folk."

Sitting back against the bench, Harpis wondered how he would convince Aanaman to let him depart again so soon after the man returned from the council.

*****

The council chamber in Mer was a squat, one-story, one-room, stone structure at the center of town with solid iron doors and no windows. The room inside was sparse. At the far end was a row of bookshelves against the back wall with six small writing desks in front of it, one each for the governor's clerks, should they choose to bring one along and a sixth for the clergy scribe who made a recording of every meeting for the histories. Along one side of the room were four ornate chairs for the Exarch, Impresario, Arch Mage, and Death Herald, the last of which had been almost regularly unoccupied.

Governor Edwin Lurras of Mer sat at the giant, five-sided oak table in the chamber's center. He enjoyed being the first in the room. He arrived hours before the others, benefitting from having the council chamber in his home city-state. Edwin was a lender and financier before being elected governor of the economic capital of Quaj.

His brown hair encircled the considerable bald spot on the top of his head despite the man being only in his fifties. He was a physical threat to no one. Conversely, his strength in math, economics, and bartering served Mer well over the twelve years of his six biannual terms as governor.

He loved politics more than any of the others. He reveled in these meetings even if he despised some of the guests they provided.

His face pulled into a grimace as one of his militia officers burst into the chamber and interrupted the silence.

"Governor, some twenty ships from Tuath have entered the harbor, bristling with armed men, perhaps two thousand in total!"

Edwin frowned deeply. "What is that pompous son of an ass doing sailing into here with half his navy? These are supposed to be peaceful dealings, not armed stand-offs."

The officer shrugged unknowingly. "What are your orders?"

Edwin let out a long sigh of disappointment. "Empty the barracks and triple the street patrols. Activate the rest of the garrison forces, have them on standby. Move at least five hundred armed men into positions around the wharf and have another five hundred within minutes of this building. Send our reserves to the barracks."

The officer turned to leave, but Edwin gave one more order as he got to the doors. "And Lieutenant, our men are to avoid confrontation at absolutely any cost. Prevent our guests or our people from experiencing any violence today if possible. You find Captain Elliswerth and pass that along to him, won't you? I expect a full debrief from him on the handling of this childish display of aggression after the council meeting."

The man saluted and left.

*****

As ordered, the other nineteen ships stayed out in the far reaches of the harbor as the Tuath governor's flagship tied up to the Mer docks. Sirul descended the gangway to the pier, Benali Tuath in tow.

Sirul was pleased that he had convinced the Impresario to sail with him to the council. He had used his first encounter with Myrlman's second cousin as a final test. Despite knowing the bard had not spent time with Myrlman since he was a child, the risk of being called out as a pretender by Benali had exhilarated Sirul. However, after several meetings with the man back in Tuath, he had not sensed even the slightest suspicion.

Having gone almost the entire week before their departure without donning it, he felt the time was right to rid himself of the potential liability. So, the night before they arrived, he had flung the mask off the side of his ship, surrendering the powerful artifact to the deep of the sea and completing his transformation into Myrlman Tuath.

He was pleased with his well-orchestrated introduction to the island's political arena. The supposedly neutral Bard's Hall leader arriving with him should at least put the other governors on their heels a little in what would be an exciting council meeting. Though he had never been in Mer during one of the meetings or witnessed it firsthand, Sirul felt confident in his ability to play the part. After all, this was supposedly Myrlman's second-ever council meeting and the first as an adult and in power.

Judging by the tantrum the man had thrown while Sirul watched from the ceiling of his office in Tuath after the last one, no one expected the man they thought to be Myrlman Tuath to make a good show of political mastery.

The experienced killer still living in Sirul sensed the Impresario's tense and measured steps behind him. Good, he thought, that the man who believed him his cousin was also on his toes.

In front and behind him marched fifty seasoned members of the Tuath militia. As they completed the short walk to the council chamber, he saw that they were the last to arrive. Perfect, everyone would notice the Impresario at his side, and he would also know where to sit.

As they walked in, his killer's senses tingled under the many eyes of the overstaffed Mer militia around him. They were obviously nervous at the presence of so many uniformed Tuath militia in their city.

Outside the squat building, there were maybe a handful of guards from the other city-states. They clumped together, telling war stories, and milling about until they saw the contingent from Tuath.

The twenty-some group of armed men and dwarves from the other three city-states drew together and faced the Tuath contingent. Their tight faces revealing their concern at the numerical disadvantage despite the ten well armored and well trained dwarven soldiers among them.

Sirul strode from his protective entourage with Benali slightly behind him and shoved open the iron doors with both his hands. They slammed like a gong as the stone walls inside abruptly stopped their swing, and all eyes drew to him. His hundred-strong guard contingent was a daunting backdrop for his intimidating show of force.

Flawless, Sirul thought to himself as he took the empty seat at the five-sided table. Benali Tuath made his way between the Exarch and Arch Mage, both of whom met his gaze with raised eyebrows.

Edwin Lurras addressed the table. "Now then, welcome all to Mer and this delayed meeting of the council. Governor Tuath, we all offer our condolences for the losses your people took in the attack against your ship on the way to this very meeting. We are glad you arrived here safely this time."

Sirul loudly scoffed at the man, and the table grew tensely

quiet.

Edwin gave him an annoyed look. "If you have finished your dramatics, Governor Myrlman Tuath, I would like to list our agenda for this quarter."

Sirul slid his chair loudly backward as he stood furiously, placing one palm on the table so he could lean over farther.

He pointed his finger at the chest of their host. "There is but one item on the agenda for this meeting of such a distinguished council. That is your outright apology and reparations for the murder of my father and the attempted kidnapping and resulting personal injury to myself."

Edwin Lurras of Mer looked genuinely flabbergasted. "How dare you bring such accusations against me without evidence or motive!"

A tight smile slowly drew across Sirul's face, but it looked more like a dog baring its teeth. He slid his hands into his tunic, causing more than one at the table to tense.

"You want proof and motive then here," he said, throwing two blood-covered gold coins stamped with the seal of Mer and a dozen letters from Edwin Lurras of Mer to Seulman Tuath onto the table.

All eyes sank to the items now strewn in the center of the table.

Edwin simply glared. "What of it? Pray, tell me, have you been party to any of the threatening letters your father often sent me in return? Our economic struggles are no secret amongst this council, and what do two coins from my city prove of anything? I had nothing to do with either tragic event!"

Sirul slowly sat down. "And yet, I have produced these letters to our peers here at this council, and you have produced nothing. The coins I took from a chest in the hull of the ship that attempted my kidnapping. The blood on them is my own."

Edwin looked beside himself in bewilderment. "This proves nothing. Again, I had nothing to do with this."

Crossing his arms, Sirul addressed the entire room. "I, Myrlman Tuath, of the Tuath city and state will hear no other agenda item from this council. Neither will I forgive these transgressions until Edwin Lurras and Mer meet my reparation demand for their injustices against my people and me. Ten thousand gold coins and ten ships delivered with them should suffice."

Governor Edwin Lurras' mouth hung open as he looked around the room desperately for support. "Mer does not even have such wealth in coins, nor have we committed any crime!"

Sirul was unflinching. "Well, distinguished governors of Quaj, what say you?"

The first to speak was the dwarven governor of Fjall, Ingar Hammersmith. Unlike most of his kin, Ingar had a clean-shaven face and head. The lack of hair showed the anvil and hammer tattoos on either side of his head as well as the many pocks and scars of his face.

Had his hair grown, it would be the same snowy white as his eyebrows, currently furrowed over his wrinkled face and reddish-brown eyes. Eyes that burned with barely bridled rage at the spectacle before him.

The dwarven governor slammed his fists into the table before locking his fingers together tightly. He looked each of the other governors in the eyes for a moment before speaking.

"Hear me well. The lot of you are sons or grandsons of men who were yet twinkles in their father's eyes when war between the human-run city-states last ravaged this island. That tragedy is the reason we meet here four times a year to settle our differences politically. I will not suffer the ill-proven threats of an impudent spoiled brat to disrupt the peace of this island."

Ingar paused, making sure his words sunk in. "Myrlman Tuath, you will be keeping your mouth shut on such absolute horse dung unless you've evidence Mer has moved against ye. Only then will this council be forced to act."

The dwarf emphasized his last comment by jamming his finger into the table in front of him with each word. "Forced to act politically!"

Sirul's simmered. He was no politician, and the warrior dwarf across from him had stared him in the eyes for the whole tirade. It was a challenge that Sirul would typically answer with death. His entire frame quietly shook as he flexed and unflexed his muscles, trying to dissipate his rage. He was afforded a distraction as the Kalt governor, pale, dark-haired, and weaselly Jaeryl Innisgrath, spoke.

"I, for one, support the claims of Tuath. Unless Mer can inarguably prove they were not involved and that the evidence shown here today is not viable, I have no choice but to agree that Myrlman Tuath and his people are deserving payment for their grievances."

The issue was seemingly a tie. All present stared at the figure of Aanaman Reaper, who was sitting quietly at the table rubbing his hands on his temples.

He stopped abruptly, laying his hands on the tabletop. "Part of my state lies in between Mer and Tuath, and I'll not have the blood of either or both city-states spoil my crops. Nor will I suffer my people's homes and fields becoming battlefields!"

Forcing himself to lower his voice Aanaman continued. "Due to the delay of this council meeting, the next one is barely two months away. I say we return at that time, giving Governor Edwin Lurras and Governor Myrlman Tuath time to make their cases eloquently and defensibly. Only then should we vote on the claims made. The two concerned will have no vote, and we will decide then with a majority rule."

The room was deathly silent for a few long moments before Ingar Hammersmith spoke. "I second Aanaman's proposition and the peace it keeps. All those in favor say aye."

Jaeryl Innisgrath of Kalt answered a begrudging, "aye," and Edwin Lurras an enthusiastic one.

Sirul sat silently seething at the bureaucracy around him. He was frustratingly unable to navigate the situation politically. As much as he wanted to kill the others in the room, that would not get him what he wanted. He stood abruptly and sneered at the table, which had begun a tense and hushed conversation.

"Farewell, governors!" he shouted as he left, and Impresario Benali obediently stood and followed behind him.

With the door closed behind the two men from Tuath, Ingar Hammersmith spat at the ground in their direction. "That spoiled boy from Tuath will have the lot of you dragged into war before the year is up, mark my words. Do ye think you'd be spared down there in the south, Jaeryl Innisgrath?"

The man from Kalt stood out of his chair and glared at the dwarf. "Do you think war will not come to your mountain hole, Ingar?" Jaeryl left, slamming the iron doors behind him.

The dwarf's retort went unheard by the departing governor. "Bah to him too, on puppet strings from the Kalt clan. I am betting their lumber industry would boom from a war, and who knows, maybe he is safe in the south. No one else besides his people and that forsaken tribe of elves can stand the wind and cold of southern winters."

The dwarf got up to leave, as did Aanaman, who was clenching his fists in thought. The dwarf and man gave parting courtesy to the still silent and wide-eyed governor of Mer.

After short whispers between themselves, the Exarch and Arch Mage stood, offering comfort to the governor.

"Logic will lead us to the proper solution," voiced the Arch Mage.

"Daybreak's judgment is above our own," the Exarch followed.

As the day had begun, Governor Edwin Lurras of Mer sat alone at the table. For once, he was not so fond of politics or the meeting of the council.

*****

If not for the Exarch's white robe and cowl, or the black-embroidered flowing orange robes of the Arch Mage, an onlooker could easily mistake them for any other two old friends taking a stroll on the beach. They paced the private area south of the college as they had countless times. This time though, they were not catching up on the news and discussing the weather.

The Exarch stopped suddenly and faced eastward to where the day would break tomorrow and for every day to follow. "Uridyll, my friend, we must ensure our institutions are neutral in this. Whatever the outcome, there must be no bias from the winner against our actions. Otherwise, we lose the ability to save lives."

The Arch Mage stopped too, looking up at the college to the north. "The annals of history are painted with blood spilled in past conflicts at the hands of mages. I'll not allow us to become implements of war once again."

He paused and looked down at his robes and the candle sigil of a college instructor hanging from the gold chain around his neck.

"If it comes to it, and the rule of law fails this city, the mages will protect the academics of the college and the clerics of this island as they work to save and rebuild her," he said.

The Exarch put his hand on his friend's shoulder. "Perhaps it

139

will not come to that, maybe men will see reason, and perhaps we can avoid more violence."

Turning his head to take in the expanse of Mer city behind the college, Arch Mage Uridyll shook his head. "Always trying to see the best in people, aren't you, old friend."

The Exarch smiled and shrugged as he turned to leave. His parting words made the Arch Mage crack a tiny smile despite the day's grim circumstances.

"You have your logic and research, Uridyll. What am I without my hoping and praying?"

*****

It had taken barely three days for Governor Aanaman Reaper to return from Mer. Harpis heard the gate open and slam from his apartment window across the dirt street from the governor's home and saw the man disappear inside.

Some might feel that living directly across the street from their employer was stifling and maybe even bothersome. To Harpis, though, it was the first time he had living quarters to himself. Shortly after Aanaman had gone into his home, a guard made his way across the street and shouted at Harpis' window that his presence was requested.

*****

Entering the governor's lantern-lit office after being shown in, Harpis was greeted with Aanaman's back as he poured three glasses of whiskey. He walked one over to Harpis, handing the other to Captain Kilannry, and then collapsed into his chair.

Throwing his booted feet up on his desk, he stared at his ceiling. "Take a seat, bard."

Harpis did so and took a long sip from his glass. He could tell the governor was frustrated, but it appeared the captain had as little idea about what was going on as he did.

"Gentlemen," Aanaman said. "I think that there is likely to be a war on our island in two months. He slammed his feet from his desk to the ground and sat up in his chair, facing them. He recounted the scene that had unfolded before his eyes at the council meeting.

Harpis quietly shook his head, and the captain let out a long, low whistle.

"Captain Kilannry, activate any reserves we have and begin drilling the men and shortening shifts. I want them sharp. Send a contingent of men, a number you feel comfortable with, to our north expanse trapped between Mer and Tuath," Aanaman ordered.

"I want the people to know we have not forgotten them. Spread the word. If a conflict arises, we will welcome those willing to come to the city from the farmlands. We will not participate in this bloodshed that is likely to come, but we will do what we can to protect the lives and livelihood of our people."

The captain raised his glass in acknowledgment, and Aanaman turned to Harpis. "I've never much cared for the bards, but truth be told, I need eyes and ears where mine can't be."

The governor of continued. "I need as much information about the inclination of the other city-states as possible, especially what is transpiring in Tuath and Mer. You will leave in the morning on one of our ships bound for Tuath and gather news from your fellow bards as frequently as you can until you deem it unsafe. You have my thanks in this endeavor."

Harpis similarly raised his glass. "I will leave in the morning then, sir." He did not verbalize his thankfulness at not having to concoct a reason to travel post-haste to Tuath to meet up with a particular dress-wearing gnome.

"Do you think we are under direct threat?" Captain Kilannry said, putting his now empty glass on the table and reaching for a decanter.

Aanaman swirled the little drink left in his glass, staring at it thoughtfully. "Well, I am not the greatest politician, but a blind and deaf man could have read that room. Ingar, to his credit, seems presumably fed up with the bickering of humans. He vehemently supports a non-violent resolution."

Finishing his drink, Aanaman placed the cup back on the table and shrugged. "If threatened, I imagine he will just hole up in Fjall and wait us all out. Mer and Tuath are likely to fall into an open conflict of some sort. Besides impacts to our people who happen to live on their borders, I doubt we will suffer direct ramifications."

The captain filled the empty glass in front of his governor

while giving his own opinion on their southern neighbor. "Now, Jaeryl Innisgrath to the south, he is a snake if ever I have met one. The Kalt family and their control on the lumber trade holds sway over him."

Aanaman nodded. "It is probably the worst kept secret on this whole island, if I am honest, that he does not make his own decisions. We will keep a weather eye on Kalt for now and do what we can for our people in the north. Given our lack of a navy, perhaps we should consider the docks our biggest concern."

After a few vigorous shakes of his head to clear his mind, Aanaman continued. "Now, those are problems for tomorrow. If we are all in agreement with our missions come morning, I would prefer some company in drinking the memory of the bureaucratic circus I just witnessed right out of my mind."

Chapter 15
War Drums

Harpis regretted the expense of the next day's ship from Ravnice to Tuath. He also lamented the price of renting a horse that morning to make the trip to the Hall, but the spent silver had allowed him to make up considerable time. He resisted the urge to outright look for Wren as he made his way out of Tuath city and to the northern road to the Hall.

He decided he would spend the night in one of the transient rooms and catch up with the other bards to maximize the amount of information he might get from this excursion.

Arriving at the front doors of The Hall as daylight began turning to dusk, he was shaken by the quiet. There wasn't anyone playing music or singing songs. There wasn't anything.

Harpis dismounted his horse and pushed open the great doors to the main concert hall. His skin prickled as the only sound he heard was the creaking of the doors coming to a stop.

He thought of calling out, but the hair standing up on the back of his neck encouraged him to maintain some amount of stealth. He made his way to the Impresario's quarters in hopes that he could at least gain some information to take back with him.

Thumbing through the pile of parchments on Benali's desk, he found a note from Myrlman Tuath. The message was nothing short of an order to Benali to use his bards to spread the news to every city that Mer had perpetrated his father's murder and his attempted kidnapping.

He made his way out onto the third-floor balcony and took in the evening sun and the song of the wind rushing up the giant cliff face from the sea.

Looking down at the water from the balcony railing, the sight that greeted him took his breath away. In the sheltered bay at the base of the cliffs were some sixty ships moored in a giant flotilla. They appeared to be navy vessels with Tuath banners flying from their masts and Tuath seals on their sails.

Distracted by the surprising sight, Harpis almost did not hear the door creak behind him or the man speaking to him.

"Well, well, looks like we have ourselves an unwelcome visitor!" said an unknown voice.

Harpis spun around, putting his back against the railing of the balcony. Two uniformed militiamen from Tuath approached him, sword and spear pointed his way menacingly. He guessed they were here to make sure people did not wander in and see the giant naval force like he just did.

"Just a lost bard, I was looking for the Impresario, no need to be hasty here, boys," he offered.

"Lost indeed, but soon to the sea, unfortunately. We are under strict orders regarding people snooping around this building. Your choice, fly like a bird of your own volition or be cut down and have your corpse suffer the same fate."

Instead of jumping from the balcony, he faced them fully and set his feet.

"I reckon this will be more fun than listening to you scream the whole way down!" the swordsman to Harpis' left yelled as they ran in.

With adrenaline roaring through his veins, they seemed to move slowly, raising the sword, and pulling back the spear to strike in unison. Harpis threw his forearms into the swordsman's upraised arms, blocking high to keep the man from chopping him down while stepping around him swiftly.

Once behind the swordsman, he exerted his weight against the man's shoulder blades while holding the sword arm above the attacker's head.

The move rolled the man's arm downward, forcing him to bend over with his sword arm fully extended, sword uselessly away from his body.

The spear wielder, now with his partner between Harpis and himself, missed wide.

Harpis yanked the man's wrist lower, causing him to step forward in pain.

He simultaneously kicked the bent swordsman as hard as he could in the back, sending the man into and over the balcony.

The swordsman's screams lasted for what seemed an age as the man with the spear became much more cautious and measured. The spearmen circled Harpis, who once again had his back to the railing. He thought of going for the knife in his boot but was not sure it would offer much of an advantage to the other man's six-foot-long spear.

Harpis had another idea, one he liked only slightly more than sure death. He put his hands on his hips and taunted the man. Years on a fishing vessel had made him quite proficient at slinging curses and stinging remarks, and soon, the man roared at him and charged the mouthy bard.

As the man rushed in, Harpis' hand went to his left hip and unhooked the belt. When the boat hook hit the ground, he quickly kicked with his heel, sinking it into the wood of the railing post. The man was soon upon him. He reacted by grabbing the man's spear and pulling them both over the edge of the railing.

The man flew past screaming. Harpis was spun twice from the rope unwinding around his waist before his breath was squeezed out of him by the belt noose halting his fall. Thinking it best not to look down, Harpis scrambled up the rope. While he climbed, he thought to himself that it might have been wise at some point before this moment to have tested the integrity of his makeshift belt.

Coming over the railing and back onto the balcony, he saw Maestro Bravit step onto the balcony. Seeing no weapon in Bravit's hands, he went to a knee and drew his knife just in case. Remaining in a kneeling position, defensively clutching his knife, he tried to steady himself.

"Peace! Harpis! Peace!" Bravit said, not coming any closer and holding his hands up. "They were here to babysit me, and there were only the two of them."

Harpis slowly sheathed his knife back into his boot and stood. "Bravit, what in the world is going on here?"

Bravit looked Harpis up and down curiously before answering. "Dealt with those two goons right efficiently, didn't you? I expected to find the idiots gloating over a corpse when I got up here."

Harpis' mind raced for an excuse for a long moment before

looking back at Bravit. "Years fighting drunk sailors on the Kalt wharf, those two northerners didn't stand a chance."

The portly bard snorted. "I do recall quite the rough crowd when I would spend time in the south during my nomadic years."

Bravit peered back into the Impresario's quarters almost mournfully. "The governor tried to demand we use the bards to further his machinations. Before objecting, Benali ordered all the bards to leave, and The Hall closed for at least a few months. He wanted to avoid people viewing us as favoring one side or the other regarding this whole Mer situation or being utilized for nefarious reasons."

Harpis looked around the quiet and empty grounds. "What are you still doing here then?"

Raking his hand through his dark curls, Bravit sighed in disappointment.

"Benali told me to stay and keep the place from falling over, and he left for the city to be with his cousin. I am not sure what is going on in his head, Harpis. Written on his face of late has certainly been an inner struggle. His cousin and his loyalties to this city-state have been at war for his will. Shortly after Benali left, those two idiots showed up to keep an eye on me."

Bravit walked to the balcony's edge. Standing by Harpis, he shook his head as he looked over the railing where Harpis had sent the attackers tumbling down the cliffs.

"Myrlman Tuath is a paranoid one. I tell you truly, Harpis. I've no idea what the flotilla below is for, but I am thinking they will be spilling blood wherever their course is," he explained in a warning tone while looking back at Harpis.

Harpis put a hand on the maestro's shoulder. "Bravit, if more Tuath militiamen come after those two, say that an agent of Mer showed up looking for information and that they'd chased them into the countryside."

Bravit let out a low laugh. "Not like they'd believe me if I told them poor, old, unarmed, lute-playing Bravit killed them both and threw them over the cliffs!"

Harpis chuckled with the man. "Bravit, if you don't mind, I might catch a short rest up here before heading back. I will lock the Impresario's quarters and stay out here on the balcony in case someone comes around in the night. I will be gone at morning's light, and I will leave the horse, so you have ample evidence about the agent from Mer. I'd do my best to stay off the main road anyway."

*****

The following day in Tuath, Wren arrived in the city and made straight for the diocese. Knocking on the domed building's door, he glanced around, looking for anyone paying too much attention to him. It seemed to him that the city itself was tense with anticipated conflict and bubbling anger.

A young cleric answered the door and glanced Wren up and down suspiciously. "Our Lady's blessing to you this good morning, sir, can I help you?"

Wren gave him a short bow. "My Mistress' blessing to you, cleric of Daybreak, please, be a good lad and fetch the vicar for me." Confused, the cleric looked around and nodded, slowly closing the door.

A few moments later, the door opened again, and the vicar stood, perplexed at his cleric's description of their visitor. "Ahh, I see," he said, patting the cleric's back. "A pleasant day to you, Death Speaker," the vicar said. He then turned to the priest. "We don't get such visitors very often, but this is a senior necromancer. He worships Our Lady's sister."

The vicar turned back to Wren. "To what do we owe the honor?"

Wren gave another short bow, this time to the vicar. "Please, Wren is fine. I come at the behest of The Herald. Rare is it for such atrocity to visit a city governor, and we wanted to offer an attempt at communing. Perhaps we may find some information to aid in bringing justice for his soul in The Great Dream."

The vicar seemed pleased at the offer. "But of course, we would be thrilled to observe a necromancer at work."

Wren stepped inside the diocese with the two men. "I just need to know where his body spent the most time since death prior to being burned."

"Right this way," the vicar said as he took Wren down to the second basement mortuary and bid the young cleric gather any of the others about the diocese to observe Wren at work. "I must tell you something odd about this man's death if you can swear on your Lady to secrecy."

147

Wren nodded at the man. "I swear it."

"Our autopsy found he had a large amount of poison in his blood, enough to kill several men, despite his throat being also slit," the vicar whispered.

Wren gave the man a surprised look and a raised eyebrow. He knew he could trust the medical methods of the clerics and decided this might be quite the interesting question and answer of the man's spirit if he could contact it.

Wren's instincts made him more than a little uncomfortable at the thought of going deep into a prayer trance with so many around him as he noted the dozen or so clerics now gathered in the basement mortuary,

He reached into the air and pulled his scythe from it to several wide-eyed looks. When he snapped his fingers, and Xissay came screaming out of the sulfuric smoke over his shoulder, hands engulfed in flame, the entire room recoiled, and one of the men let out a shriek.

"Xissay!" Wren commanded, and she came to a halt floating in the air in front of the gnome.

Wren shook his head at her, and her shoulders slumped at the missed opportunity for some mayhem.

"I uh, need my familiar here to channel my prayers to The Sleeper," Wren offered to no objection.

Xissay rolled her eyes at Wren and took up a position floating over his shoulder. He climbed on the stone mortuary pedestal in the middle of the room where the governor's body had lain before funeral rites ceremoniously sent his soul to The Great Dream.

He sat cross-legged with his scythe laying across his lap and began praying to The Sleeper, slowly rocking side to side. When he opened his eyes again, Wren saw the room devoid of color and bathed in grey save Xissay's bright red hair and purple eyes. Being undead, she was more of this plane than the living one. Slowly the incorporeal white form of a handmaiden approached him, pausing a few feet away.

"A question for Seulman Tuath," Wren said to the spirit, which nodded in return and faded away.

In the realm of the living, the clerics just heard mumbles and saw Wren's slow swaying.

A moment later, the bristly memory of Seulman Tuath's spirit appeared before the gnome.

"How did you die?" Wren felt the outpouring of his gift, channeled through his scythe, shake his whole body as he asked.

To the clerics watching, the lantern-lit room seemed to grow almost entirely dark.

The spirit fought angrily against Wren's command but eventually succumbed to the gnome's will.

"Poison," was all it whispered.

"Who?" he asked. The spirit battled his will even harder, and Wren could not hold his concentration as he wondered why someone cut the man's throat after his poisoning.

The gap in concentration allowed the spirit to steal itself back into the eternal dream, and Wren opened his eyes to the silent and gawking crowd of clerics around him. "Seulman Tuath's spirit is as incorrigible in death as he was alive. I am sorry, friends, but I could not command him to answer."

The clerics and vicar especially looked more than a little disappointed. "Thank you for at least trying, Death Speaker."

Wren climbed off the pedestal and met Xissay's gaze. She, in turn, gave him a doubting look and rolled her eyes again as he dismissed her. He thanked the clerics again for letting him try and apologized for not offering them anything. Once outside, he made his way for the North Winds Tavern to wait for Harpis.

*****

Wren had been sitting inside for several hours when Harpis finally arrived, panting and sweaty. The man plopped down out of breath across from the gnome and asked the server for water.

He gave Harpis a concerned look. "There are these things called horses, you know?"

After guzzling the whole glass of water and asking for another before the server could even leave, Harpis shook his head and took a long breath to steady himself. "Had to return on foot, couldn't trust the roads. I think we have a big problem."

Wren laced his fingers together on the table. "I learned some troubling news as well," Wren said in a quiet and mumbling tone. "It seems the governor died from poison, and someone slit his throat after. I am still trying to make sense of it."

He became more somber and shook his head slightly in resignation. "Also, we will not have to inquire after Eiyna. She

149

was the victim of a murder some nights ago. Someone painted a message from Mer in her blood on the wall of the inn where she worked. The governor ousted all his father's staff for fear of spies from Mer, and she took a job out in the city. Her murder is all these folks in this bar have seemed to talk about since I got here."

Harpis leaned in across the table, sliding a parchment to Wren. It was a note from Myrlman, demanding Benali Tuath be at his side for a war meeting at the naval docks in Tuath, taking place later that night.

"I think we should see if we can listen in," Harpis said, burning the parchment.

Wren sat back in his chair, crossing his arms. "That is risky business, Harpis, and we've no other help in the north now, but I fear you are right. We must know what they are up to."

Harpis leaned in again. "It's worse than that, I counted some sixty naval ships tied together in the bay at Bard's Hall, and in case you haven't noticed, it looks like they still have half their known navy still sitting here in the Tuath harbor."

Wren seemed to cringe. "Sleeper below us, you're telling me Tuath has upwards of eighty or a hundred naval ships? It looks like we will indeed be doing some sneaking this evening before getting out of here."

*****

It was over an hour after nightfall when the Tuath navy and militia leaders gathered with Sirul and Benali. They crowded on the second floor of the naval headquarters building, which sat on the harbor.

The windows were all open to let in the cooling humid air of the tropical autumn night. Harpis had no trouble hearing what the men said. He was primarily concerned with staying quietly in place on the slippery clay tiled roof of the building that was surrounded on three sides by the harbor waters.

Wren and Xissay sat on the roof across the street, watching Harpis cling desperately to his perch.

The sprite sat on Wren's shoulder and whispered into his ear, "Didn't know he was an experienced thief, better he than your ancient bones and joints complaining up there, giving you away."

Wren's face wrinkled. "I don't think he has ever done this

before, to be honest."

Xissay gave Wren a bewildered look and raised both eyebrows as she stared at Harpis prone on the other roof. "What could go wrong?"

Wren shrugged hopelessly.

*****

Harpis listened in while a man's voice reported to those in the room. "The twenty ships carrying out the mission to the south departed yesterday morning and should arrive at their destination sometime tomorrow."

Harpis could hardly believe it. That meant the sixty ships he had spotted from The Bards Hall balcony were all together in addition to the known Tuath naval forces.

Straining, he could barely hear the response. "I expect a full report of the outcome of our little raid as soon as the men return!"

"Of course, governor," the first man snapped.

Harpis did not presume twenty ships would do much against the already on edge Mer. On the other hand, hitting Ravnice or Kalt with such a force could undoubtedly be impactful. He lamented that he could not give Aanaman a timely warning with the ships already gone and hoped Ravnice was not the intended target.

He was pulled from his thoughts by Myrlman's raised voice as he spoke to the others in the room. "Gentlemen, how many ships and men do I have at my command?"

"We have seventy-eight ships still in the north. All are fully crewed," the admiral answered proudly.

The militia captain followed suit. "There is a growing feeling among Tuath of fearing Mer. There is also anger at your family having been so casually attacked and insulted. These emotions have led to record numbers of applications to the militia. With the reserves called up and the new men, we have roughly fifteen thousand men."

Harpis silently let out an exclamation. Tuath now had a navy over twice the size of Mer's, even with twenty ships supposedly already deployed south. Its men would now just outnumber the militias of Kalt, Ravnice and Mer combined. As Myrlman voiced his approval, Harpis found it odd he had yet to hear Benali speak.

The voices inside became hushed as they started discussing some other plan, and as he strained to hear them, Harpis accidentally kicked one of the tiles with his boot. The tile loudly cracked in half, and the voices below him went silent.

"A spy!" Came the cry from below.

Thinking quickly, Harpis grabbed a loose tile and threw it over the peak of the roof towards the street in front of the building. Letting go of his grip, he drew his knife from his boot and hoped that Trilia had been accurate in her accounting of its enchantment. He stabbed himself in the arm and held the blade tip in as he rolled off the roof.

The silence around him was thankfully complete as he fell the two stories to the water and splashed into it without making a single sound. The Tuath men rushed out onto the street and did not see the silent, human-sized shadow fall from the roof into the bay.

The feeling of the knife feeding off the life in his blood was surreal. He could feel his heartbeat slowing and becoming more labored the longer it pierced his skin. As he hit the water, he pulled the tip from his arm and began swimming underwater until his breath would not hold.

He wondered how long it would take for the knife to kill him if he had let it continue to nourish its enchantment from his blood. The thought made him shudder as he swam quietly down the shore away from the commotion.

*****

Watching the catastrophe unfold from the other roof, Xissay began wringing her hands in anticipation of a battle, her fingers glowing ember red as she did. Wren held up a hand to calm her and pulled his scythe from the air while murmuring.

Down the street, the fresh corpse of an alley cat suddenly lifted itself out of a garbage pile and shot hissing and meowing across the road in front of the naval building before turning up another street and falling once again lifeless.

Wren stopped his chant just in time to hear one of the men below.

"It was just a damn cat," the man said as they returned to the building.

Wren turned to Xissay. "If you wouldn't mind floating down and letting our bumbling idiot of a friend know, I will meet him at the merchant docks. Tell him to get dried off. We will book a room at a wharf-side inn and make south on a ship in the morning."

The sprite gave him a dissatisfied look. "All the things you could have beckoned, and you went with a bloated corpse of an alley cat?"

Wren shrugged at her. "The entirety of Tuath is on edge and ready to march to war. I think making it look like it was just a cat would be better than tipping the entire city-state into hysteria. Letting you catch a house on fire or me call forth the corpses of dead men to distract them from catching Harpis was unnecessary."

Xissay floated off to find Harpis with a dismissive wave of her hand. "You are no fun. Maybe we'd scare some sense into these foolish humans."

Chapter 16

Abandon Ship

Trilia sighed. "I grow worried, Qarn," she stated from the triangle table. The words were directed at the gnome's back as he stood in his usual spot, looking out over the courtyard through their office window. He did not visibly react or turn to face her as she continued.

"Turin has not responded to our last two queries. We have not heard from Eiyna in weeks, and with Niverna gone, we are blind in Tuath. Our ship servicing the northern ports is over a week late, with its last known tasking being to pick up Eiyna's messages in Tuath harbor. The Brewer went silent after his supposedly blundered killing of Seulman Tuath. Which we set him to because The Needle failed to accomplish the same mission," she said.

She rubbed her temples in thought. "We have to assume also that The Brewer was unable to clean up this whole mess between Tuath and Mer as instructed. The letters we forged as if from the Tuath governor apologizing to the governor of Mer for their history of fighting were likely undelivered. I fear we may be at odds with Tuath. Did we perhaps underestimate them and are now being undone in the north? Have we sent Wren and Harpis to their deaths?"

There was no answer to her questions, and Qarn did not seem to notice she had begun or stopped speaking to him. She slapped the table and yelled at the old gnome in frustration. "Qarn!"

Had the gnome snapped back at her and told her to stop being paranoid, she would have been comforted. Instead, Qarn turned slowly and walked over to the table. Sitting in his chair, he reached over and squeezed her hands.

"My dear, I've watched the rise and fall of several generations of Tuath leaders. Sadly, I cannot fathom them running an intelligence operation capable of unweaving our presence in their area so completely. Though Eiyna was young, Niverna was one of our most experienced operatives. She never communicated the slightest inkling of anyone being on to them. The Brewer had been a Shadow off and on for decades and, well, we both know what Sirul was."

Qarn let out a long slow breath before continuing. "I have been giving it thought for some days now. No matter what way I try and come at it, the only way we could have been caught so completely flat-footed is if someone with knowledge of our inner workings and tradecraft was actively helping hunt for Syndicate members in Tuath."

Trilia squeezed her forehead in frustration. "Who could be that methodical and cruel?"

Qarn crossed his arms and locked eyes with her. "I think you know the answer to that question."

Trilia cursed under her breath. "If Sirul Amun has turned on The Syndicate, then none of us are safe in the plane of the living."

The gnome was nodding his agreement when suddenly a horn blared from the lighthouse outside, startling them both. It was followed quickly by two more blasts, signaling an attack on the island.

Qarn uttered several ancient gnomish curses as Trilia put a hand on his shoulder. "Stay here and lock the door behind me, dear gnome."

She grabbed the sapphire encrusted scepter from beside her chair and made her way into the winding tunnels of their dormant volcano home.

*****

Hearing the horn, the ship's crew tied to Lodestar Island's docks looked about frantically until they spotted ten ships minutes from the small harbor. They knew their responsibility was to get away, spread news of the attack, and try and return later.

Urgently, the captain ordered the mooring lines to be cut with hand-axes rather than untied, and they shoved off immediately,

155

but the ships were almost upon them.

The Syndicate vessel barely made it out of the harbor without being run down.

Three of the much larger Tuath flagged ships broke off and followed it around the back of the island. Four others crowded into the tiny harbor and unloaded scores of militiamen via the lone dock while the other three waited further out in the harbor.

The larger, many sailed brigantine ships were gaining on the smaller Syndicate schooner and would soon have it engulfed. The Syndicate crew went from saying final prayers to cheering in victory as a colossal octopus made entirely of seawater climbed itself onto the deck of the lead ship. It ripped the masts off like dead twigs and went about whipping men overboard like rag dolls before making its way onto the second ship. On seeing this, the third vessel turned abruptly and seemed to run away.

Thinking themselves saved, the men on The Syndicate ship turned towards the island cheering at the sight of Trilia Saboghan standing resolute on the rocky slopes, her orange elementalist robe rippling in the wind.

Their joy was short-lived as they came around the island's far side to the sight of ten more Tuath brigantines. The Tuath naval force did not even bother to board The Syndicate vessel. Their lead ship simply slammed into the broad side of the schooner as it attempted to turn away from them. The collision ripped The Syndicate boat in half, and its men were shot dead in the water by crossbow bolts.

Trilia was enraged at the sight of the ship sinking and the growing sense of inevitability she felt about the fate of her beloved Syndicate. She turned from the sea back to the harbor of the island. Drawing the jewel-encrusted cynosure scepter from her belt, she made a broad sweeping motion from the open sea towards the docks while melding her mind entirely to the water.

As the sweeping of her hand approached the offloading militiamen, a monstrous fifty-foot wave appeared, following her command and motion. It went crashing over the seven ships now trapped in the harbor. The swell ripped most of the men from their vessels, throwing five of the seven ships onto the rocky volcanic beach.

She focused almost all her thoughts and whispered this time to the sea. Her giant, octopus-shaped water elemental crawled out of the ocean behind her and made its way towards the wreckage to finish off the survivors. She grinned thinly and held her scepter out to the sea again.

She began another sweep of her hand, and the sea followed. A hammering on her back, neck, and head abruptly broke her concentration, and the sea subsided. The cool metal tips of crossbow bolts punctured her warm flesh in cold explosions of pain.

Try as she might, her lungs would not pull air, and her hand would no longer follow her command.

If she could have breathed around the dozen crossbow bolts buried in her back and neck, she would have screamed as her mind splintered into madness as she lost control over the enchantment. The elemental octopus dissolved into a mist just as her sanity had.

The threat from the mage dealt with some twelve-hundred surviving Tuath militiamen offloaded for an hour, their ships taking turns at the small docks.

On strict instructions from Myrlman, the Tuath militiamen climbed the face of the volcanic crater from every direction, taking with them rigging from the ships. Fifty at a time, they rappelled into the crater, all under the protective fire of crossbows which hummed down into the courtyard like a rain of angry wasps.

*****

Arken Hester and Braffen Frothbrew had taken up positions at the top of the curving stairway to the Navigator's office, hoping to give Qarn as much time as possible to destroy their secrets.

A train of corpses going up the stairwell made it difficult for the Tuath militiamen to get up to them, and the curves of the stairs nullified the usefulness of the crossbows they carried with them.

It was a beautiful dance of death the two wove. The militiamen could only take the stairs one at a time, and as soon as they got to the top, Braffen would deftly twist and turn them, exposing a throat, or armpit, or face to Arken. Across the opening from Braffen, the man was surgical with his rapier, taking only the blink of an eye to open a throat, pierce a heart or scramble the brain of an enemy.

The man and dwarf grew slick with sweat, and the hallway

and stairway became slippery with blood. Militiamen came until the top of the stairwell was so clogged with bodies that they had to pull corpses out of the way so more could attack.

The stench of death in that stairwell was enough to make many militiamen grow pale and vomit. So it was that after an hour of dying, the Tuath militiamen started refusing to go up.

Arken and Braffen stood, bent at the waist, with their hands on their knees, heaving with the effort of sucking air into their lungs. Dying men were stacked higher than Braffen was tall, the topmost corpse that of a crossbowman who had tried crawling over the other carcasses to get a shot at them.

"I am thinking they are getting a bit smarter, Master Arken. I don't know how much more of this fun we will get to have," Braffen said when he finally caught his breath.

Both were covered head to toe in the blood of their enemies. They heard bookcases in the Navigator's room behind them toppling to the ground and the loud curses of Qarn within it as he burned the histories of The Syndicate.

If their efforts and operatives on Quaj had any hopes of surviving, Qarn needed to destroy everything they had documented.

The door to the Navigator's quarters flung open, and the roaring flames behind Qarn made Braffen and Arken flinch.

"It's done. Daybreak forgive us and preserve these confounded idiots we've tried to steer towards the right over the years." The gnome said, smacking the head of his small iron mace into his palm.

"I am guessing that these particular idiots, the gods take them, aren't taking to our efforts these past decades," Braffen said.

"One last chance to educate a few then?" Arken said, wiping blood from his rapier. The gnome and dwarf nodded at him in agreement.

A commotion from the bottom of the stairwell drew their attention. Corpses were being hauled down the stone spiral under cover of dozens of crossbow bolts sent ricocheting upwards. When the assailants finally cleared the stairwell, a stream of men came surging up.

The first among them was holding in front of him a piece of one of the tables from the kitchens, and he simply let the men behind him push him right into and on top of Braffen as they turned right at the top of the stairs, the next five men all had crossbows and sent them firing into Arken's chest.

Despite the hail of missiles, the spy master's rapier took three more to The Sleeper with him.

Pinned under the wood table and the weight of three men, Braffen Frothbrew snapped the bottom man's neck and relieved the next man of one of his eyes before darkness closed around him.

The last to die on the island, Qarn crushed the kneecap and face of a man who fired upon Arken before being killed himself.

*****

The admiral ordered that the crews take the bodies of their fellow Tuathian sailors and militiamen onboard the thirteen surviving ships for burial at sea. He also ordered them to gather the island's dead and pile them in the crater to burn in a single pyre. He might well suffer consequences for ignoring Myrlman's order to let them rot, but he would not let the young governor change his views on the etiquette of warfare.

Once the bodies of The Syndicate members were piled and lit ablaze, the admiral shook his head sadly. He had planned on letting the women surrender, but the stubborn islanders would have none of it. One of his officers informed him that the womenfolk had taken at least twice their number with them in the sacking of the small island fortress.

One of the ship's captains walked up behind him as the funeral pyre burned. "I'll be damned, a Mer spy outpost off the southern coast of Kalt just as Myrlman had said, though as to why there was Quaji folk, a dwarf and gnome amongst them, I've no idea."

The admiral turned to the captain. "How many?"

The officer cleared his throat uncomfortably. "One hundred and forty-seven lost at sea, two ships sunk. One hundred and twelve lost at the harbor with five ships scuttled on the rocks, sir."

The admiral went from looking at the officer to staring at the pyre burning in front of him. "And how many of our fine men did these brave folks take with them?"

The captain hung his head after reading the number on the parchment in his hand. "One hundred and eight in the tunnels, another thirty-two in the stairwell, sir."

The admiral spat at the ground in disgust. "Well, it's done. Nearly four hundred of our city's men lost for the effort. Never have I seen such slaying. Burn the scuttled ships, tell the men we depart at once. Let us hope this whole plan falls together for Myrlman, and our people will be better off for this sacrifice as he says they will be."

*****

Making their approach from the western side of Quaj was Turin Deadeye and his three-person crew. They sailed on the sleek and narrow schooner *Open Ocean* and could see the smoke coming from Lodestar Island as soon as it came into view over the horizon.

"I fear for our compatriots," Turin said from the bow of the ship.

His heart sinking into his stomach, he turned to his crew. "Prepare to make a run. We may be sailing into a trap."

The *Open Ocean* sailed a sweeping curve around to the island's far side, hoping to stay far from any threat. If an enemy vessel still at the island spotted them, they could outrun it easily, already having some distance between them.

Turin still stood on the ship's bow with a spyglass held to his eye. He closed it and stepped down to the main deck. "Take us in. There are no threats I can see from here."

Tears rolled down the elf's weathered face. "I think we will be the only ones alive on the island."

The *Open Ocean* tied off to the remains of the dock, and Turin bid the crew stay prepared to flee at once.

The scuttled ships had been burning for hours and would burn for a day yet. Tatters of Tuath standards and uniforms littered the lava rocks around him as he made his way to and through the lighthouse and into the courtyard.

Turin Deadeye had seen the deaths of hundreds of friends and enemies over his centuries-long career, but he could not help but weep like a babe when he made the courtyard and saw the smoldering pyre at the center. He wanted to run away and turn his back on the people he felt he had personally doomed to die.

He could not help but think if he had just planned better,

designed their system better, that his Syndicate family would be here now to warmly greet him instead of the dreadful nightmare before him.

Tears continued to stream down his cheeks as he made his way into the stone hall at the far end and up to the Navigator's office.

He could not believe the amount of blood in the stairwell and the tunnel leading to it. The ancient elf, a veteran of countless battles, was visibly shaking with grief as he walked through the ankle-high lake of blood.

Despite the carnage before and behind him, there was small comfort that the contents of the Navigator's office lay completely burned in ruin. The courageous acts of those who lived and died on the island had saved their fellow operatives on Quaj.

Chapter 17

Vengeance

Slowly, Lorkin took in a steadying breath before pushing his way through the doors of his private chamber below Fjall and making his way into the annex's main cavern. The squat stone cave comfortably fit several workbenches and tables and was lined with bookshelves carved into the surrounding wall that stretched to where the ceiling began curving. His four apprentices, a young gnome, two fellow dwarves, and an eager and peculiar human boy, sat in silent anticipation as he made his way to the table in the center of the room.

He slowly clenched both his fists, cracking his knuckles as he did before gingerly pick up the platinum wrist band and thumbing the priceless amethyst depiction of The Sleeper.

"Rare is it that we get to embed such powerful anamnesis into so beautiful an item as this. Since the War of Magi, few have needed such powerful enchantment, let alone had the means with which to pay for it," he said, addressing the room without lifting his gaze from the item.

"Stone Mage, are you concerned that this might conflict with The Treaty of Mer?" the boy asked.

"No, young Emurillo. This may be the most effort I have spent on an anamnesis in over a century. However, I cannot fathom how imparting the memory of resonance into the jewel of this bracelet qualifies as an implement of war. I can't even figure out why Death Speaker Wren requested the odd enchantment," Lorkin answered, "Now all of you be silent."

In one hand, Lorkin held the plain, slim grey-stone scepter that he had spent two full years enchanting as his cynosure almost two centuries ago, the other he placed over the bracelet after putting it back on the table.

First, he called to mind the memory he had already etched twenty-two times onto the jewel. The memory wasn't his own. It belonged to the stone, the rock, and the jewel itself. It was the memory of an iron mining pick ringing against the hefty purple gem. It was the consciousness from the stone itself of the rolling toll that echoed across the cavern it was mined from, and it was the rock's remembrance of the clanging reverberation when the final strike freed the jewel from a million-year-long grasp.

Lorkin's recollection had to be perfect and took over a week to commit to his mind each time. Every layer of the lattice had to be as like the previous as possible, or the whole thing would collapse in unstable imperfection. He sensed the towering magical structure that was his memory lattice. Sweat rolled down his face but, he did not feel it. He knew only the jewel and the anamnesis lattice. With the care and patience that came from decades of practice, he calmly and deliberately used his gift to lay the memory one last time onto the amethyst. It took the better part of the day, and finishing, Lorkin nearly collapsed.

Using his stone-scepter cynosure like cane, he gave his charges a smiling look of smug accomplishment that did not entirely hide the weariness in his eyes.

"Well, my friends, I don't know the purpose of Wren's request, but this enchantment should last at least a human lifetime, with the layers withstanding multiple activations from each separating," Lorkin said with a smile and wink at Emurillo.

*****

The twenty Tuath men had made it into Mer the day before on a merchant vessel flagged out of Kalt. They had made their way around the wharf area during daylight hours, milling about in small groups of two or three to avoid attention.

It was nightfall when the burly leader addressed the small groups as he meandered his way around the wharf to each of them.

Reaching the last small group, he spoke sternly and quietly, "Let's go, lads, there is a tavern just down the road from the governor's mansion called Fisherman's Feast. We will gather there, keep to yourselves, and order dinner and a drink or two to avoid suspicion. Do. Not. Get. Drunk."

The Mer governor quarters were not the stately mansion of Tuath but still quite befitting a ruler. Out in front of its doors on the street, several guardsmen patrolled the grounds. It blended in with the rest of the city easy enough, save being a story taller than the other buildings around it.

When the late hour arrived, the men made their way out of the tavern in the same small groups as when they had entered and took up positions along alleys near the governor's mansion.

There were guards outside at the gated fence, three of them, and one more inside. During the day, the party from Tuath had taken care to have at least one person from their group walking past the mansion every half hour or so, taking note of how the Mer militiamen were operating.

The leader gave the silent hand signal after looking up and down the street. It was quiet and empty save the guards in the late predawn hours. Ten men and nine streamed out from alleys on either side of the mansion, and the guards barely got their hands up to halt the men on either side of them before they realized they were in serious trouble.

Myrlman had instructed the men from Tuath to avoid killing anyone if possible. Consequently, the guards would wake up hours later with pounding headaches but alive all the same.

The trailing member of the raiding party did not follow them in and had instead climbed to the top of the building and lit the oil-soaked rags on the end of his arrow before firing it straight into the sky. The signal sent, there was no longer an option for turning back.

They kicked the door in and rushed upstairs towards the governor's chambers. There was only a lone guard sleepily leaning against the wall outside their bedroom. He challenged the men flooding up the stairs, and they knocked him unconscious with a brick from the alley outside.

As they burst into the governor's quarters, his wife screamed hysterically. One man threatened her with a knife, and another clamped a hand over her mouth to keep her silent.

Governor Edwin Lurras had his nose broken for his trouble before being choked unconscious. Then, he was unceremoniously rolled into the rug from the middle of his room and hefted onto the shoulders of four men.

"Keep his face downwards, ya daft idiots, lest he drowns in his blood thanks to the greeting ya gave him!" The leader shouted after them.

He nodded at the man covering the wife's mouth, and he used his other hand to pinch her nose until she passed out. Within minutes from the flaming arrow shooting into the sky, the men were gone from the mansion.

The guards were left tied together on the first floor, pillowcases over their heads, and the unconscious wife was left locked in her room.

The horse and small open carriage the Tuath men had bought earlier were waiting in the alley. The governor, still rolled in the rug, was thrown into it.

On top of him were piled sacks filled with every parchment, book, and note from his office and bedroom.

The leader jumped into the carriage while another man jumped into the driver's seat, and they pulled away on the short trip to their ship moored in the wharf.

With half an hour left before the dawn sun would start throwing light over the sea and onto Mer, the governor was bound and gagged below decks.

The sacks holding any evidence against Myrlman's claims, merchant orders, militia reports, and much of the business of Mer that Edwin Lurras had in his possession were now on their way to Myrlman Tuath.

After untying the boat, they lit a fire on the docks they were tied to, piled high with wet leaves to make as much smoke as possible. The crew was ready on deck to unfurl their sails with haste at the response to their signal. But, for now, two of them were pushing it along quietly in the harbor using long oars. When moments later, chaos erupted around them, they hastily let out their sails.

*****

Sirul stood on the steering deck of the lead ship with Benali Tuath and the admiral of the twenty-ship formation. The ships were utterly dark. No light lit between any of them as they floated silently. Before dawn's first light, the ships were virtually invisible to each other and would have been impossible to spot from the Mer harbor before them. Almost a hundred Tuath militiamen were on each vessel, a force of two thousand men. Every one of the men was standing silently still on the ship's decks, awaiting the signal from the admiral.

"We will shortly seize the opportunity to return greatness to our city, state, and our family name, Benali. Despite your lack of cooperation regarding The Bard's Hall, we will succeed." Sirul whispered almost fervently at the bard.

Benali Tuath was not sure of the man Myrlman had become. He assumed that Myrlman brought him along because the young governor did not trust him enough to leave him behind. Before he could respond, they heard an owl hoot from the crow's nest above.

"There, the second signal, time for our little distraction," the admiral whispered.

Sirul nodded at the admiral for them to proceed. Then, with a shout from the admiral, the entirety of the twenty ships sprang to life. Each of the hundred militiamen crowding the decks lit a torch and began screaming and hollering at the Mer harbor.

The crews of the ships lit lanterns and unfurled sails as they began heading towards the harbor. Confused shop owners and merchant ships lit their lights upon being awoken, horns started blaring, and bells began ringing all over the city in sets of three, signaling an attack.

A lone merchant ship unfurled its sails in all the commotion and flew an oversized Tuath banner as it made a sprint for the twenty boats. Seventeen military vessels of the twenty-strong Mer navy were tied up in the harbor when the chaos began. Almost immediately, the three thousand Mer militiamen on station and duty when the horns blared began making their way to the wharf.

Lieutenants were directing many to pile on to hurriedly unmooring Mer navy ships that were hastily making way to try and intercept the twenty ships from Tuath. The rest of the Mer militiamen were saturating the wharf in anticipation of a landing from the Tuath ships.

Instead, the Tuath vessels halted just out of range from any bows or crossbows that might show up on the wharf docks. They dropped their anchors while in a line to take up a large portion of the inner harbor.

The ships from Mer turned as one and began unfurling all their sails in a race to get across the harbor from their docks at the east end of the city peninsula. As the ships tried to catch the wind, the morning's first light revealed the other Tuath ships. They had been waiting just out of sight around the peninsula, also blacked out and silent. The sixty ships were now full of screaming and hollering Tuath militiamen and quickly approaching the Mer ships from behind.

The second more considerable group of ships from Tuath enveloped the seventeen from Mer on either side. The militiamen from Tuath far outnumbered the men from Mer. On most ships, surrender was immediate.

On two of them, fights broke out, and the Mer militiamen were peppered with crossbow bolts and arrows until they lost the will to fight. Then, finally, the surrendered Mer sailors and militiamen were thrown off their ships after dropping what weapons and armor they had. Men from Tuath replaced them, and the sixty-strong flotilla that had come from the south was now seventy-seven.

The Mer wharf was now bristling with the city's militia but also full of thousands of its citizens. The seventy-seven ships anchored in a longer line further out of the harbor behind the twenty, blockading the entire harbor.

Amid the fray, the Tuath merchant ship had tied up alongside the flagship with Sirul, Benali, and the admiral aboard, quickly offloading its human and intelligence cargo.

Sirul made his way to the bow of his ship and addressed the large crowd below.

"People of Mer, I wish nothing but peace and that which you owe my people and me. The militias of Mer or Tuath need not shed further blood today!"

After spending nearly every moment of his life for over a decade purposefully avoiding the attention of even a single individual, having thousands hang on his every word was intoxicating.

With the dawn sun breaking the horizon behind him, his armada cast long shadows over the wharf and entire harbor.

"Where is the captain of the militia!" Sirul shouted.

A short time later, a very tan and leathered brown-haired, green-eyed man in expensive-looking armor and a long blue cloak appeared at the wharf's edge in front of the ship.

"Where is our governor?" The captain shouted, glaring up at

167

Sirul. His rough face looked as if the wind had carved it from a mountainside.

Sirul smirked. "We will get to that in a moment, but first, I must deliver to you some information and evidence, peacefully, before we can continue."

At Sirul's signal, a small rowboat crewed by two unarmed Tuath sailors made its way from the side of his ship to the wharf edge and threw a satchel up to the militia captain before pushing off.

In the satchel were forged letters written by Sirul implicating the dead governor directing threats to Seulman Tuath and several authentic letters from Edwin regarding the economic strife between the two city-states.

Sirul gave the militia captain several minutes to flip through the documents. "Now you have the evidence regarding the heinous acts your revered Governor Edwin Lurras ordered in secret. You are aware of the cost to my family and city-state that has been the result of his actions!"

Oddly enough, the more he played the role of Myrlman Tuath, the more he felt slighted by the people of Mer and the governor. Although Sirul had precipitated it all himself, he disrespected at the lack of response from the council weeks ago.

He was angered further that Mer had disrespected his now adopted city-state in response to what he viewed as valid seeming claims of wrongdoing. Valid, at least, in the face of all the manufactured evidence presented, of course.

"What of it then?" shouted the militia captain from the wharf.

Sirul smiled down at the old captain. "I will take what is due. I will get what the council refused me and deliver my justice!"

Nodding to the Tuath sailors behind him, Sirul waited as his men brought Edwin Lurras before him and the people of Mer, still bound and gagged. Sirul grabbed the man's hair in one hand and tilted his head back. Then, staring into Edwin Lurras' eyes, he drew a dagger from his belt and slowly cut the man from ear to ear. All the while holding him upright and staring into his eyes as the life faded from them. He had not blinked or flinched while being showered in the blood that sprayed him with each dying pulse of the man's heart. Some of the Tuath sailors and militiamen even turned away or lost the contents of their stomachs.

Drenched in red, he spoke, spitting Edwin Lurras' blood from his lips as he did. "You may retrieve your murderous leader's corpse. I have handed out justice for the murder of my father and the attempted kidnapping he had ordered for myself."

Sirul's gaze settled on the militia captain. "Through the irresponsible actions of the now-deceased governor, Mer has been relieved of its navy. In compensation for the suffering of my people, I must collect financial reparations. Life in Mer will continue as it always has."

He turned his head, taking in the gathered crowd. "You may elect whomever you wish to run your city-state. As for your trade leaving this harbor, patrols from the vast navy of Tuath will protect it. We will collect tolls in fair amounts for such protection. The collections will continue until you have repaid Tuath for the debt owed."

Sirul motioned back at the armada behind him. "Twenty of Tuath's ships, each carrying one hundred militia, will always remain in the Mer harbor. The remaining ships of Mer's navy may peacefully surrender without consequence when they return. Otherwise, they will be appropriated violently or sunk."

He wagged his finger, chastising the gathered people of Mer. "At the slightest sign of disobedience, or an attempt to rebuild a navy, my forces will disembark and wreak havoc on this wharf. If there is widespread upheaval to this rule I am imposing on your harbor, I will crush Mer. I will march thousands of Tuathian militiamen south. I will sail one hundred Tuath naval brigantines into this harbor, and I will burn this entire city to the ground!"

Benali Tuath could not believe what he was witnessing. How could the once pampered lover of arts, who had aspired to attend his own Hall, just cut a man from ear to ear in cold blood.

The captain shouted up at Sirul, shaking his fist, trying to make a show of strength for the people of Mer. "This oppression will not last. The council will see you brought low for what you've done here! You won't succeed in taking what you want from our people!"

Sirul laughed. "Old man, I already have succeeded! Look around you. Do you think these folks would rather go back to their normal lives and pay the deserving people of Tuath a pittance for protection and reparation? Or do you think they have the stomach to see their city destroyed in an attempt at vengeance against a justified capital punishment? I assure you, if the terms I have laid out are not acceptable, that I will take what actions are necessary to make Mer state an extension of Tuath state and Mer city just another subject of Tuath rule."

With a signal from Sirul, the ships began to disembark. First, his flagship and other nineteen in the inner harbor turned one at a time and filed out through the seventy-seven strong flotilla that blockaded the outer harbor.

Next went the seventeen commandeered vessels. Their Mer flags now hung upside down with a Tuath banner flying above them. Finally, all but twenty of the outer vessels headed for Tuath.

The entire procession took half the day as the ships turned one at a time to sail away in a line that stretched to the horizon. The statement of naval power from Tuath could not have been more impressed upon the people of Mer.

Sirul made his way to the steering deck to rejoin the admiral and Benali Tuath.

"Why the long face, Benali? Look at what the great Tuath has just accomplished!"

Benali gazed into the grey eyes of the killer he thought he had known. "How could you just kill that man in front of his people without a trial? The council will surely respond!"

Sirul didn't blink. "Don't be a child. For the life of one man, we have bought the compliance of the biggest city-state on the island. As a result, Tuath will be much wealthier for it and our navy, militia, and people more respected. As for the council, what response would they be willing to muster?"

With no answer forthcoming from the bard, Sirul went on ranting, "No other city has any kind of navy to speak of, and less than three hundred merchant vessels are sailing around this entire island. Take from that our own, and there is what, two hundred and some seaworthy vessels left?"

Benali's shoulders sank in resignation, and he shook his head. "Cousin, this still seems ill-advised and an unnecessary risk to our city."

Sirul spat at the bard's feet for his lack of confidence. "Even if amassed all at once, it would be an unorganized and inexperienced coalition. We own the sea, and since we own the sea, who would dare send an army north?"

Benali was beginning to sense his opinions were not going to be heeded, and it was best to let Myrlman finish his monologue uninterrupted.

Sirul carried on unabated. "In the week it would take to march a unified army to our lands, we could sail a hundred ships and ten thousand men to the heart of Ravnice or Kalt or Mer in a day, and I don't see it as likely that they find the courage to unify against us. Kalt benefits more from supplying us than they do going against us. Without blood spilled on their lands, I doubt Ravnice cares at all. No Benali, the question you should be asking yourself is, why has Tuath for so long been in the shadows?"

The bard decided that he was better off keeping his doubts of his cousin's grand plan to himself.

Chapter 18

Preparation

Harpis made his way across the street from his apartment after receiving the summons from the governor. There was little guesswork involved as to what the reason for the meeting was.

The entire city of Ravnice had been abuzz with the story of Myrlman Tuath killing the governor of Mer, taking their naval ships by force, and sailing off into the sunset with a hundred strong armada of brigantines.

Harpis noted that instead of two guards in front of Aanaman Reaper's home, there were now twenty. Some were patrolling. Others were manning makeshift guard huts at the wrought-iron gate.

Inside, there were several more guards posted than there had been. Harpis tried to spare a smile to Shanowen Reaper. In response, her face tightened into a manufactured calm for her children's sake as they played in the living room under the protective gaze of several uniformed militiamen.

Upstairs he passed another guard and noted the two crossbowmen at the end of the hall. The usual guard stood at the door and let him into Aanaman's office with a mumbled greeting.

The governor addressed him as he took his now customary seat at the small meeting table with Captain Kilannry.

"Welcome bard, I need your knowledge of this forsaken island and current events as we come up with a strategy for Ravnice moving forward."

The surly militia captain gave Harpis a nod in greeting.

"I trust you've heard what that butcher in the north did at Mer Harbor?" Aanaman asked.

Harpis nodded his head slowly. "This whole thing seems to have originated as a blood feud between Mer and Tuath. How concerned do you think we should be?" he asked Aanaman.

The governor sat at his desk, drumming his fingers for a moment. "In general, I worry that with Mer in the palm of his hands and a hundred ship armada at his disposal, Myrlman Tuath may start looking further south."

Taking a sip from the glass in front of him, he paused in thought. "I doubt that he would directly strike us, and it seems like Kalt was favorable towards his claims at the last council meeting. However, I saw rage burning in that man's eyes when I stalled his plans. He was unhappy with me suggesting we reconvene the issue at the next council. He is impatient and rash enough to decide that two months was too long, and a vote was too much chance."

Captain Kilannry shifted in his seat. "Still, I'd like to step up recruitment and try to expand our militia. Maybe we should also begin some form of a regular military drill with them."

Harpis nodded at the man, filling his own and the captain's nearly empty glasses with whiskey before speaking his piece. "I am sure that improving our military posture through the militia is a good step towards the safety of Ravnice. However, I think the most likely outcome, if Myrlman Tuath's gaze turns south, is a similar blockade of our harbor and a tax on our vessels as well."

Aanaman motioned for the bottle, and Harpis handed it to him. "Well said, I have a similar fear. I think that he could also establish a similar practice here. If he decides to occupy Mer with his militia, he could simply set up patrols on the roads at our northern borders and tax our farmers and merchants as they try to take goods north by land. To the south, I fear Tuath could too easily persuade Kalt into allowing their harbor and their roads at our southern border to suffer the same fate."

Captain Kilannry let out a soft whistle. "I'll let the two of you commiserate on how not to lose an economic war. I'll concentrate on keeping us safe from the enemies that bleed blood and not coins."

"We may have reason to keep our attention to the south. Kalt has an elected governor, but the clout and the city-state's economy still rest firmly with the Kalt family and their lumber business. So maybe they see an opportunity in allying with the now

173

emboldened city-state that embraces hereditary rule as a way back into direct power?" Harpis asked after responding.

"Now that, good Harpis, is a well-made and frightening point. Perhaps we should focus militarily on the potential enemy we can hope to defeat to the south instead of the one that hopelessly outnumbers us to the north," Aanaman said, kicking his feet up onto his desk.

"As for the economic troubles, we will deal with them if we have to. My people can live without timber from the south or spices and other pleasantries from the north. I wonder how long the people in either region would suffer through a lack of grain or salted meats, or worse yet, whiskey."

Harpis shook his head. "Their people would suffer just long enough for them to decide that they could just relieve us of those goods at the end of sword and spear points instead of paying for them with silver or gold coins."

Aanaman held his hand up in acknowledgment of the bard's point. He stood from his desk and joined them at the small table. He poured them each one last drink. "That's enough depressing talk for one evening, thank you both. Captain, call up our reserves and send a few battalions of our more seasoned militiamen to the southern border while we train up our recruits in the city."

The governor raised his glass. "Now, no more talk of war, I demand we share this last glass with a conversation regarding the fine product of my distillery and its rightful place among other great whiskeys."

*****

Wren flipped the sign in his window and locked his shop doors long after the sun had set. He had been so busy at work in the basement amongst the dead that he had lost track of time. He always felt a little better when there were many corpses in his second basement morgue awaiting burial.

After all, if someone attacked him in his apartment above the mortuary, his assailants would be hard-pressed between fighting Wren and Xissay above and repelling the risen dead answering Wren's call from the basement.

After ascending his creaky stairs, he shut and locked his apartment door and searched for a candle to light. Wren did not mind the dark, but he could not read or write in it. Setting the lit candle on his small table, he reached for a bottle and glass.

"Well met, gnome." A familiar voice stated quietly from his comfy chair.

Wren nearly dropped his glass in surprise. He spun around, scythe already in hand and Xissay over his shoulder before he recognized who had spoken to him. Turin Deadeye sat in his cushioned chair next to the fireplace and began setting kindling up to start a fire.

"Gods above, Turin, how did you get in here!" Even as he asked it, Wren knew he probably could not ask a more ridiculous question of the master spy and founder of The Syndicate who could have broken into his home a thousand different ways.

"Your front door was open. I came down to the basement, but you were so lost in the grey between life and death with the dead downstairs, I came up here to wait," Turin answered nonchalantly.

Xissay shot Wren a concerned look and felt his forehead with the back of her hand.

"No fever, and you don't smell drunk, I am wondering what excuse you've got for being so irresponsible?"

Wren glared at her. "The shop was open. After all, I am trying to run a legitimate business here sometimes."

Wren dismissed the sprite back to The Great Dream as she began offering him further insult. He was afraid of the answer, but he asked the old elf anyway.

"Turin, what cause have you to throw away all caution and find me here in my home?"

Turin described the carnage he found at Lodestar as the flames grew in the fireplace. Wren could not do more than gasp at the elf's description of the nightmare he walked through upon reaching Lodestar Island.

"Before coming here, I stopped in Kalt and informed our helmsman and operatives there that their service was at an end. Not knowing if you and Harpis would yet have returned from the north, I made for Mer. I discovered that our Hand has died. He was captain of one of the Mer naval ships that initially resisted the Tuath armada. The Tuath forces rewarded him with his death. Our Eye in Mer still lives and may be of use to us yet. I told the helmsman there to walk away, as I did the one here when I arrived. Our entire presence in Tuath has been slain, including one of our three Shadows."

Wren could not believe what he was hearing, the sorrowful news of his friends and information that only the Navigators had known for so long. How many Shadows, who the other operatives were, what they did, all of it a stream of mental and emotional blows while he tried to concentrate and take in what the elf said.

When Turin finished, the gnome shared the sad news he had learned on their trip to Tuath. "Harpis and I did not have to inquire about our Hand's whereabouts in Tuath. Eiyna, it seems, was grimly murdered, and her blood used to paint 'FEAR MER' on the side of a building to stir up the Tuath populace."

The elf shook his head sadly. "I think that it is likely fair to assume that she was caught by those in Tuath with the former Shadow Sirul's help. They likely used her death to further this propaganda push that Mer is the one who killed Seulman Tuath and tried to kidnap his son. Truth be told, Wren, it was the decision of Qarn, Trilia, and I to bring an end to the rule of Seulman in hopes that Niverna could guide the rise of the son."

Wren looked Turin in the eyes. "It appears we may have erred there, for the act of murder seems to have galvanized the son."

Turin shrugged slightly. "That is what is odd about all of this. First, we had sent Sirul to murder the man and make it look like an accident. Then, when he went dark to us, and Seulman Tuath still lived, we sent in The Brewer. The man was a master of poison with decades of experience. However, it appears something went wrong because it looked like an assassination after all, and we have not heard from The Brewer since. Assumedly he was caught or killed, thanks to Sirul."

Wren was staring at nothing and rubbing the white stubble on his chin. "That explains one thing but leaves me with more questions. I went to the diocese in Tuath and was successful in asking one question of the fading spirit of Seulman Tuath. He said he died of poison. So, The Brewer was successful, and the dead man did not know someone slashed his throat. So that must have happened after he left the living. Who slashes a dead man's throat Turin?"

It was the elf's turn to stare off in concentration. "Perhaps Seulman's throat was slashed after he died to make the assassination that was supposed to look like an accident appear as outright murder. Like Eiyna's death, Seulman's was used to galvanize the people. I will tell you, though, over twenty years of good information Niverna passed to us about Myrlman Tuath. I do not think the son would have played any part in the murder. By all accounts, he wanted nothing to do with controlling his city-state. It seems Sirul Amun is running quite the operation in Tuath."

Turin went on staring into the fire. "Our organization has been brought low, Wren. I fear the time for quiet action is at an end. We must bring the folk of this island together so that they may openly shake free of Tuath's grasp. I think it is best that Harpis joins us. We have much to discuss and little time."

Wren snapped his fingers, and Xissay appeared, staring grumpily at the gnome.

"What?" she asked indignantly

"I need you to fetch Harpis for us, quietly," he said to the undead sprite.

She crossed her arms at the gnome and elf but, as bid, floated towards Wren's small window.

"Yes, master, right away master, of course, master, with much haste!" she said exaggeratedly. Pausing at the window, she angrily addressed Wren before departing. "Dismiss me when I return without at least a proper drink and being brought up to speed on whatever cloak and dagger the two of you are cooking up, and I will burn this corpse barn to the ground when summoned next!"

With Xissay gone from the window, Turin could not help but chuckle. "Well, she is charming."

Wren looked at his ceiling in exasperation. "I'd like to say you get used to her attitude, but I would be lying."

*****

Whether with keen and sober senses or those dulled by the governor's whiskey, Harpis probably would not have heard the tiny sprite. She heated one of the glass panes of his window with her hands until it turned to liquid and pooled at the sill.

Stepping into his apartment, she pinched her nose. "It smells like a pig farm in here, Harpis. Are you looking at beginning a new profession? Barding and sneaking about been wearing on you?"

177

Harpis shrieked like a young girl as he fell sideways out of bed while trying to get up. With nothing else nearby, he threw his blanket in the direction of the voice. The blanket seemed to hang there in the air, the visage of a spirit. He reached for his boots and drew his dagger in time to see the blanket fall to the floor. The now smoldering hole Xissay burnt in it allowed her floating form to be free of the drape.

The glow of her fiery hands lent light to the room, and Harpis became immediately uncomfortable at the way she eyed his unclothed body up and down.

"Hurry now and get dressed, or don't," the sprite said, grinning. "Wren sent me to gather you. Don't get followed."

With that, she went back through the hole in his window and disappeared into the night.

Harpis stared dumbly at the smoking blanket for a moment as he stood naked in his room clutching his knife. Then, he slapped himself with his other hand before getting dressed to make sure he was not dreaming and headed out of his apartment.

*****

Even knowing Harpis was on his way, Turin and Wren still jumped when there was a knock on the door downstairs. After going down to get him, Wren and the bard stepped into the gnome's one-bedroom apartment.

Harpis gasped when he saw the elf in Wren's comfy chair. "Turin, what has brought you here like this?"

Wren was going to hand a drink to Harpis, but when he smelled the whiskey already heavy on the bard's breath, he decided better of it and slid the glass to Xissay instead.

The elf recounted his tale a second time. Harpis could not help but weep for losing those recently endeared to him at Lodestar Island.

Turin then spoke to both the Hand and Eye of Ravnice. "Besides us three, there remains one Shadow abroad and the Eye in Mer."

Harpis raised an eyebrow at Turin. "And what of the other Shadow?"

Turin gulped down the rest of his glass. "I believe the Shadow known as The Needle, Sirul Amun, is in league with Myrlman

178

Tuath. It is the only explanation that makes any sense regarding their ability to completely catch us off guard in the north."

Wren sat back slowly and thoughtfully in his wooden chair.

"So, let me get this straight," Xissay said from her tabletop perch. "The most famed dealer of death in the storied history of your organization is currently unhinged. He is helping a vengeful spoiled brat who is the son of a now-dead, borderline tyrannical governor to destroy The Syndicate and conquer the island?"

Wren shot a glare at Xissay for so casually speaking of their dead friends but calmed quickly. After all, what pity did the dead have for the dead?

"That is an accurate summation," Turin said.

"What are we to do?" Harpis asked the gnome and elf. "And what of our presence in Fjall?"

Wren and Turin exchanged glances, and the elf spoke first. "No matter what plan we concoct here and now, we must execute it from the safety of Fjall. As to your other question, young bard, I will reveal that last secret to you when the three of us are safely delivered there and cannot be captured and brought to divulge it. It is one piece of information that Sirul does not already have."

Wren was shaking his head and staring at the brown liquid he swirled in his glass. "If we can get to Fjall, I can also consult with the Death Herald. She may have information or opinions of value to our cause. Still, what can five members of a nearly destroyed organization that isn't supposed to exist affect? We need to change the course of this island's fate one last time. Sadly, I believe there is no time left for plotting in the shadows."

Turin gave the gnome a reassuring look. "Our plight is desperate. However, if we can bring enough influential members of this island into our confidence, maybe we can undermine the foul plans unfolding in the north. Our goal then should be to gather those who can help us. Whatever we decide to do, it will probably require synchronization and actions across every city-state."

A tiny cough from Xissay interrupted the flow of their conversation. She shook her empty glass at Wren. "Well," she said. "I'm not running any more errands, so you boys are going to have to figure this bit out for yourselves."

Turin turned to the gnome. "Wren, are you quite sure you are not the familiar in this relationship?"

Earning a snort from Wren, Turin returned to the task at hand. "I will set sail in the morning, headed up the Fjall River from the Ravnice coast to Fjall city, and await you. I will trust our Eye in Mer to convince the Exarch to make a trip to Fjall. If we are to be successful, I truly believe we will need the minds of the Exarch and Arch Mage. We need them to contribute to our cause, even if only in the form of ideas and not direct action. The two confer too much for us to think, even if we wished, that one would come without the other. So how do we get the Arch Mage to Fjall? The Exarch already travels the island often, so that should be easy enough."

"Well, I know the stone mage of the college annex in Fjall. I could convince him to send dire summons to the Arch Mage and bring the man to Fjall," Wren offered.

All three men nodded in agreement, but Harpis felt he had a final recommendation. "I think we should also bring Benali Tuath in if possible. I am not convinced that he has turned himself towards supporting the tyranny in the north."

He explained the situation he encountered in Tuath at The Bard's Hall and insisted that the Impresario could help concoct the eventual plan.

Wren seemed doubtful, thinking that Benali Tuath must assuredly be in league with his kin.

Turin stopped their debate shortly after it began. "Harpis, I bid you travel to Tuath and try to reach the Impresario, but only if you think you can do so stealthily. If you talk to him and press him hard about his allegiances and believe the answers, you may bring him to Fjall. Know this, though, if he disagrees with whatever we all decide in the dwarven city, we will likely have to confine him. Also, his absence will cause some paranoia in Myrlman and Sirul. Either way, bringing him in poses a risk, but I will trust your judgment. Make your way to Fjall as quickly as possible."

"What about the other human governor or whatever formal leadership Mer now has?" Wren asked.

Harpis spoke first. "Well, I don't think we can rightly trust Governor Innisgrath of Kalt. We do not know who Mer has put in place or that person's potential allegiances. I trust Aanaman Reaper with my life, but if our enemies noticed any absence, it would be if the governors were not at home in their cities. They have another council meeting in less than three weeks, and I assume that they will all want to be present and that Myrlman Tuath expects them to be,"

Turin Deadeye gave him an approving smile. "Well, my friends, it seems like we three have work to do. I look forward to meeting with you in Fjall in a week or so, and hopefully, we can come up with a way to save this island we call home. From this moment forward, consider every situation a potential trap until you are safely in Fjall."

The three decided it best to stay at Wren's apartment and leave at differing times before dawn.

Harpis wrote a letter for Aanaman, explaining that he would be attending a meeting of dire importance with several other bards regarding Benali Tuath. He would leave it with the militiamen on guard when they set off.

Wren looked around the small apartment. "The two of you will have to sleep on the ground by the fireplace, my apologies."

The gnome disappeared down the stairs to the mortuary and returned with a stack of linens.

When he reappeared in the apartment, Xissay slapped her palm to her forehead.

"You lot look like you are off to a great start. Such confidence Wren has to bring you the linens he uses to drape corpses for bedding!" she said, laughing uncontrollably.

"It's all I have," he said, glaring at the sprite.

The man, gnome, and elf were quickly snoring thanks to the empty bottle of whiskey laying on its side on the table.

The sulfuric smoke that heralded Xissay's departure from the living realm soon appeared, and she strode through with a fond look at Wren.

"Quite the exciting afterlife I am having," she said to herself.

"And I hope to continue the excitement, so let's not go meeting in The Great Dream anytime soon, old gnome," she whispered to Wren's slumbering backside before disappearing completely.

Chapter 19

Congregation

The boat Wren rode made its way fully into the dimness of Fjall. When his eyes adjusted to the dark interior, he noted the addition of a giant ballista on the dock nearest the entrance. The dwarven crew tracked the small ferry as it docked, and two armed guards greeted and inspected it before the ballista turned back to face the river and cave mouth.

Stepping off and approaching the entrance tunnel of Fjall city, he saw there were ten dwarves where months earlier, there had been only two. He had to hand it to the dwarves. Their military-mindedness was nothing if not impressive. He was allowed to proceed after explaining his reasons for his visit to an officer amongst the group.

Wren took a moment on his downward trek to stop in and greet his fellow gnomes at their jewelry shop before he got to the college annex at the end of the downward sloping tunnel. Then, scythe in hand, he knocked on the door, and the booming voice of Stone Mage Lorkin hailed him from the other side.

"Come to collect that trinket, Death Speaker?" the dwarf asked as he welcomed Wren into the cave structure. For years this expanded cave served as a workshop and home to the small contingent of the Tower of Stone. Since he was there on more urgent business, he had nearly forgotten that he had left the bracelet with the mage.

"Ahh, yes, of course, can we please discuss payment…in private?" he asked.

Lorkin stared at him a moment with a raised eyebrow. "Surely, Master Gnome, right this way."

Lorkin took them deep into the annex, through his private quarters, and then into the library and office in the tunnel off its deepest section.

Closing the thick iron door behind them, the dwarf turned to Wren. "You already paid me for the work on the bracelet, Wren. What's this about?"

To avoid being overheard, Wren spoke in hushed tones. "I need you to get the Arch Mage here. Lie or do not, but hundreds of thousands of lives depend on us, and we need him here soon. I am afraid I cannot disclose more than that right now, but you must trust me. I swear to The Sleeper and the stone of her mausoleum, which we both have an affinity for that I would not ask this of you if I had any other option."

Lorkin eyed him up and down. "I can get the Arch Mage here in a hurry, but you're paying for the ferry trip and passage on a ship for one of my apprentices to get to him. Also, when he arrives, you're the one who's going to explain to him why I did not discover some relic in the mountains of exceptional power and mystery that requires his immediate consultation." The dwarf paused for a moment in thoughtful consideration. "And you are to include me in whatever situation requires these measures."

Wren nodded his agreement. "I apologize for the haste, but I must depart at once for The Sanctum."

The dwarf shot him an impressed look. "The Death Herald will be attending as well then? This will be quite the gathering indeed."

As they walked back out into the main annex, Stone Mage Lorkin motioned to one of his apprentices, who brought the amethyst and platinum bracelet to him.

"It was a good thing you were long in returning, the enchantment took much longer than anticipated." Lorkin stated.

He fondly turned the amethyst visage of The Sleeper over in his hand before handing it to Wren. "Layering the memories of the gem's resonance as it was struck and hewn from the rock by metal was quite taxing. I am confident in the enchantment, but the number of uses may be limited. It should allow for several dozen amplifications. Odd enchantment to ask for a necromancer, especially on such an exquisite piece."

Wren took it, still in awe. He marveled a moment at The Sleepers beauty cut in pure amethyst. "Thanks to you and again

183

for your help. I should return to Fjall in a few days."

Leaving the annex behind, Wren made his way past the now heavily guarded gate to the tunnels deep beneath the mountain. Then, when the darkness of the stone had surrounded him, he summoned Xissay to join him on his trip.

"Oh, I do miss being beneath the world, a shame we can't go to the deep places!"

The two made their way quickly through the tunnels, enjoying the subterranean silence. Finally, reaching the door to The Sanctum, Wren was ushered in as he dismissed Xissay to many complaints and drew his scythe.

Though time was precious, Wren still slipped quietly into the reliquary and joined in the evening prayer to The Sleeper.

When the necromancers finished and filed out, he stayed seated in the back. Once the door closed behind the last of the departing worshippers, the Death Herald, who had been acting as if he was not there, gave him an inviting wave.

Making her way to sit in front of The Dreamer's Door, she lay her great scythe across her lap and spoke. "Death Speaker Wren, to what do I owe the pleasure of your visit, my friend?

Wren approached the Herald and joined her at The Dreamer's Door. "I have troubling news and an important request."

He proceeded to recount what had happened to The Syndicate and the goings-on in Tuath and Mer.

The Herald listened, the entire time her eyes were closed, deep in thought. "Many souls of late have made their way to The Great Dream, Wren. Our Lady is happy for the company, but she is troubled. Those joining her have Konflict's name on their lips. They have his rage in their hearts and his conflagration in their eyes. To have another god so prevalent in her domain keeps her from sleeping deeply. She disapproves of the battle and war to come. She feels that they might bring her more souls with a stronger embrace of Konflict's spirit than her own, which would disturb the peace within The Great Dream."

How mind-altering it must be to share thoughts and moments of conversation with a god, Wren thought to himself before making his request. "Will you come to give us council, Herald?"

The giant troll gave Wren a toothy smile. "I will attend, and I will avail myself of whatever plan comes of this. Our Lady would never forgive me if I missed an opportunity to shepherd so many to her. I will be there this week as you have asked."

She turned back fully to The Dreamer's Door and began murmured prayers. Wren gave her a quick bow and made his way out of their temple and back to Fjall as quickly as possible.

*****

The chill of the pre-dawn hours in late autumn caused Ezera's body to shake every few moments. Nevertheless, she patiently awaited the fast-approaching sun that would bathe her in warmth.

Sitting on the jagged rocks at the very edge of the Mer peninsula, she sat with her back against the seawall of The Archdiocese of Daybreak.

The Exarch's voice spilled out of the central spire tower. Barely five words into his prayer, she saw the sun peak above the ocean, its morning rays bringing welcome heat to her face. She quietly prayed with the Exarch until the bottom of the sun cleared the horizon, and high above her, the Exarch concluded.

She had hoped the routine of performing her daily ritual would bring some comfort to her troubled mind, but it did not.

She was glad to see Turin after the ten years since leaving Lodestar, but the news he had brought in the waning hours of the night had made her heart heavier than she thought possible.

One last mission then for The Syndicate, destroyed as it might be. She hoped her unequaled favor and gift from Daybreak would be enough to convince The Exarch of her claims. Brushing her blond hair out of her face, she gave one last look at the rising sun before turning to enter the building.

Ezera caught up to the elderly Exarch as he finished his descent from the spiral stairs of the spire.

"Your Holiness, please, an urgent word," she said, grasping his leathery hands.

"Ezera, but of course, my child, of course. Join me as I break my fast."

She followed him as he made his way out of the worship area under the dome and to his quarters, the easternmost of the rooms ringing the circular chapel. Sitting together and alone, she thought she would have no better chance.

"Hameki!" she said, causing the older man across from her to straighten at the use of his name and not his title. "Daybreak spoke to me in my dreams last night, and when I woke, her intentions were still within my heart. We must hurry to Fjall. It is time to bathe the cave city in her light!"

The Exarch stared at her, forgetting to chew his food.

"Please, Exarch." She said, reaching across and squeezing his hands. "Let us go and see. Let us talk with the dwarves at once."

"This is wonderful news. For centuries, the dwarves have refused our presence in Fjall, yes, yes, of course, you may depart at once, my dear!" he said excitedly after finishing his food.

Ezera almost panicked. "No, Hameki, it was you in my dreams. You are to be the one to convince Ingar Hammersmith to let Daybreak into his home!"

The older man beamed with pride. "Then we shall leave this day!"

As they finished their breakfast, Hameki could not stop smiling.

Ezera felt bad for manipulating him. However, given the potential for the massive loss of life and everything Turin had said, she knew it was necessary. Somehow, she felt that her goddess would be content with what had been done in her name to protect and save lives. Whether her actions invoked the wrath of Daybreak or not, Ezera was at peace with her decision. She had served The Syndicate many years before she formally served the goddess at Hameki's side. She owed her fallen companions one last lie.

She knew that upon arriving in Fjall and seeing that others like the Arch Mage were present there, the Exarch would likely accept it as divine providence.

She and Turin had discussed as much. If necessary, Turin had also told her he would convince Ingar to grant them a diocese in Fjall. Thus, making her lie as near as a truth to the Exarch as possible. She was not sure how the elf would prevail where five Exarchs had not. All things considered, though, those clerics were no masters of intrigue like the old elf was.

*****

Harpis gawked in awe at the vastness of the amassed armada as the merchant ship he booked passage on made its way into Tuath Harbor. Although usually ships would have sailed a straight line into the docks, the merchant's vessel had to pick its way around anchored brigantines and makeshift docks.

Tuath had constructed a spider's web of floating wood and sunken piers to enable resupplying and the movement of militiamen onto the ships as quickly as possible. If what Aanaman had told him was right, there were still twenty brigantines posted in Mer to keep watch over that city's harbor. Even with them gone, almost a hundred ships crowded Tuath Bay and the city harbor.

Harpis' heart was beating so hard he worried the other passengers could hear it as the ship made the dock. He had decided that his best bet for accomplishing his task would be to play a lost bard. He would profess that having visited the empty Hall, Bravit had sent him there to inquire after the Impresario. Harpis had tradecraft and courage aplenty, but still, he doubted he would be able to happen across Sirul without somehow tripping up.

The possibility of potentially letting the man know at best he was lying or at worst have the truth tortured from him was not acceptable. Instead of deciding to march straight in and ask to speak to the Impresario, Harpis felt much more confident in lying to a mansion guard.

He had no idea how close the handwriting he used for the letter was to Maestro Bravit's own. He hoped that the Impresario would not care too much for the penmanship in his excitement at reading the words.

He wore baggy white sailor pants, a black leather tunic, and his boat hook belt around his waist. With his fiddle case slung across his back, Harpis hoped he looked every bit the traveling bard. He approached the gate of Tuath Mansion and took a moment to glance behind him at the beautiful, gentle slope the tropical city took down into the bay.

"What's your business up here, southerner?" One of the guards shouted.

Harpis turned from the cityscape, feigning surprise, and held his hands up in peace to the olive-skinned Tuath native.

"Renau Holden, nomad bard of the Hall," Harpis introduced himself, using the name of one of the few wandering bards he had met at the Hall.

"For Impresario Benali Tuath, an urgent message from

Maestro Bravit at the Hall!" he said with a sweeping bow while extending his hand and the letter it contained.

The guard took the letter and scoffed. "All right, bard, we'll get your letter to him, now begone from the gate."

Harpis decided to press his role as traveling bard a little further for good measure. "Are you sure you wouldn't want to hear a fiddle piece or a song of Tuath, master guards?"

The men waved him off, and one went to the gate of the mansion wall with the letter.

Arken's frequent words rang in his head. "Always be who they expect you to be," the spymaster would say.

Feeling he had done his lie justice and honored his teacher, he quickly made for the road to the Hall.

Some hours later, he blew a sigh of relief at the sight of Benali Tuath making his way out of the city. His tree branch perch provided him a good view of the three miles or so it would take Benali to reach his position.

The time gave him ample opportunity to see if anyone followed or escorted Benali. Harpis had made sure that the letter he left for Benali would equally motivate Sirul or Myrlman, who were likely to read it first, to send the Impresario to the Hall.

Come quickly. I discovered a gifted song in my readings. It may drastically aid the forces of Tuath in coming battles.

-Bravit

The Impresario rode alone. Harpis fought off paranoia and decided this was not surprising given that the man was deep in his state and headed on a half day's ride to a place that had Tuath militiamen posted as guards.

Once Benali passed immediately below his tree branch perch, Harpis whispered to him, "Impresario."

Benali Tuath nearly fell off his startled horse as Harpis dropped from the branches into the road and looked around in surprise. "Gods above! Harpis, what in the name of The Siren are you doing here? Did Bravit write to you, too?"

Harpis cleared his throat awkwardly. "I need you to trust me, Impresario. I penned the letter, not Bravit. I needed you out of the city."

Benali glared at Harpis and began worriedly looking around.

"Impresario, do you still serve the island, or are your loyalties to Tuath alone?" Harpis asked as the two men made their way into the woods off the road.

Benali looked insulted. "Of course, I serve the island above my home city. I swore an oath to the people of our land when I became Impresario. All the people. I am admittedly in a tough spot with my late cousin's paranoid son as governor. I had to close The Hall just to avoid the abuse of the bards. Why would you ask, and why would you believe me, regardless?"

Harpis watched every movement of the man's eyes and face, looking for any sign of dishonesty.

"I believe you because I have trusted you since the day I began at the Hall. I also have no choice. If you choose to leave here and tell Myrlman what I am about to tell you, my life is forfeit. Without a horse to outrun you, I do not think I would make it out of Tuath alive if I could not trust you. Most importantly, the people of this island need you, and I cannot deliver you to aid them if I could not trust you enough to come deep into Tuath myself to find you," he answered.

The Impresario's shoulders relaxed a little. "What then, Harpis, why all the secrecy?"

Harpis first told of his encounter at the Hall. He hoped that in revealing his actions against the Tuath militiamen and the fight at the Hall, he would be able to gauge further where Benali's loyalties were.

"I need you to be at Fjall in a week. It should be doable with the horse you ride, take the back roads out of Tuath and into Ravnice to avoid detection. Will you do that?" He asked, satisfied he could trust the man.

Benali Tuath tilted his head in confusion. "Why would I go to Fjall?"

"Because without you there, we may not be able to save this island from the tyranny of your cousin. Thousands, if not hundreds of thousands, of people, may die if he carries on, and people will forsake The Hall for having not acted on behalf of the people," Harpis answered.

The Impresario stiffened at the threat to his institution's reputation and his legacy.

"Myrlman won't expect you back until tomorrow at the

earliest. You should have plenty of a head start on anyone he sends after you. He does not know where you are truly heading, and that ignorance, most of all, should keep you safe," Harpis said to reassure the Impresario.

Harpis desperately wanted to ask about Sirul but until they were safely in Fjall he knew it wise not to inquire about the assassin.

"I will ride for Fjall. It is the one city I have never visited, and the fate of men on this island seems as good a reason as any other," Benali said before giving a concerned look at Harpis. "How will you get there safely?" he asked.

Despite the trust conveyed in the comforting smile that he gave the Impresario, Harpis' training at The Syndicate stopped him from being too revealing. "I have my ways. I will see you in a week."

*****

Arch Mage Uridyll was reading quietly in his quarters when the knock at the door interrupted his concentration.

"Come," he instructed. When he saw Stone Mage Vennil and Stone Sage Mara, he visibly perked up. He had been hoping they would return with news of the mask for some time. His expression changed to one of confusion when he saw Stone Mage Lorkin's dwarven apprentice from the annex in Fjall walk in behind them.

"Arch Mage, we have word from Stone Mage Lorkin," Mara said.

Uridyll immediately straightened in his seat. "Well, get on with it."

"It seems the dwarves have unearthed an enchanted relic deep in the mines beneath Fjall. It is said to have unknown power, and he seeks your consultation immediately," Vennil explained.

The Arch Mage shot a look at the apprentice standing between the sage and mage. "Well, what is it that has our usually demure and secluded friend flustered enough to send you here and ask for me in person?"

The apprentice only shrugged. "My apologies, Arch Mage, but he won't even tell any of us. He has been in his office for days. He says the aura of magic around it is blinding but wouldn't offer any other details."

The details did not matter. It was enough to hear that the typically immovable, unemotional rock of a mage was stirred to such excitement.

Besides, Uridyll would also like to have a conversation at length with the dwarf mage regarding a particular mask the staff in the Tower of Stone had so recklessly lost. After all, Lorkin and his small contingent of dwarves and gnomes had been practicing stone magic longer than most humans in the college had been alive, and Lorkin was the only mage still living who had fought in the War of Magi.

Pulling himself from his contemplation, Uridyll addressed his visitors. "We leave tomorrow, and all three of you are coming with me. Perhaps Lorkin will be of some help regarding our other concerns as well."

The last sentence was said while shooting a glare at Stone Sage Mara and Stone Mage Vennil.

After they left, he let his gaze fall to the leather bag of oil and the tinder striker, lying unused on his desk for years. Given the violence of recent days, perhaps it would not hurt to bring it along.

In his quarters and around most of Mer, he could call forth his maelstrom of a fire familiar from the tiniest of flames. But, in Fjall, where enchanted stones and not torches or lanterns lit most rooms, or on a ship on the sea or river, the Arch Mage would struggle to find a flame from which to beckon it.

Chapter 20
Strategy

Over thirty Tuath brigantines were anchored in loose formation at the outskirts of the Kalt harbor. Unlike when the Tuath navy sailed into Mer, no horns called out an attack at the sight of them. No alarm sounded nor rush of militiamen occurred as three of the ships finished mooring to the docks in Kalt harbor. The docks that they were visiting belonged to the Kalt Family Lumber Company, and not the city itself.

Sirul still hated Kalt. He hated it, especially on these late autumn days. The only thing more miserable to him than Kalt weather in the autumn was the rare times he had been to the south in mid-winter.

He had important and somewhat pleasant business to attend to, so he smiled thinly despite the cold. No one flinched or panicked at the company docks when over two hundred Tuath militiamen made their way into and around the company headquarters.

Sirul walked directly into the Kalt Family Timber owner's office and shut the door after letting himself in. Alone, without protection, his situation made the militiamen outside nervous. However, the Tuath governor did not seem distressed sitting across the small wooden desk from Svenus Kalt, the current head of the Kalt family and, subsequently, the Kalt Family Timber business.

Svenus was fair-skinned and dark-haired like many of the island's southern inhabitants. He stared across his desk at the overly bundled and tan northerner in his office with measured discontent.

Sirul knew full well what the old man wanted. Help in attaining control of the city-state that bore his family's name.

"Svenus, I must say that I am impressed. When you agreed to the amount of lumber I needed, I had seriously doubted there was a possibility you could deliver it all."

Svenus smiled at him. "But of course, Myrlman. Anything for my best customer. My family has been at this for well over a century. So why shouldn't we be able to provide what you seek."

Sirul cracked a smile. "In that case, I will need to double the number I previously gave you. I have brought gold and silver plenty enough, thanks to our efforts in Mer, to pay for it upfront."

Sirul had many plans for Kalt's lumber, from siege engines to a giant wall around his city as well as more brigantines to impose his will upon the island.

"You can keep your gold and silver for this next order, Governor Tuath. I want your support in my efforts." Svenus said.

Sirul began drumming his fingers slowly on the wood of the desk until he saw Svenus visibly fidget in his chair.

Satisfied at the other man's newly cautious demeanor, he continued, "I will place you back into the council seat of Kalt shortly. However, we must delay that for now. I have plans to enlarge my borders to include all of Mer, and eventually, we can extend Kalt across Ravnice and deal with the cursed dwarves in their hole together. In the immediate future, I have one last council meeting to attend. I must have it pass in a relatively civil manner. If too much has changed at once, the politicians will never accept my aims. I need this to happen so I can complete my ascension to power in the north. Such an ascension will enable me to help you in restoring your family's rightful place."

Sirul did not want to reveal too much to the old dolt, but he did need his lumber. Paying for it with a future hope as opposed to gold and silver suited him just fine. However, he required Svenus Kalt to stay in line until he had finished his business at the next council meeting.

"Do we agree then? Myrlman Tuath and Svenus Kalt allied?" Svenus asked, reaching his hand across to take Sirul's.

Sirul shook it, but before he let it go, he conveyed a parting threat.

"Allies, unless you prove yourself a liability to my plans. This alliance must remain between us until I am ready to place you in

193

power. So do not become a danger to me or my intentions, Svenus Kalt."

Svenus had lived a long life amongst the hardy people of the subarctic southern end of the island. He knew the promise of death when he saw it in a man's eyes. He nodded, and Sirul released his hand and got up to depart.

"Oh, and some of my brigantines will remain behind to provide a protective escort for the lumber. Remember, they will take the route up the back of the island and at night. I prefer this done with as much stealth as possible," he said, leaving.

*****

Svenus sat at his desk watching the Tuath militiamen vacate his premise, and all but ten of the brigantines eventually turned back to sea. The last of the men from Tuath was not gone for more than an hour when several Kalt militiamen knocked on his office door. He waved them in cheerily.

"How may I help you, gentleman?" he asked.

The militiamen looked at each other nervously. "Good day Master Svenus. Governor Jaeryl Innisgrath has ordered us to come and bring you before him. If it pleases you, sir, we will gladly escort you to him."

Like most others in Kalt, each of the three had many family members, friends, and acquaintances employed by the Kalt family business. It was the economic lifeblood of almost everyone in the city. Despite their jobs as Kalt militiamen in service of the governor, none of them wanted to incur the wrath of Svenus Kalt.

"I figured he might. All right then, let's go and see the governor," Svenus said matter-of-factly.

Like those of the other city-states, the wharf area of Kalt had a cobbled outdoor space ringed by shops. Where it differed was in its dedication to the lumber trade above all others.

Some fishing vessels made their way in and out of Kalt harbor from time to time, trying to work the dangerous southern fishing grounds. Most crafts though, were large lumber transporting ships.

The cobbles in Kalt were almost always clear of tents and vendor stalls in part due to the much more frequent inclement and harsh weather of the chillier city-state. It was also because the

194

maneuvering of lumber from mills on large cumbersome wagons that made their way to ships using the wharf prevented even semi-permanent merchant stalls.

To any observer of the party making its way across the Kalt harbor and to the governor's office, it would have looked more like the militiamen were Svenus Kalt's personal guard than his ordered escort.

Svenus entered the governor's building in a similar manner that Sirul had his own.

He flung open the door without a knock and sat in the chair across the desk before Jaeryl could offer it to him.

"That will be all, thank you, guards," Jaeryl Innisgrath said to the escort while looking past the man seated across from him. in obvious irritation.

"What do you want, Jaeryl?" Svenus spat.

The governor fixed him with what he hoped was an intimidating glance. "You are aware, yes, that I am the governor of this city and state?"

Svenus put his boots on the governor's desk and reclined. "Oh yes, of course, Jaeryl, democratically elected by the folk who live in it."

Jaeryl reached over the desk and shoved the older man's shoes off his desk. "Then surely you understand that any business between Kalt and the Governor of Tuath will go through my office. The governor's office!"

Svenus crossed his arms at the increasingly agitated governor. "Jaeryl, it was just a transaction between business partners, nothing to fret that little head of yours about."

Jaeryl's face tightened in frustration. "What kind of business dealing requires the presence of thirty naval ships?"

Svenus sighed at the governor. "Jaeryl, you are pretty daft for a politician. Myrlman Tuath brought thirty naval vessels to our harbor for a business dealing to let everyone know who is really in charge."

"And were those Tuath naval ships made with Kalt family lumber?" the governor practically snarled in response.

Svenus only shrugged.

Jaeryl Innisgrath was growing red in the face. "And did this business transaction result in the appropriate taxes for the betterment of our people? Or have you once again cut an

195

underhand deal to the detriment of our city and state?"

Svenus smiled as he spoke, knowing what he was about to say would send the governor over the edge. "No taxes, none, we've made another arrangement, ye see."

The governor leaped out of his seat, and his loud tone turned to outright shouting. "I should have you arrested, and your business forfeit to the state for the insolence you show to the rule of law and the damage you've done to this city!"

Svenus stood now, too. He swept the glass the governor had been sipping wine out of off the man's table with enough force that it shattered off the far wall rather than the floor. In response to the noise, the door swung open. Two guards stepped in behind Svenus, and several more outside watched intently.

"Listen here, you wet behind the ears, useless excuse for a politician," Svenus began, shoving his finger in Jaeryl's startled face. "How well do you think these men will listen to you when you can't pay them? When their families cannot make money, and their children cannot eat? How well will they listen to me when I offer them triple their wages? Years ago, you came to me asking to help you get elected and promising to keep my family business as the highest priority in this city-state. Do not ever forget who made you governor, Jaeryl Innisgrath. I can just as easily destroy you and place some other perfumed politician in your place!"

Svenus Kalt glared at the militiamen, who already had averted their gazes before he stormed out of the governor's office.

*****

It had been Harpis' first time into Fjall, and the marvelous and expansive dwarven city under the mountain was awe-inspiring. More impressive to him still was the gathering he was now a part of in the meeting room of Ingar Hammersmith.

The room was long and narrow, with a stone table of similar dimensions within it. Harpis figured the table sat probably thirty, but it only needed to seat thirteen today.

Down on the other side sat Ingar Hammersmith and Okliff Shieldborn, the fierce and bristly, blond general of the dwarven army.

Next to them was Stone Mage Lorkin, The Arch Mage, and the two who arrived with him from Mer, whom he had yet to meet.

196

On his left sat Turin, the Impresario, Wren, and the Death Herald, and to his right was the Exarch and a woman cleric who wore the stoles of a vicar.

Turin had told him that she was The Syndicate Eye in Mer and that they would not mention her involvement. Harpis had noticed a rather heated conversation between the Arch Mage and Stone Mage Lorkin, whom Wren had introduced Harpis to yesterday. The argument ended in a shrug from Lorkin, who then pointed at Wren, resulting in a frustrated shake of the head from the Arch Mage.

The fist of Ingar Hammersmith pounded the table in front of him, interrupting the chatter around the table.

His gruff voice shattered the growing silence. "Welcome all to Fjall and my own council room. I plead with you to listen well to what you hear next in this room. Heed all of it and be understanding. The fate of all in this room and all they care about on this island hangs in the balance. Particularly at risk is the fate of those humans amongst us and their charges."

The dwarf's gaze settled on the old elf. "Know that I trust Turin Deadeye, the elf who has seen a thousand years and sits now across from me. I trust him with my life and the lives of every dwarf, gnome, and human in my city and state. You'd do well to mark his words and trust him also."

Wren made a conspicuous cough into his fist and made a gesture with his head at the Herald.

"Er, and troll too, forget we have one of those here in Fjall, apologies Herald." He then raised his hand in Turin's direction and bid the elf speak.

Turin stood and surveyed the room with his one eye.

"First, I think introductions are in order. I will name you all if there are no objections," there were none, and Turin continued. "Of course, there is our gracious host who has just spoken, Ingar Hammersmith, Governor of Fjall. Next to him are General Okliff Shieldborn, leader of the Fjall Army, and Stone Mage Lorkin. Between the three of them, I think they have seen more war and elemental magic than any other living beings on this island."

Turin turned next to the humans. "We are graced with the presence of the Arch Mage of The College of Elements, as well as Stone Sage Mara and Stone Mage Vennil of the Tower of Stone. From The Archdiocese of Daybreak, there is Exarch

197

Hameki and his senior-most gifted attendant, Vicar Ezera."

The elf then faced Wren. "This is Death Speaker Wren; he is the longest living worshipper of The Sleeper on this island and next to him The Sleeper's chosen, the Death Herald. Nearest me is Impresario Benali Tuath of The Bard's Hall, and Harpis, court bard to the governor of Ravnice."

It occurred to some in the room that the elf addressing them knew their name with great familiarity, even though they had never seen him in their life.

"As to the reason I have brought you all here today, I think part of that is obvious. Tuath has made moves, some of them violent, on the rest of the island. Sadly, it looks as though neither the governors nor their city-states can resist them without war ravaging this island. The other reasoning, I am afraid, is less obvious to some of you," Turin explained.

He took a moment to let the others gather their thoughts. "It is true what Ingar said, I saw my thousandth year almost a decade ago, and I am indeed old, even by the standards of my people. Many of my centuries have been spent here, on this island I too call home."

The elf's expression became sorrowful. "I was there all three times that open war has devastated it in the past. Some of you here also remember that last and greatest war. The one where mages used their gifts for such savage devastation that they afterward swore their institutions forever to neutrality and peaceful practice."

Turin's eyes now glinted like steel as he looked around the room while he spoke. "So, I used my greatest resource, time, and bent my mind and will to the creation of a small organization of spies and assassins that I could deploy throughout the island of Quaj and keep her from tearing herself apart again."

There were audible gasps from several in the room and baffled silence from others.

"It was called The Lodestar Syndicate. I had two operatives posted in each of the city-states, and a small base on Lodestar Island, an island unknown to most, far off the southern coast of Kalt. Through espionage and subterfuge, we acted to deal with the dangerous and evil folk as they came and went."

He dropped his gaze to the tabletop. "At times, when necessary, we killed such evil folk. Until recently, that is. We have suffered our own great loss. Tuath slaughtered my friends who lived and worked on Lodestar Island, killing men, women, and the elderly indiscriminately."

Impresario Benali grew very still and stared blankly ahead, listening to the one brutality of Myrlman he had not yet discovered.

Arch Mage Uridyll interrupted Turin angrily, "Who were you to decide anyway? Who were you to play god to the people of Quaj?"

Turin held his hands up in peace for a long moment. "I promise you, Arch Mage Uridyll, we had not but the best of intentions, with a mind for the greater good always. If my word and that of others here at this table are not enough to appease you, at least respect our losses. The deaths of those involved may serve as justice to you and as punishment for our lofty aspirations and actions."

He glanced at Wren and Harpis. "Aside from those on Lodestar Island, we had two operatives, as I said, in each city-state. The two in Kalt are no longer anyone's concern. The two in Mer were both killed in the Tuath strike at Mer harbor," he said, lying to protect Ezera.

"The operatives in Ravnice are at this table. Harpis and Wren, who helped gather you all here today, are members of The Syndicate."

He stood again and walked to the head of the table. "Which brings me to the reason I am sharing all of this with you all. It seems that one of our assassins has become involved with Myrlman Tuath and helped him to track down and kill our entire presence in Tuath. We believe he is working with Myrlman Tuath to turn the people of Tuath against the rest of this island and pursue an outright war. You see, the actions of Tuath are frightening enough of their own accord. Adding in the fact that a Syndicate produced master assassin and tactician is working in concert with him, the nightmare may yet be inescapable if we cannot come together to end it."

"You forgot to mention your agents here, in Fjall! And how, good governor, are you not enraged that this man has been spying on you!?" The Exarch shouted in concern.

Ingar Hammersmith stood for a moment after being addressed and stared the Exarch back into his seat.

When the Exarch sat, Ingar spoke. "I have known Turin some two hundred years. After the last great war, he discussed his plan with me. I had lost many a dwarf to human plotting in that War of Magi. I told him I would support him if he ever needed it and offer protection if I could. He never needed an operative here, he is a friend of Fjall, and I freely discussed the goings-on of my state with him." Sitting again, the dwarf crossed his arms grumpily.

"Thank you again, good Ingar, as I said, think what you may of our now dead organization and its operatives. It may be gone, but its mission is no less relevant. So, I ask you here with us now to help in ending the threat of outright war and the tyranny taking place at the hands of the Tuath governor."

The out-of-place troll and Death Herald turned toward the elf warmly. "Turin, ever have The Sleeper and I appreciated your efforts for the people of this island."

Turin gave her a short bow with his head.

"What of your folk? There are a few hundred elves left in Kalt forest, no? Will they not join your cause?" the troll asked.

The question seemed to sadden Turin. "My people, for the most part, do not care for the other folk on this island. They care least of all for humans, thanks to their feud with the people of Kalt. They are impossible to stir to action unless under direct threat themselves. It is much easier for them just to wait until the currently troublesome generation of humans dies than risk elven blood, I am afraid."

The Impresario clapped his hands together in front of him and pushed his forehead into them. "Master Turin, how does this assassin helping Myrlman look? Perhaps I have seen him. However, I must say that I have been around Myrlman a lot of late, and I have seen no one aiding him in his decisions or his dirty work. I even watched, feet away, as he slit the Mer governor's throat and was showered in his blood, smiling the whole time."

Turin paused thoughtfully. "Sirul Amun, our deserted assassin, is a thirty-year-old human of Tuathian descent. He is of medium height and athletic build. His skin was olive and often tan. He has blond hair and grey eyes."

At the description, the Impresario's eyes shot open, and he looked directly at Turin. "Good elf, you have just described my cousin's son, Myrlman Tuath, to me!"

It was Turin's turn to be caught off guard and confused.

"Sirul had a long scar from his right eye down to his jaw from a lost fight at a young age before he came to us."

Benali Tuath sat back in shock. "Myrlman recently received the same scar at the hands of his would-be Quaji captor's attempted kidnapping."

Everyone in the room was silent, searching for an answer to the questions the conversation between Turin and Benali had just raised. Finally, Turin acknowledged the Arch Mage's nervously raised his hand and motioned for him to speak.

Uridyll looked almost frail with worry, "I am afraid I have my own, potentially related, and troubling revelation for this group. Someone stole an enchanted artifact of considerable and relevant power from the college earlier this year. It was known as the Clay Mask of Breyva."

At the mention of the mask, Stone Mage Lorkin sucked in his breath sharply, momentarily interrupting the Arch Mage.

"It can allow the wearer to duplicate the face of another living person they see and wear it for some time. We do not know much of its enchantment other than that," the Arch Mage continued.

Lorkin had become visibly bothered by what the Arch Mage had said. "It's more powerful than that, Uridyll. That mask was the Apotheosis of Stone Magus Breyva, her life's work. It will wear the face chosen indefinitely, pulling from the wearer's life energy to keep up the illusion. The mask would only show itself as red clay on the wearer's face upon their death."

At first, Benali Tuath's reaction was one of joy that the second cousin who had a love of the arts and music might not have turned into the monster he had been spending time with as of late.

"It would seem then perhaps that Sirul Amun is wearing the face of Myrlman Tuath and playing at ruling a city-state and attempting to rule much more," Turin said.

The Impresario's demeanor grew mournful as he realized that having seen no person working closely with Myrlman, the young man was likely dead.

Benali looked hopefully at Lorkin. "If Myrlman has recently received this scar, in kind with the one Sirul had, then the raid where he received it is perhaps where Sirul took his place. Until recently, it had been years since I visited with my nephew. I cannot rely on my memory of an adolescent's voice to prove the man I have been around lately is a fraud. Stone Mage Lorkin, do you know if the mask would hide or show scars?"

The dwarven mage shrugged unknowingly, and the Death Herald spoke. "If we could shepherd this Sirul into The Great Dream, his death would reveal the mask. Perhaps then we could show the people of the island the truth of what he had wrought. It might be sobering enough to bring peace."

The elderly Exarch raised his hand. "In either case, I will have Ezera use her Daybreak gifted powers to disenchant the mask when we recover it. Such a powerful artifact has no use for any good or just purpose."

Harpis stood to speak and almost sat down without opening his mouth as the gathered figures stared at him. "I think that it would be unwise to lay our hopes on avoiding all-out war by killing Sirul alone. I agree that we need to remove the mastermind driving the north into war. It may be that showing Myrlman Tuath was an imposter might sober some, but the entirety of Tuath is against Mer. As Wren and I made our way through the city, tension and ill will were everywhere. Later I saw the same when I visited Tuath alone. At every corner, tavern, and inn, folk talk of the injustices Tuath has suffered and how Mer deserved their wrath."

"What Harpis says is true, even if what he first told me about himself was not. I trust him, and I have lived in Tuath these past months. All people talk about is when we will enact our vengeance on the south. I don't think they will stop until we show them it would be a hopeless endeavor," the Impresario concurred.

The Exarch shifted uneasily in his seat, the talk of war and bloodshed making him nervous. "How do we make war and conquest seem hopeless to them with as few lives lost as possible?" The Exarch pleadingly asked the room.

Turin retook control of the gathering. "For that Exarch, I will need to rely on yourself and the Arch Mage. We will also need the fighting prowess of the dwarven army. First, though, I must know from each of you that you are with us. That you will keep the trust and secret of this council held under the mountain."

He looked from person to person as they nodded or verbalized their agreement. Finally, when he looked at Benali Tuath, the Impresario spoke his piece. "That animal running my city and state is likely the killer of both my cousin and his son. You have my word for the secrecy of our intentions here."

It was lost on none in the room that with Seulman Tuath long dead, and Myrlman Tuath proved to be Sirul Amun, Myrlman himself was probably deceased. With them dead, Benali Tuath was next in line to the hereditary rule of Tuath.

Turin stared at the Impresario for some time before speaking again. "Then it is settled. We must remove Tuath's grip on Mer. They currently hold sway with their flotilla and their ability to offload their militiamen at a moment's notice to quell any uprising. The dwarves will march to Mer and take it back from Tuath. They will then make an obvious show of marching towards Tuath. The flotilla, seeing this and being unable to land in Mer, will assuredly turn north to aid in the battle for their homeland. Exarch and Arch Mage, we will all depend on you. We need the militiamen of Mer to understand that the dwarves are not invaders and instead are there to liberate their city and draw the Tuath force away to the north. We need the men of Mer to stand down as they approach."

The two older men looked at each other and nodded their agreement to help save the city they called home.

"Impresario, you will return to the man playing at Myrlman Tuath and tell him you will reinstate the bards and reopen Bard's Hall. Tell him he can use them to facilitate the spreading of propaganda and information to the greater conquest of Tuath. In truth, we will lean on you to pass up-to-date intelligence to us via Harpis if necessary," Turin said.

Benali Tuath nodded at both Turin and Harpis.

"Lastly," Turin said. "We need to find a way to depose Myrlman if possible. We will hit Tuath from the south with the dwarves and possibly with the militia of Mer and Ravnice. Harpis will bring Aanaman Reaper into the fold after the next council meeting. However, the death of Sirul Amun may bring the whole conflict to a swift end. Myself, Wren, and Harpis will sail north on my ship when Harpis returns. With the last assassin of our old organization, we will try and remove the head of this snake. I am aware that Kalt may be falling under the control of Tuath, directly or indirectly. I am confident that if we deal with the threat in the north, Kalt will resume its infighting between the city, the Kalt family, and the elf tribe in the Kalt Forest."

Turin surveyed the table once more. None could refute the plan's logic, and all had their roles to play.

Before they left the table, the Death Herald stood, her hulking form half again as tall as most men present. "If you'll have me along, Master Turin, I don't think I could miss the opportunity to be there when so many are making their way to my Lady's Great Dream."

The elf grinned at the troll and gave her a bow. "It would be our honor, Herald."

Chapter 21
Demands

Sirul had close to his entire fleet with him when he arrived in Mer for the council meeting. Once again, the impressive line of brigantines created an almost complete blockade of the whole harbor as his lone flagship approached the docks.

He despised the bureaucratic event he was bound for, but he was not yet ready for the military conquest of the island. He felt comfortable in confrontation with any one of the human city-states or the dwarves individually, but not all at once. Not yet. There was work to be done before he would have Tuath prepared to fight on multiple fronts, though if everything went according to plan, he wouldn't have to fight on any.

As much as he hated politics, he did see value in one last attempt to get what he wanted out of the council. If today went well and he could turn the other governors on the dwarves. Even if not, Sirul felt confident he could slowly control more and more of the island and the four primarily human city-states until he was ready to face down the dwarves in their mountain home.

It pleased him that the wharf, docks, and city, in general, were bristling with Mer militiamen. He brought with him the clear and immediate threat of an unknown number of militiamen aboard his vessels.

Then there were the thousands of Tuath militiamen who would march south if their governor were murdered and made a martyr. He felt safe indeed as he disembarked his flagship with his contingent.

As his procession snaked its way to the squat council building, he smiled at the nervousness and tension among the Mer citizens and militiamen alike. Upon arriving at the council building, Sirul also smiled at the scores of militiamen from Ravnice and Kalt, who were also present. Curiously, he did not see any dwarven guards outside.

After flinging open the large doors to the council chamber, he tried to calm his facial expression. He wanted to prevent himself from revealing the thoughts and emotions that ran through him as he looked from seat to seat.

The Arch Mage, Exarch, Death Herald, and Impresario seats along the wall were all empty. He struggled to bury the rage deep within him. The two old geezers from the Mer institutions had earlier refused to answer his calls for a private meeting and now snubbed him openly by not attending this pivotal council meeting. He didn't know not to expect the Herald. The Impresario's seat was at least expectedly empty as he assumed Benali was researching what the letter from his contemporary had mentioned.

He decided it was not surprising after all that the dwarven governor had not shown up. If he were Ingar Hammersmith, he would not come to the beck and call of Myrlman Tuath either. It was better this way, he reasoned. Without the dwarf here to speak against his claims and intentions, he might have an easier time influencing the other governors.

The captain of the Mer militia occupied the seat of the Mer governor, which Sirul had been almost sure would remain empty. He eyed the older man he had spoken to weeks ago after slaying their leader.

Without taking his seat, Sirul addressed the other men, leaning forward with his hands on the table in an aggressive posture.

"It would seem that the dwarves no longer seek to keep council with the likes of men. We must not let this disrespect go unanswered. Too long has a dwarf dictated in a place where humans should have the only voice. Let him rule below ground, and we will rule our lands above it!"

Aanaman Reaper of Ravnice crossed his arms and raised an eyebrow. Governor Jaeryl seconded the statement. The militia captain from Mer said nothing and kept his silent stare fixed on Sirul.

Before attempting to force the first decision on the other men, Sirul first addressed the man from Mer. "So, the people of Mer

206

have already found a new governor? You are, Governor who?"

The man stood and met Sirul's aggressive stance with his own. "I am Captain, not Governor, Elliswerth, and I am here because none of our civilians have the nerve to sit in this small room with a cold-blooded killer like you. They have yet to elect a new governor."

Sirul found the man's statement entertaining. "Well then, good captain, if you could re-take your seat, we will get started on the business of this council."

The governor from Ravnice then turned towards him. "Well, Myrlman, you called us here after we were certain Tuath would never again attend a council meeting or suffer it to happen at all. So why are we here?"

Sirul took a moment to glance at the other three. "Well, seeing as how the gifted institutions of the island have abandoned us, we governors alone must make this decision. Given Ingar Hammersmith's disrespect and failure to attend this council meeting, I would like to put forth a vote disavowing the dwarven city-state of this council. I would also like to put forth a vote on a more formal alliance between the four city-states of men so that we may best stand against dwarven meddling."

The captain from Mer was the first to answer. "I cannot speak for the people of Mer. We cannot agree to either proposition as a city or state without an elected official."

Sirul ignored the man completely. In his mind, Mer was already a part of Tuath. He assumed he could impose his will upon the people and leadership of Mer if necessary. Whoever they elected would be no match against the will or scheming of Sirul. Now, he was more concerned with forcing Ravnice into compliance, or if necessary, outright opposition.

"I, for one, am in favor of both!" Governor Innisgrath of Kalt said. His answer and enthusiasm drew a glare from both the Mer captain and Aanaman.

"My position on the road to conflict is the same now as it was when we spoke of Mer and Tuath. That was before you decided to take matters into your own hands in case you don't remember." Aanaman said, indicating the Tuath governor.

"Is there a purpose to this vote? Will you just impose your will at the end of a dagger? Or with your navy if you once again do not get your way?" he asked.

Sirul was happy enough to have Aanaman openly turn against the other city-states in the face of the decision. Such an act would give more time to increase his influence over the others. In truth though, it would all be easier if the former farmer would just fall into line.

"I respect your concern. The justice given to the late Governor Lurras was a personal matter. The tithes the merchants of Mer now pay are in reparation from their fellow citizens' acts at the bidding of the man they elected. Your opinion is requested, and your decision will be respected, noted, and counted towards a simple majority or minority here," Sirul said to the Ravnice governor.

"Given that Kalt seems to be deeply in your pocket, I doubt it matters either way. No. I do not support alienating the dwarves. The only path to Fjall city is through Ravnice. I do not want the blood of men or dwarves to soak my people's lands," Aanaman replied in angry resignation.

Sirul shot a chilling smile at the man. "I vote with the governor from Kalt. I believe that we must excommunicate the dwarves from our council and form a stronger alliance and a nation of men. When Mer elects their new governor, they will decide whether to join this alliance or not."

He continued with a smug look at Aanaman. "We have our vote. A simple majority of this council is clear. Therefore, we will move forward without the dwarves, and we will begin to protect ourselves from their actions. Governor Aanaman is entitled to his opinion. However, he will have to make the choice of going along with the majority rule of this council or else risk being forced from it for not complying with its politically determined decisions."

Aanaman stood from his chair, and it kicked out behind him before falling to the floor. "What a pile of horse dung. You force me to either voice my opposition to Tuath and Kalt or allow your decisions to dictate to my city-state and her people."

Sirul stood and stopped him before he could continue. "I caution you to think on this decision and perhaps think on it until the next council meeting. The dwarves are no longer welcome in our audience. Mer will provide a governor to the next meeting, and that person will speak to the decision of Mer. I will also remind Ravnice of the implications if it decides to neither remain with this council nor join this formal alliance. You and your

208

people would directly oppose your neighbors to both the north and the south. I will also remind you of our naval forces and that Ravnice has the longest coastline to defend of any of our city-states."

Aanaman spat at the ground near Sirul and stormed out, with the parting comment of "patsy" to the governor from Kalt.

*****

The day after the forced council meeting in Mer concluded, those who met in Fjall finished disbanding. The small force sailing for Tuath gathered at the docks by the city's cave mouth entrance. The odd company was finalizing preparations and boarding the *Open Ocean* in a desperate attempt to depose Sirul Amun.

The Exarch and Arch Mage had left on separate ships hours ago in the early morning. Both were bound for Mer with their instructions clear to them. Impresario Benali Tuath had left the night before with different but similarly essential instructions and an excuse and explanation for his absence that was well-rehearsed with Harpis.

Turin faced Harpis, Wren, and the Herald. "We've one more who will be joining us. I would like to introduce you all to my niece, the only remaining former Shadow of The Syndicate, besides the alienated Sirul Amun, of course."

From Turin's above deck cabin on the small schooner walked a lithe female elf. She shared the tan, almost brown skin of Turin and other wood elves.

Turin's hair was stark white with age, but hers was a reddish-brown and stretched down her back to well below her waist. She had the steely look of one who gives death in her blue, almost grey eyes. If she were wearing a dress, one might have mistaken her for an elvish princess. But, instead, she wore simple leathers like her uncle and a gigantic crossbow across her back.

"This is my niece, Gwenolyn Amura, to The Syndicate she was known as The Bow," Turin said, introducing his kin.

"Well met, friends of Turin Deadeye," she said with a nod to the gathered party.

Turin named the others for her. "This is Harpis and Wren. They were former members of our Syndicate. This is the Death

Herald, head of The Sanctum and the necromancers in service to The Sleeper." At the mention of her position, the Herald gave a low bow.

"This is the famed assassin known to us as The Bow?" The gnome asked, looking at her incredulously. In response, Gwenolyn removed the weapon from her back. It looked to be a crossbow stock that was as long as she was tall.

She undid two clasps with a flick of her foot, and the crossbars snapped out in an arc that was near six feet wide. "When drawn, this can fire a bolt as far as a ballista."

Harpis stood open-mouthed and eventually pointed at Gwenolyn. "You, you were the one who paid me a visit in Tuath!"

Turin put a hand on her shoulder. "Yes, Harpis, I sent her to watch you and to watch over you. We five are bound down the river, with a quick stop in Ravnice for Harpis to confide in Governor Reaper. We will then make for the north and our mission to remove the head of the snake constricting around our island. Herald, Wren, I will have to ask you to remain either below decks or in my cabin to avoid suspicion for much of our trip. A schooner sailing down the River Fjall and into open waters crewed by two elves and a human is one thing. With a gnome and a mountain troll in our company as well, I would imagine word of us might travel faster than this ship can sail."

They boarded the *Open Ocean*, and as the ship drifted out of the mouth of the caved harbor, the dwarves at the defenses gave them a solemn parting salute. Once they were entirely out of the cave mouth, Gwenolyn nimbly climbed the mast and manipulated the rigging to let out the sails. Turin took up his place, as he had for a millennium, at the wheel.

Before he went below decks with the Herald, Wren went to Harpis. "Look here, lad, in thanks for your help months ago on the *Sea Goat* and for not failing your Syndicate indoctrination and embarrassing me. I've got you something."

The gnome reached into his robe and produced the bracelet.

Harpis took it from him with a silent awestruck thanks. He was astonished by the beauty of the sunlight glittering within the amethyst vision of The Sleeper.

It was the most beautiful thing Harpis had ever held in his hands. "I do not know how to thank you, my friend, it is an amazing piece, and one I don't deserve but will well cherish."

Wren took it back for a moment and handed it back upside down, showing Harpis the word of activation etched into it. "It is enchanted, say the word, and sing one of your gifted songs. The bracelet will attune to your voice and amplify it whenever you repeat the activation. The enchantment will afford you several dozen uses, so see how it behaves and keep it only for dire situations. Stone Mage Lorkin is confident in its work. However, I am eager to see its power, so this one unnecessary time, I must see it in use."

As the ship passed the first bend in the Fjall River, the mountain's mouth disappeared behind them. The road that ran alongside the river until it reached Ravnice came into view, as did the column of dwarves marching on it, bound for Mer.

Seven hundred and fifty strong, the column was three-quarters of the Fjall army. At their head was the grizzled General Shieldborn. While the weapons they carried varied, every single dwarf held a shield almost as wide and tall as they were.

They all wore the polished plated armor crafted by the finest smiths among them. Almost half had a crossbow, or compound bow and quiver slung across their back. They marched in silence, but their footfalls slammed the ground in complete unison.

Harpis looked for a moment at the bracelet and uttered the activation phrase, "Discordium."

He stared at it, almost expecting it to glow or warm or vibrate, but at the look Wren gave him, he decided he was probably just supposed to give his voice to the enchantment.

He sang one verse of the fishing song his father had taught him and paused. It had not sounded any different than he expected.

"It should be attuned to you now, lad, go ahead," Wren encouraged.

Harpis uttered the word a second time and again began the fisherman's work song that had saved them on the *Sea Goat*, doing everything he could do weave his gift into it. The resonance of his voice, amplified by the bracelet, surged through him as the notes encompassed his very being. His pulse became a thunder in his ears. In his chest, he felt the beating of his heart pound like a drum.

His voice boomed across the river and the valley through which it ran. The echo rolled off the out of view mountain behind

211

them, and birds and animals for a mile around them startled and fled.

The dwarves' march became faster, their muscles seemed ready to explode with energy, and their footfalls fell in tune with the song that thundered from the deck of the *Open Ocean*. Hands clasped pommels and handles of weapons more eagerly, and the dwarves who had never before heard the song began singing along too.

As Harpis ended the song, he received cheers from the column as they passed the front lines of dwarves. Harpis spotted Stone Mage Lorkin marching in the front with the General.

The dwarf mage shouted across to them, "Looking like the magic in your bracelet worked out just fine then, Wren! I now am seeing why you asked for such an enchantment!"

Wren, Turin, and Gwenolyn all shook off the goosebumps and chills that were running up their spines during Harpis' entire song. Wren looked at Harpis and then the bracelet and nodded approvingly.

"Now, that lad, that was quite the song."

Harpis could only smile as he pulled his tunic sleeve down to cover the invaluable gift.

He could barely hear the troll speaking to him as Wren made his way back out of sight below decks.

"It has been some time since I have heard the gift so woven into song. Bracelet or not, it has been sad ages since the bards have used magic so. A song can be a gift to wield stronger than any of us worshipers of dark or light could hope to command. Stronger even than gifted elementalists can dream to call upon. Have a mind for the ears that might be listening when you weave your words," she said.

Chapter 22

Roles

Making his way through the mansion that was once his cousin's home, Benali Tuath felt like he was helpless prey. Though the smooth marbled floor, white walls, and ceiling stretched openly around him, it somehow felt like a cage he had willingly entered and may never escape.

He thought back to fond memories, chasing his older cousin Seulman on these very tiles. They had spent many days running after each other, playing knights and dragons or fighting imaginary battles as pirates and sailors while their fathers meted out rule over the northern state that bore their name.

There was small comfort to Benali in the knowledge that the young man he had watched grow up had not turned into the monster he had gotten to know these past months. The thought did little to calm his nerves as he knocked on the office doors of the Tuath mansion, and a voice from inside beckoned him to enter.

Sirul was alone in the office. Curtains swayed in the breeze with the balcony doors open wide to the sunny expanse of Tuath sprawling below them. All but twenty of the Tuath armada's ships were moored out in the deeper reaches of the bay. From the mansion, they looked like so many bobbers in a pond.

It was a surreal moment for Benali, looking upon the man known as Sirul as if it was for the first time. He had rehearsed the coming conversation for hours with Harpis in Fjall, and he was undoubtedly one for remembering lines. He would have been a poor excuse for a bard if he could not, but he was nervous all the same. After all, this was the first time his life depended on his ability to perform.

"You have been gone long, cousin," Sirul said from across the giant desk without rising to greet him. "Please take a seat."

Benali did as asked and hoped his nervousness around the assassin would not draw any suspicion. But, if he was honest with himself, he had been quite uneasy around the man for some time, even before he knew it was no longer Myrlman Tuath.

"So, Benali, where have you been this past week? Was your compatriot successful in finding new songs imparted with the gift of magic?"

The Impresario shifted hesitantly for a moment before steadying himself for perhaps his life's most important verses.

"I was gone longer than expected trying to find our gifted nomadic bard, Virtuoso Mahala Shelta. Maestro Bravit did indeed find a book with several gifted songs contained within it. Still, I fear it was beyond the skill of he and I. Mahala is the bard most experienced in weaving the gift into music. Sadly, I was unable to find her, but I did find several of my bards abroad and have sent them to task in finding her and sending her to us."

Sirul searched the man's face for several agonizing moments. "You look like you have something else you wish to say, Benali?" he asked, leaning back in his chair.

"I do, cousin," he said, the familial label catching in his throat. He forced composure into his voice and continued. "I have decided that I want to do more to support the return to power you are orchestrating for our family and city-state. I have also instructed the bards I did encounter to ultimately return to the Hall. We will gather and spread information at your request Myrlman, for the greater good of Tuath."

It was hard for him to get the name out without choking on it. At his last statement, Sirul raised his eyebrows approvingly.

"I am glad to see you fully in the fold, cousin. But, of course, you may return to your Hall at once and begin your operations there. I will send a company of militiamen to garrison with you and keep the new eyes and ears of Tuath safe."

Benali almost got up to leave. The conversation had gone as Harpis had said it would. He now had his chance to get safely to The Hall as had been the plan.

His conscience would not let him. "If it is all the same to you, I think I would like to spend a night or two in the city. After all the traveling I have just finished, a few days here would do me well. I will make for The Hall in a couple of days."

Sirul dismissed him with a hand wave. "Do as you wish. It makes no difference to me, though I am excited for you to finish this work with your fellow gifted bards."

Benali Tuath was almost through the door when Sirul stopped him. "Why weren't you at the council? You knew ahead of time that I had sent for the other governors to meet me last week."

"I, uh, my apologies Myrlman, by the time I remembered it in my quest across the southland for the Virtuoso, I was too far to make it in time. I thought it more useful to our cause to carry on the task at hand," Benali answered, trying not to shake at the thought of further interrogation

Sirul did not seem concerned with his explanation. Benali had forgotten to tell Harpis that he was supposed to be at that council meeting, so they had not come up with a reason for his absence. Any further excuses or answers would be unrehearsed and of his own creation.

Sirul looked at him inquisitively for a moment. "It is just that your opinion would have been valuable. I feel comfortable controlling the pawn from Kalt or Svenus Kalt himself should it be necessary to put him in that seat. Similarly, I think that whoever the people of Mer put in that room with me will bend to intimidation easily enough. However, what are your thoughts on Aanaman Reaper of Ravnice?"

Benali chuckled, in part in relief at realizing why Sirul was pressing him and at the frustration in Sirul's voice as he said Aanaman's name. "If ever there was a fish out of water in politics, it would be the farmer turned governor from Ravnice. If you can work around him and let him alone, he does not care for anything outside of his state and will likely leave us to our own devices. Try and pull that stick out of mud, though, and you may find it pulls back."

With that, Benali made his exit from the killer's cage, but not the city, as had been the plan.

*****

The guards in front of Aanaman Reaper's house nearly stabbed Harpis when he snuck up and told them he needed to meet with the governor and that it was a matter of the utmost urgency.

"By the gods, bard! You scared me half to death! Where have you been these past weeks?" one of them asked him.

Harpis did not have time for much explaining. He needed to return to the ship in the next few hours before dawn arrived. Inconveniently, due to his love of the fields, the governor's house was on the city's far side from the coast.

He pressed the men. "It is urgent, and it is for his ears and the ears of Captain Kilannry only. Can one of you men wake him and send him this way as well? Thousands of lives hang in the balance."

One of the men took off at a run to get the captain, and the one who had challenged him brought him hastily inside.

Aanaman Reaper had not bothered to get dressed and now sat behind his desk shirtless in cloth pants. "I did miss you Harpis, but I tell you, I could have waited until morning to greet your return. So where in the world have you been anyway? You've been gone for weeks."

Harpis lifted his hands apologetically and was going to ask the governor to wait for Kilannry when the much grumpier man walked into the room without knocking.

"This had better be good, bard," He muttered and dropped into his chair opposite Harpis at the small table.

Aanaman looked at him with a grin. "You see, Harpis, we've all missed you so," he said with a wave at the captain before becoming more serious. "So, what is it that demands our attention before dawn?"

Harpis hoped his assessment of the faith his present company held in him was accurate. "As to where I have been, I don't know that you would believe me."

Captain Kilannry interrupted him, "Bah, enough intrigue boy, spit it out."

Harpis squeezed his eyes shut in a momentary cringe and then went on. "Well, sirs, I was in Tuath, convincing the Impresario to join me for a secret meeting with the governor of Fjall. We worked out a plan with the help of the Exarch, the Arch Mage, and the Death Herald. We were there at the request of a millennium and some years old elf who was the founder of a clandestine organization called The Syndicate. I was a member of said Syndicate until Tuath raided our island south of Kalt and slaughtered every person there."

216

After he finished, there was a long, empty silence that was finally disturbed by the sound of the governor pulling a cork from a bottle.

"If you aren't drunk in the telling of that tale, then I am sure to be needing a drink to hear the rest," Aanaman stated as he poured all three a glass.

"That does explain the absence of certain individuals at our last council meeting. It would seem Myrlman Tuath has eyes for unifying the human city-states against the dwarves and choking every ounce of power and influence he can from us. I feel I may have endangered our people by my response. However, I don't know that our people would have been safe for long, no matter how I handled the situation."

Harpis hoped the surprising ease with which they accepted his first statement would hold for the next one. "It is not Myrlman Tuath. It is a former assassin of The Syndicate gone rogue. His real name, the one he had as a child, was Sirul Amun. He stole an enchanted clay mask from The College of Elements some months ago and used it to impersonate Myrlman Tuath. We believe Myrlman died in the raid where he was supposedly almost kidnapped, after which all of the recent conflicts began developing at the supposed hands of Sirul."

Captain Kilannry almost choked mid-sip as he drank. "A magical mask that lets you look like someone else, hah!"

Harpis shot the older man a stern look. "The clay mask of Breyva can hold the illusion until its wearer dies. Thankfully, we have a plan to hopefully bring Tuath and her people to their senses. In the meantime, I think there are actions Ravnice should take."

Aanaman sat up straight and dropped his bare feet from their regular spot propped up on his desk. "This does sound like quite the fantasy. However, I had met Myrlman Tuath on several occasions when Seulman would try to bring him along to council meetings. The perfumed and pampered young man I met years ago bore nothing but a physical resemblance to the keen-eyed killer I sat across from at the last council meeting. So, bard, what would you have us do?"

Harpis sighed aloud in relief at being heeded before describing the plan. "I am to sail north with a small force and sneak into Tuath in hopes of dealing with Sirul directly. The dwarven army from Fjall will liberate Mer. We plan to destroy their docks, for now, to prevent Tuath from unloading thousands of militiamen onto their shore in response. We think it would be best if you would also destroy your docks this morning."

Captain Kilannry scoffed at the notion. "Destroy our own city docks? Why don't we just invade ourselves for them?"

"We do not know the location of the Tuath Armada or if there is more than one flotilla. But, with your docks destroyed or inaccessible, Ravnice's harbor could be easily defended from landing parties with a few groups of archers," Harpis said, unfazed.

The captain finally nodded in agreement. "Admittedly, we could easily defend our harbor that way."

Harpis was less confident the men would accept his next request. "We also think it would be best for everyone if a large portion of Ravnice's militia marched south to the Kalt border. It will serve Ravnice and our efforts in the north well to have them there in case Sirul has some contingency in place to have Kalt climb up our backside."

"Well, I would be fairly confident that without Tuath to back them, the Kalt family, or the governor, or whoever is really in charge down there will not have the stomach to go into battle," Aanaman said.

Harpis was more than glad the governor was following. "That is our presumption as well and with Mer liberated, there will be another ten thousand militiamen, maybe more, to join our cause if this does turn into a real war. In either case, this plan offers at least the chance for minimal bloodshed. After liberating Mer, the dwarves will march on Tuath to draw all enemy forces north and away from Ravnice and away from being able to support Kalt."

Captain Kilannry blew a loud whistle. "That is quite the plan. The boys have been itching for a march and some proper military activity since all these tensions began. I think the young bard is right, Aanaman. With the docks unusable, we could pepper even a large landing party as they approached from the ocean."

Aanaman stared hard at Harpis. "How long can I think about this?"

The bard stood from his chair, turned his glass upside down, and met the governor's stare. "I need your answer now, sir."

Aanaman stepped around his desk and clasped Harpis on the

shoulder. "Then you have it, don't worry about looking over your shoulders for the spineless tree cutters to the south. We will ensure that they do not make it across our lands and will destroy the harbor docks before dawn, as you have asked. I felt hopeless that violence was coming to us. You have given me hope for continued independence and eventual peace where I did not think we had any."

"Don't go dying up there in the north and leave me alone with this drunk. If the three of us are honest, he's better at running a distillery than a city-state," Captain Kilannry said, glass raised.

Harpis nodded his appreciation of the captain's toast and met the eyes of each man for a moment. "Until next time, gentlemen."

*****

His morning prayer and greeting to Daybreak complete, Hameki made his way down the spire and dome and straight for the front doors of his institution. With Vicar Ezera in tow, they went outside to greet the militiamen who patrolled outside.

Captain Elliswerth had made sure to keep men constantly posted at the institution for added security since Tuath had attacked.

He held up a hand to halt the nearest group. "Excuse me," the Exarch said to one of them. "I need to speak with Captain Elliswerth immediately."

The men snapped to attention. "Of course, Exarch!"

Several moments later, when Captain Elliswerth eventually arrived and climbed to the top of the five-story structure, Ezera and the Exarch greeted his labored breaths with a smile.

"How may I help you, Exarch? My man made it sound quite urgent."

Hameki faced west and took a moment to survey the expanse of the Mer peninsula below them. "Captain, we live in troubling times, and I fear that if we do nothing, then all people will suffer. I have returned from a meeting with some who will be able to liberate our city with little bloodshed. However, for them to be successful, I am afraid that it will require you and your men to play a part."

Elliswerth straightened, and when he spoke next, there was resolve in his voice. "My men will fight to a one to shed this city

219

of our current oppression if that is what is necessary, Exarch!"

Hameki sighed and shook his head. "What we need is for your men to be sure that they do nothing and let the column of dwarves that will approach from the south and west later this day pass uninterrupted through our gates."

The captain looked quite perplexed, and he stared at the Exarch as if the older man himself had just turned into a dwarf in front of him.

"Why would a column of dwarves be marching to our gates, and why are we letting them through?"

Ezera grew impatient and answered for the older man. "They are coming to relieve us of the Tuath militiamen and sailors on the brigantines in our harbor. First, they will demolish our docks so that the thousands of men aboard those brigantines cannot easily disembark and wreak havoc on our wharf. Then they will turn north for Tuath and make sure the northerners see it so that they may draw them out of our waters. This way the whole thing looks like dwarven aggression against Tuath and not insurrection from Mer."

The captain nodded slowly in understanding. "With the docks destroyed, we can easily defend ourselves at the harbor if necessary. Do we then send our militia north to follow the dwarves?"

This time the Exarch spoke for himself. "With no governor to lead us, we cannot send the militiamen of Mer anywhere. There may yet be a need for a martial law captain, but I hope we have avoided it."

*****

Uridyll sat at his desk, unable to concentrate since returning to the college. He had thought of warning the merchants of what was about to happen at the wharf and to the docks, but he did not trust they wouldn't simply flee to preserve their interests.

There was a good chance that in warning them, many would depart all at once. Their actions would be suspicious and force them to be inspected and potentially interrogated by the Tuath ships out in the bay and responsible for tithing them as they came and went.

In frustration, he put down the book of enchantment he had

been trying to read for distraction and almost knocked his leather flask of oil and striker off his desk.

An idea struck him as he stared at the objects. He and the Exarch had talked at length upon returning to the city from Fjall about needing to keep their respective institutions neutral in the coming conflict. This way, when things went back to normal, the people would still see them as unbiased institutions that worked for the benefit of all on the island and not one city-state or the other.

Still, though, the Exarch and his vicar did have a part to play. He expected that this very morning Hameki was doing as he had been asked in Fjall and was informing the city militiamen to stand down at the approach of the dwarves. He grabbed a lit candle and went to the ladder in the back of his quarters. He climbed it to the roof of his living space and office above the library below.

Placing the candle on the rooftop, he backed up a few paces and spoke words he had not spoken in years.

The tiny flame atop the candlewick danced and then grew and spiraled into a tornado of fire twice again as tall as a man. Then, the swirling tongues of flame slowly calmed and took the form of a giant owl. The clay tiles of the rooftop were charred black under the bird's talons as it spread its wings and shook its head before staring at Uridyll.

The Arch Mage looked fondly at his elemental familiar. "It has been too long, my friend; I think today we may have some work to do."

Chapter 23

Provocation

It was just after midday when the column of seven-hundred and fifty dwarves arrived at the city's inland-facing gates. Stern-faced Mer militiamen nodded respectfully. Some even saluted from the gate tower as the dwarves arrived.

General Shieldborn held up a gauntleted fist, halting the army as it reached the gate and hailed the militiamen operating it. "One of you lads want to walk ahead of us and take us on the best route to the wharf? Preferably one where we can approach out of eyesight from the sea before taking it back from those Tuath ships you've got babysitting your every move?"

A young man stepped from his post at the wall with a look from one of their officers.

"Lance Corporal Grimmins, happy to show you down to the docks," the man said, saluting.

General Shieldborn motioned for the young militiamen to join him and Lorkin in the front of the column, and they marched on. The three-wide column of dwarves snaked its way impressively down sideroads and alleys towards the wharf.

After a few tense moments, Lance Corporal Grimmins halted them. "Sir, about ten feet beyond the next building, you'll be in the center of the wharf and probably visible to the ships."

General Shieldborn gave the young man a salute. "Be getting back to that gate now, lad. Some proper violence is about to unfold here."

The militiamen returned the salute. "If it is all the same to you, sir, I don't know that I could stand idly by and let you all fight for my city-state."

The dwarven general gave the young man a toothy grin in response to the fiery statement. "All right then, you see this dress-wearing dwarf standing next to me. He is going to cause all kinds of mayhem here shortly, and I want you to stay at his side and watch his back."

Stone Mage Lorkin shot the general a sour look and accepted his new bodyguard grumpily.

"All right, lads, quiet and calm as you like," he said as loudly as he dared.

The quiet shuffle and grating of armored boots replaced the rhythmic drum of dwarven feet as the column of dwarves tried at stealth.

He pushed the top of his helmet down, tightening it on the top of his head, and gave a parting nod to Lorkin. "Been a long time since we've had some proper fun, old mage. Remember to watch yourself. That dress of yours won't stop arrows or bolts!"

Lorkin scoffed at his old friend. "Not my first or last tussle, Okliff. Mind yourself and the lads."

"First Company with the Stone Mage, Second and Third Companies on me, shield formations," he said, the fire of battle growing in his belly.

The column then split; the right rank followed Lorkin straight towards the water's edge. The other five hundred dwarves began forming into five rectangular phalanx formations, five abreast and twenty deep, as they made their way along the wharf's edge closer to the Tuath vessels.

*****

Lorkin looked around at the two hundred and fifty-some dwarves that protectively encircled him with a shield wall. Then, rolling up the sleeves of his orange mage robe, he gave Lance Corporal Grimmins a wink. "Don't be soiling yourself!"

He began to murmur the activation of his elemental enchantment quietly. Then, as he finished the phrase, he kneeled to the cobbles and placed his hand on a stone in front of him. His pulse pounded, and the stone thrummed along with it into the active enchantment that consumed his concentration.

The stone he touched began to expand rapidly, twisting and rumbling like thunder until it grew to the size of a small house and

223

took the form of an elemental bear made of entirely smooth grey stone.

He opened his eyes and gave the elemental a fond pat and motioned for the dwarves nearest the water to part ways. When the twenty or so dwarves moved, and he had a clear view of the many merchant ships and fishing vessels still tied off at the docks, Lorkin frowned.

"Well, Uridyll, I tried to let you save the Mer ships, but I can't be suffering these docks much longer lest they allow the Tuath forces to disembark easily."

*****

Arch Mage Uridyll had joined the Exarch and Ezera in the top of spire to watch the day unfold. Seeing Lorkin's elemental appear on the wharf, Uridyll knew it was time for him to play his part. Still busy gawking at Lorkin's magical summoning, the clerics did not immediately notice Uridyll's efforts.

He poured a tiny amount of oil from his leather flask onto the stone floor and sparked it to life with his striker. His whispered incantation coaxed the small flame into a whirlwind that grew with the tempo of his chant. Eventually, it spouted out of the spire window and into the air above, where the roaring flames swirled and twisted until they formed into his elemental owl.

He motioned for the docks and imparted his instructions.

The two clerics were now staring at him, awestruck. He offered only a shrug. "I'll only be freeing the merchant vessels from the docks Hameki, not lighting the Tuath ships ablaze," he explained.

*****

Lorkin looked on approvingly while the flaming maelstrom that was Uridyll's elemental plunged from the top of the spire. It skirted the docks, setting mooring lines ablaze as it went.

"The favor of Daybreak is with us! An omen of fire from the goddess herself!" exclaimed townsfolk from a small crowd nearest himself and First Company.

Shaking his head at the comment, Lorkin grinned at the flaming owl. "Well done, Uridyll, and many thanks!"

His elemental bear then took off for the far end of the wharf, each step shaking and cracking the cobbles of the harbor. Charging the docks nearest the Tuath ships, it began ripping piers from the water.

In response to the calamity on the water's edge, horns began blowing among the twenty Tuath vessels, and their sails began unfurling. Half the ships broke from formation further out in the harbor and dashed the docks.

"Just a few more moments if you would!" Lorkin shouted at the soldiers encircling him.

A few of the dwarves rushed to the stone mage, throwing their shields above their heads, as did all but the outermost row of the shield wall formation. A few crossbow bolts and arrows bounced off the shields overhead as the Tuath ships closed.

His elemental had barely finished ripping the last of the planks from the water when he quickly dismissed it. He shot a smile at the human militiaman staring mouth agape at his side. "Magic is a hell of a thing, is it not?"

Even though the docks were now gone, the ships were unwilling to stop their sprint. They slammed into the wharf's edge with enough force to knock many a dwarf from their feet.

To a one, the brigantines began sinking the short distance to the harbor bottom, and the militiamen and sailors disembarked like ants from a kicked over an anthill, some thirteen hundred militiamen and sailors abandoned the ships. He snorted as they charged wildly at the five formations under the command of General Shieldborn.

He quickly turned to the red-haired dwarf next to him. "Commander Shatter-Hand, engage the men if you would."

The officer took the horn from his belt and blew two long reports. "Five-by column! March!" he shouted, and the dwarves seemed to move as a single entity. In a matter of seconds, the circle around Lorkin transformed into a column of dwarves five across and fifty deep. One more report from the horn of Commander Shatter-Hand and the dwarves marched off.

He clapped Lance Corporal Grimmins hard on the shoulder. "My thanks for your help and watchful eye, but you're apt to be in the way in the ugliness to come, go home to your family."

The man started to protest, but the look in Lorkin's eye made him sure he was leaving whether or not he wanted to.

*****

General Shieldborn and his warriors had barely regained their footing when the men from the ships were upon them. The five dwarven phalanx formations stretched the three hundred feet from the water to the shops that ringed the wharf. There was enough room between each rectangular formation for one or two men to pass between them.

He slammed his ax into his shield and barked at his soldiers. "Only about three of them for each of you by my reckoning. Try not to embarrass yourselves by letting this take too long!"

The light leather armor, minimal training, and complete disarray of two thousand men met with calm, plate-armored dwarven fury. The wave of Tuath militiamen and sailors crashed into them, and the shield wall summarily broke it.

In utter desperation and with nowhere to run, the men died in waves against the dwarven shields. The writhing mass mercilessly crushed those closest to the dwarven formations against their shields.

He spat defiantly as many men made futile attempts to slip their swords or spears through the shield wall. The front line of militiamen facing the dwarves had no defense against the crushing blows of dwarven weaponry.

General Shieldborn swatted aside a haphazardly thrust spear that slipped over the top of the shield wall directly in front of him. He grinned as the perpetrating militiaman had his chest caved in by the war hammer of a dwarf in the second rank.

Noticing that the immense weight of so many men was beginning to strain his lines, he grabbed his command horn and blared it loudly four times. Pausing a moment to let his formations prepare, he then blew it twice more. In sync, the dwarven lines backpedaled two steps and reset their shields.

He nodded approvingly when the crush of men pushed many that were close to the dwarves to the ground as the sudden lack of resistance led to an awkward and forced advance on the part of the Tuath forces.

While more Tuathian forces continued to engage, many along the front lines were naturally forced between the front face of the dwarven phalanxes by those behind them. However, General

226

Shieldborn was not concerned for the men that made it through, as he knew they would meet the line of dwarves that had been protecting Lorkin.

As the initial frenzy died down, he noticed the enemy officers had gained a semblance of control. The humans pulled back from the slaughter of the deadly dwarven formations and began organizing into their own lines. Few men had shields but those who did joined those who had longer weapons such as spears and pikes at the front.

The Tuathian militiamen formed up in lines as broad as the dwarven formations, and the two forces were now not more than a hundred feet apart. He usually would not have let the enemy gain the initiative, but he had hoped they might surrender and spare themselves further bloodshed.

Hearing one of the Tuath officers commanding the men, he shouted at his own, "Rain's coming boys!"

Shields snapped overhead as arrows and crossbow bolts started falling around them.

Peeking through the slits where shields joined, General Shieldborn frowned as he heard enemy officers screaming orders and saw the rear half of their forces start heading down the back streets of the city. Not wanting to be encircled, he quickly decided to relay new instructions. "Column Right!" he shouted.

The general's middle formation held fast, and the other four moved out in perfect synchronization. Then, without relenting the shelter of their upheld shields, the dwarves got into lines parallel to the harbor sea wall. Lorkin and Commander Shatter-Hand's phalanxes joined them at the rear.

With a glance to confirm his entire army was in a single column again, he pointed his ax at the militiamen. "Right at 'em!"

They began slowly stepping their way towards the humans still in front of them.

What had once been some semblance of an organized Tuathian tactical formation soon fell into disarray. The dwarven column moved seemingly unimpeded by the panicked attacks of the men. It had pushed so far into the human lines that it had split the force that had remained on the wharf entirely in two. Half had their backs to the water, and the other had their backs to the shops.

He blared on his horn. "Pass it down the lines. Then, on my next signal, ranks one, two, and three push inland, ranks four and

227

five push them into the water!"

Amidst the din of a halfhearted assault on all sides by the militiamen, his soldiers passed the message down the formation, and he then gave another horn blast.

The sides of the box formations became the front lines. The dwarves resumed their slow step advance. The men inland of the were pinned helplessly against the shops. A few had attempted pushing back against the dwarves and died for it, but the rest threw down their weapons. The advance of the other dwarven lines simply pushed those against the water over the edge and into it.

A commotion from one of the side streets emptied onto the wharf and drew his attention as he made ready to order his soldiers to engage the hundreds of militiamen who had disappeared from the waterfront earlier. But, instead of raising his horn to his mouth, he flashed a grin as almost two thousand Mer militiamen escorted hundreds of surrendered Tuathian sailors and militia out onto the wharf.

Waving a greeting to Captain Elliswerth at the head of the Mer militia, he called a halt to his forces.

He then addressed the still thousand-strong group from Tuath that stood trapped on the cobbles and the upper decks of ships sitting on the harbor floor. "Look here, men of Tuath, I've no want for any more death, but I've no problem in dealing it. We have you outnumbered, out equipped, and out trained. Surrender here to the men of Mer, and they will treat you fairly."

Even if the lopsided fight was not enough, the fact that they had witnessed a house-sized stone bear shred the docks was enough to convince them that an offer of surrender was the better option.

"Captain, you and your men can handle these northerners, I assume?" he asked.

Captain Elliswerth gave the dwarf a nod.

"Have our thanks for what you've done here today, good dwarves!"

The general returned the man's salute. "And have mine for cleaning up those that made it out onto your streets, sir."

General Shieldborn turned to his three commanders. "Form them up in a column of five, only those truly able to make the march north in haste," he then turned back to Captain Elliswerth. "I've got a few wounded that I'll leave here for the clerics if you don't mind. Wish there were the time for ale and tales of the battle, but we've business in Tuath I best be attending."

Captain Ellisworth sent some of his men off to hasten the cleric's arrival. "Safe travels and good fighting."

General Shieldborn bid farewell to the man and his wounded and made his way to the head of the column. "All right, boys, we're turning north. Let's make sure the rest of the northerners still out on those ships in the harbor hear ya chant!"

*****

From his position on the steering deck of his ship, the Tuath admiral responsible for policing the Mer harbor could hardly believe his eyes. He had lost half his ships and watched his numerically superior force's complete devastation against the dwarven formations.

He feared that if they tried to land more forces, he risked not only defeat but the return of the rock elemental and the destruction of his ships and slaughter of potentially all his men. He witnessed the dwarves reforming their column and turning to the north. As they entered the city's alleys, the chant of over seven hundred dwarves echoed out into the harbor.

"North to Tuath!" The chant reverberated across the waters of the harbor until the dwarves were entirely out of sight.

"Your orders, sir?" the helmsman of his ship asked the seemingly distant admiral. Then, wrestling with his options, the officer made his decision.

"With no docks, we've no good way of deploying our other militiamen, and even so, it seems the Mer militia has found the will to fight, which would have us quite outnumbered. So instead, we must warn Tuath of the dwarven approach. Homeward at once!"

As the ten ships turned and left the harbor, cheers rang out from across the Mer waterside.

*****

Gwenolyn sat on the steering deck of the *Open Ocean* as it bobbed in gentle waves anchored near the barren rocks of the western Quaj coast. She did not care for the lives of other races as her uncle did. However, pointless death was something she did not embrace. She hoped they could break the people of Tuath from the hypnotism of war with the south. If they did, the whole island of Quaj, including the woods where her people lived, would be better for it.

With the late morning sun finally making its way over the mountains, she stretched and looked around at the natural beauty and silence of the empty and rocky western coast bathed in quiet sunlight. Then, she spotted dark smudges on the horizon that could only be ships. She immediately went and woke Turin and the others.

The older elf climbed to the top of the mast with his spyglass before shouting down to them, "Lumber ships from Kalt, destined for Tuath no doubt. They must be using the island's back to avoid detection while they supply the north with lumber. Unfortunately, they have several Tuath brigantines for escort. I am hoping that our own ship is hard enough to spot against the backdrop of the rocks that they pass right by us. We are not due to make our presence known in Tuath for another day yet. The dwarves likely just made camp there last night."

Far from civilization and any worry of being noticed, the Herald and Wren made their way above decks with Harpis.

"Should we be pulling anchor and preparing to sail just in case then, Turin?" Harpis asked sleepily, approaching the wooden wheel that wound the anchor.

"I do think it wise," Turin said, dropping nimbly from the riggings, he made his way to the helm with his spyglass, and Gwenolyn climbed up the mast to replace him as the lookout. She was ready to unfurl their sails at any moment.

"We could always just deal with the ships if you wish, Master Turin," The Herald said to the elf in the guttural troll accent.

Turin shook his head. "Powerful and favored as you and Wren may be, there are ten lumber vessels and five brigantines. I am less worried about destroying them and more so that we would be unable to stop all of them before they made Tuath Bay and warned of our presence."

Wren was not so confident as the Death Herald and raised his eyebrow questioningly at the leader of the necromancers.

Noting his concern, the Herald patted his balding head. "Fear not, Wren, The Sleeper is with us."

Turin's curses cut off any response from the gnome as the elf held the spyglass to his face. "The brigantines are turning this way. We must trust that the dwarves have already arrived by the time we get there. Let's hope they notice our arrival in time to provide some distraction."

Gwenolyn quickly let the sails out, and the *Open Ocean's* sleek hull practically leaped over the waves as it caught the wind funneled northward by the rock face of the Fjall mountains.

Turin's assessment of the situation came in an almost mournful voice. "We shouldn't have a problem staying slightly ahead of those brigantines despite the number of their sails they have let out, but they'll be right on our backside as we make the bay. I lament at losing the element of surprise, but it is too late for anything else."

*****

Benali had been watching Sirul pace the Tuath Mansion balcony like a caged animal all morning. A stream of his officers had been in to see him every hour since the dwarves had arrived at his city gates last night.

Sirul suddenly stopped and turned to him. "What in this five-be-damned world are they doing outside my city!?" he asked for probably the hundredth time.

Benali could only shrug in response. He, too, was surprised. Not that they were there, but there were so few of them. Sirul went to the balcony railing, and for a moment, Benali imagined shoving him over it. However, his fantasy was interrupted at the return of the Tuath militia captain stepping out onto the balcony.

The old man snapped to attention in between Benali and Sirul. "How may I be of assistance?"

Sirul tore himself away from the view of his city and the distant dwarven encampment. He looked the captain up and down like wounded prey. "You can assist me, Captain Plonius, by removing those Five-forsaken dwarves from my city gates and sending them to The Sleeper!"

The captain nervously spread his hands in apology. "Sir, it would be unwise to engage them outside our walls. It would be to their advantage."

"Advantage? We outnumber them almost twenty to one with

the reserves called up!" Sirul seethed.

Plonius looked to the bard for help, but Benali stared at his feet, not wanting to draw attention to himself.

The captain made another effort to make his governor see military logic. "Governor Myrlman, we may have fifteen thousand militiamen, but only a third of them have experience policing our city. Another third is reserves, and the rest are recently signed up volunteers who haven't drilled or trained a day in their lives. Worse, we wouldn't have the element of surprise as the dwarves have run regular patrols since arriving last night."

Sirul had dismissively turned back to glower over his city and at the dwarves.

Hoping the governor was calming, Plonius offered one last point. "They have also masterfully picked their location, where the mountains run to the sea, flat ground is barely wider than the coastal road, our numbers would mean little if we went out to them, sir."

Sirul refused to face the captain. "That will be all, captain. I expect you to return to me before nightfall with a plan to defeat those filthy dwarves. I will not abide us hiding behind our walls for much longer," he said in a growl.

Benali quietly let out a small sigh of relief as bloodshed of his countrymen was for now avoided. He was glad Plonius had proved his point, but as he watched the man depart, paranoia at being alone with the killer that was not his cousin set in once again.

Chapter 24

Desperation

As the *Open Ocean* came around the final northern turn towards Tuath Bay, the crowded harbor came into view. Glancing behind them, Harpis saw that they had been able to maintain some distance from the brigantines chasing them, but not much.

Within moments after they rounded the corner, so too did the Tuath ships. With the bay in view, those pursuing them began sounding horns of alarm. It did not take long for the armada anchored in Tuath bay to take notice and spring to life.

Harpis pulled a frown as ships began unfurling sails and dragging in anchors all over the bay. He looked up to Turin in dismay. "How can we hope to keep outpacing those behind us, let alone make our way through the flotilla ahead?"

The elf did not stop scanning the waters ahead of them. "We will have your answer soon enough," he responded tersely.

The Death Herald and Wren climbed onto the steering deck and flanked Turin on either side. Gwenolyn remained in her perch above the riggings. Harpis stood on the main deck below Turin and the others, unable to tear his eyes from the visage of a hundred naval ships in various stages of turning to attack them that was awesomely terrifying.

"If I can keep their grapnels off us, I might be able to crash us into a dock at the wharf's edge and get you lot running off into the city before the crews of these ships or the militia are on us," Turin shouted from the helm.

The troll and gnome made their way down to Harpis in preparation for the landing hopefully to come. The Death Herald looked down at Wren from across the steering deck. Her calm

233

toothy smile in the face of their impending doom was unnerving even to the stalwart gnome.

Harpis' hope improved some as he heard the Herald speaking to Wren. "Wren, do you think that perhaps Xissay may join us and slow our pursuers a bit?"

Wren pulled his scythe from the air and snapped his fingers, a grin appearing on his face as well.

"Finally!" Xissay screamed as she appeared above his shoulder. "For once, are you going to let me play?"

He pointed at the ships behind them. "See what you can do about that lot."

Harpis saw the sprite's small hands begin to glow red, and the air around them smoked and smelled like burnt dust. She gave a grin to Wren and a bow to the Death Herald before darting after the ships following them.

"Will she be all right?" Harpis questioned Wren with a look of concern.

The gnome's only response was to laugh and shake his head. Harpis gasped moments later when sails on one ship after another began bursting into flames. The men aboard were running around terrified, and he could hear some screaming about demons and omens. Some of the men abandoned the ship in terror, and some tried hopelessly to strike Xissay with arrows from the rolling decks of the Tuath brigantines.

Without the wind caught in their full sails to propel them, the Tuath vessels began slowed to an almost complete stop before listing helplessly in the breeze.

Wren turned away from the fiery spectacle behind them dismissively and smiled up at Harpis. "Quite impressive when she wants to be!"

Despite agreeing with the effectiveness of the fire sprite's display, Harpis still felt helpless as he looked upon the hundred or so ships headed right at them. The lead ships were barely a thousand feet from the schooner as the *Open Ocean* entered the harbor proper from the outer bay.

Though he had seen Wren perform a similar summoning, he was in awe as The Death Herald drew her eight-foot scythe from the air in front of her and slammed the butt of its shaft into the decking so hard he could hear the echo from the hold below. The sculpted platinum skull of a hunting cat caught the midday sun brilliantly, and the fiery sunlight dancing in the fist-sized rubies of its eyes made him wonder if it was somehow alive.

Harpis struggled to hear her murmured prayers to The Sleeper and almost jumped when she snapped her enormous green fingers. What looked like a small storm cloud formed in the few hundred feet between the *Open Ocean* and Tuath armada. The smell of sulfur filled the entire bay for a moment so thick that Harpis choked on it.

He could not help but join the collective gasps from those aboard the Tuath ships as the decayed remains of a black dragon with a rotting body the size of a warship emerged in mid-flight from the cloud. It greeted the realm of the living with a rattling shriek that shook the exposed bones of its throat.

Harpis stared open-mouthed at the dragon and then the Herald, who had her eyes squeezed shut in concentration. "What in the Five-be-damned world is that?" he asked aloud.

Not getting an answer from the troll as she struggled to maintain control over the undead familiar, Harpis looked at the equally astonished gnome.

Wren shook his head in amazement. "I haven't a clue how many centuries have passed since a dragon was in the realm of the living, but it appears The Herald found one in The Great Dream!"

The wingspan of the Death Herald's undead familiar was twice again as long as the giant Tuath brigantines. It flew straight at the first of them. The dragon smashed the masts aside like they were saplings. Then, grabbing both bulkheads of the ship with either claw, the great creature beat its wings mightily and lifted the entire boat out of the water.

Harpis heard screams of horror from Tuath sailors as the undead dragon threw the brigantine into the next nearest ship. The impact ripped both vessels nearly in half.

Arrows and crossbow bolts began flying from the other ships as they closed.

"They're out of range for now, but the air around us will soon be thick with their missiles!" Turin shouted.

Harpis could hardly hear Turin's warning over the sounds of men dying to the burning acid breath and shredding claws of the undead dragon.

The Death Herald stood unabated, absorbed in the effort to keep the great undead familiar amongst the living. A ballista bolt fired from one of the lead ships knocked her hulking form from its feet. The five-foot bolt drove into the deck behind her after obliterating her heart with an impact so heavy it knocked Harpis and Wren from their feet as the ship's momentum momentarily lagged. At once, the familiar disappeared into a black cloud as the troll hastily dismissed it.

Cheers erupted from among the Tuath ships, and Harpis' heart sank as he struggled to find his feet while Turin had the *Open Ocean* nearly on its side to angle them away from the armada. Even with the maneuver, and the ships the dragon had destroyed, he knew they were in an unwinnable race to the Tuath wharf.

Finally getting his bearing again, Harpis knelt with Wren at the Death Herald's side as she took heavy, gurgling breaths around the ballista bolt in her chest. The missile was the width of a man's arm and held her firmly against the ship's deck. The light fading in her eyes with each wheeze, she dropped her scythe with a heavy thud. The troll then grabbed him and Wren off their feet and held them inches from her face.

"I am coming, Lilynth. At long last, I am coming," she said, dropping them to the decks as her arms fell slack and her great scythe disappeared.

Harpis' voice trembled as he finally pulled his gaze from the troll's corpse and looked to his friend, whose eyes were closed in prayer.

"Wren, who is Lilynth?" he asked, shivering as he felt a foreign stirring of his gift as the name left his lips.

When the gnome opened his eyes, he looked afraid to answer. Instead of speaking, he reached over to Harpis and pulled his sleeve back, pointing at the amethyst visage of The Sleeper on the man's bracelet.

Harpis shook his head in bewilderment at The Herald's death and what she had said. Then, a crossbow bolt smacked into the deck inches from his foot, snapping his attention back to the situation at hand as arrows plunged into the water around them.

He looked at Turin, and the elf gave a forlorn look at The Herald, which turned to rage as he faced the Tuath Armada. "Get below decks, I'll try and get us to the shore, but you're no use to any of us if the three of you are pincushions!"

Gwenolyn dropped from the riggings above after firing one

last shot from her great crossbow at the nearest brigantine.

Harpis looked from the elves to the gnome. "Wren, we are lost. What do we do?" he asked, fear in his voice.

Wren spat at the hopelessness in his question. "We fight, and maybe we die!"

With that, he turned to the troll's corpse and closed his eyes while speaking in hushed tones. "All things considered, Herald, I do not think you would mind. Enjoy Our Lady's long overdue welcome. Thank you for this and everything."

The gnome then chanted for a moment while clutching his scythe. The reanimated body of The Herald pulled itself from the ballista like roast from a skewer.

Harpis could not help but wretch at the sucking sound the corpse made sliding free from the bolt. Then, at Wren's bidding, it moved between them and the ships. The gnome nodded Xissay's way and then pointed at the boats encircling them. "If you wouldn't mind, my dear! Harpis, get that look off your face. There will be time for panic and mourning when we are dead!"

"I'd be happy too!" Xissay's answer flitted back on the wind as she sped off.

Harpis was still struggling to process what had happened on the deck of *Open Ocean*.

Wren snapped his fingers to get his attention. "We'll keep you from harm as long as we can, so sing damn you!" As Wren finished, there were several thuds from arrows striking the reanimated corpse. Gwenolyn dropped to a knee and undid her crossbow with a glare at the bard. "Well?"

"I don't even know what to sing!" he said hopelessly.

"I don't care what it is. Just do something like you did on the *Sea Goat*!" Wren returned. "Preferably something that sends these gods forsaken Tuath sailors right back to their mother's teat!" he shouted sarcastically.

Rubbing the amethyst depiction of the goddess with his other hand, he uttered, "Discordium."

He pulled his fiddle from his back and played the slow, sorrowful wails of someone unable to wake from the torment of a nightmare. With desperate resolve, he began a lullaby used by mothers in his village to scare their children to bed.

Over the whimpering of his fiddle strings, his voice cracked and broke as it crashed across the harbor. He struggled to maintain control while giving in to fear and despair. Raw emotion and his gift alike poured into the verse as tears streamed down his cheeks.

It was with the helpless dread of a terrified child that he wept the chorus and her name. He could barely hear himself for the pounding of his pulse in his ears. As his voice called her name, the maelstrom of her power dominated his own. It tore through him, threatening to erode his very flesh and bones as it hungered to consume his body.

With each utterance from his wavering voice, the sky itself seemed to dim, and darkness closed in.

By the time Harpis sang the third chorus, the harbor had disappeared before him and became a dark grey, nearly black fog. He sang on, though now it sounded to him more like he was whispering.

The receding mist revealed The Sleeper's nude figure. She lay as hillsides of pale flesh draped in wisps of raven hair that at times were indiscernible from the haze of The Great Dream. Behind her, a moonless night sky full of entrancing starlight bathed her form in a cool silvery glow. Suddenly her eyes shot open. They were pools of inevitable blackness that seemed to seduce every fiber of his body towards their promise.

*****

Wren looked around wide-eyed as the sky greyed and color seemed to fade from everything. At each mention of his goddess' name, Wren felt swelling pulses from his scythe as it vibrated with her influence.

When Harpis sang the third chorus, the waters beneath the boats began to churn and roil, tossing the brigantines into each other. As the fourth chorus came from the bard's mouth, it echoed off the entire hillside of Tuath.

Shrill, wordless wails poured forth from the brigantines, the harbor, and even further into the city. Wren could hardly believe what he saw as the sea under the brigantines was teaming with the reanimated remains of sailors, fish, sharks, crabs, and every other no longer living denizen of the harbor.

The undead mass of deceased creatures and body parts was ravaging and shifting the Tuath ships. The undead sank or capsized a third of what was the fleet of Tuath. Wren whistled as some of the vessels were under the assault of several animated whale corpses that had answered the beckoned call of Lilynth and came in from the deep to attack the brigantines as Harpis sang on.

Xissay returned to her position, floating at his shoulder with an impressed look on her face. "Quite the necromancer your bard is!"

Wren found no room for argument as the ships that were still able fled away from the city towards the sea and presumed safety allowing the *Open Ocean* to speed unimpeded towards the Tuath wharf. On the docks, the entire market came to life. Wren chuckled at the display as stalls were suddenly full of reanimated crabs and flopping undead fish, causing several Tuath citizens who had been gawking at the assault on the harbor to scream and flee.

Finally able to peel his eyes from the spectacle of his goddess' might, Wren looked to the man whose voice was resonating across every corner of the bay. Harpis' face looked older. His skin looked like the weathered and wrinkled features of a man thirty years his senior, and the hair around his temples was now almost pure white.

The bracelet on his wrist shattered into molten pieces. Each layer of the magical lattice imbued within it was torn apart simultaneously, burning the silhouette of the goddess' visage into his wrist. The man's eyes were filled with blackness as he sang on to her. With their deaths no longer imminent, the gnome tried to interrupt the bard. As he went to shove Harpis, the power flowing through the man almost overcame his senses. The will of his goddess pulsed so strongly through his hand that Wren almost lost consciousness.

He thought better of trying again himself and imparted instruction to Xissay. She grabbed Harpis' knife from his boot and stabbed him hard in the ass. The bay became weirdly still. It was as if a thunderstorm had disappeared in an instant at the very height of its fury.

The magical silence around Harpis kept his pained curses from reaching any ears. But, on the other hand, the facial expressions he was making at Xissay made clear enough his opinion of having the tip of a filet knife in his rump.

Harpis pulled the knife from his skin with a cringe. He stared out at the calming sea around them and the corpses of thousands of dead things floating on its surface. The sun's heat made the smell almost unbearable, and so large was the mass of death now on top of the waters the stench was inescapable.

Rubbing his scarred and burnt wrist, he looked lamentingly at his friend. "Wren, what happened here?" he stammered. "I was…I was somewhere else, it was dark, and I saw her Wren, I saw the eyes of your Lady, and they were so beautiful, I could not wrench my gaze from the darkness of their void."

"Find yourself some religion in that song, did ye? Well, I would not be calling her name too often; you have aged decades in the minutes you spent singing that song to her. If you gain too much of her attention, she may decide to keep you in her Great Dream."

Harpis took the filet knife in his hand and turned it so he could see his reflection in its blade. He almost dropped it to the deck when he saw how his face had aged.

Wren looked him up and down with concern. "There is a price to pay for such power, lad, you weren't conscious of it, but I reckon hundreds of thousands of dead things as far as the eye can see were heeding The Sleeper's call. She was using you as a conduit. I felt her powers channeling through me while you sang. It is perilously reckless to bridge the planes of the gods to the mortal realms," he said somberly.

*****

General Shieldborn walked towards the front of his encampment. Try as he might, he could not see why the Tuath ships across the harbor had begun blowing their horns or why the men at the top of the gate had turned towards the sea.

When a giant undead dragon appeared from the dark cloud over the harbor and began its devastation, he had his answer. His soldiers began frantic conversations with tinges of fear in their voices.

He stomped his feet grumpily. "Hey now, tighten up, it looks like we will be starting the festivities a day early. Yonder commotion is from our friend The Death Herald, or I'm a goat's ass!"

The officers began forming the dwarves into their phalanxes. They then started walking the ranks, inspecting weapons and armor as they went.

Okliff ran a finger against the edge of his ax, growling after distractedly cutting himself while staring at a ship being thrown from the sky by the dragon.

He looked back at the formed-up army. "Might as well get to it!"

The five-dwarf wide column set out for the gates of Tuath. Once it was nearly at the doors to the city, they were half-heartedly peppered by arrows from the wall.

He turned to Lorkin. "Care to knock?"

"Happy to!" Lorkin said as he scanned the ground around his feet.

Lorkin knelt to the ground and, grabbing a pebble, uttered the summoning incantation of his enchanted stone elemental. Then, as the stone began to grow, he threw it towards the gate where it landed as the giant bear with a thud that shook the Tuath walls as much as it did the militiamen's courage.

The distant screams of terror from the bay had already sent half those at the wall fleeing. The other half were busy scrambling to address the fact that a house-sized bear smashed their city gate into splinters before disappearing as quickly as it had appeared.

Amongst the fear of a mythical dragon and a formidable stone elemental, there was no organized response to the dwarven advance.

*****

Sirul could not believe his eyes. Benali Tuath and he both stood slack-jawed and in terror at the scene that had unfolded in the bay. The fleeing naval ships of Tuath had all but disappeared over the horizon.

"Where do they think they are going!?" Sirul shouted at the city below him as much as to the bard.

"No will of mortal man is capable of sailing back into the death and darkness of those waters," Benali offered poetically.

Sirul turned to him with eyes that burned with rage. "Siren, take the lot of them!"

Their gazes shifted from the lone vessel approaching in front of them to the city walls to their right. There they saw a dwarven column entering through what was once its main gate.

241

Sirul screamed for his officers as a man possessed. "Every single one of their militiamen is to engage and push the dwarves back and out of my city, or I will take them to The Sleeper myself!"

*****

Turin broadsided the dock near the fish market, and Wren, Harpis, and Gwenolyn disembarked at a sprint. Gwenolyn pointed to a taller two-story building further up the slopes of Tuath, about five hundred feet from the mansion balcony.

As they ran to her mark, Harpis enveloped them with the cadence of *Panoryla's March*. The notes of his song reverberated off the walls of buildings and down alleys as they passed.

Several of the militiamen and citizens of Tuath they passed on their run to the building of choice recoiled in cowardice at the thunderous notes. When they finally made the building, Harpis ended his song but not before a group of twenty militiamen spotted them and began heading their way.

Gwenolyn immediately went into a flurry of action, dropping four of them with her crossbow before they got within a hundred feet.

Wren turned to her and Harpis. "Get to the roof, and you watch her back, lad. I've enough help now to deal with the rest of them."

Gwenolyn was still looking at the gnome confusedly as Harpis shoved her inside and up the first flight of stairs.

Scythe in hand and Xissay at his side, he began his prayers to The Sleeper as the men rushed in. They did not notice their four recently killed companions were almost upon them from behind. Xissay flew straight at the first of the men. One of them had a crossbow and aimed for the whispering gnome but fired instead at the sprite.

The crossbow bolt struck her square in the chest and passed right through her without any effect. Such was the benefit of already being dead. She grabbed the helm of the first man in the group and turned it to liquid. The man screamed as the molten ore burned through his skull and silenced him forever.

The sight, smell, and sound caused several of the group to soil themselves, pass out, or flee screaming, right into the animated corpses of their fellow militiamen. When the final militiamen rose as a corpse, Wren opened his eyes and stopped his spell. The no longer reanimated corpses fell to the street, and he made his way upstairs to join Harpis and Gwenolyn on the roof.

The three of them could hear the screaming of Sirul hundreds of feet from them, incensed and enraged at the poor performance of his militiamen at the city walls. Despite asking the man to get to the Hall, Harpis was positive that it was the Impresario beside Sirul.

"Perhaps the man from Tuath has betrayed us. Why else is he here at Sirul's side and not away at The Hall as instructed?" the gnome asked.

Harpis' face showed his disappointment as he could find no reason to argue Wren's point despite desperately wanting to as he looked across at the balcony.

Chapter 25
Wages of War

Benali Tuath looked at the back of the man who was not his cousin, commanding the people of his beloved Tuath to their deaths for his own gains. He felt hot rage washing over him at the sight of Sirul.

Benali remembered what Stone Mage Lorkin had said beneath the mountain in Fjall. The mask would appear, and the wearer's face beneath it would be back to normal when there was no more life left to sustain the mask.

Benali left Sirul's side and went to his cousin's desk, grabbing the knife he knew was there. A gift the bard had himself had given the former governor when he was named ruler of Tuath. Benali walked silently behind the distracted imposter.

"Sirul Amun, I sentence you to die!"

Sirul had not heard his real name in years. He subconsciously turned towards the man who spoke it. He did so without understanding the implications of its utterance from the bard's lips. The trained killer with decades of experience looked in silent confusion at the dagger handle sticking out of his chest. His eyes closed forever to the sight of a vengeful Benali Tuath.

Benali knelt beside the dead man and waited. Moments passed like ages while he watched for the mask to appear and beneath it Sirul's natural face.

Benali began to panic. The man dead before him was supposed to be wearing an illusionary mask, playing at his cousin. Benali clawed desperately at the dead man's face, trying to remove a mask that was not there as dread grew within him that the dead man was Myrlman.

Officers reporting from the front line entered the office and saw their governor dead, a dagger in his chest and Benali Tuath kneeling at his side. They drew their swords and rushed at the Impresario.

Something whistled past the lead officer and hit the second so hard it lifted him from his feet. The man died before hitting the ground, a crossbow bolt between the pieces of what was once his heart.

Benali did not hear the yells of the officers. He did not see the missile that seemed to come from nowhere strike one of them down. The world went dark. Impresario Benali Tuath, the last living heir to the hereditary line of Tuath city-state, went to The Great Dream at the hands of a Tuath militiaman. He went not knowing if the man he had just murdered in cold blood on his cousin's balcony was Seulman Tuath's son or the imposter Sirul Amun.

*****

Harpis, Wren, and Gwenolyn saw the tragic series of events unfold from their perch a few streets from the mansion balcony. Thoughts of Benali possibly betraying them had fled from their minds as he took it upon himself to take Sirul from the land of the living. Gwenolyn cursed as she had attempted to reload her crossbow quickly enough to strike down the second officer attacking the Impresario but was unable to fire in time.

The second officer took the Impresario's life at the end of a spear before she reloaded and readied her shot. Harpis struck the stock of her crossbow and sent the bolt wide.

Wren held a hand in peace at her glare. "That man was only avenging what he thought was the assassination of his ruler. Killing him now that Benali is sadly gone from us will do nothing but rob another family of a father, son, or brother."

Gwenolyn's expression softened as she resigned to the necromancer's logic.

She and Wren had already turned to head back down to the streets when the gnome realized Harpis had not moved, still staring at the distant balcony.

He walked back over to the young man, tapping him lightly on the shoulder with the butt of his scythe.

"C'mon then, lad, there isn't anything you can do for the corpse yonder."

Harpis looked down at his friend with tear-rimmed eyes. Needing to keep the young bard's mind to the task at hand, Wren cast aside his typical gruffness. He patted the man's leg and shook his head as if to dismiss Harpis' emotional thoughts for him.

"I know the Impresario was important to you, Harpis, but the best thing you can do for him now is to ensure he did not give his life in vain. There are many we may yet save if we can end this little war today."

Harpis nodded at him and somberly made his way to the stairwell off the roof. As they reached the cobbles below, the sounds and screams of men dying and killing drew their attention to the gates of the city. With the haste of *Panoryla's March*, keeping the burn from their lungs and aches from their legs, they made for the city entrance and the battle there.

*****

The dwarven column was barely into the city when General Shieldborn noticed an increase in the volume and ferocity of resistance they encountered. He raised a fist without looking behind him, and to a dwarf, they halted their advance.

Hearing and seeing no further commotion from the bay, he turned to his army. "All right then, I am not for fighting men who have their backs against the walls of their own homes in a city we do not know. Let's get this thing turned around and back out to our camp!"

Noticing the disconcerted looks from his commanders, he snapped at them, "Well, out with it!"

Shatter-Hand was the first to respond. "We've got them on their heels, General. Why not break them?"

The general placed an understanding hand on the other dwarf's shoulder. "We were here for a diversion, nothing more. Let's hope Turin and company were able to get to the head of the snake. I am for seeing if we can't get out of here without having to kill too many more of these fools or risk the livelihood of our own."

The dwarves made their way out of the city, and the Tuath forces seemed to become inspired by the thought of them retreating. The several thousand who were around the city wall and gate doubled as those fleeing the wharf and harbor area bolstered their forces.

The dwarven column passed through what had been the gate while the men along the wall jeered and taunted them. Shortly after leaving the commotion behind, General Shieldborn once again halted his force. He surveyed the battlements behind them and the coast road ahead that narrowed significantly outside the city's wooden wall.

He removed his helm and rubbed his short blond hair in thought. "All right, warriors of Fjall, we are not for breaking camp just yet. I think we will wait and see what came of our companions' approach from the bay."

Plopping his helm back atop his head, he summoned his officers with a wave. "Thoughts, gentleman?"

This time it was one of the younger commanders who spoke up. "Sir, it looks like they've some six or seven thousand atop those walls peacocking at us. If they decide to make good on their threats, I'd prefer we meet them in the narrows ahead."

General Shieldborn nodded in agreement. "Me as well. Get your troops into smaller phalanxes. Five by fifty should do. I want two lines of them at a place where a line of eight stretches from the rising hills down to the seaside. Another line of seven formations behind them, any archers and crossbowmen in the second line only."

He dismissed them with a salute and made his way to the center of the front line as they quickly and efficiently carried out his commands. Safely out of distance from any ranged weaponry at the wall, he walked in front of the two formations. "At ease, for now, stay in your formations in case these men decide to try their luck. Hopefully, they are just as happy to mock us from within their walls."

Before he finished addressing the dwarves, bells began tolling frantic rings from the governor's mansion atop the hill overlooking tuath bay, and horns began bleating across the city. It seemed even more men had made their way to the walls, and they animatedly began to point and scream at the dwarves.

The yelling at the gateway hit a crescendo, and thousands upon thousands of Tuath militiamen charged for long minutes out of it.

General Shieldborn sighed to himself before giving his next orders to this army. "Shield walls up. Keep the formations tight. Bows and crossbows engage at will!"

The defensive structure of the wall and gate became a deadly detriment to the Tuathian forces. The men were forced through a bottleneck that only let a dozen through at a time. Men were hardly making it through the gate before bolts or arrows struck them from the dwarven lines.

After several minutes of slaughter, the mass of humans outside the gate and walls was beginning to grow. Despite the enormous amounts of casualties, the Tuath militiamen were simply more numerous than the dwarven missiles.

The lethality of the gate area became painfully obvious, and men quickly started jumping from the ramparts up and down the long wall. Once over it, they recklessly made for the narrowing land between the hills and sea that was occupied by the dwarven formations.

A thousand men died before they had any chance at engaging in melee with the dwarves. Eventually, the majority of the Tuath force was on the other side of the wall, but only a couple hundred at a time could engage with the dwarven front line.

Some made attempts at taking to the waters to go around the dwarves and were picked off. The weight of the men began to push the front formations of the dwarves backward. Not many dwarves were wounded or killed, but they could not stop the simple trampling advance of so many men.

General Shieldborn had been hoping to avoid outright slaughter in Tuath, as he had in Mer, but the desperate men gave him no choice. He grabbed Commander Shatter-Hand and shouted in his ear above the fray. "Commander, on my signal, set up a feint and then retreat into the teeth!"

Commander Shatter-Hand sent a runner to the rear line of seven phalanxes. Shortly after they passed the word, General Shieldborn grabbed his horn and blew three long signals before shouting, "Retreat!" with the rest of his men in the first line of formations.

The rear line of phalanxes went from ten wide and five deep to the opposite dimensions, opening wide gaps for the dwarves of the first line to rush past them. In the sudden space that grew between the running dwarves and confused men, dwarven arrows and bolts began to rain in. The men charged after the dwarven retreat to close the gap and avoid the airborne missiles.

General Shieldborn blew his horn again as they reached the last row of dwarves in the line behind them. "All right then, chew them to pieces!"

The dwarves from his lines fell into their own five wide ten-deep formations. The two lines now created a toothlike pattern that provided wide cavities that the blindly charging men filled.

Once the men filled in, those in the front of the massive assault realized their folly as they were engaged on three sides by heavily fortified dwarven shield walls. At the same time, arrows and crossbows continued to assault more distant ranks of the Tuathian militia. Ignorant of what the formation meant for their front, the men in the back kept pushing onward, hoping to stop the aerial onslaught.

The teeth of the dwarven formation churned on them until a swamp of mud, blood, and urine formed where the two forces met.

Coppery scents of sun-heated blood fought their own battle for dominance amongst the smells from men soiling themselves.

The air that had become thick with sweat and carnage causing General Shieldborn to breathe heavily while he surveyed the bloodshed.

Horns blew an alarm down the dwarven ranks from the direction of the sea. His gaze snapped towards the water, where some twenty of the Tuath ships had landed. They had run their ships aground and were launching volley after volley at the dwarves from their makeshift brigantine fortresses.

He furrowed his brow angrily. "Siren curse their sailors for finding a spine!"

He grabbed the two dwarves nearest him. "Run down the lines, first horn, form back into a single shield wall, second horn, right flank back step into a wedge formation with the hills behind us!"

He went for his horn, but as he got it to his lips, a crossbow bolt from the mass of men in front of him blasted it into a hundred pieces, burying itself into his palm.

With a snarl, he bit the tip of the bolt and pulled it the rest of the way through his hand.

"Shatter-Hand, sound once then twice, now!" he shouted.

The nearby commander quickly obeyed. They had finished

249

forming back into a solid shield wall. At almost the same moment, the dwarves to his right began falling back. With his forces formed into the wedge, it became painfully obvious just how vastly outnumbered they were.

Under the press of bodies, the point of the triangle formation was slowly being driven back towards the hills. Gradually it was becoming more of a rounded half-circle.

He cursed as he noticed dwarves were getting hurt by the crush of their fellow soldiers being pushed back against the hillside more so than they were by Tuath weapons.

A pike pole made it over the first rank, momentarily stealing his attention as he forced it away with his shield.

Spitting at their opponents, he vented his frustration. "If they flatten us out too much against this hill, their numbers are going to become a real threat," he shouted to Commander Shatter-Hand.

The old dwarf nodded and pointed his mace at the narrowing road to their right, where more and more of the men were beginning to swarm. "We might be wanting to try for the narrower position and just back our way out of this Five-forsaken state. Let them die on our shields as we do."

General Shieldborn grabbed some dirt and squished it into the bleeding hole in his hand before gripping his ax handle again.

He answered his officer through a clenched jaw. "We are going to lose more than a few pushing through them that way, but if we don't, we might all be fondling The Sleeper's bosom tonight!"

As Shatter-Hand went for his own horn, others blew from amongst the dwarves backed against the hillside to their right.

General Shieldborn craned his neck to the right. "Now what!?"

Instead of cursing in frustration, General Shieldborn cheered with his ax in the air. Captain Elliswerth and over three thousand Mer militiamen behind him rounded the coast road and slammed into the rear of the Tuath forces to his right.

He bellowed new commands at his army, "Flatten out against the hills five ranks deep!"

The chaotic push of the men from Tuath surged towards the flattened dwarven line. The move allowed Mer militiamen and Fjall dwarves to engage the Tuath force on two separate fronts simultaneously.

Once the militia forces had fully engaged each other, General Shieldborn sent two runners down his lines. "Now we break their back! Forward! March!"

Dwarven muscles bulged and strained against the writhing horde in front of them but slowly began pushing the Tuath militia towards the ocean waters.

*****

Harpis, Wren, and Gwenolyn arrived at the city gates in time to see the entirety of what was left of Tuath's militia out on the narrowing land in front of them. Hundreds of men died each moment against the dwarven formations and amongst the unorganized melee with the men from Mer.

"So much death." Harpis mourned at the carnage before them.

"So many bound for my Lady and her Dream," Wren said in matter-of-fact acknowledgment.

With grim determination, Harpis drew his knife from his belt and handed it to Gwenolyn. "You prick yourself, and you and Wren stay within the sphere of silence this creates," He paused, looking sadly at the ongoing battle. "When they stop, stop me."

The elf took it, turned it over once in her hand, and gave a sad look to the now older-looking Harpis. "Go on then, bard."

Wren looked as if he was about to argue, but Harpis could not hear his mouthed words inside the silence created by his enchanted dagger as it pierced Gwenolyn's flesh.

Harpis began a song. Not for The Sleeper this time, but still, he wove every ounce of his gift into *Clario's Cacophony*.

The irregular notes and nonsensical words rang out from the bard's mouth and tore across the battlefield before they were amplified and rebounded by the narrowing hills.

Thousands of men and hundreds of dwarves began losing concentration. Cries and the shouts battle of began to subside. It was then that Harpis entwined the dying notes of *Clario's Cacophony* into the delivery of a song that was as unknown and nameless as it was intimate and sorrowful.

*****

251

General Shieldborn slapped his hands to his ears, dropping his ax as he did. It felt like someone had dumped cold water on his face, hit him with a gauntleted hand, and then put a pot over his head, beating it with a hammer as hard as they could.

"What kind of gods sent racket is this?" he tried to shout at the dwarf next to him,

If the other dwarf heard a word he said over the constant clamor, he couldn't tell. He couldn't even discern if he had spoken over the percussion that was as much in his head as it was around him.

Once the commotion seemed to lessen, and he again became conscious of the men around him, he noticed many dwarves and militiamen looking around quietly and confused.

Almost immediately, he heard distant singing pick its way through the silence towards him. The words were lost to him as quickly as they reached his ears. Everything around him vanished, and darkness filled his mind. He sent commands to his limbs to move or his mouth to open, but they failed him.

Suddenly he was lying down with a blanket pulled up to his chin. He saw his mother weeping over him, a younger vision of him and his sisters at her side. He felt the aching pain in his chest and tingling in his arm as his heart pumped its last. His eyes struggled to shed a single tear. Just as his father had on his deathbed, one single sad droplet rolled from his cheek before shattering on the stone pedestal. His mother's wail, the same one she cried at his father's passing, faded from his ears.

Just as quickly, he was amongst battling dwarves and giants on mountainous slopes of a frigid land he had only heard of in tales. Looking down at the broadsword in his hands, he barely had time to react to the frost giant, four times his height as it swung a club at him so hard it went right through his hasty block. The broadsword flew from his grip, and the club crushed his spine. The impact cracked nearly all his ribs in an explosion of pure fiery pain across his chest. His sight began to fade again as he saw the giant take a step towards him, his collapsed lungs tried to suck in precious air but instead pulled in only blood, and he felt the blackness of death again.

Unable to close his eyes or his mind, General Shieldborn lived countless more deaths. Some he had witnessed, some he had heard of, and some he was at a loss to reconcile.

*****

Wren and Gwenolyn watched dumbfounded as men and dwarves alike fell to their knees crying like scared children, writhing in terror on the ground. Gwenolyn pulled the dagger from her thigh and looked to prick Harpis and end whatever he was doing to the dwarves and men. Instead, she saw what looked like a century-old, white-haired, and frail man wearing Harpis' clothes collapse in front of her.

*****

General Shieldborn was among the first of the dwarves to shake free from the nightmare. He tried unsuccessfully to speak around the lump in his throat. Slapping his face a few times, he finally sputtered orders to his warriors. "Form up between the two militias. I reckon they will come out of this a bit slower than us. Let's use whatever goddess inflicted torment that was and end this now."

Several among his men could not find the strength to rise, but for the most part, stoic, ashen-faced dwarves formed a line between the two groups of men from Mer and Tuath.

When most of the humans had regained some semblance of consciousness, he shouted towards the city, "Parlay men of Tuath, send me those who would represent you!"

Captain Elliswerth called back his men, and he walked forward to join the general. Several older men from Tuath met them, as did Wren, who had made his way through the confused masses.

The gnome was first to speak. "Men of Tuath, Impresario Benali Tuath has slain the imposter who had taken the identity of Myrlman Tuath to advance his desires.

Several of your officers, who did not know that it was an imposter and thought Benali a murderer, were the ones who killed the bard. You are free of the tyranny of your leader and know well and enough with no hereditary heir among you. You may, for the first time, elect a leader."

General Shieldborn thanked the gnome and then faced the men. "I will withdraw my forces as will the men of Mer if you agree to a truce. Further, in a week, if you see fit to send an elected governor south to a meeting of the island council of city-states, we may conclude this affair without further bloodshed."

The Tuath officers looked at each other with demoralized but thankful looks before agreeing with the dwarf. They shook hands with the general and Captain Elliswerth before turning to what was left of their broken militia and directing them back into their city.

With the immediate threat of further open war ended, Wren returned to the fallen form of Harpis. Gwenolyn was at the bard's side, and she met the gnome's bitter gaze with sorrow in her eyes.

Wren looked down at the man he had sent to The Syndicate less than a year ago. Gone was the young man in his early twenties. There was now a greyed and lifeless form of a man four times his age. He no longer breathed, and his wrinkled, parchment-like skin was growing cold to the touch.

Wren sat at Harpis' side and began uttering the most ancient prayers to The Sleeper he knew. For the first time in his hundreds of years as a necromancer, Wren whispered them using the goddess's true name.

The world began to turn grey, and he saw the white form of one of The Sleeper's handmaidens beginning to kneel beside Harpis, preparing to take him fully into The Great Dream. Without thinking, he told the handmaiden to stop.

Since becoming a death speaker, he had been able to see the goddess's handmaidens as they used the grey fog in between life and death to take souls from the realm of the living. He had prayed to them too, in the past, and he thought they had heard him at times.

Never had they acknowledged him, but this one did. It stopped kneeling and stood, facing the gnome, and gave a slow bow. Suddenly the world around him got darker, and he no longer saw the battlefield in shades of grey or the handmaiden at all. He was entirely within a thick blackish-grey fog, with Harpis' corpse still lying next to him. Out of the mist, The Sleeper appeared enormous before him. She was naked and asleep with her head in her hands as she lay on her side facing him.

Wren's heartbeat was in his throat, and tears streamed down his face at the pure and holy beauty of his goddess. He was breathless at being for the first time in the presence of one he had fervently served and worshiped for centuries.

"My Lady, Lilynth." He said, for the first time addressing her and not just speaking to her. He saw her form shift and a smile creep across her face. She did not open her eyes upon him. She spoke to him in a voice that echoed around him and inside his head like falling trees.

"Yes, Herald?"

Her words nearly shattered his mind into a thousand pieces, as did their implication. Reeling, he almost lost track of his sanity and the question he had intended to speak to her.

"May the living keep the bard a little longer?"

The black pupil-less eyes of Lilynth snapped open, and Wren felt his very being melting away under their gaze.

"Long have I waited to hear my name once again in a melody so sweet. However, your years are but passing moments to me. I will leave him to you for a while yet then, Wrennulmatlkuonoksug Svatnurlak, if you will trade your years for his"

Wren fell to his knees, head bowed, in the grey fog. He felt the eyes of The Sleeper close again, and everything went black.

*****

Gwenolyn was entranced watching the seated gnome age a century and collapse before her. She jumped, almost shooting Harpis dead again in surprise as the man coughed back to life and began breathing next to her.

Chapter 26

Penance

The autumn council meeting took place as the seasonal chill had almost finished creeping its way northward on Quaj. The dawn air in Mer was a mix of dry cold from the south and the stubborn, heavy, tropical climate that never left northern Tuath.

It had been several months since the dwarves and forces of Mer returned from Tuath. Such was the cheering that echoed throughout the streets that the dwarven column making its way through Mer might as well have been its own parade.

Harpis, Wren, Turin, and Gwenolyn were the last to arrive at the squat council chamber. As they entered, the room grew quiet, and Aanaman bid them take the row of seats for observers that now sat in front of the scribe desks. For the first time since the death of Edwin Lurras, the council table was full. For the first time ever, each seat was occupied by one elected to it by the people they represented.

The Exarch and Arch Mage sat together, and next to them was the now empty chairs of the Impresario and Death Herald.

With the chamber doors shut, Arch Mage Uridyll stood from his seat. "Before this council meeting begins, a word, please. I think it appropriate that with the deaths of the late Impresario and the Death Herald, whose name none knew, we invite Harpis and Wren to sit in their seats. They may do so representing their institutions as the senior-most members present."

Harpis and Wren solemnly rose and went to the chairs next to the two old men, who greeted them warmly. Wren had yet to tell anyone of his experience talking with his goddess and being named Herald. He had not spoken much at all in the time since that day. Although the gnome still looked much the same, he was now completely bald, and the short beard he kept was stark white.

Even after Wren had traded years to The Sleeper for his own Harpis still wore the cost of the power he had channeled. Despite seeing just over twenty years, the bard could pass for fifty.

Even with what he had given, the gnome still had a century or so of life left before being considered ancient by gnomish standards. As he climbed into the chair next to Harpis. The man coughed a chuckle at the sight of the old gnome scaling the chair like a small child. Wren glared and harrumphed at the bard once he was finally situated.

Aanaman addressed the gathering. "As some of you are in this chamber and attending this council for the first time, I do believe some introductions are in order. We, of course, have the Exarch and the Arch Mage, Harpis the bard, and Wren the necromancer representing their organizations. I am Aanaman Reaper, Governor of Ravnice. There is Governor Ingar Hammersmith of Fjall, Captain Elliswerth of Mer."

The captain held a finger up to interrupt. "It is Governor Elliswerth now, actually," he said, smiling proudly.

"My apologies, Governor, and congratulations, from Kalt, of course, we have Governor Jaeryl Innisgrath, and for the first time, we have Governess Isra Rashida from Tuath, elected by her people just last week, congratulations as well," Aanaman said.

The olive-skinned woman raised her hand in greeting. She sat tall and stately in her chair. The widowed owner of the Tuath shipyard was by far the most popular and well-known Tuath citizen to volunteer for the council seat ballot and had won the nomination easily.

Governor Elliswerth spoke first after the introductions. "Our first order of business is regarding The Syndicate and the role they played in the recent conflict that spread across this island. First, have our thanks, deeply, for your efforts in bringing the battle of Tuath to an end. Further, the peoples of this island are ever indebted to the goodwill of the dwarves for the part they played," he said with a nod to Ingar before turning back to Turin.

"However, what cannot go unanswered is The Syndicate's role in creating the monster that was Sirul Amun. There must be punishment for that, and the other clandestine actions carried out against the people of Quaj without due justice or law. Despite

257

your intentions, Master Turin, your judgment was not perfect, and we have all suffered for it. As punishment, we sentence you to confinement in The Archdiocese of Daybreak."

Turin hung his head at the thought of imprisonment, even in the company of the Exarch.

Governor Elliswerth looked at him comfortingly. "You will only remain there as long as it takes you to recount everything you can recall about the actions of your Lodestar Syndicate to the historians of the clergy so that all may judge the good and the bad you have done over the centuries. It will do well for the people of this island to know what has transpired, so mistakes like those that enabled Sirul Amun don't happen in the future."

Turin looked the man in the eyes and gave him a slight bow of respect from his seat.

"All in favor?" Aanaman asked the council, to which there were only "ayes" in response.

Governess Isra stood after the vote and addressed the gathering. "The lies of Sirul Amun have cost the people of Tuath as dearly as they cost those of Mer. Still, there must be some price paid for the damage caused at the hands of my people. There remain some forty brigantines left in our navy. Fifteen of them and the thirteen ships that survive which Tuath commandeered will sail to Mer upon my return to Tuath. That is if that suits Governor Elliswerth."

Again, there was only agreement from the group. As she took her seat, Jaeryl Innisgrath nervously raised his hand and was acknowledged.

"The Kalt family of my city-state willingly aided in the supply of materials to Sirul Amun's war machine. I believe they dealt with the man to restore their seat at this table if Sirul was successful in his campaign. I fear their influence in my attempts at lawful rule would have been impossible to resist. They have a large amount of forestland and wealth. All of which stems from the preferred timber areas that the Kalt people cannot work without their permission," he stated

The governor from Kalt did not know it, but the representatives of Fjall, Mer, and Ravnice had already discussed Kalt and the Kalt family's role in the conflict and agreed.

Aanaman turned to Jaeryl. "I think we have a solution to the issues you have mentioned. I put forth for a vote that almost half of the Kalt family forestland will be forfeit as penance. Further, Ravnice will forfeit an equal portion of uninhabited and unworked forestland in the south to the elf tribe that lives in the woods of Kalt. This land will form a new elven state. In addition, this will force the forestry industry in Kalt to look to lands not owned by the Kalt family. A fact which should considerably lessen their sway over local politics and the people."

Jaeryl Innisgrath opened his mouth to argue but quickly closed it, recognizing that his people had not given up much, and he would no longer have to suffer the wiles of Svenus Kalt.

"Aye," was his only response.

Aanaman looked at the seated Gwenolyn. "Mistress Elf, would you be so kind as to bring the news to your people and ask them to provide a representative at this council's next meeting. Henceforth our meetings will have ten around this table instead of five. The sides are large enough to hold two seats each instead of one. With six governors and four representatives from the institutions that serve the whole of the island, perhaps we can begin to bring the city-states together through a more island-wide agenda."

Gwenolyn nodded in shocked silence.

*****

Later that same day, Harpis and Wren boarded a Ravnice vessel with Aanaman and had made Ravnice city as night fell.

Aanaman invited them to his office for a respite, but the man and gnome had a tradition to keep after battles won and survived.

They parted ways with the governor at the wharf and made their way into the musty air and dancing candlelight of The Siren's Scream. Tucked into the back booth, stew, fresh bread, and whiskey before them, Harpis finally decided to prod his small friend.

He laced his fingers and let out a long breath. "My thanks many times over for saving my life."

Wren shook his head at the bard. "Just returning the favor. Who knows how many lives you saved that day at the cost of your own?"

"Just trying to live up to your lofty expectations," he said, cracking a smile.

259

Wren shook his head at the attempted humor. "She had you, you know? She had sent one of her handmaidens to gather you to The Great Dream. It seems she has an ear for that mediocre singing voice of yours."

He smiled at his friend's gruffness. "You saw her, too, then? Gods above, Wren, she was beautiful to behold and terrifying to be beholden by."

The gnome crossed his hands and sat back. He was silent for several moments. "She was more beautiful than I could possibly have imagined, and her voice shook me to my core."

Wren grew silent again, staring off blankly at their table.

"Well?" Harpis inquired. "What did she say to you?"

Wren's gaze drifted from the table to look up at the man. "She named me Herald."

Harpis let out a long slow whistle and raised his glass. "Well, congratulations then, no higher honor and none more deserving!"

With the distant look still in his eyes, Wren joined his toast. "It is more than I ever could have hoped for from Her."

"I suppose you are bound for The Sanctum then?" he asked with a touch of remorse.

Wren shrugged. "I must return for a time and consult with the death speakers, but no, I have no plans for staying beneath the mountain praying away eternity. Perhaps the Herald was right in joining us before she left. Maybe the Herald's place is where there is death and not hidden away in the mountains. I think I may consult with the Exarch about how best to bring our worship to more folk and places. What of you, bard? The Impresario is gone. Will you go to The Hall in his place?"

It was Harpis' turn to sit silently for a time. "I think no, but I do think some things need to change for bards in general. I will leave soon to find Virtuoso Mahala and return with her to Maestro Bravit at the Hall. We have much to discuss regarding the future of our institution. We must explore with more rigor the magical potential of our craft and spend less of our time spreading news or rumor. I believe Bravit is likely to be the best choice for the next Impresario of the bards, but whatever The Hall will become, I plan to be a part of."

Harpis stared at the gnome for a few moments, "I did think of a name for that song, by the way, the one I sang to stop the fighting, *The Sleeper's Serenade*. The first new gifted song in decades."

Wren raised his eyebrows. "Well, maybe keep her name out of the singing of it, so I don't have to go and try arguing with a goddess again for your mortal soul."

Harpis nodded his agreement. "I have no desire to be a conduit to the Lady of Death again, no disrespect intended. The gift I was born with is more than enough for me."

Wren raised his glass in a final toast. "To gifted songs and the betterment of bards then."

Harpis held up his own. "To The Sleeper, Her Herald, and our next drink together."

Chapter 27
Outcomes

The ferry's hull rubbed against smooth river stones as it came to a rest on the waterside. Ezera paid for the transportation and stepped lightly off the bow and onto the grass. She waved the ferry off as it made its way the short distance from where she stood to the mouth of Fjall city, where the river went into the mountain. She stood at the point of the natural bend where the city entrance first came into view for those traveling the Fjall river.

Turning to put the river at her back, she looked at the small clearing where she would meet the dwarven governor. The river made up two sides of a natural triangle, with the woods making up the third. The grass she stood on stretched for a hundred feet before ending at the thick forest. She thought the spot was perfect.

Exarch Hameki was ecstatic about the prospect of bringing regular worship and a diocese to Fjall. However, they agreed that it would best serve the state's people if it were outside but near the mountain city. The nomadic human communities who herded goats on the mountain edges would find them more readily above ground than within the mountain city.

Besides, it would make for challenging morning prayer to Daybreak if the diocese were in the mountain and away from dawn light.

The arrival of another ferry drew her attention to the riverside. Governor Ingar Hammersmith jumped off and motioned for the four guards with him to stay on the boat as he made his way to her.

"Good morning, Vicar Ezera. Welcome to Fjall. I hope the trip from Mer was easy enough."

She gave the dwarf a short bow.

"Daybreak's blessing to you, Ingar."

The dwarf stood at the point of the river bend with her, facing inland with the cave's mouth to his left barely in view.

"We'll be building your diocese right here, a two-story domed structure of solid stone from the mountain Fjall herself. I will have them put quarters for you and two attending clerics on the left side and four hospital rooms for the ill or visitors on the right. I think that the domed chapel will hold enough room for fifty or so of you light worshipers to sit at a time, and we'll cut a skylight to the east so you can greet the dawn."

Ingar kicked loose soil in front of him and surveyed the land. "We will also dig a three-story deep basement so you can keep foodstuffs and then lower down perform any necessary autopsy and rituals on the fallen away from the heat of the sun. You'll also be needing a dock. The spot just after the bend here should work, so ferries and boats can more easily come and go. The road from Fjall passes not far into the woods from here. I suppose we could cut a clearing to it as well."

Ingar crossed his arms and surveyed the area, making mental images and notes to pass along to his workman when he sent them out.

She put her hand on the dwarf's shoulders and gave him a warm look. "The Exarch and I cannot thank you enough for your generosity. I also personally cannot thank you enough for allowing us to establish worship here finally. I know Turin did much to convince you, but still, have my appreciation as well."

The dwarf looked up and spoke in quieter tones to avoid being overheard by his guards on the ferry. "It is good enough that you are out here instead of within the city. If I am honest, the farming and herding folk of Fjall could use your healing and your religion. I owed Turin much and was happy to oblige him in this. However, I also have a personal reason for supporting this diocese. The dwarven army will patrol out each day and night just as they do other areas at the mouth and entrances to the mountain."

He paused for a moment in consideration. "I ask for your confidence in something."

She fully faced Ingar and noted the seriousness in his face. "You know of my former employment under Turin. I can more

263

than keep a secret, if necessary."

Ingar gave her a nod. Blowing out an uncustomary nervous breath, he continued.

"I'll be sending you a dwarf to be one of your two attending clerics. I want him trained here and not in Mer. He is overly interested in medical practice, and I can think of no better opportunity for him than here with you."

Ezera nodded her agreement, but her eyebrows remained furrowed in confused thought. "Why the secrecy then? I don't think it is all that odd that a dwarf is interested in medicine and healing."

Ingar crossed his arms and looked at the sun in the sky for a moment. "The dwarf is my son. Dobry Hammersmith will be your apprentice. More than the medicine, he is gifted, and I believe it is Daybreak given."

Ezera was silent in surprise for a moment before shaking her head in wonder. "Well, he would certainly be the first dwarf or any dweller of the deep that Daybreak had gifted to my knowledge."

Ingar shrugged and raised his hands unknowingly. "I sent him to Stone Mage Lorkin, who said the boy was hopeless at commanding any of the four elements despite sensing his obvious gift. I sent him to The Sanctum, and the necromancers confirmed his gift and said The Sleeper knew him not. I will tell you the lad is no bard. Dwarves have an affinity for singing drinking songs and beating shields with weapons but no more music, magic or otherwise, graces our halls. Given his appreciation and want for healing, Daybreak makes the most sense. I appreciate your discretion in teaching him."

With that, Ingar patted her on the shoulder and headed back towards his ferry. "Come, enjoy a night or two in the city and have some good dwarven food and ale. We will begin work in the morning, and I expect to have it done in short order."

She smiled at the dwarf and followed him towards his ferry. It was the start of an exciting chapter in her life indeed. Any fear of boredom now that she no longer served The Syndicate flew from her thoughts with Ingar's revelation.

*****

Gwenolyn had traveled south and west from Mer on foot and off the road enjoying the silence and solitude of walking in the forested lands of southern Ravnice and northern Kalt as she neared the woodland village of her fellow elves.

The trees grew taller and fuller, the animals were more at peace, and the smell of pollen on the salty southern breeze brought her calm. Finally, after a few more steps, she stopped. Slowly and without looking up, Gwenolyn removed the cloak hood from her head. Her reddish-brown hair tumbled down past her waist, and the point of her ears showed just above the braids.

In response, she could almost feel the calming exhale of breaths around her and the easing of pulled and knocked arrows and bows. She looked up and spotted half a dozen wood elves in various branches of the trees around her returning arrows to quivers.

A black-haired elf from among them dropped the thirty feet from her perch to the woodland floor barely a foot from Gwenolyn. The lead scout stared hard into Gwenolyn's face before speaking.

"It has been a long time since you have walked beneath our boughs, Gwenolyn Amura. What brings you back to the people you forsook and away from the sea you embraced?"

Gwenolyn resisted the urge to flatten the pointed nose of the elf with the butt of her crossbow. "I have important news for the chieftess. I need to see her at once."

The scout eyed her up and down again. "All right then."

The black-haired elf stepped back and waved Gwenolyn ahead. A few steps past where she was confronted, Gwenolyn looked back at the utterly empty forest floor and soundless, motionless branches above.

Shaking her head at the ever-impressive way her people moved about the woods, she made her way to the elvish village. Then, not far from where the scouts had stopped her, she looked up into the branches and began to see the wooden huts and rope bridges that made up the village of Glasduille.

She found the entrance after a few more moments of walking beneath the populated canopy. It was less a gate or door than a staircase that spiraled up a three-hundred-year-old oak tree some sixty feet into the canopy above.

Because that was the only easy way up to the bridges and

platforms, the village was incredibly simple to defend. A few skilled archers could pick apart any force trying to gain the canopy. There were over twenty armed elves that always kept watch on the stairway entrance and rope bridges. Glasduille Village was relatively safe from armed invasion but was less so from the infringement of Kalt loggers.

Though platforms and bridges stretched across the top boughs of many trees, the tops of large pines contained the small living quarters. The most extensive of these pines held the meeting room that the chieftess occupied during most days. The circular room was almost twenty feet across and at the center of the canopy structures.

Two elves armed with swords stood guard at the entrance. After a suspicious inspection from their eyes, they waved Gwenolyn into the circular room. The white-haired elven chieftess sat at a large circular table with several other village officials who paused to glance up at her as she entered.

"If it isn't the niece of Turin Deadeye, come home to roost," the chieftess said, sitting straighter in her chair and locking eyes with Gwenolyn.

"Good day to you, Chieftess Ceanna. I bring important news," Gwenolyn replied.

The older elf scoffed loudly at her. "What, have you and your uncle given up on playing nursemaid and grandpappy to the lot of ungrateful humans that infest this island? Where is the vagabond sea elf? Are you not ever at his side or working his machinations?"

Gwenolyn strode forward and took a seat at the table without being asked. The action drew shocked looks from the few other elves in the room. She crossed her arms and looked the chieftess up and down. The woman had once loved Turin, and Gwenolyn doubted she had ever truly forgiven the elf for loving the sea more than he loved her or the trees.

"I am here because the council of governors has seen fit to award the elvish people of Quaj their own state. The northeastern corner of Kalt we currently sit in and an equal portion of southwestern Ravnice will now be the elvish state. So, we will have a seat at the table, and they ask that we provide a representative or our leader to the next council meeting in three months. The elves around the table exchanged dumbfounded looks, and the often clever and snide Ceanna was caught flat-footed in a conversation for the first time in years.

Gwenolyn kicked her muddy booted feet up onto the circular table and crossed her arms. She shot a grin at the chieftess. "Well then, what say you, Governor Ceanna of the Glasduille State?"

A smile slowly crept its way across Ceanna's face.

"I will be honest. I did not think I would live long enough to see the likes of humans come to their senses and rule justly. Truly this is great news you bring our people, and sorely would I have wished to share the triumph with Turin. I am sure he is quite pleased with the outcome of his little espionage and meddling experiment."

Despite the joyous atmosphere now overtaking the meeting hut, Gwenolyn pulled a sorrowful look. It lasted but a moment before she regained her calm demeanor.

"The cost to The Syndicate was grave. The organization is no more, and Turin holds himself accountable for the scores of Syndicate lives lost. He also holds himself responsible for the countless lives lost in the recent conflicts. He has banished himself to Lodestar Island."

It was Ceanna's turn to look saddened. "A shame then. He should have enjoyed his retirement here among the trees and with his people. Celebrating the fruits of his centuries laboring for the sake of this island."

*****

Harpis' feet ached from the cold of the snow-covered terrain seeping through his boots. Clutching his cloak around him to ward off the chill of the southern winds, he looked up at the golden light spilling out of the tavern windows ahead. As dusk fell in southwestern Kalt, he smiled to himself in nostalgia. The shadows chased the sun across the highlands and up the distant Fjall mountainsides as the sun set. Bobbing in the seas off the nearby coast as a child, he had often imagined the same visage was The Sleeper playfully chasing her sister Daybreak each evening. Happy as he had been to get away from the cold of southern Kalt the past year and a half, the approaching winter solstice was most appropriately enjoyed amongst the white snow and blistering winds.

267

Nearing the tavern, he could hear the faint sounds of a well-played violin rising and falling amongst the cry of the wind. He had been pursuing the nomadic bard Virtuoso Mahala Shelta since he had returned to The Hall after Benali's death. She always seemed to be a week ahead of him as he had picked his way southward from Tuath on hints and rumors regarding where she was going next.

The violin's sound faded entirely and was replaced by appreciative applause as he shoved open the tavern door. Near the hearth of the room was the petite bowing figure of the woman he sought. He had never seen her or met her, but Mahala Shelta was undeniable in her form-fitting fur-lined leathers. Waist-length chestnut hair bounced in curls around a face that seemed to rest in a constant frown.

He struggled to maintain his composure and not stare at her like some lustful sailor. Her eyes were captivating pools of green and hazel filled with mystery and sadness. Despite her unapproachable demeanor, there was an intoxicating curiosity about her melancholy that he could not help but yearn to avail.

She fixed him with an intense gaze as the cold from the recently opened door pushed its way into the warm wooden tavern. She quickly pulled the room's attention back to herself. Placing one hand on her hip, she pointed with the other at a particularly burly and heavily mustached patron who sat unimpressed with his arms crossed.

"You there, big man," she said in a voice that was raspy and smooth like the rustling of silk curtains in a breeze.

"I bet you payment of food and drink for the night that my next performance will make you weep," she challenged, stabbing the bow of her violin at the man as if she were a fencer in a duel.

"Sure thing, sweetheart, I'll take that bet, have at it!" he said with a laugh while exchanging doubtful looks with his two drinking companions.

She sat in a chair across from him, and with a tight grin, she began playing. Her slowly sawing bow conjured forth an instrumental from the violin that Harpis had never heard before. He kept waiting in strained anticipation to listen to her voice invoke enough sadness to make the man cry. But, instead, she pulled forth such sorrowful tones from her violin strings that it sounded as if the wood of the instrument itself was sobbing in

268

some unknown grief.

Harpis straightened in surprise as he felt a tickling tug at the edge of his senses that was undeniably reminiscent of his gift but much fainter. The feeling came and went like the scent of distant flowers on a wet spring breeze, so light and fleeting that he wasn't sure it was even there.

He watched her hypnotically sway as she played. The patron began looking around in a nervous confusion at his friends. He placed his hands flat on the table in front of him as if to steady himself while moisture began to rim his eyes.

Mahala dragged the last keening note out with a draw of her bow that seemed as unending as it was unrelenting. The final note finally faded, and the man's face twisted in anguish while tears rolled down his cheeks for a long silent moment before he shook his head clear of despair and gawked open-mouthed at her.

"Daybreak save me, I have never been so saddened in all my life, woman!" he shouted. He indicated to the barkeep regarding her tab. "I cannot believe what I have heard. Had I not wagered against you, I still would have paid for your drinks tonight. How about one more song for us? Something happy!"

Mahala gave him a slight bow and stood from her seat, surveying the room before looking apprehensively at Harpis. Her fingers waltzed across the neck and strings of the violin as she began an airy and rhythmic tune. Harpis immediately recognized the notes of one of the few songs written for and by gifted bards.

After the first few measures of *Panoryla's March*, she began to snake her way between and sometimes across tabletops. She became an entrancing dervish, spinning, and twirling as she stepped and leaped with the nimble grace of a doe. Each note was punctuated by the flick of a foot, the strut of a leg, or swing of her hips.

Harpis could no longer resist as the invigorating energy of her gifted song pulled him in. He began singing along with her. A half measure behind, his own words followed the rise and fall of her voice. Their harmonies interlaced in an amplifying resonance that pulled both their gifts into a rippling weave of magic and music.

Mahala was briefly caught off guard. Mid-stride, she came close to stumbling as she passed between two chairs, faltering for a single note as her face revealed a glimpse of surprise as Harpis' gift enveloped her.

With the last words of *Panoryla's March* still echoing off the walls, the twenty-some patrons of the tavern roared in shouts of delight and applause at the two of them.

For her part, Mahala simply glared at Harpis and beckoned with an angry finger for him to join her at an otherwise empty table. Then, as they both took their seats, she ordered her supper and mead from the barkeep before turning her smoldering eyes to him.

"Well met, virtuoso," he said, unable to keep the excitement from his voice.

"Harpis the bard, I presume," she returned tartly.

"You know of me?" he asked in unmistakable surprise.

"Oh, the others at The Hall wouldn't shut up about the man who sings to the gods themselves," she said, eyeing him up and down. "I must say, based on their descriptions, I expected you to be young enough to be my child, but you look nearly old enough to be my father."

She hadn't meant it as a barb, but the statement hit Harpis like a kick to the stomach. Each time he passed a mirror, it pained him with the memory of what he gave that autumn day in Tuath half a year ago. Hearing it from the lips of a beautiful woman in her early forties who could easily pass for half that age was a new form of suffering.

Seeing the woeful expression appear and flee from his face, she leaned towards him. "Was the price worth it?" she asked with some compassion.

"What, are you not into older men?" he said sarcastically.

Snorting at his display, she crossed her arms in front of her and looked down her nose at him. "Do people usually think you clever, Harpis the fool? Or do they see through the charisma of your gift and know you for the ass that you are?"

The challenge steeled Harpis, and he shed his typical snark. "I would give it again and again for the people of this island," he said, resolute and confident. "I have followed you for many days and many miles, Mahala Shelta, to ask for your help."

She slammed her fists on the table angrily at the statement. "Virtuoso. Mahala. Shelta," she said in a near snarl.

He raised his hands in peace, "My apologies, Virtuoso, with Benali gone, we need your help. I need your help."

She sat straighter in her chair and glowered at him. "And what help might I be to the man that sang to a goddess?" She said, leaning in towards him again with her fists clenched tightly. "I have spent the better part of two decades roaming this entire island. I have listened to every sound this world makes, working, striving, and practicing in wandering solitude to master the art." She paused, staring him in the eyes. "Everything. Everything I have ever done or could hope to achieve pales in comparison to your singular, goddess channeling performance."

He stared back at her dumbly for a moment before regaining his composure. "I truly and honestly hope that you are never in the position to pay the cost of such a performance," he said gravely.

In an attempt to break through her surliness, he changed his expression from somber to smiling and his tone became bombastic. "I have witnessed you for only brief moments and can happily admit to being an unschooled knave in the presence of your erudite grasp of gifted verse and song."

Anger eased slightly from her demeanor, and she rolled her eyes at his pivot to flamboyance.

Becoming serious again, he looked at her violin resting against the table-leg. "For one, I did not have the slightest clue a bard could summon the gift without the use of the voice. I also am unknowing of how you could affect only the one man amongst all our ears. I felt your gift in the song as it floated on melody past me, but only just. All Bravit and Benali, The Sleeper keep him, ever taught me were a few songs like the one we just sang together."

She shook her head dismissively and then blew a stray curl out of her face. "That is because that is all the two of them could ever do, barely gifted and rarely practiced as they were. They were but ignorant children playing with candlelight, unaware of the raging wildfire it can convoke."

271

Epilogue

The deep winter wind was beginning to howl across the seas south of Kalt. The endless breath from the Arctic would go on unabated for months. Turin Deadeye was crewing the small schooner *Open Ocean* himself, and the going was more difficult in the years of his second millennium than it had been in the first. Yet, despite his eleven centuries, experience and unrivaled skill allowed him to guide the vessel into the small remnants of a dock at Lodestar Island.

He drew his cloak in against the cold as he walked solemnly from the dock to the lighthouse. The stairs of the light tower creaked against the silence and the howl of the wind outside. The old elf lit a fire inside the chamber at its top, which held the giant polished brass reflecting mirror.

The beacon lit; Turin Deadeye gazed out at the roaring winter sea. After centuries of helping Quaj navigate through troubled seas, he would guide her people and her ships through the night and keep them off the rocks a bit longer yet.

*****

Enky watched the battle raging in Tuath through several of the frames on his walls and the one he kept on his desk. To him, typically surprises were mundane. He nonetheless clapped with giddy excitement while watching a frame on the wall as it showed an undead dragon picking a ship out of the water and hurling it at another.

Wringing his childish hands in excitement at the conflict taking place, he stopped suddenly and violently snatched the lone unhung frame from where it sat on the desk in front of him. He looked on in despondent disappointment as the events it showed unfolded. A human man, his marionette, went lifeless. He threw the frame to the ground in disgust. After a moment, the shattered pieces disappeared from the floor, and the silver inlaid black wooden frame reappeared on top of the desk, devoid of any display.

Only then did he calm down enough to notice that his coin had stopped spinning without falling on either face. Instead, it sat defiantly on its side with the edge towards him. Throwing his hands up in frustration, Enky then slammed them on the desktop, causing the coin to fall flat.

"Chaos writ and chaos wrought, but not the outcome that I sought," he said mournfully. He picked the coin up and stared affectionately at his reflection in its blank, polished face.